ADRIFT

Al Parker

SterlingHouse Publisher, Inc.   Pittsburgh, PA

ADRIFT

ISBN 1-56315-412-9
978-1-56315-410-0

Trade Paperback
© Copyright 2008 Al Parker
All rights reserved
Library of Congress #2008924343

Request for information should be addressed to:
SterlingHouse Publisher, Inc.
3468 Babcock Boulevard
Pittsburgh, PA 15237
www.sterlinghousepublisher.com

Broadmoor Books
is an imprint of SterlingHouse Publisher, Inc.

SterlingHouse Publisher, Inc. is a company
of the CyntoMedia Corporation

Cover Design: Brandon M. Bittner
Interior Design: N. J. McBeth

This is a work of fiction. Names, characters, incidents, and places, are the
product of the author's imagination or are used fictitiously. Any resemblance to
actual events or persons, living or dead is entirely coincidental.

Printed in the United States of America

Dedicated to Phyllis

To my wife, my love, best friend, and most trusted confidant, whose help, support, and encouragement throughout the years made possible the writing of this book.

ABOUT AL PARKER

Al Parker knows his subject matter. A young man in the 'Fifties, he lived in and experienced the times. The life of a Navy seaman and related military details in *A Touch of Sadness* are also drawn largely from the author's own personal and naval experiences during the Korean War.

Now retired, he and his wife, Phyllis, live in Chesapeake, Virginia. This is his first work of fiction.

In Memory of Mom and Dad

PART 1

CHAPTER 1

A GENTLE BREEZE FROM THE Gulf blew across Florida's "Panhandle" and into southern Georgia, its warm currents rustling the leaves of the pecan trees in the backyard of the dilapidated, clapboard house sitting on the edge of the quiet little town of Thomasville.

Soft gusts caressed Eve Allison's thick, dark-blond hair, stroking it lightly against her pretty face. Her attractive, high cheekbones attested to a trace of Indian lineage, probably Seminole. She was holding two wooden clothespins between her flawless white teeth. Standing barely five feet tall, she stood on tiptoe to hang clothes nearest the pole, but as she worked toward the center, the weight of the wet wash caused the clothesline to sag, making her task easier.

At her feet, her small tow-headed two-year-old son played contentedly, his vivid blue eyes keeping a constant vigil on his mother. He never allowed her to move more than a few inches away before grabbing the hem of her dress with his small hands. Two large galvanized washtubs sat on a makeshift platform near an outside spigot at the rear of the house. One tub contained soapy water and an old, metal washboard with a partially used bar of "Octagon Soap" sitting on the ledge; the other brimmed with rinse water.

Shoulders aching from the strenuous morning chores, Eve reached up to hang her husband's work shirt; she peered over the line and saw her husband entering the yard. Her forehead wrinkled. It was too early for Ben to be coming home. Something was wrong. His large, broad frame seemed to droop and his strong, squared-jawed, handsome face was grim. "Ben, are you sick? Who drove you home? It's too early for your regular ride…."

"Honey, Mr. Etheridge says he won't be needing me at the dairy anymore 'cause they got that new milking machine. I told him I out-milked the first one they tried, but he says with needing to milk them cows two times a day, he can't afford to lose money in wages the machine saves." Ben reached down and picked up his young son. "Eve, I ain't got a job no more."

"You're exhausted. Come inside and I'll get you a glass of ice water."

"I'm tired, honey. I walked home."

"My God!" Eve brushed aside his wavy blond hair to touch her hand to his forehead. "That's over eight miles in the middle of the day."

"Walking home, I kept thinkin' this area's all played out since the Depression. There's no work here." Ben Allison spoke softly as he hugged his baby boy in his arms. "It's best I send you to your folks and I head up North to find work. Your brother in C.C. *Camp* and the one in the Army send money home to help them get by on, and I'll leave you with my last week's pay from the dairy to help pay for your keep. You said your sister wrote about getting work in New Jersey. If she's right, I'll get work and send money for you to come." He looked away from her anxious eyes.

Tears began streaming down her face. "Ben, my family doesn't want extra mouths to feed, and they'd resent me and the baby being there. You're a good mechanic. Remember you fixed that farmer's tractor and he paid you for it? I don't want to go up North. My first baby's buried here. I can't leave him."

"Honey, we've got to eat, and I can't wait for a piece of farm equipment to break down. I don't want to leave our first boy here, either. I had to build that little pine box to bury him in. Hell! I still owe the doctor for this baby. All I could give him was a quart can of cane syrup for payment. I'd join up with the Army, but they're not takin' nobody now. Guess with the whole country out of work, everybody is trying to join.

Eve placed her head against his strong chest and listened to his familiar heartbeat. *How will we manage,* she wondered. *How can our lives be so full of happiness one moment and so empty of joy the next….?*

The sun was barely turning the dark sky to charcoal the next morning as Ben strode away with less than three dollars in his pocket. He would hitchhike to Florida, there hoping to catch a ride on one of the citrus trucks. Helplessly, Eve watched him gradually disappear down the dirt road. Despite her worry, she couldn't help admiring his courage. If there was work, she told herself, Ben would find it.

Ben found work and then sent for his family. Eve rode a Greyhound bus from Georgia to New Jersey holding her small son, Paris, on her lap.

In the next nine years, Ben worked many unskilled jobs before he and his family settled in an Italian area of Paterson known as "Little Italy." Here, he did auto repair work as a side-line to earn extra money. Speaking with an alien southern accent, he brought about hostility at first, until his honesty and mechanical capabilities cleared the path for acceptance.

Paris was 10 when he witnessed his father in a fist-fight provoked by a large Italian man. Ben beat the man to the ground and later explained to his son, "Don't fight unless you have to, but if forced, hit hard and fast. The first punch usually decides the outcome."

The outbreak of World War II found Ben Allison frozen in a "Series E" (Essential) job classification, with a company manufacturing asbestos pipe coverings for ships needed for the war. The small blue pennant with an "E" insignia flying below the U.S. flag on the plant's flagpole kept Ben from being inducted into the Army.

CHAPTER 2

IN THE SUMMER OF 1948, the nation basked in a brief tranquility before entering into the Korean War. Three years had passed since the fighting ended and a blissful peace reigned throughout the country following the end of World War II.

Today had been hot, though a gentle breeze rippled the tall grass and fluttered the smaller branches of the red oaks, making the day more bearable. The air felt thick and mosquitoes were beginning to swarm as evening approached. The late August sun inched westward across a cloudless, azure sky to begin its majestic decent into the distant New Jersey horizon, heralding the close of another day. With a final burst of brilliance, its rays streaked through the clustered leaves of the trees surrounding the grassy clearing where the two boys played. The radiant beauty of the sunset was passing unnoticed by the two youths engaged in a make-believe duel. Perspiration and grime formed black beaded rings around their throats as they thrashed at each other with sticks fashioned into crude wooden swords. In their imaginations, time had rolled back to an earlier era and these were the finest rapiers in France with which they were defending, unto death, their maidens fair. The battle continued to wage until, in their zest, one delivered a painful blow across the knuckles of his foe.

"Ow! I told you not to hit near the hands, Mike. Now I think you've broken my hand." Wincing in pain, Paris Allison dropped his makeshift weapon and cradled his wounded hand with the other. Nausea rose in his stomach and he swallowed repeatedly against the sour, burning bile erupting in his throat.

Using his forearm, he wiped his face to conceal the unbidden tears stinging his deep blue eyes. A sudden gust whipped the mass of light blond hair crowning his head and helped cool the hot flush that coursed through his slender frame.

"Gee, Paris, I'm sorry. I got carried away and swung too hard. But see, it's not broken. You can still move it." Mike Johnson's hazel eyes, set in a round, freckled face framed by copper-toned hair and punctuated by matching eyebrows, mirrored his concern.

"Yeah! I guess its okay…no thanks to you."

Only five months separated their eleventh birthdays, but standing next to each other, Mike was almost a head taller. He was wider and stockier than Paris, who was slender and lithe.

"Let's sit here on the ground," Paris said settling on the sedge grass. "I still feel a little sick to my stomach."

"That sick feeling will go away soon," Mike assured Paris as he plopped down.

For several minutes they sat silently, their legs outstretched and crossed at the ankles, while Paris flexed the fingers of his injured hand. The pain was subsiding, but the reddened surface was slightly swollen.

Then Mike turned to Paris and cleared his throat. "Uh…do…do you ever get feelings?"

"What kind of feelings?" Paris retorted sullenly.

"I mean…do you ever get really hard down below?" He looked away, a flush creeping up his neck to his cheeks.

Paris shrugged. "That's a normal feeling, a part of growing up. That's how grown-ups make babies. Sure, I get them too."

"How come you know so much, Paris?"

"'Cause I read a book my mom got me called Father and Son. It explains everything, so when we grow up we won't make any mistakes."

"Wow," Mike sighed. "I wish I were as smart as you. I know I'll foul up and never will be able to make any babies."

Paris grinned at Mike's worried face. "Hey, don't worry. I'll read it and explain it step by step. That way we'll both learn everything there is to know and neither of us will ever make any mistakes when we grow up."

Hope brightened Mike's face. "What sort of girl do you want to marry when you grow up, Paris?"

"My mom says there's a very special person waiting for each of us. I'm going to marry a girl with blond hair and blue eyes, but she's got to be really beautiful."

"I'm going to marry a dark-haired girl. One like the movie star we saw in the Arabian movie last week. When I grow up, I'm going to kiss her just like in the movies."

As though a curtain had been drawn, the sun disappeared behind the trees and dusk mantled their surroundings.

"We'd better head back home," Paris said. "We'll be in hot water with your mother if we're not home before dark."

7

Paris spent many summer weekends with Mike, his first cousin on his mother's side of the family.

The Johnsons lived in Mountain View, a small rural town north of the industrial city of Paterson. The surrounding woods had been a playground for the boys, and there they grew up together, bonding with the closeness of brothers.

That evening the gentle movement of the warm, summer breeze stirred the thin curtains hanging over the open window, while outside the crickets and frogs, sounded their vigilant mating calls. The two boys lay restless in bed, unable to fall asleep, their minds filled with the bursting vitality of youth.

"Paris, if it's normal…you know, what we were talking about, what you said…to get feelings…. If that's part of making babies when we grow up, where do they come from? The babies I mean?"

"The girl carries them in her stomach. You've seen girls they called pregnant. Their bellies get real big and fat."

"Oh, shit! I know that. I mean, how do they get out? You know, out of their stomach? It has to take some large opening. I've seen babies and they're big, even new babies. How do they get out?"

"Let me think about that, Mike. It shouldn't be too hard to figure out." Paris placed his arms beneath his head and peered up through the darkness at the ceiling. After a few moments of deep thought he answered, "That's easy. The only opening big enough for a baby to get out is through their mouth. They just cough them out when they're ready. They open their mouths and cough real hard."

"Gosh! Yuck! You must be right. But now that I think of it, I'm not sure I want to kiss a girl anymore, at least not one that's had a baby."

"Sure, I'm right. It's got to be that way. There's no other spot big enough."

"What about their…you know…." Mike snickered. "What about…from their behinds?"

"No! Use your head. If they came from there, they'd smell awful, and who'd go around kissing new babies and talking about how sweet smelling they are. No, they cough them out, like I said before."

"Did you read that in the book?"

Paris hesitated, not wanting to lie. "No, I haven't gotten that far yet. I think that's explained in another chapter." He thought about it some more. The mouth was the only place big enough. "Yeah, Mike, coughing them up is the only way.

That's why married men don't kiss their wives on the mouth. If you notice, they always kiss them on the cheek, and usually it's just a peck."

"Yeah! You're right. When they're dating, they always kiss on the mouth with big, long kisses. But after they're married and have kids, they stop kissing anymore. I see that all the time."

CHAPTER 3

AT TIMES, TWO SILHOUETTED SHAPES were cast upon the giant movie screen as the young men's movements unknowingly blocked the flickering lights coming from the distant projection booth. In the darkness of the drive-in theatre, they maneuvered cautiously between the parked cars, balancing flimsy cardboard trays loaded with cups of sloshing soda and hot dogs.

At seventeen, Mike towered six feet, with a broad chest and wide shoulders. His once coppery red hair had darkened to a rich auburn, and the youthful freckles once marching across his round, pleasant face had yielded to a tanned complexion. As he trudged along, his feet shoved deeply into the graveled road, causing small stones to scatter, sounding like splashes of rain.

A few feet ahead, Paris led the way in the semi-darkness. Balancing his weight on the balls of his feet, his graceful cat-like movements created little noise on the uneven surface. His lean physique was four inches shorter than Mike's; square shoulders tapered down to a small waist and narrow hips. His head was crowned with wavy light-blond hair, which framed his penetrating blue eyes, sensual lips and straight nose. Altogether, his was an undeniably handsome countenance, which attracted admiring glances from women of all ages.

A bright scene from the large projection screen lit the area, just as Mike was throttled by a speaker cord stretched from its post to a car window.

"Damn!" He'd sloshed soda into the cardboard tray and down his shirt. "Let's give up and wait until sunrise."

Paris tried to suppress his laughter as he scanned the darkness in search of the pale yellow '49 Ford convertible. "I should have kept the parking lights turned on to help us locate the car. I parked closer to the screen...at least two rows further over."

Mike whispered, "How are you making out, Paris? Will she let you get a good feel? I've had my hand on my girl's tit through the whole first movie. I think she loves it."

"I can't do much in the front seat. I think Anna's afraid, with you two eyeballing us from the back."

Their dates' giggles rose out of the darkness at their stumbling antics.

"Ah geeze, they saw us. I wonder if it's all worth it," Mike muttered as they retraced their steps back two rows.

"Boy! What took you two so long?" Mike's girl flashed a pixy smile.

"We were unavoidably detained," Paris answered, opening the car door while carefully balancing his tray.

"He means, he got lost as hell, Loretta. I knew where we had parked all the time, but Paris wouldn't listen to me," Mike teased.

Paris tilted the back of his driver's seat forward toward the steering wheel to allow Mike to crawl in alongside his girl. Paris then leaned into the car to dole out the food and drinks before sliding behind the wheel.

"I was afraid you two had found other dates," Anna whispered, her long, dark eyelashes accentuating the pouting expression on her small, delicate face. Wisps of deep brown hair tantalizingly brushed Paris' nose as she shifted toward him.

"My hot dog's cold, Mike, and the soda tastes diluted. The ice is all melted."

"Oh hell, Loretta! It's not all that bad," Mike said defensively.

Paris detected a spoiled streak in Mike's girl and now regretted their double date arranged for this Saturday night. He wanted to be alone with Anna, to see how far she would allow him to go. He draped his right arm around her shoulder and pulled her closer. Despite knowing she wouldn't want to do any heavy petting in the other couple's presence, in the darkness of the car, he inched his left hand cautiously toward the bareness of her legs above the top of her stockings.

Anna's parents held her with a tight rein, and definite rules were set, to which she was expected to adhere. Any indiscretions now were against her moral upbringing and permitted only because of her affection for him.

His arm cradled her shoulders as she snuggled up to him. Unconsciously, his right hand stroked her hair as his thoughts drifted back to their first encounter.

It was during the last semester of their senior year they began to date. He was stunned when a close buddy asked him who he was taking to the senior prom. "All the pretty girls have already been asked, Paris," Greg said with a grin. "What 'dog' you planning on taking?"

His mind raced. He should have already gotten a prom date by now. There was still time to ask someone, but as Greg said, the better looking girls had already made prior arrangements with his fellow students. "You can bet your last dollar I won't be taking a dog," he replied.

The next period, as the European History class was in session, Paris scanned the classroom. His gaze fell on Anna Kersler. It was rumored she would be voted the prettiest girl in the graduating class, and everyone knew she had been one of the first girls to be asked to the prom.

He hurriedly tore half a page from his notebook and scribbled, "Will you go to the senior prom with me?" Folding the note and shielding it in his hand from the eagle-eyed schoolteacher who stood before the class, he waited until she turned to face the blackboard, then he hissed quietly to catch Anna's attention. Her pretty face seemed startled when she opened the note passed along to her by several of her classmates.

Paris watched anxiously as she read its contents. He detected no indication of rejection or acceptance in her expression. Then, she quietly ripped a small piece of paper from her notebook and wrote her reply. Waiting for the instructor to face the blackboard again, Anna passed her answer back to Paris. His heart pounded as he unfolded it and read her reply. "I've already been asked by someone else, but I'll go with you."

For the remainder of their senior year, she rejected any other boy's advances and was known as Paris' steady girl. On weekends, they went to the movies, then for White Castle hamburgers in Clifton, where orders were taken at your car window by girls on roller skates, their tight blue-and-white short-shorts leaving little to the imagination.

Anna's classes ended before Paris', and if the weather was fair, he'd leave the convertible top down. She'd perch herself upon the back rest of his front seat and wait to be driven home before he headed to his part-time job at a retail store in downtown Paterson.

The movement against his chest as Anna shifted her position brought his mind back to the present time. During the remainder of the movie, Anna sat with her head resting in the crook of Paris' right arm, while Mike and his girl appeared locked in a perpetual embrace in the back seat. Paris' left hand began toying with her garter strap. Receiving no resistance, his fingers inched upward until they touched the moist silkiness of her panties. Damn, he thought, his heart beginning to pound. If only we were alone. If she allowed me to go this far, she wants to go all the way.

When the movie ended, Paris removed the speaker from the driver's window and hung it back on its post. Looking toward the rear, he kidded, "Well, I hate to break up your wrestling match in the back seat, but I've got to get Anna home." He turned on the ignition, pressed the starter button and the powerful engine whirled over and started. Backing out of the space, he nosed the Ford out of the lot. He had no intention of taking Anna straight home after dropping Loretta and Mike off.

Although Paterson was an old industrial town, the view at night from the steep cliffs surrounding Paterson's northern edge made its twinkling lights sparkle like jewels. Toward the eastern horizon loomed the distant shadows of the huge sky-scrapers forming the New York skyline.

On warm nights, young lovers frequented this secluded site atop the bluffs. With the lights of the car turned off, they were enveloped in darkness. They could feel the gentle night breeze and hear the sound of frogs and crickets in the woods around them. It seemed they were in a world removed.

"I've never let a guy get fresh with me before," Anna breathed against Paris' neck.

"Do you think I'm being fresh?"

"Well, you shouldn't touch me the way you're doing."

"Should I stop?"

"Yes," she said hesitantly. "I think you'd better."

Her head still cradled in his arm, trying to arrest the excitement they had stirred in each other, Anna began to talk. "I've heard you're not going to college when you graduate. I expected you'd go on to college, but everyone says you're enlisting in the Navy. You never told me of your plans, but then you never talk about yourself, at least not to me."

"It's better that I get away. My family's not well off financially, and college would be a burden they don't need."

"Then you really mean to do it…to enlist? When will you go?"

"Right after we graduate. I'll try to get into the Navy and see more of the world."

"I'll miss you," she said softly, "if you're sincere about it…about joining."

"Oh, I'm sincere all right. I've made up my mind." He withdrew his arm. "I'd better get you home. It's getting late," he said, reaching for the ignition.

"Wait, Paris! Hold me again."

Startled by her sudden forwardness, Paris pulled her to him. He kissed her, feeling the hot excitement again flooding his loins as he pressed her back across the seat. Hands fumbling under her dress, he turned and lifted his body to wedge his hips between her legs. As her knees lifted and parted, her dress slid to her waist, revealing her stockinged legs. He could feel the soft, moist pubic hair as his hand pulled aside the crotch of her panties. Then he unzipped his slacks and attempted to enter her.

"Oh! Paris it hurts!" she gasped.

Initial pain rapidly abated, replaced with erotic sensations she had never felt before. Anna pushed her pelvis to meet the rhythmic thrusts as soft moans emanated from her throat. She climaxed just as Paris withdrew.

Fear of the consequences now cooled the hot desires they had felt.

"Why did you change your mind? I never expected you to give in," Paris said.

"You'll think I'm crazy, and my parents would kill us both if they found out, but I suddenly felt I wanted you to be the first. That not to know you…." She hesitated, groping to find the words, "would…would be worse." She shook her head, helpless to explain. "I think I've stopped bleeding now. I've used up all the paper napkins left from the drive-in. I guess we're lucky we didn't throw them away."

"Are you sure you're going to be all right?"

"Yes, I'm okay. God! I just hope nothing shows through my dress."

CHAPTER 4

THE ICY NIGHT WIND WHIPPED the powdery snow across the ground, dusting the tops of the parked cars. In the cold moonlight, the whiteness gave an eerie iridescence to the surrounding landscape. Silvery icicles hung from the eaves of the house in which the small gathering of friends and relatives had come to give their best wishes to Paris before he left. Some were stunned at his decision to enlist in the Navy, feeling he should be going to college, but Paris wanted to avoid *adding to his parents' financial struggles.* His father's formal education had ended in grade school, and the family's meager livelihood was made by his dad's long hours of hard, physical work repairing trucks and automobiles.

Paris started working at 16, but realized as a youth that he was expected to do the same work as an adult, for lesser pay. Sure, his future opportunities would be limited without a degree, but since the Korean War Armistice wasn't yet signed, he argued, it'd be wiser to enlist and have a choice of the branch of service. Not going to college meant that when he reached nineteen, the mandatory draft would force him into the military anyway. By entering now, he'd be eligible for college benefits under the G.I. Bill. When his enlistment was over, he'd get his diploma.

Leaving Anna inside to help his mother tend to the guests, he slipped out to the front porch for a needed break from the constant barrage of questions. Shivering in the cold January air, he stuffed his hands deep into his pants' pockets and hunched his shoulders. His breath became clouds of crystals hovering in front of his face, then dissipating. His thoughts were as distant as the infinite stars in the blackened heavens, and he wasn't aware of the door opening behind him.

Mike's voice startled him and he spun around, with his right fist raised.

"Wait! Hold it!" Mike held up his palms. "Save that hostility for the *Gooks.* Boy! You're edgy! Getting a little scared? You got doubts about going?"

"You scared the hell out of me. I didn't hear you sneak up behind me. No," Paris answered slowly. "I've thought it all out, and it's the only way to go."

Mike released an exasperated sigh. "Why the hell did you do it? You've got everything going for you. I wish I were in your shoes. Just look at Anna. I can tell watching the way she looks at you that she's ape shit over you. I wish I was half as sure of Loretta."

"Ah, she'll come around. She's just a little spoiled, used to getting her own way. She'll be okay."

"She's spoiled, all right." Mike agreed, nodding his head.

"Mike…about my car. I want you to take it. You can pay me a little at a time, without getting yourself in a bind."

"Shit! I can't do that. You and your dad put a hell of a lot of work in that ragtop."

"I've talked it over with Dad and I don't have any brothers to give it to, so first cousins are the next best thing. I want you to take it, but keep it in good shape. When I get leave, I may want to borrow it a few times."

They both gazed affectionately at the pale yellow Ford convertible parked by the curb, the wind-blown powdered snow dusting its raised canvas top. *I could shave using those chrome bumpers as mirrors*, Paris thought.

"Here are the keys. Take good care of her. I don't have a garage, so it's better if she's being used. Just watch your speed; the tires are getting pretty thin and you'll need new ones soon. I wanted to get white-walls, but my money got kind of scarce."

"Can I take care of Anna for you while you're gone, too?"

"Get the hell out of here." Paris elbowed him the ribs.

"Well, you said it yourself. No good to have her sit around…better if it's used."

Mike abruptly stopped his joking as the front door swung open.

"Oh! There you are," Anna chided them, stepping out onto the porch. "What are you two doing out here? The party's inside."

"We were just talking about what you and I are going to do while Paris is gone," Mike bantered.

"Oh, good! I'll go and tell Loretta right now," Anna teased, turning to go back inside. Mike's hands gripped her upper arms, stopping her in her tracks.

"You want to turn this party into my wake?" he kidded, then released her. "Yeah, I'd better get inside. I saw one of your pals zeroing in on Loretta just before I came out. Anyway, you two want to be alone."

When the front door closed behind Mike, Anna put her arms around Paris' waist and snuggled her head against his chest. "Hold me close for a moment; I'm freezing."

He tilted her pretty face to look up at him. "Anna, I want you to go out. Have a good time. Don't wait for me. You can do better."

She shook her head fiercely. "I'll wait." She pulled his head downward, her kiss filled with passion and promise.

CHAPTER 5

STEVEN BAKERMAN HUNCHED HIS SHOULDERS, shoving his hands deep into the torn pockets of his frayed coat. The rough, wooly fabric bristled against his neck and cheeks, but warded off the cold January wind and snow sweeping across the U.S. Naval Training Center located on the Maryland shore of the Chesapeake Bay. Snow crusted the thin soles of his tattered shoes, and he stomped his feet to increase circulation and ease the burning pain in his toes.

"I look like a bum." He unconsciously spoke aloud, his thoughts betrayed by the movements of his lips. "Why worry how I look now? We'll all be like peas in a pod when we get uniforms. I just hope I haven't stepped in shit up to my ears."

He was only seventeen, but his brown shaggy hair was already thinning above his high forehead, accentuating his prominent nose and angular face. Tight lips parted as he exhaled into the frigid night air, revealing a missing lower front tooth.

Experiencing cold was familiar to Steve, but nothing he remembered equaled the agonizing chill now penetrating his shaking body. Remaining apart from the crowd of nervous young men, he stood just outside the door of the empty bus that had transported them from New Jersey and watched as another bus-load of recruits pulled into the depot.

It was the largest enlistment for the United States Navy since the outbreak of World War II. Anyone out of high school not going to college and near draft age had hurried to join to get the Government entitlements, which would cease with the foreseeable end of the Korean War.

Steve Bakerman's ambitions were more immediate. He wanted to get off the corners of Paterson's lower Main Street, predominately inhabited by low-income blacks and a fast-multiplying Hispanic population, all housed in decaying cold water apartments, surrounded by open produce markets.

Living in a slum neighborhood had been a humiliation. During his school years he had watched his family's failure to pull themselves from this mire as a result of lack of education and work skills. Enlisting was the surest exit he knew to escape this embarrassment. *Just this morning,* Steve thought as he eyed the other men, *I was sworn in with this crowd of wimps. Look how they herd together like cows going to slaughter.*

He'd chosen to stand alone at the National Guard Hall in Newark, though he had to confess to having pangs of envy seeing hundreds of relatives and girlfriends come to witness the swearing in ceremony and see their loved ones off. No one had come to see him leave.

Loneliness had been his only companion during the long bus ride from Newark to Bainbridge. Now, standing in the cold night air looking at the ominous gray military base, he was convinced. "Yeah, I've made a mistake."

Above the gusting wind, a petty officer in a Navy pea coat over a dark blue uniform, a white "dixie cup" hat resting above the bridge of his nose, began bellowing orders in a southern, nasal drawl.

"All you goddamned shitheads...get over here and form a column of twos. Move your asses, now! I ain't got all night. There's another bus load of you rejects coming in."

The new recruits scrambled to obey the order, but not fully understanding, began assembling in a single column.

"Goddamn! I said twos...not a single file, you assholes."

"The bastard wants us to form a double line. Stand alongside me and the rest will begin to follow suit." Steve was aware someone was speaking to him and moved forward to stand next to the stranger.

"My name's Bakerman...Steve Bakerman," he said quickly, welcoming the friendly overture.

"Mine's Allison, Paris Allison."

"Where're you from, Allison...er, you said 'Paris'?"

"From Paterson. Yes, Paris."

"Hey, I'm from Paterson too."

"Yeah! What part?"

Steve felt the familiar embarrassment reddening his face at having to admit his slum origins.

"In the lower...."

"Shut up, you shitheads. This ain't no tea party. Keep your traps shut or you can stand out here all night and freeze your nuts off. It's too late to handle all of you tonight and I didn't have time to book y'all in at the Ritz, so when you're through the first stage of processing, I'll march your asses over to the Main Drill

Hall. There ain't no cots or mattresses available yet, so you'll have to make do and flake out on the floor 'til morning."

Following the initial processing, Paris, Steve and the first wave of new recruits bedded down on the floor of the Drill Hall, cradling their heads in their arms and using their coats for cover.

Steve tossed uncomfortably, unable to sleep. With the cold hardwood floor pressing his worn clothing into his bones, he dwelled on the day's happenings leading up to the strange alliance he had come to make with this stranger. *Paris*, he thought. *What an odd name.* He never needed anyone to survive in the harsh environment in which he grew up, yet at this time and place, he found he was drawing an unexplained strength–perhaps courage–from this newfound companion.

"Christ," he muttered beneath his breath, "I thought Uncle Sam could at least afford a place for us to sleep. My recruiting officer didn't tell me it would be like this."

"It won't get any better," Paris grunted.

"Sorry, I thought you were asleep," Steve apologized.

"Who in hell can sleep like this?"

The following days were chaotic. Each man was issued a complete sea bag, and the newly formed company marched into the large drill hall where instructions were given for stenciling personal identification on their clothing. Countless mistakes resulted from poor instructions and misunderstandings.

"If the asses in charge did less swearing and more explaining, there wouldn't be so many mistakes," Steve moaned.

"Just remember, white paint is for winter dress blues and work uniforms, and black paint is for summer whites," Paris reminded him.

In the confusion, and to the disgust of the instructing petty officers, some recruits mistakenly stenciled names and service numbers on the outer sides instead of the *insides* of garments. As they placed the white caps on their heads, a few had stenciled the outside brims with their black-inked identities.

On the third day of inoculations and processing, the recruits marched to the barbershop. Amid mixtures of laughter, protests, and often tears, the company got its first close-cropped G.I. haircut. Until now, they had been sleeping in the drill hall on hastily distributed floor mats. Today, they were assigned barracks with sleeping arrangements assigned alphabetically.

Both Paris and Steve breathed sighs of relief when they heard their names called out: "Allison, bunk one, top rack. Bakerman, bunk one, lower rack."

Donald Orloski was big, half again as broad across the back as the average man, and his neck was thick and weather-creased below a crop of short, dark hair. The curled bottom lip on his ruddy face suggested a cruel disposition. His size intimidated those in his charge during 12 years at sea; but this was his first shore duty assignment, and his scowl hid the fact that he was unsure of himself. His stomach tightened as he recalled the past hour at the regimental meeting. The base commander had pulled no punches while sitting at his desk, the "scrambled egg" visor pulled low on his forehead.

Commander Reed had outlined the progress he expected in a deep monotone, never wavering or hesitating. "The base is at full capacity with this surge of enlistees coming in at the end of the Korean Conflict. Time is money. Without going into budgetary problems, I'll only say this once. Basic training is designed to prepare recruits for usefulness to the Navy in just eight weeks. Any longer is a waste of money and manpower. You'll be given all the help and administrative guidance possible to have your company graduate on time. Failure to achieve this will reflect directly on your military record." With that, First Class Petty Officer Donald Orloski had been dismissed.

The Duty Watch snapped his piece to *Present Arms*, yelling, "Attention on deck" as Boatswain Mate First Class Donald Orloski cleared the main ladder and stepped onto the top landing. The young recruits in the barracks froze at attention as their new company commander stood in the doorway. He scanned the neat rows of double-tiered cots and upright gray metal lockers, now occupied by Company 74. His duties had been mandated: ready these recruits for use to the Navy in just eight weeks.

Paris and Steve jumped to their feet, standing as straight as possible on hearing the command from the duty watch. Paris' attention focused on the eyes of the first class petty officer in charge of the newly formed Company.

"What are you staring at? You seem like you're off in another world," Steve whispered out of the corner of his mouth.

"I was looking at his eyes. Dad taught me to study the eyes; they're a dead giveaway. That bastard doesn't have all his marbles."

"Shit. He's a boatswain mate. All they need is a block of wood between their ears. He's been assigned our company commander. Name's Orloski."

Company 74's new commander, never before experiencing control over a large group of men, couldn't organize or follow the necessary training agenda. Orloski became frustrated with his men and ordered forced marching about the asphalted parade grinder in retaliation for any lack of progress.

He attempted to train the company in semaphore and the handling of a *piece* using the Basic Manual of Arms, but his poor leadership qualities bogged down the company and they found themselves marching again on the grinder.

"You know, if they hadn't shaved my head so I'm afraid to be seen in public, I'd have gone over the fence by now," Steve said. Sincerity rang in his voice.

"With heads like yours and mine, I think we'd better stick it out here, at least until our hair grows back out," teased Paris.

"Yeah! But this bastard don't know shit about handling a company. All the others that started out at the same time are way ahead of us. They're done with the semaphores. All this prick knows how to do is march. I don't think the Army does as much marching.

"You're right. It's march or stand watch with a damned rifle that won't shoot." Paris glanced down at the antiquated Springfield rifle he held.

"We have to call it a *piece*, and it's like most pieces I've run into; they don't put out either," Steve chuckled.

"I'm beginning to get worried though," Paris pondered aloud. "I don't know how much longer Regimental Headquarters will allow us to keep falling behind. They said we should make it through Basic in eight weeks time. We're behind the other companies by at least two weeks, and we're losing ground fast."

Their concern was not unfounded. The first regimental inspection was scheduled shortly after the third week. Company 74 failed miserably. Headquarters had the group set back two weeks for retraining.

Called on the carpet for his company's inept performance, Orloski resolved to set some examples.

His hostility focused on a young Italian boy from Brooklyn, named Angelo DeMarco. DeMarco barely squeezed through the required physical because of his slight size. His dark complexion and long face earned him the nickname, "House Mouse." DeMarco performed no worse than anyone else in the company, but Orloski needed someone to use as an example to shape up his deteriorating command. He pounced on the recruit with sadistic pleasure.

"You skinny assed guinea! Can't you do anything right? Hold that 'piece' straight or I'll put my foot up your macaroni bending ass. You're the biggest problem in this company, and I'll either make you into a sailor or break you in the process."

By Tuesday of the fourth week of Basic Training, DeMarco showed signs of cracking. In the chilly, early morning hours everyone lined up at attention for dress inspection. Orloski slowly scrutinized the men, stepping up to face each man so he could look him directly in the eyes, searching for any fear a recruit's eyes might betray.

The Company stood in two parallel lines, allowing a walkway to enable Orloski to pass, giving him a frontal and rear view of his men.

The bastard, Paris thought. *He's enjoying this.* The company commander was peering into his eyes, his face so close that Paris could smell his acrid breath. Without meaning to do so, he turned his face away slightly.

"You got a problem, sailor?"

"No, sir!" he snapped back.

"I say you got a problem, shithead. Looks to me like you're letting your sideburns get a little long. You think this is the Old West? You trying to be a nonconformist?"

"No, sir!"

"What'd you say, Skinhead?"

"No, sir!"

"Bring your razor tomorrow. Don't shave at reveille; just bring your razor to quarters. You're going to dry shave before the whole Company. You'll learn to cut those sideburns according to Navy regulations."

"Yes, sir!"

Their eyes locked. Orloski sensed no fear in the youth's unwavering stare.

Dislike, but not fear, he thought with grudging respect, and moved to the next recruit. "Well, Bakerman, you look like inspection material to me."

Steve stared straight ahead; perspiration began forming where his white cap met his brow. A small droplet trickled down his forehead to his temple.

Orloski studied the young recruit; his lips curled in a sneer as he watched the sweat run down Bakerman's face.

"You hot, sailor?"

"No, sir!"

"Either you're hot or you're scared. I think you're scared. You scared of me, sailor?"

"No, sir!"

"Uncover, shithead. I want to see if your hat is clean or if you tried getting by, washing only what you thought would be seen."

Steve removed his white cap with his left hand, inverting it so the inside was visible for inspection. He stood rigid, his right hand still about the barrel of his piece, resting with its stock alongside his right leg.

"You goddamned scrounge. Look at that ring! I bet your ass is as dirty. You'll stand an extra four-hour watch for being a pig. Cover, sailor!"

"Yes, sir!"

Steve squared his white hat back on his head.

Orloski continued down the column, growling obscenities at each recruit. No one escaped unscathed. When he reached DeMarco, he unleashed his full fury. The Italian youth was trembling visibly, his slight frame shaking uncontrollably. Orloski grabbed the front of the recruit's T-shirt showing above the dark, v-necked wool jumper. "You dirty Dago bastard. Your T-shirt looks like it hasn't been washed in weeks. You're a walking garbage bag."

He stretched the undergarment out in his hand, tearing the neck band and revealing the G.I. dog tags around DeMarco's neck. Orloski's eyes narrowed as they fixed on a smaller chain. His fingers pulled it up from beneath the white T-shirt. A small crucifix hung from a tiny gold chain. With a violent yank, he broke the chain from about the sailor's neck and threw it to the ground. "It'll take more than rabbit feet and crosses to save your ass in this man's Navy. Do you see that garbage Dumpster at the end of the grinder?"

"Yes, sir!" Angelo DeMarco's voice quivered, tears streaming down his long face.

"Double-time your ass over to that Dumpster and crawl inside. Close the hatch behind you! You understand me, *Dago?*" Orloski screamed into the youth's face.

"Sir?" Angelo's voice was barely audible.

"Get your black *guinea* ass inside that garbage Dumpster. On the double…go!"

Angelo sprinted from the file. The Dumpster seemed a welcome reprieve from Orloski's tirades.

"All right, dress up!" Orloski yelled. "Get into a marching column…two abreast."

Orloski marched the Company toward the metal Dumpster. "Company halt!" He lifted the heavy lid and peered inside. The young recruit was huddled in a squatting position with his "piece" across his knees. There was barely room above his head to clear the lid. "Whew!" The stench of the decaying garbage assaulted Orloski's nostrils and he stepped back from the smell.

"You should be right at home, DeMarco. Let me hear you. You at home down there, sailor?"

"Yes, sir," came the weak reply.

"It's too quiet in there. I think we need some noise to keep you company. I'll see what I can do for you."

Orloski closed the hatch and turned to the men. "March forward, breaking to the left and right of this shit-can. I want to hear the butts of those pieces hammer the sides of this Dumpster."

Three times, the Company marched past the huge garbage container, each man repeatedly pounding the butt of his ancient rifle against its walls.

Within his malodorous prison, young DeMarco crouched in a fetal squat, his hands covering his ears, his pitiful screams muffled by the deafening resonance.

"You cruel son-of-a-bitch," Paris said loudly, marching abreast of Steve.

"Shhhh!" Steve whispered to his friend. "If he hears you, no telling what he'll do. They say there's a newscaster on the radio who had a nephew die down here while going through Bainbridge Basic. He's been heard broadcasting to the people that if their sons are in Korea, write to them, but if they're in Bainbridge, Maryland, pray for them."

"What's this newscaster's name?"

"Gabriel Heatter," Steve replied, trying not to be overheard. "He's one of the top newscasters on the radio."

25

"Shit! The things Orloski are pulling on poor DeMarco should be reported, but who'd really give a fuck?"

Two hours later, Company Commander Orloski released the slim Italian youth from the Dumpster. "House Mouse" was never the same. When the company returned to the barracks after daily drilling, Angelo DeMarco would seek a hiding place in the far stall of the barrack's head. He'd sit fully dressed on the toilet seat, starring at the back of the closed stall door.

By late January, morale reached an all time low. Standing at attention, extreme fatigue, mid-winter cold and icy winds blowing across the parade grounds compounded the recruits' depression. Orloski yelled to be heard above the noisy gusts. "Today, General Classification Testing will commence. Pass with high marks. The higher your G.C.T. score, the better your chance for advanced schooling. Fuck up on it and you'll be swabbing a deck aboard some ship in the Fleet. 'Class A Schools' means faster advancements in the Navy...if you can hack it."

Steve whispered, his lips barely moving, "Orloski must have fucked up on this testing. He looks like he's been trained in deck swabbing."

Orloski continued. "Two new recruits will be joining this company. They're being sent down for retraining. When they report in, it might be wise to let them know I don't tolerate any form of disobedience."

"The poor bastards don't know what they're in for. Out of the frying pan and into the fire," Steve mumbled.

"Maybe they'll take some of the heat off DeMarco," Paris responded quietly.

The following week, Paris and Steve watched the two recruits unshoulder their heavy sea bags upon reporting to Company 74. They stood on the landing outside the barrack's entrance, waiting to be assigned bunks and upright lockers.

Studying them as he heard both identified by the master of arms, Paris concluded, "I've never seen two more opposite-looking characters."

The one named Madison was over six feet tall with penetrating eyes, recessed like dark bits of coal into a hawk-like countenance. His head was capped with the remnants of straight black hair. His profile resembled the Indian found on a Buffalo nickel. Broad shoulders indicated considerable strength in his upper body. His surly expression oozed hostility.

Steve drew Paris' attention to Madison's hands. "Damn, when he closes his fists, they look like sledge hammers. I'd hate to have to take him on before breakfast."

"Yeah. That one's not going to be easy to get to know."

"The shorter guy looks scared," Steve noted.

"I've seen that same wide-eyed expression on a startled deer when Dad and I hunted," Paris said, studying the recruit's bristle-like brown hair and his long, swarthy face with its flared nostrils. "He looks like a frightened deer. But then I guess we're all scared. I try to imagine how Dad would act when things get real rough. Let's see if we can take the two of them under our wings. Sometimes a little bit of friendliness goes a long way. They look like they could use some."

"This is going to take some time."

"Lately, time is the one thing we seem to have plenty of," Paris responded dryly.

Tyrone Madison set his heavy sea bag onto to the deck. He felt the thud of another bag drop heavily beside him and glanced disgustedly in Michael Crowley's direction as the recruit straightened his back, rubbing his shoulder muscles.

"That damned bag weighs a ton. I think I pulled my arm out of joint," said the smaller youth.

"You bitch too much. There's no difference in your bag's weight and mine," said Madison.

"Yeah, Tex, but just look at your size. If I were as big as you, I wouldn't mind the damned weight, either."

"Like I said, you bitch too much," Madison repeated.

"You sure aren't the friendly type. You'd think we'd be pals with having things in common, like being set back to the same company."

"I ain't looking for any pals. I keep strictly to myself. Pals get you in trouble. That's why I'm here now," said Tex.

"You're here now 'cause you threw your piece across the company commander's foot."

"That was never proven, so button your lip, Mickey, or I'll be getting another set back."

Madison scanned the crowded barracks, his thoughts momentarily drifting back a few months ago. Things had been good for him in El Paso. He was making more money than needed, until a snitch blew the whistle and he was caught red-handed stealing cars and selling them across the Mexican border.

What was it the judge said? He mused. Oh, yeah: "You have a choice of becoming government property or going to jail. Because you're nineteen, I'll show some leniency. Voluntarily serve your country or do hard time in prison." But, hell, the judge said Army, not Navy.

Standing alongside Tex Madison, Michael Crowley felt the familiar uneasiness that constantly hounded him. Acutely aware of his lack of confidence and being separated from his previous company after a bout of "walking pneumonia" and a week in sick bay only made matters worse.

Paris and Steve perceived Michael Crowley as an extremely nervous, average-sized individual, possessing a glib tongue that usually got him into trouble. They took him under their wing, but often criticized him for "rattling like an empty garbage can," but "Mickey" gratefully accepted their friendship.

CHAPTER 6

FIRST CLASS BOATSWAIN MATE ORLOSKI stood with Company 74 before the Olympic-sized pool, listening to the briefing from Chief Petty Officer Winters, the swimming instructor. "Now," he ordered, "go into the locker room and shower before you put on your swim suits. The corpsman is going to check your peckers; I don't want any dirty horsecocks contaminating this water. I'll ask for volunteers to qualify swimming the necessary distance. You are required to complete two events: first, swimming the outer circumference of this pool; second, jumping off that 25 foot tower." Winters pointed to the high platform above the far end of the pool. "Anyone failing to qualify gets set back two weeks for retraining. Uncle Sam wants his sailors to know how to take care of themselves in case they have to abandon ship. My job is to make sure you have this basic knowledge. Now, hit the showers and scrub those dicks. On the way out of the locker room, you'll each be checked for cleanliness. You got five minutes."

The young seamen stripped quickly, placed their gear in the upright lockers, then showered beneath the long row of nozzles.

Paris lathered his body, scouring his genital area before joining the line-up for the "pecker check." A single file formed at the entrance to the huge pool, and Paris quickly moved up to the seated corpsman who, with a long flashlight, studied his penis.

"Okay, shithead, peel it back."

Paris pulled back his foreskin, revealing the sensitive head of his penis.

"All the way back, I said."

Paris had never pulled his foreskin completely back. It was so tight that tears involuntarily came to his eyes.

"Shithead, *all* the way back or I'll cut the goddamned thing off. Come on! All the way back. You're holding up the line."

"Goddamn it! I've never pulled it back that far. It hurts like hell."

Paris heard Steve and Mickey snickering behind him. Bastards, just you wait, he thought. He pulled carefully, feeling soreness around the stretched skin. With a sigh of relief, he entirely exposed the head.

By now, his two buddies were roaring. Mickey yelled from behind, "He needs a good piece of pussy to pull it for him."

The corpsman sprinkled powered detergent over his exposed area.

"Go back to the showers. You got less than a minute to clean the crotch cheese off your wang."

As Paris passed his two friends, they continued teasing him. "See! If you were circumcised, your cock would be clean. We don't need a shroud over our dicks."

"I hope you bastards drown."

He was busy scouring himself when Steve and Mickey returned to the showers with their genital areas sprinkled with powdered detergent.

Steve looked serious. "Shit, man! That 'pecker checker' wants us to draw blood scrubbing our dicks. This powdered shit is like sandpaper. My dick's shrunk two inches."

With the sanitary inspection completed, the three sat alongside the pool with the rest of the recruits, listening as Winters called for volunteers for the swimming qualifications. "Anyone thinking he can swim around this pool three times, fall in over there."

Several in the company stood up and walked to the starting point.

"Shit," Tyrone Madison addressed the trio for the first time. "One rule I've learned is never volunteer for anything."

"All right, anyone thinking he can swim twice about the pool."

A few more stood up and walked to the starting edge.

"Hell! It's wintertime," Mickey whimpered. "It's been over six months since any of us has done any swimming. I'd drown in a bathtub now."

"Okay," the instructor yelled, "party's over. Each man's got to make it around one time or its back for retraining. Every sailor's got to be a qualified swimmer to make it through Basic. The rest of you pussies fall over here in single file behind the volunteers."

Reluctantly, the remainder of the company stood and formed a long, curving line about the edge of the pool.

"No diving. Jump feet first into the water and come up in the same spot, then swim free-style along the outer rim, finishing back where you started," Winters said.

"I'll never make it," Mickey whined. "I can't swim that far."

"Sure you can." Paris grinned. "Just think, you don't have the weight of a foreskin to hold you back."

One by one, the recruits jumped into the water. Some were called back to start over when they attempted to spring forward from the bottom to gain extra distance. Each was forced to surface exactly at the point of entry.

Most showed signs of tiring before reaching the half-way mark. Even those who had believed they could swim well enough to make it around two and three times were showing fatigue in the last lap. All were long out of practice.

Tyrone Madison's strokes were even and smooth as he began the last lap; the strength in his shoulders proved advantageous and he finished easily. Paris and Steve were a short distance apart nearing the final lap, but both were exhausted. Mickey dropped far behind and was thrashing the water with short, uneven strokes.

Salvation came from behind with a verbal alarm. "He's had it! Pull him out, quick! Get him before he goes down again!"

Instructors on both sides of the pool used long poles to aid the struggling swimmers. Further back, one yelled, "Grab that one...he can't make it! Use the pole to pull him out!"

Steve called ahead to Paris, "I ain't gonna make it. I'm winded...got to get out," and he stroked his way to the side.

Now within 15 to 20 feet of their starting point, in the confusion, Steve and Paris swam unnoticed to the side and scrambled out of the water.

Madison grabbed Mickey Crowley, a few yards behind them, and pulled him from the water. "Quick," he breathed heavily, "get over there before anyone sees you. All those qualifying are in that area." Hoping their deception had not been noticed, the four recruits mingled with the qualified swimmers.

When the swimming event was completed, a dozen had failed to qualify. After resting, they would be given a second attempt, but anyone failing again would be sent back for retraining.

Now, the recruits stood gazing up at the tower looming high above them.

"I ain't jumping off that thing. I'd rather go down with the ship. I get afraid stepping off the curb," Mickey said.

"Just grab your balls, shut your eyes and jump. If you don't come up, no one's going to miss you," Steve joked.

"I'd rather dive. At least you can control how deep you go," Paris said, studying the structure.

"You don't want to dive. If there's debris in the water with a ship sinking, you'd kill yourself diving," Tyrone Madison remarked calmly.

The test simulated an "abandoning ship" procedure. To qualify, it was compulsory to don dungarees and jump from the tower feet first, one arm across the face and the other shielding the groin. Underwater, it was necessary to remove the dungarees, surface and knot each of the legs. Holding the waistband, the recruit was to flip the trousers over his head to capture air in each leg and form an inflated water bag. When the waistband was held below the water, the legs retained enough air to support the man's body and keep it afloat.

In groups of five, recruits climbed the ladder to the tower platform while the rest of the company watched from below. The height was overwhelming, and anxiety showed on every face. This ordeal was the worst yet.

High up on the platform, Chief Petty Officer Winters randomly picked the first man to jump. "All right, alligator bait, let's see if you can do a 'jive step' on the way down. You're first."

Booker Jones was the only Negro in the Company, and the whites of his eyes seemed to enlarge against his dark skin. "Oh, shit!"

"What was that you said, sailor?" the instructor snapped.

"Thank you…sir, I said thank you."

Booker Jones was not sure which he dreaded more: the drop or his swim instructor.

"Now, for the last time, don't look down. Jump keeping your legs and knees straight. You'll hit the water with less impact. Don't worry, you'll surface and be able to get the dungarees off. The body has a natural tendency to float, just like a piece of wood."

The instructor gave the visibly trembling recruit a gentle push. "I don't think ebony floats," he joked, as the young Negro plummeted to the water.

Surprisingly, he hit the water with very little splash. In a few seconds, he broke the surface, white teeth flashing against a dark face as he smiled relieved at having survived. The company cheered.

Jones, submerging several times and struggling to remove the dungarees and knot the legs, finally slung the wet trousers over his head and formed an air raft.

The young recruits clapped and cheered as he floated between the inflated legs. A broad grin on his face, he yelled hysterically across the water to his cheering buddies, "Ebony floats! See! Ebony floats!" The swim instructor, openly pleased at the recruit's performance, joined in the cheering.

As each group successfully made the jump, they assembled at the base of the tower, shouting encouragement to the remaining recruits waiting to complete the rigid requirement.

All went well, until "House Mouse" Angelo DeMarco began climbing the ladder. A third of the way up, he froze, shaking visibly as he clung to the rungs.

"Goddamn it!" yelled Orloski. "Get your ass up that ladder."

The frightened recruit hung in the same place.

Orloski shoved through the staring onlookers and mounted the ladder, ascending to DeMarco. With sheer brute force, he pushed the slight figure toward the top of the platform.

"Jesus Christ!" Steve cried out, "He'll cause him to fall."

The recruit finally scrambled onto the platform. There on top, Winters spoke to him in an unusually soft voice. "Look, son, it's really no big deal. Everyone has made it with no problem. You'll do fine. Just step a little closer and feel your way for a couple of minutes. It looks higher than it actually is."

Angelo DeMarco moved cautiously toward the instructor. He was about a foot from the edge when his company commander blurted, "This shithead's scared, and I won't coddle a coward!" This unexpected blast caused the frightened lad to turn. Orloski surged past the swim instructor, shoving the young recruit. "You yellow-bellied runt! I'll make you jump!"

Angelo screamed as the sudden shove cart-wheeled him over the side. He spun uncontrollably through the air, hitting the water flatly on his side, mouth open. The hard impact echoed through the hall. The horrified recruits stood at the edge of the pool, staring at the water, not believing what they had witnessed, waiting for DeMarco to resurface. He did not.

"Shit! He's drowning," yelled Paris.

He and Tyrone Madison dove simultaneously into the water, propelling their bodies to the spot where Angelo had entered. Shrill whistles sounded a "drowning alarm" as Winters made a clean dive from the top of the high platform.

Paris swam toward the dark blur at the bottom of the pool; a burst of bubbles suddenly engulfed him as Winters knifed into the water. Through the bubbles, Paris saw a blurry image with an inert form swimming toward the surface. Madison, one arm under Angelo's chin, broke the surface alongside Paris. An instant later, Winters emerged next to them, yelling between coughs, "Get him to the side."

Orloski descended the platform, and the recruits saw a guilty expression on his face. The company commander helped hoist DeMarco's limp form out of the water.

"You dumb, crazy bastard." Madison spat. Ordinarily, this would have landed him in the brig for insubordination.

The company commander ignored the blatant onslaught. "Give him room!" Orloski shouted, pushing the recruits aside to allow Winters to attend Angelo.

For what seemed an eternity, he worked frantically on the unconscious sailor as everyone stood watching. "He's coming around! He's breathing. Go ahead...cough. Cough out as much water as you can. You're going to be all right."

Angelo's eyes rolled as he tried to regain his focus.

"Is he going to be all right?" Orloski asked, visibly shaken.

"Yes. He'll be okay, but I want to have a few words with you," Winters hissed through clenched teeth, "in private, in the locker room."

The instructor's irate voice chastising Company Commander Orloski's conduct was easily heard through the closed locker room door. When the door opened, Orloski's face was flushed. He walked over to Angelo DeMarco, who sat hunched over, the color drained from his face and still coughing up water. "You okay, kid?" He said hesitantly. "Look! We've decided to mark you down as qualifying on the tower jump. Don't want another 'accident' like we just had to happen again."

"Accident! Hell!" Madison's voice was distinctly audible. Orloski again elected to ignore it.

"Be careful what you say, Madison," Paris warned quietly. "Orloski's not the type to forget."

He studied Paris for a long moment. "Thanks for the warning. I'm from Texas." He extended a hand. "You can call me Tex."

CHAPTER 7

THE TWO SAILORS MARCHED ALONG the icy path, the frigid early morning wind from across the Bay making their teeth chatter. At 0200, in the cold darkness, only the dim lights above the barrack entrances gave any illumination.

"Shit! We're freezing to death in the middle of the night on Roving Fire and Security Patrol. This has got to be the most stupid thing the Navy could come up with."

"If we could just turn up our collars," Paris muttered. "What in hell's the sense of having a pea coat with a large collar to keep the wind off your neck and ears, if you can't turn the damned thing up?"

"That's typical Navy logic; it's called 'uniform of the day.' This is horseshit! I'm so cold my feet don't have any feeling. The asses shave our heads to make our ears stick out, then march us out in this freezing cold so they'll fall off," Steve ranted.

"Look! There's a washhouse. Let's go in and warm up. I can't take this cold any longer."

"They'll hang our asses up to dry along with the wash if we're caught," Steve warned.

"Who in hell would be dumb enough to be out this time of night, in this cold, checking on us?"

"Okay. Let's go in, but just long enough to thaw out."

Inside, they dodged through the lines of wet clothing stretched across the walls of the steam-heated structure. Paris positioned himself at one of the foggy window panes. "I can spot anyone coming from here; we should be safe for a few minutes. What time is it? We have to report in every hour."

"There's still time. It's half-past two," Steve answered. "This hot, moist air sure takes away the chill. There must be three or four of these steam houses handling the base's washing and drying."

"Steve, we're in a hell of a mess. How much longer is Orloski going to keep our company on restriction? We're in our seventh week and still haven't been allowed to see a movie or use a telephone to call home," Paris whispered, rubbing at the fogged window.

"We do nothing but drill and fall further behind. Company 73 is already graduating next week, and they started out the same week we did."

"I know." Paris shook his head. "We've been at it a long time. I'm beginning to forget what the outside world is like. I haven't seen anything feminine for so long, I wonder if there're still any girls out there."

"Who are you kidding? You keep on getting perfume-scented letters from that girl, Anna. I'll bet she always kisses the envelope when she seals it. I get a hard on just smelling your mail," Steve teased, the warmth gradually restoring his sense of humor.

"If we ever get a visitor's day, I want you to meet her. She's promised to come."

"Great! Maybe after we get out of Basic and get some leave, we could double date. I know a few girls I can get in touch with back home."

Paris wiped the glass with his hand and scanned the dark area outside. "I lucked out last week. I got picked to go to the PX on a *gee-dunk* run. Orloski assigns one of us to go for razor blades, stationary and soap for the company. There's a piece of tail working in the PX I'd give my left nut to crawl in the sack with. You ever see her?"

"See her!" Steve laughed. "I've been beating my meat each time I think of that beautiful ass bending over behind the counter."

"You *what?*" Paris feigned a shocked expression.

"No shit, man. I saw her twice when I made two of Orloski's necessity runs. I'd drink a gallon of her piss to see where it comes from."

"I'll bet you would, too." They laughed, then Paris ducked away from the window and raised a warning hand. "I thought I saw someone coming this way. Let's get the hell out of here…quick!"

The freezing air hit them like a slap in the face. "Shit, it was a false alarm," Steve grumbled. "No one crazy enough to be out here but us, and we ain't got a choice."

"What do you think about what that sadistic bastard is doing when a fire drill is sounded? Orloski ordered the last man out of the barracks to march the next day, carrying two buckets of bricks."

"We've been lucky so far," Steve said, already shivering. "He always grabs DeMarco.

"The House Mouse stays in the back shower stall and is always the last one out. He's acting crazier, never talks anymore. As small as he is, I know those bricks get real heavy lugging them around all day."

Wondering what time it was, Paris looked at his watch's luminous dial. "Hell! It's time to go into the Brigade Office and report. I went last time. Now it's your turn."

"Paris…you go. Please," Steve pleaded. "I get nervous just thinking of sounding off. I'll probably shit in my pants. You do it one more time, okay?"

"All right, Steve. I'll do it again, but at 0400, we both have to go in to be relieved from watch. You should try it at least once, for practice."

"Oh! I don't sweat both of us going in together. It's just this hourly bullshit of having to do it alone that shakes me up. I'll be all right at 0400."

Throughout their watch, Steve had coerced his buddy to make the hourly reports, but as Paris said, both had to sound off at the end of the watch to be relieved. The moment of truth came at 0400.

Paris and Steve entered the Brigade Office and both brought their pieces to present arms as a salute to the gunnery chief behind the desk. Paris sounded off first, easily gliding through the procedure after hours of practice. "Good evening, sir. Allison, Seaman Recruit 4117710, Company 74, Roving Fire and Security Watch. All safe and secure. Asking permission to be relieved."

"Permission granted," the chief acknowledged.

Now, it was Steve's turn. "Er…Bakerman…I mean, Good evening, er. Bakerman, Seaman Recruit, 4118711, Comp…Comp," he stuttered, sweat pouring down his face.

Paris couldn't help smiling at the dumfounded expression gradually appearing on the gunnery officer's face. Up to now, the officer had watched nonchalantly as he leaned back in his chair, chewing on a cigar stub.

Steve tried to regroup and brought his piece down to his side, then snapped it back again to *present arms*. "Good evening, Sir.…er…Bakerman, Seaman Recruit 4118.… " his mind went blank. He brought his piece down again and swung it back to a salute position. Each time he tried to sound off his report, he dropped another word. "Good evening, sir…Bakerman…er…er."

The Chief tried to control himself, but the harder he fought to hold back his laughter, the more comical the situation appeared. He poked his stale cigar back into his mouth, trying to stifle the swelling laughter in his throat. His face turned red, not with anger, but hilarity, as he attempted to appear stern and grim.

Paris couldn't restrain the convulsive chuckle in his throat.

Steve Bakerman was the only one not finding the situation amusing. Still stuttering, he attempted once again to come to *present arms.*

The chief roared from across the room, attempting not to grin as tears flowed down his face, but his eyes betrayed his true feelings. "You goddamned shithead. You go outside and you practice. You hear me?" He wiped his eyes with the back of his hand. "And if you give me one more 'er,' I'll have you stand the next three watches. I want it letter perfect." He glowered at Paris. "What are you grinning about? This a joke to you, sailor?"

"No, sir." Paris snapped to attention, unable to erase the grin on his face.

"You better help your buddy or he'll spend the rest of his enlistment on Roving Patrol. Now! Go outside, and when you come back in, I want it perfect."

"Yes, sir." Steve saluted.

Once outside, Paris erupted with laughter.

"Paris, you got to help me. That bastard means business. He's out to get my ass. I know it. Come on, stop laughing! This ain't funny."

They practiced for some time before Steve summoned enough courage to go back in and face the chief. He never divulged what happened inside. When he returned, both walked silently from the building. Once outside, they dropped their "pieces" to the ground and rolled against the building, holding their sides, laughing.

CHAPTER 8

THE MELTING SNOW SPARKLED LIKE countless diamonds strewn over a crumpled, white blanket. The air was cold, but in the early March sunlight, sloshing sounds beneath the Company's marching feet foretold the end of the long winter.

Apprehension ate at them like a malignancy, eroding what little morale was left as they filed into the Drill Hall. Fear of the unknown was ever present. Each day summoned another challenge, but offered no meaningful advancement as the group fell further behind.

"I wonder what's in store for us today," Steve whispered, as the company commander's attention focused on the rear of the column.

"Probably more shit to pile on us," Paris said with a shrug. "I'm beginning to regret not joining the Army; we'd do less marching. My dad wanted to join the Army…he wanted to see the Hawaiian Islands."

"Did he ever get there?"

"Nope! He met Mom and then family responsibilities took priority. All he ever did was work. Down South, after the depression, there wasn't any work. I had a brother die of pneumonia…no money for a doctor or medicine. Dad made the casket and buried him. Finally, Dad hitchhiked north to find a job. That's how we wound up in New Jersey."

They halted abreast of another company waiting in the hall. On command, both units were to turn and form a single line facing each other. Both company commanders instructed their men that each recruit now faced his opponent, regardless of size.

"You'll be fitted with 16 ounce gloves and paired off to fight," Orloski stated. "You'll be timed for three minutes and must fight within this five-foot square painted here, on the deck."

"Oh shit!" Mickey Crowley moaned loudly.

"This is a part of your basic training…where I can tell if you've got shit in your blood…or enough guts to make you a sailor. When I blow this whistle, the first pair of you shitheads will go at it. Try to beat the piss out of your opponent. If I catch you killing time or dancing around, you'll get in the square with me." Orloski smiled sadistically.

Company 74 did well. Most of the recruits came from large cities where there was some knowledge of street fighting and boxing. The only novice to this type of fighting was Cleve Johnson. From rural Pennsylvania, he found himself facing "street smart" young men. It was obvious he was no match for his sparing partner. Johnson continued to hold his heavy gloves at his sides after the starting whistle blew. The first series of blows hit him in the face, and he tried to cover up with his arms, leaving his mid-section wide open.

His opponent hammered at his unprotected stomach, and Johnson's face had a shocked, hurt expression as the blows belted his solar plexus. He tried to ward off the onslaught by flailing wildly, leaving his face unprotected. Johnson went down under a hail of blows to the face and nose, his jaw broken in two places. It turned out that his opponent had been a contender in semi-professional boxing competitions.

"You looked pretty good, Allison," Orloski said. "I liked the way you handled yourself with the gloves…good offensive and defensive boxing. You scored some good hits without taking any damage to yourself. Where did you learn to fight?"

"I grew up in a rough Northern neighborhood with a southern accent, sir."

When Tex Madison quickly outmatched his boxing opponent, the time was ripe for the company commander to retaliate for his insubordination during the swimming drill.

"I think you were just dancing around, Madison. Now, I'll let you take a crack at me." He stepped into the square.

"I'd like nothing better, sir," said Tex, gritting his teeth. "Where are your gloves?"

"I don't need any." Orloski struck without warning. His bare fist caught Tex in the cheek below his eye and sent him staggering out of the square.

As Tex tried to shake off the impact of the blow, Orloski, pointed his finger at him. "You had your chance. Now fall back into ranks."

The large recruit crouched, about to spring at his assailant, when Orloski repeated his order. "Fall back into ranks. That's a direct order. Your instruction is over, unless you think it's worth some Brig time?"

Tex stared at Orloski, hatred glittering in his dark eyes. He spat on the hardwood floor, then turned and walked to his place among the ranks; his cheek was cut and already swelling.

Grumbling rippled throughout the group. "The bastard sucker-punched him. The prick didn't forget what Tex called him."

"Attention!" Orloski commanded.

When the boxing exercise ended, both companies marched away with their allotment of bloody noses, cut lips and swollen faces. Company 74 marched away with more than its share of bitterness.

Mail call came on Sunday. Paris received three letters. One was unmistakably from Anna; her red lipsticked kiss was on the sealed envelope flap. Another was from his mother and the third, from Mike. It wasn't often Mike took the time to write. Paris opened his first and waded through the almost illegible handwriting, but the message was clear enough: Mike and Loretta had gotten engaged.

Steve looked over, detecting the frown on his buddy's face. "Bad news?"

"I hope to hell not. It's my cousin...the one I told you about. He's planning on getting married."

"Hell! That ain't such bad news. It's the best way I know of getting a steady piece of ass."

"I hope you're right. I just wonder if they're ready for this. She's spoiled rotten. Can be a real bitch at times."

He glanced down at the letter and hit it lightly with the back of his fingers, finalizing his thoughts. "I hope she comes around...or his problems are just beginning. You think Orloski can be a pain in the ass? You should meet Loretta."

He opened the envelope from his mother and read its contents. *"Things are about the same. Dad is working hard. We miss you and worry about you."*

When he got to Anna's letter, he smiled. "I saved the best for last."

"Shit, man. Please read it out loud so I can have a wet dream tonight." Mickey knelt and pressed his palms together.

"You little bastard. The only kind of wet dream you've ever had was waking up with your cock in your hand," Tex laughed.

At the end of the ninth week, Company 74 marched out on the parade grinder for its second regimental inspection. The group was to march four abreast before the stand of regimental officers, snapping their heads toward the officers on a given command from their company commander, while at the same time, bringing their "pieces" to *present arms* as a salute. The men carried this out with precision. At least in this, the Company was well trained.

Orloski intended to have his men, upon completion of the salute, take a left flank to carry them at a diagonal movement, away from the parade stand. No one knew if he was nervous or he allowed his attention to stray, but Orloski called out his order, "To the right flank...march." The unit was thrown into chaos.

Those marching nearest the bleachers realized it had to be a mistake and turned to the left to prevent hitting the bleachers. Those on the outside responded automatically to the order given. Mayhem reigned.

Failing its second regimental marching inspection, once again Company 74 was set back for two weeks' retraining. After the ninth week, the Company was in reality only in its fifth week.

On the way back to their barracks, Orloski hammered the marching men with obscenities.

"Paris," Steve whispered, "the jerk-off has gone berserk. I don't think he even realizes what he said."

Paris didn't have time to respond. Orloski had come up from the rear and in a sudden motion, slapped the piece Paris was carrying across his right shoulder against the side of his head.

"What do you think you're carrying...a squirrel gun? Keep that piece straight across your shoulder."

Paris stumbled and went to his knees.

Steve stooped to help his buddy back to his feet, trying not to break step. "The goddamned idiot. He'll wind up killing somebody."

Orloski's wrath didn't stop there. Coming up behind DeMarco, he kicked the small recruit in the buttocks. "Get your wop ass in step...you ain't on no banana boat now!"

The Company halted in front of the barracks, and there Orloski's unleashed his full fury. He ordered Company 74's marching flag to be discarded. In its place, they were to march with a mattress cover hung from the flag staff.

"You don't deserve a Company flag. From here on, everyone on this base will know you as a bunch of fuck-ups. I want a pig drawn on a fart sack. You'll march carrying that as your Company banner. DeMarco, you'll carry it from here on. It'll fit you to a tee."

"Yes, sir." The House Mouse gazed straight ahead, his eyes blank.

"After chow, we'll start over. We'll spend the next week marching with full sea bags until you shape up. I've been easy on you up to now, but all that's changed." The Company marched to the Mess Hall, with orders to reassemble after chow.

The cold March wind whipped the powdered snow across the grinder as the men formed outside their barracks, full sea bags slung across their shoulders.

Alligator Bait — Booker Jones — spotted him first. "Hey man!" Jones called out, pointing. "There's some damned fool on top of the water tower." The recruits squinted upward.

Silhouetted against the pale blue sky someone stood at the edge of the tower's cone-shaped roof. Something long and white, tied around the figure's neck, flapped in the stiff breeze.

High above, Angelo DeMarco stood looking down. The frigid air whipped the mattress cover knotted about his neck. On it, he had used his black stencil ink to paint the crude outline of a pig. He was oblivious to the cold. Far below, the gathering crowd seemed like an army of tiny ants. No longer would he fear anyone or anything. He had finally escaped as his mind snapped. *No one would ever know his thoughts as he stepped off the edge.*

Boatswain Mate First Class Donald Orloski was relieved of his command of Company 74 and returned to the Fleet to serve out the remainder of his duty. His replacement was quickly moved in to take over.

Gunner's Mate First Class William Fisher addressed his new assignment: "I'm not going to baby you sailors. There's a lot of ground to cover and a lot of mistakes to be corrected. I'll expect us all to work together and hopefully, we'll push for completion of your training in the next five weeks. One more thing…it's time you were off all restrictions. Inform your folks and relatives you'll be having your first Visitors' Day in one week."

Everyone was exuberant. The only privileges for the past nine weeks were receiving mail from home. Only a few chosen recruits were allowed to make necessity runs to the PX for the entire Company.

Under the First Class Gunner's Mate's leadership, the group surged ahead. They graduated after fourteen weeks Basic Training. This far exceeded the original prediction of eight weeks, but everyone knew under Orloski they'd never have made it. Nothing, though, could erase the brutal memories of the past nine weeks.

"Hot dog! We got a Visitors' Day," Mickey shrieked.

"Is your girl coming, Paris?" Steve grinned.

"Yeah! She's riding down with my parents. We're all going out for a good civilian dinner. Your folks going to make it, Steve?"

"Naw. Nobody'll be able to come. I think I'll spend the day at the PX looking at that girl's ass."

"Like hell! You're going to come with me. I want you to meet Anna...anyway, somebody has to keep my mom and dad occupied while I spend some time with my girl."

"You sure?" Steve's face brightened.

"Would I say it if I didn't mean it?"

CHAPTER 9

BEN ALLISON DROVE TO ABERDEEN for dinner. Inside, the small sedan hummed with continuous, amiable chatter. It was warm in the close confinements of the car, and everyone removed their coats and piled them in one corner of the back seat.

Steve Bakerman kept a conversation going, occasionally turning toward the back to include Paris and Anna, but not so often as to be intrusive to the young couple's whispering and discreet embraces. Deeply moved by everyone's friendship, he showed appreciation with compliments and gratitude for being allowed to be with the family.

Casually, Anna placed her coat over her and Paris' laps. Paris slid his hand up her dress. His fingers gently caressed her, and between their soft whispers, they'd sneak a kiss when no one was watching.

Anna's wet tongue glided into his mouth and he felt its softness against his own as he touched the moist pubic hair beneath the silkiness of her panties. He felt himself grow hard, and frustration mounted as he continued to fondle her. Her kiss, the smoothness of her thighs, and the tantalizing scent of her perfume were driving him wild.

After an enjoyable dinner, Ben drove the remainder of the day, allowing everyone to view the surrounding areas away from the Naval Installation. In these few hours, the two recruits felt a heavy load had been mysteriously lifted.

"How's Mike doing, Mom?" Paris questioned, his hands continuing their exploration beneath Anna's dress.

"Mike's pretty wrapped up with Loretta," she sighed. "I don't think it's good for children that young to get so involved." She cast a disapproving look at the back seat.

Paris pulled slightly away from Anna. "Mom, tell him when we get our leave, we're planning on going to Palisades Park. Right, Steve?" He looked for moral support, hoping Steve could pry his mother's attention back to the front seat.

"Yeah!" Steve chimed obligingly. "Mrs. Allison, did I tell you how Paris and I passed the swimming qualifications?"

The long drive with the continued caressing was paying its toll. Ecstatic passion had become excruciating pain. Paris was in severe pain, and by the time his father pulled past the sentry and onto the base, he fought hard to conceal his agony.

"What's wrong?" Anna whispered.

"Nothing...nothing."

"You've gotten so quiet?" she pressed.

"It's just that the day is over and you've got to leave now."

Mr. Allison dropped Paris and Steve off at the visitor's parking area, a good walking distance to where liberty cards were turned in.

"I'll plan a good time for you when you get leave," Anna whispered, kissing him as they said their goodbyes.

The sailors watched the tail lights of the car disappear through the gates. A dim shadow of Anna's hand was still waving goodbye through the rear window.

"Come on, Paris! We have to hurry. It's half a mile to where we have to turn in our liberty cards and it's getting late. We don't want to blow our first pass. Hey! What's wrong? You sick or something?" Steve put his arm across his pal's back as Paris doubled over in pain.

"Christ! I can't walk...my balls hurt. I've never hurt like this before."

"Your nuts are sore?" Steve laughed.

"Hey! It isn't funny. I'm hurting like hell. I don't think I'll make it. You go on. Don't be late. It's got to be something serious," Paris moaned.

"It's serious all right, shithead. You've got the worse case of lover's nuts I've ever seen. Comes from smelling too much nooky and not being able to dip your wick. I saw the way you two were playing around in the back seat. Serves you right! I thought you were going to eat each other up. Come on! Put your arm over my shoulder and I'll help you walk."

Paris grimaced as they moved forward. "Why are you laughing? It ain't funny."

"Not to you, but it is to me. Remember when you called me down for saying I had been beating my meat over that cute ass at the PX? Well, 'ol' buddy, you're going to have to try your own hand at it now, or you ain't going to do any marching tomorrow."

"I hope you get jungle rot of the crotch!" Paris snarled.

"Try to take your mind off the pain. Tell me about your folks...more, about your dad."

"It's hard to tell you everything about my dad...dammit, I hurt."

"Talk! It'll take your mind off the pain," Steve prodded.

"When he came up North, the weather was getting cold. Mom told me he only had two dollars and 80 cents in his pocket. He caught a ride on a fruit truck. Wound up in Newark and tried to sleep the first night on a bench in Penn Station. A railroad dick found him…let's stop a second. It hurts like hell to walk," Paris said weakly.

"Paris, we've got to keep walking or we'll be late. I'll hoist part of your weight on my shoulders; just keep moving your legs. We'll make it if you keep moving. Tell me what happened at Penn Station."

"The detective, after talking to Dad, got him something to eat and put him on the right bus…paid for it all. That's how he got to my aunt's home. He found a job loading heavy bags of cement. Hell! He didn't complain like us. He worked. We bitch about boot camp. My dad could have done it standing on his head…Steve, I can't walk anymore. I've got to rest."

"I see the entrance where we drop off our liberty cards. It's only a little way now. Keep talking."

"Did I tell you, bartending, he watched one Negro slice another's stomach open over a shot of whiskey? He was just a little older than we are now. Damn! Each generation gets weaker. Look at us; the Navy feeds us three squares a day and we still bitch."

"We're just about there, Paris."

"When I was a boy, I watched my dad beat this Italian man in our neighborhood until the guy cried. He wanted trouble and my dad gave it to him."

"We're at the entrance. Just drop your liberty card into that slotted box," Steve urged. "Better try wacking off tonight to lessen the pain."

Company 74 finished its Basic Training. Designation of the next duty assignments was the last process after graduation. The General Classification Test taken during the first weeks of Basic Training determined the individual's academic aptitude. Some would be sent to Class "A" schools, encompassing such fields as Radar, Sonar, Radio or Electronics. Those not scoring high enough to enable them to attend advanced training would be sent to the fleet. Each graduate was promoted to the rank of Seaman Apprentice.

Paris, Tex, and Mickey qualified for their first choice: a twelve-week Class "A" radar school at South Annex in Norfolk, Virginia. Steve Bakerman, too, had gotten his first choice. He would be sent to Aviation Mechanics School in Norman, Oklahoma. All four felt lucky, but graduation from Basic Camp spelled the breakup of Company 74 and an end to the many close-knit alliances made within this band of young sailors.

All gathered in small groups in the Main Drill Hall, shaking each other's hands, forced smiles masking their inner sadness. The Company, cemented by so many hardships, would soon be assembled for the last time with fully-packed sea bags.

Company Commander Fisher marched the group to the Disembarkment Center where they drew orders sending them to their assignments. In addition, the newly promoted Seaman Apprentices were allotted a 14 day leave.

"Look at it like this," Mickey exclaimed. "Now, we'll be rid of all this horseshit of Basic Training and finally be in a real man's Navy!"

"Yeah! Hell, before long we'll be in all those foreign ports overseas, getting laid!" Steve said with a grin.

"Or in Sick Bay, with a good dose of clap," Tex laughed.

Paris looked at his buddies. Tex and Mickey would be with him through radar school in Norfolk, Virginia. He clamped an arm around Steve's shoulders. "I'm not going to say good-bye, buddy. We're going to be together while on leave in Paterson. I'm anxious to meet your girl. I wonder if she'll give you lover's nuts like mine gave me on Visitor's Day."

CHAPTER 10

PARIS ALLISON AND STEVEN BAKERMAN boarded the train at Harve DeGrace Railroad Station, just outside Bainbridge, and arrived at Penn Station in Newark, where their folks were waiting. The sailors hurriedly introduced their families and, as everyone departed from the terminal, they each promised to call about plans while on leave.

Paris threw his sea bag in the trunk and climbed into the back seat behind his parents. Ben Allison skillfully nosed the family car onto the busy street and headed to Paterson. Paris heaved a sigh of relief. He was going home.

Memories of Paterson, which seemed so distant during the hardships of Boot Camp, returned as a reality. Everything was familiar. The movie houses on Main and Market Streets; late evening shopping downtown Thursday nights; the drive-in theater on Route 23; hamburger places with girls skating in short skirts to your car for orders, and returning with loaded trays they mounted to your door windows. The town was so closely knit that, before joining, he had easily recognized his buddies' cars, as each took on its owners identity. Older autos built in the early forties, still cruised up and down Main Street.

Paterson was an old working town filled with history; it was cluttered with tall factory smokestacks, smelly textile and dye mills, and noisy machine shops, but he loved it. Here, Samuel Colt fashioned his famous *Peace Maker*, the first six-shot revolving pistol; on the banks of the Hudson River 10 miles away, Alexander Hamilton was slain by Aaron Burr in a duel of honor. Paris could still picture the painting of that duel, hanging in the First National Bank on Market Street.

The Garden State's countryside, in full bloom, promised a long, hot summer. Mild weather was a Godsend after the icy gusts of winter sweeping from Chesapeake Bay across the open tarmacs of Bainbridge Naval Base. Here, spring had arrived early. Warm breezes caressed new buds forming on many kinds of foliage covering the hillsides of Garret Mountain. The tower of Lambert's Castle, atop the tallest plateau of the rocky mass, stood majestically etched against the sky.

The wool dress blues worn while traveling under orders scratched Paris' skin as the temperature rose. He'd soon shed the "thirteen button blues" for more comfortable dress whites packed in his sea bag.

This far inland, away from scrutiny of the Shore Patrol, he pushed back the "dixie cup" hat, revealing his fast-growing hair. He combed it in a semblance of the style he had worn before Uncle Sam had maliciously cropped it off.

The first day of his leave was almost gone. Leave, so long in coming, raced hurriedly by. He called Anna to make plans that evening, then relaxed in the living room, stretching his legs across the sofa's flower-patterned slipcover and closed his eyes.

The heavy, dial phone on the end table vibrated, it's loud ringing disturbing the peacefulness. Hastily, he grabbed the receiver to stop the nerve-shattering noise interrupting his pleasant reverie. "Hello," he growled, not fully awake.

"Paris, it's me…Mike. Sorry I couldn't be at the station. Loretta forgot you were coming home today and went ahead and made some plans she couldn't break."

The cobwebs of sleepiness began to disperse. "Yeah…I missed not seeing you. Anna couldn't make it either. She was at work. It's no big deal. I'll be home for two weeks."

"You know women…can't live with them and can't live without them."

"I was about to call you, but I dozed off lying on the couch. I wanted to borrow the convertible this evening to run over and see Anna."

"Oh, shit! I've already promised Loretta to take her shopping. She'll piss a blue streak if I back out."

"I'm sure I can get Dad's car. Don't worry about it," Paris said trying to hide his disappointment.

"Look, Paris! I'll swing by early tomorrow and we can work out some sort of schedule to use the car. Hell! It's actually yours, anyway. I haven't paid you a nickel on it yet. Maybe we can all go for a long ride."

The following day, Mike Johnson pulled to the curb of the Allison home. "Paris, you drive. Loretta and I will hop in the back to make room for Anna when we pick her up."

Paris glimpsed the exasperated look Loretta cast at Mike as she maneuvered to the back seat.

Settling behind the simulated bone steering wheel, Paris scanned the familiar dashboard with its iridescent green instrument lights. To his upper left, within easy grasp, was the ivory handled, chrome spotlight mounted on the windshield's left frame. He was back in his own domain!

He picked Anna up at her home and, after a passionate embrace, she candidly suggested they ride up Garret Mountain, to reminisce. Loretta balked at this idea. "Who wants to go up there? There's nothing to see or do."

Anna gave Paris a coquettish smile that radiated beauty. "It has a special place in my heart."

Reaching Lambert Castle, the young men recklessly scaled the tower's inside walls as high as they dared climb and, using lipstick borrowed from the girls, they drew two hearts encircling the words: "Paris loves Anna" and "Mike loves Loretta."

"No one can read anything that high up," Loretta complained, craning her head upward.

Mike looked at Paris, shrugged his shoulders, and feigned disgust. "So much for the labor of love."

Parked by the corner of lower Main and River Street, Paris impatiently tapped the steering wheel with his fingertips. Steve had promised to meet him by 6:00 p.m. He glanced at his watch; 6:30. Paris felt uneasy in this part of town. Paterson was generally safe, but from this corner the slum area worsened. He remembered an unnatural stammer in Steve's voice when he suggested picking him up at his home. Now he knew why.

He opened the door and stepped from the car to get a better view, hoping to see Steve in the distance walking toward the car. Steve would be easy to spot in his Navy uniform, but there was no sign of his buddy.

Damn! It's getting late, he brooded. *The girls will think we've stood them up*. He looked at his watch again. *I'll give him a few more minutes.*

Outside the safety of his vehicle, his white uniform attracted attention. It was a rarity to see a sailor that far inland. He started to retreat into the cocoon-like safety of his parked car when someone called to him.

"Sailor!"

He turned toward the sound. The doorway of what had once been a small store was ajar, and a pleasant, olive-complexioned Gypsy woman peered out at him. The partially open door gave only enough room for him to see her head and shoulders.

Paris scanned the strange abode. The store had been converted into a dwelling with ornate, beaded curtains covering the full, glass front to give a semblance of privacy.

"Don't be afraid, sailor. I'll tell your fortune at a special rate...only a quarter, because you're so cute." She laughed wickedly. "Come in. I'm alone. Who knows, maybe I can give you more than your fortune."

She had a sultry, provocative voice. Paris saw the top of her bare shoulders and thought she might be naked.

"I don't have time for my fortune. I'm meeting a friend. He's due here any minute," Paris said, thinking the mention of a friend arriving any moment would give him a better margin of safety.

"Look...I said I was alone," she said softly as she opened the door wide to assure him no one else was in the room.

She wasn't naked, but wore a loose-fitting, flowered blouse with an elastic top pulled low over her shoulders. A gaudy, red full skirt reached the floor, occasionally allowing her polished toenails to peep out from beneath. Dangling golden earrings hung from her small, pierced earlobes. Though crows-feet at either side of her eyes and slight wrinkles in her forehead betrayed her thirty-something age, she was an attractive woman. Paris had heard tales of Gypsies and wasn't about to be baited inside, no matter how inviting she appeared to be.

"If you're afraid, come to the doorway. You don't have to enter, and if I don't tell a good fortune, you don't have to pay me."

"I'm not afraid! Hell! Who said anything about being afraid?" Paris countered, defensively.

"Then show me you're not afraid. Come just to my doorway," she beckoned, allowing her breasts to bob sensually.

Paris cautiously stepped toward the door, glancing again up and down the street, hoping to see Steve. In the distance, he saw a white uniform.

"I see my friend."

"There's time. Let me see your palm," she whispered quickly. "If I please you, perhaps you can come back later."

She pulled his hand to her, allowing it to touch against her soft breasts. His palm grew damp with apprehension, but as her long fingers traced the inside of his palm, he felt a swell of excitement in his loins.

"You have strong hands, definite lines…I see many women and much love in your life. Your lines for this are deep and long…. "

The tip of her long index finger traced the crevices in his palm as she interpreted their meanings. "Your life…." She paused; a puzzled frown creased her forehead. She whispered now, to herself and not Paris. "The line is short. It ends abruptly."

"What did you say? I didn't understand…something about my life line being short?"

The Gypsy pushed his hand away. "Go! Your friend will be waiting. Go! There's no charge."

Paris felt a strange, inexplicable chill travel down his spine. He cursed aloud at his stupidity for giving value to this ancient witchcraft. "Goddamned con artist! I should've known not to let you coax me into this. You'll do anything for money."

"I said there's no charge. Go now."

Morbid curiosity dominated him. "I never believed in this shit. You're baiting me; you're giving me just enough to sucker me into paying. That's what this whole charade is about. Okay, I'll press it right to the hilt to prove I'm right." He reached into the top of his jumper pocket. "Here's a dollar. Give me the whole act. I want to hear all the bullshit you can conjure up, for the dollar."

The gypsy looked at him, shaking her head, slowly. "Youth…it's wasted on fools…arrogant young fools."

"I said I'd pay. Take the money." Paris thrust the bill at her.

She tolerated his belligerence, intuiting the turmoil she'd kindled in him. "Come inside," she sighed. "I'm alone. You're perfectly safe. I'll leave the door open, if you like. There's a pot of water boiling on the stove and I'll read the leaves. Then I'll know…then we'll both know," she added quietly.

Paris sat down at the small table and watched her crush the dry leaves into a cup. When she finished preparing the tea, she placed the cup in front of him. "It's hot. Don't scald your tongue, but drink it down quickly."

It took several minutes to drink the hot brew. He was aware of the pressing time and continually checked his wristwatch. "Okay! I'm finished. Let me hear your fairy tale."

She looked at the cup he set on the table in front of her. Careful not to disturb the remaining contents, she slid it nearer. Gazing into the bottom of the cup, she nodded to herself, then spoke. "I said there would be no charge if I didn't tell a good fortune. Perhaps the tea leaves are wrong...."

Her sentence was interrupted by Steve's voice, yelling through the doorway. "What the hell are you doing in there? I happened to glance inside when I saw your car parked at the curb. Man! These people'll cut your balls off. Did she promise you some nooky?"

Paris, embarrassed to be caught in this predicament, stood up to leave, but his curiosity had to be satisfied. "What did you see?"

The Gypsy looked directly into his eyes. He could barely hear as she spoke. "Beware...you will be the creator of your own destruction...by your own seed...."

"Shit! I knew the bullshit was getting deep," he said, laughing nervously while backing out the door. "Hell, Steve, you were running late," he said as they reached the convertible. "I thought I'd have time to knock off a quick piece. She doesn't look bad, even with a little age on her."

"Tell me that when she hands your balls to you in her tea cup. Let's go! We have to pick up the girls."

From the car, Paris looked back at the Gypsy standing in the doorway. Her eyes held his without wavering, and he sensed a strange tingling sensation move across the back of his neck and into his stomach. If only he had the time to question her more....

As a youth, he'd heard enough Southern folklore from his parents to place some credence in mysticism and fortunetelling. But growing older made him feel too mature and educated to believe in such things. Yet preconditioning prevented him from shrugging off the Gypsy's ominous warning. "Let's get the hell out of here, Steve."

As they reached the sidewalk and neared the car, Steve remarked, "This is some boat," appraising the yellow Ford convertible as he opened the passenger door to get in. "You just gave it to your cousin on a promise he'd pay you later? I would have hung onto it until I got out of the Navy."

"I felt he'd enjoy it and hell, who knows what Uncle Sam has in store for us. I might never get back to use it...you never know." Paris shrugged.

"My girl lives in the West Paterson area; it's not far. Where are we picking up your cousin Mike and his girl?"

"Mike called to apologize. Said he won't be able to go with us. Some excuse about Loretta…something had come up. He sounded disappointed."

"Shit! I was hoping I'd have a chance to meet him. You've told me so much about him. I feel I already know him. Is his girl sick?"

"Not sick…just spoiled rotten. She's grown up always having her own way."

PART II

CHAPTER 11

SHE SAT BEFORE THE MIRROR, a tattered copy of Edna St. Vincent Millay's *Collected Sonnets* within easy reach on her scarred, oaken vanity top. Time had eroded the mirror's silver bonding, and her reflection appeared gray and cloudy. Still, the hazy image evidenced her stunning looks.

At seventeen, Carolyn Stevens was blessed with striking, natural beauty. Deep green eyes with long, dark eyelashes enhanced her exquisite, delicate features, complemented with light blonde hair cascading below her shoulders. She finished dressing and with a few hurried strokes, brushed her long, shimmering tresses, accomplishing more than most girls did after hours of pin curls and primping.

Her heart raced with excitement and she felt light headed. This was her first date with Tony Scaletti, Regency High School's most popular and controversial individual. Friday, in the school cafeteria, he pushed several students aside to stand in line behind her and asked if she'd go for a Saturday morning drive through the Connecticut countryside.

Forewarnings by girlfriends at school of Tony's reputation, plus her mother's quiet displeasure at breakfast, didn't dampen her elation. Her friends were jealous of his attention, she reasoned, and her mother had listened to pernicious rumors involving the Scalletti family's alleged mobster connections. Recently, her two older sisters related gossip from their husbands, about Tony's relatives controlling a local union.

"All Italians are accused of some kind of misdoing," she countered. "That's ridiculous!" She knew that being the youngest, everyone was overly protective of her, especially her brother Ralph, who headed the household since their father died.

The horn sounded one long blast followed by two hurried beeps. Carolyn scampered to the bedroom window. Tony's handsome face smiled up at her. Then he waved and beckoned impatiently. Disappointed that he didn't intend to come in, breaching rules of etiquette, she frowned nervously, biting hard on her bottom lip. She turned to the mirror for a final glance. No time for primping. She'd try to explain Tony's behavior to her mother.

Carolyn's mother waited at the bottom stairs, her graying hair pulled back severely in a tight bun. Dismay was written on her aging but still pretty face. "Isn't he coming in to meet your family?"

"Oh, Mom! That's becoming old-fashioned. Not everyone does that anymore." Carolyn paused at the door seeing the concern on her mother's face. She threw her arms around her small frame and kissed her cheek. "Mom, I'm sure you'll like him once you've met properly. Next time, if he doesn't come to the door and knock, I promise never to see him again."

Using both hands, Carolyn pushed frantically against his chest and wriggled free of the weight of his body. She slid to the far side of the car seat where she attempted to smooth her skirt and regain some composure.

"Tony...I told you before: I'm not that type of girl."

"Jesus Christ! You could have fooled me. We've been seeing each other regularly since graduating and you still won't let me get any closer than I did on our first date."

"I thought you just wanted to hold me and kiss me."

"Grow up, Carolyn! You're not a baby. You don't have to answer to your mother anymore, or for that matter, to anyone. You've got a job and you pay your own way. It's not like you need permission. Couples serious about each other always make out. It's just a normal thing."

"Tony, it's not right! What you're trying to make me do should be after marriage."

"Shit! I don't need another sermon. My family wants me to start college in the Spring. I don't have time to wait years before I touch you! I can find another girl who's not scared and more understanding."

Her face paled at his threat. "Tony, if this is all you care about, take me home."

The two large wipers swept concentric arcs across the bus's windshield, unable to keep pace with the snow clinging to the outer glass. Several inches of heavy precipitation blanketed the rooftop by the time the Hartford Inter-City bus hissed to a halt at the stop. Its front door ratcheted open noisily and Carolyn stepped down into the deep snow, burying her feet above the ankles of her rubber boots. She trudged along the unshoveled sidewalk, facing into March's cold wind, snowflakes clinging to her hair like white confetti.

The storm came too quickly to cancel work at the small law firm of Cohen and Levi on Lebanon Street, but that didn't bother her. She needed to talk with her close friend and co-worker, Beverly Goodman, who was single and near her age. They shared a mutual trust, and Bev might help Carolyn with her dilemma. She hadn't discussed the situation with her mother or sisters. *I don't want them worrying,* she thought, nearing the ice-clad, wrought iron fence safeguarding the white clapboard structure housing the law firm.

At work, Carolyn and Bev were able to talk privately. "Carolyn, they don't teach any of this in school. If it's like you say, that you're both in love, I wouldn't take the chance of losing him if you two are planning to get married. A lot of girls would jump at the chance you have. Tony's good-looking, drives a new convertible, and his family is loaded with money. Anyway, it's the man's responsibility that nothing happens, not yours," Bev advised.

Carolyn sighed. "We're in love, but he talks of going to college. I'm sure he feels marriage is more important, particularly if he persists in wanting intimacy."

"Hold off if you can. But, if it's impossible without losing him...."

"You're right, Bev. Tony wouldn't let anything bad happen. He's punishing me by staying away and not calling. I've got to let him know how I feel. I have to place my trust in him. That's what love is about, and I don't think I can live without him."

Carolyn knew that as a teenager in early 1955, she had a limited knowledge of procreation, and forbidden questions hung over her like a mysterious, dark cloud. *There's a social silence concerning sexual relations or measures to protect girls from unwanted pregnancies. Should sex really be experienced only after marriage?* She pondered.

A week had passed since she had seen Tony. The euphoria engulfing her spirits during the months following graduation had faded. She missed him desperately, but how could she go against her moral upbringing. She must reconcile with Tony.

In the dark privacy of his car, fondling progressed to more intimate touching. Carolyn had guilt feelings, but couldn't deny the passion she felt throughout her body. She glowed with his touching; a strong sensation engulfed her, hiding the dark storm gathering in the near future.

By early spring, in the tight confinements of the front seat of his car, with the radio playing the soft, velvety tones of Johnny Mathis', *It's Not For Me To Say*, Carolyn gave herself to Tony, for the first time.

The small law firm planned shutting down the first week of July for vacation. At work, Carolyn made plans to spend the week in Virginia Beach, a vacation resort on the Atlantic coastline of southern Virginia, near Norfolk. Bev was only too happy to help her.

"I vacationed there last summer," Bev said. The beach is beautiful and the ocean is warm as bath water. There's so much to see and do, and so many good-looking sailors. Once you see what Virginia has to offer, you'll drop Tony like a hot cake."

"Oh! That could never happen. Not in a million years." Carolyn's heart fluttered when she thought of his touch and the heat of his body against hers when they made love.

No, she would never leave him.

CHAPTER 12

PARIS, STEVE AND MICKEY MET in Bainbridge after leave and were given orders and bus transportation to Norfolk, Virginia's Main Naval Base. A Naval van brought them to South Annex Radar School, nestled behind lavender and white azalea bushes and tall, long-needled pine trees.

Mickey stared in wide-eyed disbelief at the beautiful scene. "Look at this! It's beautiful. Nothing like that Bainbridge shithole."

"Yeah, everyone's smiling. There's green grass, birds flying and squirrels running all over the place. The barracks are painted bright white, not that morbid gray shit we had in Basic." Tex elbowed Paris' chest. "What do you think?"

"In Maryland, I don't think I ever saw a real bird, just damned seagulls. They've dropped us off at the wrong address."

Inside the main gate, the trio had a panoramic view of the small parade ground and numerous barracks. Motorized discs mounted atop high steel frameworks oscillated above what appeared to be classrooms.

"Well, Paris, how was your send-off? Did the whole family and all the wild, young pussies in town come to see you off?" Tex smirked.

"No, just Mom, Dad and my girl. Dad seemed down, almost sad. Mom told me that after I joined and left home he got real quiet and didn't go to work for three days. Dad never misses work. Mom said he'd sit in his chair staring at the floor, worrying about the war. He thought I was 'off in the government,' and he couldn't get to me if I needed him. Mom's never seen him cry in all their married years, but when he heard the Armistice was signed ending the Korean Conflict, his eyes got watery. He never got beyond the fourth grade, so 'being in the government' was like being off in some big, dark abyss."

"Damn. You're lucky to have a family that loves you. I sure envy you that," Tex responded quietly.

"Hey, guys, "Mickey chimed in, "we'd better get 'movin'. Classes start tomorrow and we have to be on our toes. Here, its three strikes and you're out. If that happens, you'll push a mop for the rest of your enlistment."

"That's not going to happen to us, that's for damned sure," Paris remarked. "I just wish Steve Bakerman were with us. Why in hell did he want to be an 'Airedale' way out in dusty Oklahoma, instead of here with us in this paradise?"

"Let's go. Tomorrow comes early." Tex started toward the barracks.

"I wish that Armistice hadn't been signed. I wanted a chance to kick those Gooks' asses," Mickey grumbled.

Paris and Tex exchanged glances. They broke up laughing. "You bullshit artist, Mickey," Tex chided him.

The first week of radar school was a breeze, with everyone in high spirits. Weather in southern Virginia was mild, and the dress code was relaxed to tee shirts, white trousers and white hats going to class. The base exuded a friendly atmosphere. Uncle Sam had a proven teaching method: ease tensions and help students learn in three-steps: read it, see it, and do it.

One instructor pointed out that, by passing the G.C. tests high enough to get into electronics, the students proved they were "above the comic book level." Radar was a wide open rate, not frozen like boatswain's mate and gunner's mate rates. If you learned quickly and kept your nose clean, you advanced rapidly. It was up to the individual.

As in Basic Camp, everyone was assigned cleaning stations to be serviced at 15:00, at the end of the day's classes. Work-stations had to be maintained satisfactorily before liberty was granted at 16:00.

Paris excelled in school, devoting any spare time helping Tex and Mickey grasp the more difficult phases being taught.

During the week when their liberty coincided, they'd finish work-station duties, study whatever time was necessary, and then hurry to shower, shave and don dress whites to head to Norfolk's Red Light section. Young faces were a dead giveaway, and proof of age was required to get served. All bars checked I.D. cards for birth dates, so they had no success getting served in the bars scattered along East Main Street.

"We can't get a drink off the base and we sure as hell can't get laid!" Mickey complained. "The bitches standing out on the street want to hustle us inside to buy drinks, and once we're inside, we can't get served. Better off to stay on base and go to the Enlisted Men's Club. At least we could drink that watered down piss called government beer and give ourselves a hand job."

"I was talking to a radar instructor between classes, a First Class Petty Officer, who's been here for a while," Tex confided. "He called Norfolk 'no fuck.' Said without a car, you're dead meat unless you get away from the Main Base, Shore Patrol and Vice Squad to make out. There's an area called Ocean View that's better for picking up girls, with an amusement park, rides and all. Tourists flock there and girls come from all over. He said the bars might serve us. They're not watched as closely as on East Main Street."

"I've got to get me some pussy," Mickey moaned.

Paris smiled. Mickey thought of having sex as if you bought it in a paper bag. Funny, he thought, the many names attached to the sex act: getting laid, getting pussy, some leg, and even hair pie. Who dreamed up all those names for sleeping with a girl? He laughed to himself. *If I'm having sex, I'm not sleeping.*

"What are you smiling about?" Tex asked.

"Nothing. I think you're right. When we have liberty this week-end, let's try this place called Ocean View."

The late April sun warmed the backs of the white uniformed young men standing outside the Ocean View bar. Down the street came the rumble of the roller coaster descending into one of its tortuous turns, shaking the old wooden frame. The men heard high-pitched screams from the amusement park above the noise of the busy thoroughfare.

"Fuck it!" Tex grunted. "We look old enough to pass for 21. With all the vacationers here in Ocean View, no one will ask to see our I.D. cards. Come on. Let's go on in."

Paris nodded. "All they can do is throw us out. For a cold beer, it's worth the risk."

Mickey hesitated. "The bartender might call the Shore Patrol and we could get kicked out of Radar School. That means hitting the fleet as a deckhand. I don't want any part of that. I'll wait outside. You guys go try to get served."

"You son of a bitch." Paris' eyes narrowed. "You'd let Tex and me take the risk while you stand out here playing with yourself? Come on, Tex! Leave the bastard out here."

"Wait, you guys! I was kidding! I'll...I'll go in with you," Mickey stammered.

Overhead fans made the bar comfortably cool. Paris glanced down the long, scarred counter. Half a dozen customers were strung along its length. Squaring his shoulders, he walked toward several empty stools and sat down. Tex and Mickey took seats on either side of him.

The bartender, wiping a spill at the end of the bar, turned to look at the three figures perched at the counter. Tired disgust tightening his mouth, he threw his bar towel over his shoulder and walked toward them.

"What'll you have, mates?"

"Three Bud drafts," Paris ordered.

"Three drafts, uh? Sure thing. First let's see your I.D. cards. They'd better show you're not still wet behind the ears or I'm going to put a size twelve shoe up three young asses."

"Let's get the hell out of here! He means business!" Mickey jumped off the stool, his thin, gangling frame bolting for the door before his buddies had time to react.

Trying to control his laughter, the bartender pointed to the door. "Get the hell out of here. I'd lose my license if I served you. Nothing personal, but git."

Outside, Paris and Tex whistled, halting Mickey's flight.

"Damn it, Mickey. You can stop running!"

They all caught up. No one noticed the two-door, black Buick slowing abreast of them until their mutual despair was shattered by a honking horn and three girls waving.

"They look like they know us and I ain't never seen them before," Mickey yelled, waving excitedly. "Goddamn, they want our bodies. Look at them smile!"

"Yeah! But they ain't stopping," Tex grumbled as the car disappeared down the street, "so you can go back to playing with yourself."

Paris gave a puzzled look, shrugging, "They're prick teasers. A wave and a smile is all we're going to get."

Dispirited, they continued walking.

"You scared wimp, Mickey. The bartender wasn't going to kick your ass. You made his day. I thought he was going to break a blood vessel laughing. Tex, you see him stuff that bar rag in his mouth to keep from going into hysterics?"

The car circled the block; intent on teasing Mickey, Paris and Tex didn't see it.

Mickey whispered. "Look, it's the cunts that just drove past."

"Goddamn!" Paris blurted as Mickey shoveled past him as the car pulled to the curb.

"Where've you gals been all our lives?" Tex questioned, pressing beside Mickey.

Both positioned themselves at the passenger door, making Paris unable to see the driver. Tex and Mickey began chatting with the female passengers riding in the front seat.

"What about taking us for a ride, girls? You'll get to love us," Mickey bragged, exhibiting confidence he had not shown in the bar room.

The tousled red-haired girl nearest the door answered irritably. "Don't wet your pants, guys. All we want is you to pretend knowing us so the three Marines following us will buzz off."

"Yeah, guys. Do us a favor?" Paris heard the driver plead.

"Sure, babe. You name it, you got it." Mickey dragged his last three words so the dirty connotation couldn't be overlooked.

"Let's get out of here! These jerks are all alike."

"Hey, wait! My buddy didn't mean no harm," Tex apologized as the big car began moving.

Paris hurried around the car's rear, hoping to reach the driver as she paused for a break in traffic. Nearing the driver's door, he saw a car pull behind with three uniformed Marines inside.

The dark-haired girl behind the wheel turned, watching for an opening in the traffic, and caught sight of the car behind. Her brow furrowed.

"Could you give us a lift back to Norfolk?" Paris called to her as he approached.

"I'd better not," the driver said, looking back at him.

"It's not fair to pull off and leave us. You're setting us up to tangle with those Marines, and your leaving won't get rid of them. They'll follow, unless they decide to stay and settle the score with us first. They're not going to like being made fools of."

She turned to look at him, becoming slightly unnerved as his penetrating blue eyes looked into hers. With the white hat pushed rakishly back and the blond hair bouncing below it onto his forehead, his face held an expression of honesty that immediately touched her.

"I don't know," she said, now less sure of herself. "It's not my car. I'm only dri-ving." She turned to the two girls beside her. "It's true what he's saying. Let's give them a lift back to the base. They might be in trouble with those guys behind us. That wouldn't be fair. Not on our account."

"It's okay with me, I guess," the girl on the far passenger side answered.

"What about you, Beth?"

"Take them to the Midtown Ferry. We're not going all the way to the Norfolk Base, Jennifer," said the heavier girl sitting in the middle.

"Okay, fellas," the driver said. "Hurry and get in the back before they change their minds."

The two female passengers in the front seat got out, and Tex and Mickey squeezed past the tilted back-rest; the driver leaned into the steering wheel, allow-ing Paris entry. "We really appreciate this," Paris said. "We dreaded hitchhiking back to the base."

"Where are y'all stationed...over at the main base by Gate One?" the driver asked in a strong southern drawl.

"No. We're at the South Annex Radar School. Just down from CE piers." Paris' tongue felt thick in the presence of the pretty, dark-haired driver. "My name's Paris, and this is Tex and Mickey."

"Hi! I'm Jennifer. These are my friends, Vera and Beth."

"So this isn't your car?" Paris asked.

"No," Jennifer replied. "It's Beth's boyfriend's car. I'm driving 'cause I'm the only one with a license."

Seated behind the driver, Paris watched her expertly steer the big Buick into traffic and away from the congested area. Turning, he glanced through the rear win-dow. The car following the girls pulled out behind them. After several blocks, it turned off at an intersection. The Marine driver gave the one-finger salute as it dis-appeared from view.

"The Marines turned off. They're not following us," Paris informed everyone.

"Lucky for them," Mickey boasted.

Tex threw a look at Paris, shaking his head. "Yeah! Lucky for them," he mim-icked.

Paris, oblivious to the conversation between the other girls and his friends, concentrated on the driver. Their eyes met as she looked through the mirror and though he couldn't see her face completely, just by looking at her eyes he knew she was smiling at him. On the main highway to Norfolk, he sensed an urgency to stall for time, knowing in a few minutes the ride would end.

"If you girls want a hamburger or hot dog, pull in at the next roadside stand. It's the least we can do for giving us a lift."

"I'd like that," Jennifer answered, nosing the heavy car into the lot beside a roadside grill.

"What are we stopping for, Jennifer?" Beth scolded her, but the red-haired Vera interrupted her.

"Good thing you stopped. I've got to go to the rest room. I'm about to wet all over myself."

"I'll walk with you. You may need help," Tex grinned, reaching over the seat for the passenger door handle. He tossed a five-dollar bill into Mickey's lap, "Here. The treat's on me, Mickey. You and Beth get some hot dogs and Cokes while we're gone."

"Hey! Why should I do all the work?"

"Because, I'm doing the buying. If you don't want to go, I'll give a full account to everyone about our last trip to a bar room."

"I'll go," Mickey said hurriedly. "Come on, Beth. Lend me a hand."

Suddenly alone, Paris and Jennifer were acutely aware of each other. "Could I come to the front and sit with you until everyone gets back?" Paris asked.

"Beth will blow a head gasket when she gets back, but it'll be all right until then."

Jennifer leaned forward to allow Paris to step out. Then she slid to the middle of the seat to let him get in behind the wheel. Turning, he looked at her pretty face. Her dark hair was accentuated by the white blouse she wore tucked into tight-fitting jeans. Her red lips smiled sensuously at him.

He gently pulled her to him, kissing her. Her mouth parted as they continued to kiss and she opened it wide, allowing their tongues to touch. She breathed hard as his hand cupped her small, firm breast.

"They'll be back in a minute," she gasped.

"I know," Paris whispered. "When can I see you again?"

"I'd better not," she answered breathlessly.

"I've got a week-end pass...seventy-two hours. I'll go home and get a car. We can see a movie...anything."

"It's hard for me to get out. I live with my parents. Now just wouldn't be a good time."

He kissed her again, feeling her body grow limp as his left hand massaged her breast. The nipple grew hard beneath the fabric and she moaned softly.

"Please…don't…they'll be back any minute."

"Let me call you. I'll bring a car back this week-end. If you don't want to go out, tell me when I call."

His persistence was too unrelenting for her to refuse. "I'll write down my number. Let me check my purse for something to write on. I'll put it on this book of matches…on the inside cover. But if I say no when you call, leave it at that. Promise?"

"Okay, I promise. Just don't give me a wrong number."

She scribbled her number on the inside of the match cover, and Paris hastily shoved it into his jumper pocket as he saw Tex and Vera approaching.

Tex opened the door for the red-haired Vera, his deep-set eyes scrutinizing the pair in the front seat. He laughingly asked, "Did you guys eat the hot dogs already?"

"No!" Paris answered. "Mickey and Beth haven't gotten back yet."

"I'd of sworn they had by all that red ketchup smeared over both your mouths."

Paris reddened and reached under his jumper for his handkerchief tucked beneath his belt. Hastily he wiped his mouth as Jennifer scrambled in her purse for her lipstick and mirrored compact.

Vera and Tex chattered amiably, but Mickey and the heavier-set girl, Beth, openly declared war on one another. While everyone was downing the hot dogs, the two shot verbal bullets at each other.

It was dusk before the petite driver swung the big automobile back onto the highway. The sailors learned the girls lived in Portsmouth and had gone to school together. As the car pulled up to stop in view of the Midtown Ferry, which would take the girls across to Portsmouth, Paris felt uncertain of his success with Jennifer. She had given him her phone number but was leaving him in doubt of seeing her again.

"Okay, fellas. End of the line." Beth motioned with her thumb. "Everybody out!"

The three sailors scrambled out of the car.

Jennifer spoke softly to Paris. "The ferry will take us to Portsmouth. You can catch the naval shuttle bus back to the base from here. I'd take you, if it were my car."

"Like I said earlier, I'm due for a week-end pass. I'll go home and borrow a car, and I'll call you as soon as I get back. I'd like to see you again. Okay?"

"We'll see. Now hurry. We can still make this ferry before it pulls out."

Before he could reply, the car lurched forward as Jennifer accelerated; tires squealing, she made a wide circular turn back toward the loading ramp, waving good-bye through her open window as she gunned the Buick. The sailors stood on the curb listening to her girlish laughter as the tail lights of the car faded down the street.

"That's the last we'll see of those bitches," Mickey said bitterly. "That fat one was really beginning to get my goat."

"I don't know," Tex said with a smile. "I liked the little redhead. She gave me her phone number. How'd you do, Paris?"

"I don't know…that is, at least not yet."

Mickey scowled. "The bullshit's beginning to get deep. I'd better put on my hip boots."

Paris hitchhiked to New Jersey on his 72- hour pass. While there, he asked to borrow the family car, hoping to return it the following week-end if he passed the weekly written examination. While at home, Mike settled with him on a price for the Ford convertible and Paris gave the cash to his father who agreed to find a more economical car for Paris while he was stationed in Virginia.

Paris knew that the trips home would be short-lived. Radar was essentially a "sea going rate." Once out of school and assigned to the Fleet, Paris might spend the rest of his enlistment off the far shores of some trouble spot.

Class "A" School, up to now, had been easy for Paris. His mind was keen and electronics fascinated him. However, this past written exam was the most difficult he'd taken, and the class held their breath waiting for their marks to be posted. Everyone knew failure of any exam meant a review before the base commander. Two more failures meant being dropped from school and sent to the deck force aboard some Fleet ship. Some of his classmates had already made one visit to the base commander. Tensions were near the breaking point as the small class of thirty students huddled in the hallway outside the Instruction Hall.

"Goddamn it! I failed this one! I know it for sure." Mickey gnawed at his fingernails.

"It was the roughest one yet," Tex said, nodding.

"I've never had to cram so much material in my head. I think my eyes are bulging. Ions and protons are dripping from my nose," Paris worried aloud.

"You're the type that never fails, Allison. I'll be dropped when they mark my test. I've already seen the Old Man twice. This one puts his foot in my ass," a freckled face youth named Baxter remarked, as he stood fretting near the bulletin board.

"Here comes the test results," someone called out as the instructor, a first class radar petty officer, made his way through the crowd of students. He thumb-tacked a list with the names and test scores to the bulletin board.

"Like they say in cards, *read 'em and weep*," the petty officer said, shouldering his way back through the crowd of anxious students.

Tex wedged his tall frame forward and shouted, "I made it! I passed. So did you Paris. You too, Mickey…by the skin of your teeth."

CHAPTER 13

LIGHT RAIN FELL FRIDAY EVENING and by noon Saturday, the heavens opened up, releasing torrential downpours. Overhead the sky darkened to an inky black. Storm clouds hovered low over the base, and heavy rain obscured all visibility.

Paris hoped to return the family car but was scheduled for duty Friday. He failed finding anyone willing to swap and make his 48-hour pass into a 72-hour weekend. Normally it would've been easy finding someone, but sailors with families living in nearby areas headed home; others were burned out with the grueling classes and needed time to relax.

Tex Madison, who could usually be relied on, had disappeared Friday when the liberty cards were handed out. Even Mickey couldn't be found.

Paris, obligated to duty Friday, couldn't feasibly make it to New Jersey and back. It took hours waiting for the ferry to cross Chesapeake Bay from Little Creek to Kiptopeake on the Eastern Shore. He resigned himself to remain on base for the week-end.

Standing at his locker, he sorted his whites, placing soiled jumpers and trousers into his canvas ditty bag. *The White Swan Cleaners*, a civilian laundry, picked up and delivered on Mondays, charging sailors a fair price to wash, starch and iron their whites; this was a definite improvement over the scrub brushes and hand soap used during Basic training.

Paris checked soiled uniforms for loose change or miscellaneous items he might have left in his pockets. Then he rolled up each article of clothing and placed it in the drawstring bag. In the top pocket of a jumper soiled with tomato stains, he found a book of matches with Jennifer's name and phone number scribbled on the inside cover. Pondering his chances of ever again seeing the dark-haired girl, he spoke aloud: "What have I got to lose?" He reached into his locker for his neatly folded raincoat.

A telephone booth was located outside the base PX, several hundred feet from his barracks. Sprinting across the soggy lawn surrounding the building, he made a dash for the paved parade ground, pulling the soaked white hat down to his eyebrows to keep it on his head. Reaching the telephone, he pulled the door shut. His pants were now soaked to the knees. Nervously, he dialed the Exmore number scribbled on the match cover.

An older woman's voice answered. He asked to speak to Jennifer and heard a disgruntled exchange of words on the other end. Finally, a youthful female voice answered. "Who's calling?"

"Jennifer?"

"Yes."

"It's Paris…Paris Allison. You gave me and two buddies a ride to Norfolk. Remember? Three marines were following you?"

"I remember."

"Would you like to go out this evening? Maybe to a movie?"

"In this rain? Thanks, but no. Anyway, I've got a toothache," she said.

"Wait! I said I'd go home and get a car. I did…this past weekend. The rain might stop later, and you'd feel better getting out. I mean…I'd take your mind off your toothache."

She gave a provocative laugh. Then she answered slowly, accentuating her southern drawl. "I shouldn't, but it is miserable and I don't feel like being cooped up here all day. Okay. I'll tell you how to get here."

She was emphatic about not coming to her door. He was to park under an oak tree by a vacant lot next to her house and wait. She'd meet him at seven o'clock that evening.

By four the rain stopped and the sky cleared, making the air feel fresh and clean after the April downpour. Paris ate at the mess hall, then hurried back to the barracks to ready himself. He left, allowing time to use the Norfolk Downtown Tunnel crossing under the Elizabeth River to Portsmouth.

Following her directions, he found Frank D. Lawrence Stadium and the side street branching off to her home. He drove slowly, checking house numbers on the ancient clapboard dwellings lining either side of the street. Some had screened-in porches, and all showed little vestige of their original dignity.

Pulling to the curb by the vacant lot, he parked under the large oak. Dusk was settling in, and the tree's canopy made the sky seem even darker. After what seemed an eternity, he heard the creaking of a rusty spring stretching on an old screen door, then the door banging shut. Approaching high heels clicked against the sidewalk, and before he could reach across the seat for the handle, the door opened and Jennifer slid into the bench seat. Wearing a touch of red lipstick, she was clad in a black sheath dress made of light summer material and wore small pearl-like earrings.

A hint of perfume teased Paris's nostrils as she settled into the seat. As she crossed her legs, he heard the swish of nylons, catching a glimpse of her pretty legs with perfectly formed calves and small ankles. She was stunning. Paris gulped, thinking of the 15 dollars in his wallet. The way she had dressed, she must expect dinner at an expensive restaurant. Sweat formed on his brow.

"I'm sorry I'm late. I bet you thought I wasn't coming," she said smiling.

"I was beginning to give up hope. Gosh! You look great. Where's a good place to go for dinner?" he asked cautiously.

"Sailors don't have money to go for dinner. I've already eaten, and I'll bet you have too. *The Blackboard Jungle* is playing at the drive-in down on Washington Highway. If you haven't seen it, we could go there. Glenn Ford's in it, and it's supposed to be good."

"Sounds great." Paris breathed easier. "If you're sure you don't want to have dinner."

"We can get a hot dog at the drive-in. Remember our last hot dog?" she teased. "Now let's get moving. I don't want to stay parked this close to home."

Paris started the engine, dropped the car into low gear and pulled off. He shifted while asking, "Do you have overly protective parents?"

"No, silly. I *do* live with my folks. They don't approve of me dating until my divorce becomes final."

"Divorce?" Paris was stunned. "You're not old enough to be married, let alone to be getting a divorce."

"Honey, I'm twenty-three. I've been married awhile and have a small son." Her dark brown eyes scrutinized Paris. "How old are you?"

He started to lie, but thought better. "I'll be nineteen on my next birthday."

She raised an eyebrow. "And when is this…next birthday?"

He answered so quietly she asked him to repeat what he said. "Almost a year off."

Jennifer began laughing, then apologized. "I wasn't laughing at you. I thought you were older. You act a lot older. Please, if we run into any of my friends, don't tell them your age."

At the drive-in they watched the images on the large white screen, neither paying attention to the dialogue. A nervous air hung over the two as Paris attempted to make conversation. His tongue felt thick as he spoke. "Was that your mother that answered the phone when I called? She sounded angry."

"Yes. She and Daddy don't approve of my dating sailors. Their minds are set on the fellow next door that lives across the vacant lot from us. They want me to settle down and stop 'living it up.'"

It amused him she called her father, "Daddy."

"I'm glad you didn't stand me up, and you're right about my not having much money. When I saw how you were dressed, all I could think of was how little I have in my wallet."

"I wanted to look good for you. You're honest as well as cute." She smiled prettily and kissed him fully on the lips. "If not for Vera seeing your buddy, I'd probably not have come tonight."

"You mean Tex has been seeing your red-haired girlfriend? Damn! I wondered where he'd been slipping off to. He never said a word."

"Some people are more private than others," she replied coyly. "More secretive."

He drew her close, kissing her as her fingers ran through the hair on the back of his neck.

"There's a place not far from here where we can go afterwards. It's quiet...no one to bother us," she whispered huskily. "We could get some beer to take with us, something to sip on. Would you like that?"

"Yes," Paris said, kissing her neck and throat, down into her small cleavage. "I can pay for the beer, but you'll have to go in and get it. They check I.D.s real close."

She laughed softly. "I forgot. I'm robbing the cradle."

They parked in a dark wooded area and caressed each other until neither could control the building passion. Jennifer pushed Paris away and, with a couple of deft movements and the graceful lifting of her knees and legs, removed her panties. As she started to unfasten the stockings from her garter belt, a mental image of Anna and their first time flashed in Paris' mind. He asked that she leave them on.

Jennifer laughed provocatively, "A woman in stockings turns you on? Seems naughtier, doesn't it? I get excited with the sailor uniform, particularly the summer whites and the black socks and shoes showing below the bellbottoms." Her tongue found his, then she pulled away and whispered into his ear, "We'll both be at ease and more comfortable with each other after our first time together. Just make sure you put on a rubber."

She straddled his lap facing him, and their bodies fused.

Paris returned the family car the following week-end. With the money from the sale of his convertible, his dad bought an efficient six cylinder, two-door, 1950 Chevrolet sedan with a fixed sun visor mounted above the windshield. Paris drove it back to Virginia.

Paris ranked top in his class in radar school, and things couldn't have been going better for him. He didn't waste time needed for studying to prowl downtown bars and local dives in hopes of finding a girl, as his fellow classmates were doing. On liberty days, he'd finish classes, maintain his cleaning station, and call Jennifer to ask when to pick her up. Afterwards, he'd study a couple of hours, content that she'd be waiting when he arrived. She always met him at the oak tree, never at her door.

It was a strange yet beautiful relationship. Jennifer asked nothing, content to be with him and, as she jokingly kidded, "live it up." She called him her "young Yankee sailor," and he'd respond that he had come from deeper South than her Virginia. He told her of his family and how his father had hitchhiked north from Georgia.

"You're my galvanized Yankee," she bantered. "My young, blue-eyed, galvanized Yankee."

Only once did he ask her about her marriage. Hesitantly, she told him how happy it had been then, as if reliving some past moments. She smiled to herself as she related how she and her husband couldn't get enough of each other. They would be driving and the urge to make love would spontaneously hit them. They'd pull down a dark road, crawl into the back seat, tear at each others clothes and "screw like minx." After the birth of her son, David, everything changed and never was the same. She never told Paris anything more.

He'd always remember the warm summer nights they spent together and would almost hear cheers coming from the Frank D. Lawrence Stadium as he drove by with Jennifer wearing tight, white shorts accentuating her pretty tanned legs as she wiggled up close to him. He could still picture her tuning the car radio as her hips gyrated to the music of Georgia Gibbs' "Dance With Me, Henry." Once, on the spur of the moment, she decided to go swimming, laughing when he said he didn't bring trunks. "Honey, neither did I."

She mischievously showed him how to avoid the constant vigil of the U.S. Navy Shore Patrol and the vice squad patrolling Virginia Beach. Jennifer had him drive up Atlantic Avenue toward Fort Story and park his car between Seventieth and Eightieth Street. Barefooted, they walked almost a mile in the sand to the private beaches belonging to big beautiful homes in those wealthier neighborhoods. They carried a six-pack of beer and an old blanket he kept in the car trunk.

She spread the blanket between two low sand dunes and quickly slipping out of her white shorts and blouse. Standing in the moonlight in just her white bra and panties, she seemed almost iridescent. She undid her bra, revealing her small, well-shaped breasts, and, still standing, slipped out of her panties. The dark "V" of her pubic hair *contrasted beautifully* against her tanned body.

"Come on, silly," she urged. "Take off those clothes. You're not bashful, are you?"

He quickly undressed, placing his clothes on the blanket. She walked up to him and pressed her body's full length against him as she kissed him. He felt himself harden as her hands gently touched him.

"With that good-looking face, those blue eyes and this beautiful equipment you're endowed with, when I'm finished with you, the young girls will be groveling at your feet," she teased him.

He asked why she wasted herself as she was doing with him. "You have so much to offer on a more permanent arrangement."

"Let's just enjoy what we have and what we do together, without questioning motives," she whispered.

He cautiously suggested they get a place for the two of them and her small son, David, to live together. He'd try to get a billet out of Norfolk after Radar School, to be with her.

"You mean shack up with you," she laughed. "No, honey. It would never work. Enjoy what we have now; don't look to the future. One day you'll meet the perfect girl. I'm certainly not that girl."

"You mean a lot to me," he tried to explain. "Just being with you. If I were a poet or a songwriter, it would be easier to express myself, but I'm not."

She kissed him softly. "Let's enjoy each other while we can." Then with a sultry smile, she asked almost shyly, "Honey, have you ever been around the world?"

"Heck, no," he answered. "I haven't been assigned to a ship yet."

She laughed coyly. "My naïve young sailor. There's so much I have to show you . . . so much for you to learn."

It wasn't love. They both knew it was more like a physical and emotional contentment. There was no pressure to say or do the right thing, to please one another. Paris stopped trying to figure out what drove her to follow this lifestyle; that was her business, not his to question.

Their last time together at the beach, he confided in her about his concern for Tyrone Madison and how his interest at school suddenly waned. His grades plummeted and he spent more time at the PX drinking, when he should've been studying. Tex failed a written and a performance test and had been seen twice by the base commander. He was warned of the outcome if he didn't improve. Paris told her he worried that Tex's involvement with Vera was on the rocks.

Jennifer gave him a subtle warning. "Honey, you keep an eye on your buddy. Vera is like a little butterfly. She goes from flower to flower. I've never known her to stay long on any one flower. I'd hate to see your buddy get hurt. No one should ever get hurt," she added, as though speaking from experience.

"God! What the hell is that?" Paris yelled, heaving his freshly opened beer can into the sand. "It's a giant spider."

Startled, she jumped to her feet. "It's a fiddler crab, silly. You've just wasted a good can of beer. Haven't you ever seen one before?" She laughed.

"Gosh, no. It ran across the sand right at my feet. I've never seen anything like that before."

"That comes from living so far from the ocean, my sailor who's never been to sea."

"You're right about that. But while we're on the subject of travel, Jennifer, I want you to know that this weekend I should head home to see my folks. It's been a while since I've made the trip."

"Go, honey. Just be careful driving. I'll be here when you get back."

For the remainder of the week Paris tried to reason with his buddy. He attempted to get Tex to go to New Jersey that coming weekend. "Tex, don't throw your chances away. There's just a few weeks before we complete school and we're so close to graduating. Shit, man! Pull yourself together. No girl's worth it. If you wash out now, you'll have three and half years left in the Navy to spend with a mop in your hands."

"I never cared much about being a 'radar pussy', so having a mop in my hands don't scare me. Somebody's got to mop," Tex answered sullenly.

Mickey chimed in, "Tex, don't be an ass. Once we're radarmen aboard a ship, there'll be pussy in every port. Forget that bitch and stay off the booze."

"Paris, take him with you this weekend or I'll have to put a foot up his ass while you're gone. Go see your folks. I've got things to sort out in my mind. Don't worry. I'll be all right."

CHAPTER 14

PARIS WAS RUNNING LATE WHILE he waited for everyone to draw liberty cards. He'd have left without them, but he needed four passengers to finance the round trip to northern New Jersey. Finally, with everyone aboard, Paris sped toward the ferry landing.

At liberty call Friday, the main road to Little Creek became a raceway. Cars loaded with sailors from the bases and ships headed north; every driver wanted to be first in line at the ferry crossing at Little Creek landing.

Pulling in line behind the waiting cars, Paris estimated an hour's wait before getting onto the next shuttle ferry crossing the bay. An hour of travel time was wasted before he drove onto the *Princess Ann*. It would take more than 3 hours to cross the bay.

Evening stars twinkled in the darkening sky as he pulled off the ferry at Kiptopeake Landing on the Eastern Shore. The three sailors in the back seat slept and Mickey, sitting alongside, snored, his head against the backrest. "I could use a nap myself," Paris mumbled. Tex Madison's predicament was uppermost in his mind, and the two beers he drank on the ferry once it reached the three-mile point in the bay absolving Virginia's alcohol jurisdiction, coupled with the engulfing darkness and unusual silence, amplified his fatigue.

He pointed the Chevy north on Route 13. It'd be a seven-hour drive to Newark, where he'd leave his passengers. There they'd take buses or trains from Penn Station to their homes. He'd pick them up Sunday at the drop site between eleven thirty and twelve noon to be back at the school before "Cinderella Liberty" expired at midnight.

Most traffic headed north, and Paris seldom met headlights coming in the opposite direction on the lonely stretch of road. This section was a narrow two-lane road with railroad tracks running parallel just off the right shoulder.

Night settled in as he approached the small town of Exmore. He'd traveled no more than fifty miles since leaving the ferry. A dark comfort formed around him as everyone slept. The only illumination came from the instrument panel and his headlights beaming on the black asphalt ahead of him.

Approaching a slight bend in the road, a sudden bright glare momentarily blinded him. Refocusing, he saw red rear reflector lenses on a car sitting near the shoulder of the road, blocking most of the north-bound lane.

"Damn!"

Instinctively, Paris swerved left to go around the parked vehicle but saw two headlights meeting him head on. He cut the wheels to the right, only to see a single high beam from a locomotive rumbling south on the tracks parallel to him. Yanking the wheel to straighten up, his right foot slammed hard against the brake pedal as he jerked the parking brake to its last notch.

Tires screeched against the road's surface with brakes locked, and the car's nose dipped downward in a forward skid. There wasn't enough stopping distance; Paris braced himself for the impact.

The sickening sounds of metal crumpling and glass shattering intermingled with startled cries from his passengers as they pitched forward out of their seat. Paris was hurled over the steering wheel, striking his head against the windshield. The impact jolted the parked car forward and off the right shoulder as it was struck from behind. It continued up the gravel embankment supporting the railroad tracks, toward the path of the oncoming train. The engineer sounded his whistle in a futile effort to ward off a head-on collision. Miraculously, the car came to a stop within feet of the speeding locomotive.

Gingerly, Paris touched his face. His forehead hurt and an egg-sized lump was forming over his right eye. A quick check of his passengers confirmed that no one was seriously hurt. Now his concern focused on the car he had rear-ended.

He started to get from behind the steering wheel but stopped as flashing red lights approached. A Virginia State Police cruiser arrived at the scene, apparently called by the engineer of the train.

A tall trooper got out and approached, carrying a long flashlight. Running its beam over both cars, he examined the site. Paris rolled down the window as the light scanned the occupants' faces.

"If anyone is hurt, I'll call for an ambulance," he said, studying everyone closely. Assured that any injuries were minor, he ordered everyone to remain in the car while he inspected the other vehicle.

A second cruiser appeared, its red dome lights flashing. Using a spotlight mounted on the trooper's door-post to illuminate the area, the first trooper to the scene scaled the railroad embankment and called out to the officer just arriving on the site. "This vehicle's empty…lights are off and no key in the ignition. It's apparently abandoned. Whoever left it might have broken down or run out of gas."

"I've got to be in complete control…can't show signs of being rattled when they check me for alcohol," Paris muttered, focusing on the glittering gold buttons and belted tunic worn by the tall trooper who leaned close to smell his breath.

"I've got a whiff of beer on your breath. You been drinking?"

"Yes, sir. I bought two beers on the ferry…drank one and threw half of the second can away."

"Well! You're honest about it. I'll need you to sit in my car while I finish my report and take a statement as to what happened."

The second trooper placed flares on the road to warn traffic and measured the skid marks with a long, retractable tape measure.

Cautiously, Paris explained the blinding light from the train and how he tried to avoid the collision after the unexpected appearance of the vehicle on the bend in the road.

The lanky officer escorted Paris to his cruiser and, once inside, finished his notes. "There's been a lot of complaints about those trains running with high beams parallel to this road. Whoever abandoned the vehicle you hit set up this accident to happen. We'll find out soon enough."

The officer measuring the skid marks returned. "Appears he was driving within the speed limit. If it was as he told you, about a car meeting him in the oncoming lane, he had no place to go but right into the rear of the other car. You've got a good-sized lump on your head. Sure you're okay?"

"Yes sir," Paris answered.

"If you're up to taking a ride, State Trooper Headquarters is a few miles up the road. I'll check out your license and registration and put a trace on the plates of the other vehicle to find out who owns it."

Paris rode with the tall trooper, leaving the four sailors at the scene with the other officer. Within half an hour, they were back. "Allison checks out. There's information on the other car. It's stolen; probably out of gas and abandoned. I've given Allison a copy of the report for his insurance company."

"I've got one question to ask," the taller officer said, looking at the New Jersey license plates on Paris' car. "You know there's a hundred-mile radius allowed from your home base. If you were headed beyond that limit, I'd have to radio the Shore Patrol for assistance. Be careful how you answer. Where were you sailors headed?"

Paris understood the importance of his answer, sensing that the troopers were trying not to involve them with the Shore Patrol.

" Just into the next town. Mickey's girl lives there."

"…My *girl?*" Mickey stammered.

"Based on what we've found," the tall trooper interrupted, "I'm not issuing you a ticket. What do you want to do about your car?"

Paris' stomach churned as he scanned the damage. He got in and tried turning the wheels. The front end was a mess, but luckily the steering was still intact. "If I could get it off the road for tonight, I can make arrangements to move it in a couple of days."

"Okay. You boys push it into that field on the other side of the highway. You can leave it there, but only for a couple of days. As for the other one, we'll call a wrecker for it."

Red lights still flashing, the State Police positioned their cruisers to ensure that traffic in either direction wouldn't interfere as the sailors pushed the disabled vehicle across the highway and into the vacant field.

"Man! What are we going to do now?" Mickey whined.

Paris' head ached. He was in no mood to listen to Mickey gripe. "For now, Mickey, just shut the hell up."

The troopers approached Paris for a final assessment. The taller one spoke. "We're going to patrol south of here for an hour. One of your buddies asked that we drop him off at an all-night truck stop a few miles back. Said his ankle hurts. It's sprained a little, so he's going back to the base. Might be a good idea if all of you considered heading back."

"Thanks, sir, but we'll head north…." Then Paris remembered the subtle warning already given. "Just to the next town."

"Like I was saying, we'll patrol south for a while. Hitchhiking in Virginia is against the law, but our patrol will keep us south for some time. Good luck."

The night was hot and by the end of the first hour they were thirsty. They came upon a restaurant and motel complex about five miles from the mishap. Entering the foyer, the manager approached them. "Sailors aren't welcome," he said and asked them to leave. Up to now, they were naive to the abrasive feelings of many citizens and businesses toward the U.S. Navy. Paris asked to use the phone and was told to find one down the road.

Their thirst grew as they tired from the exhausting trek. Farther down the road, passing a closed gas station, they peered inside, seeing an inverted clear glass water bottle on top of a cooler. They contemplated breaking the glass in the door to get the water, but Paris' better judgment prevailed and they continued to walk. This late, there was no traffic and, except for the moonlight, it was pitch dark.

"Jesus Christ! I think I stepped on a snake lying beside the road," one of the sailors yelled.

"Shit! We could get bit and die out here," Mickey screeched. "I'm going to stay in the middle of the road...next to you, Paris."

"Damn! It's a piece of recapped tire," Paris remarked dryly.

Morning was beginning to cast a gray light along the deserted highway. They were too tired and thirsty to talk, and the only sound was the shuffling of their no longer shiny black shoes. Heads swiveled as a creaky door on an old farm house opened, then slammed shut. Onto the rickety porch limped an elderly black man.

"I'm going to ask him to give us some water," Paris said.

The old black man, clad in tattered bib coveralls, shuffled to the edge of the porch, straining his tired eyes in the direction of the four sailors coming across the field. "What you boys doin' walking de road at dis time? Ain' no boats dis fer frum de sea an sure ain' none 'n my field."

"We had an accident quite a ways back, sir, and we've been walking. trying to catch a ride to the bus station in Salisbury, but haven't had any luck. We could sure do with a drink of water. Been walking for hours."

The old man studied the youths, nodding. "Y'all come on in. Ah keeps a water jug 'n de ice box, right long side a block o' ice."

He opened up the ancient ice chest and removed a clear bottle of water. After filling two empty jelly jars with ice water, he passed them around to the parched sailors.

"Ah gotta ol' Ford sedan," he said, when they'd quenched their thirst. He pronounced it *cee-dan*. "Ah can take you boys to dat Greyhound statsun in Salisbury, but's more 'n sixty miles frum here. Ah can take you, dat's, if'n you cum up wit 'pense money."

"How much expense money would you need?" Paris countered. "We don't have much money between us and we still have to get bus tickets to Newark."

"Ah can do it fer...maybe fifteen dollars? Dat'd pay fer my time an' gas dere an' back."

Paris looked squarely at his companions. "I'm responsible for this mess we're in and you've paid in advance for the trip. I'll pay this gentleman to take us to Salisbury. What's your name, sir? Mine's Paris Allison."

"Name's Willie," the old man said in a deep voice, reaching out his hand.

His rough calluses felt like a coarse emery board to Paris, who then made hasty introductions.

"Well, we best be goin'. Ah got's lots o' work to do soon's ah gets back, an' we gotta find a gas pump soon. My ol' cee-dan's settin' 'bout empty." Willie reached for his battered straw hat as he motioned to the door.

Willie dropped the four sailors at the Salisbury Greyhound Bus Terminal, where they bought tickets and made arrangements for getting back to the base Sunday night.

"Give me a few minutes. I've got to call and get my dad to pick me up at Penn Station," Paris explained as they sat on the benches in the waiting area.

Ben Allison took a towing chain with him and asked a brother-in-law to help pull the wreck to New Jersey. It was a long drive through Virginia to Paris' car. Examining the vehicle, Ben's voice was calm. "Son, you tore the hell out of it. Knocked the engine off the motor mounts. Thank the Lord nobody was hurt. The car's fixable."

Paris watched his father's scarred, calloused hands tie the tow chain to the bent bumper bracket. Ben had Paris' uncle back close enough to fasten the other end of the chain to the family car's rear bumper.

"There ain't time to cross the bay and come back. I've got to pull your car home before dark. You sure you can thumb a ride from here?" Tiredness and worry were in his father's voice.

"Sure, Dad. A lot of sailors are headed back about now. I won't have any trouble, but I hate to put all this on you and not stay to help."

His father spoke quietly, so that Paris' uncle wouldn't hear. "Your mom found a pair of fancy woman's step-ins under the front seat after you brought our car back home. She was pretty upset."

Paris thought of Jennifer and their first intimate encounter and how quickly she'd gotten out of her panties, or, as his dad so quaintly called them step-ins. In their excitement, Jennifer's panties were shoved under the seat and forgotten.

"You're old enough to be off in the Government, so I ain't trying to tell you what to do. I'm just giving you some sound advice." Ben Allison gazed at Paris with his steel-blue eyes. "A good woman can make you, but sure as hell, a bad one can break you. Son…be careful. Don't hurt your mom."

It only took a couple of minutes for Paris to thumb at several passing cars before some sailors headed to Kiptopeake gave him a lift. Aboard the ferry, he found a ride headed to the main base and was dropped on Terminal Boulevard, within walking distance of the school.

Monday, he called home. It took his father and uncle twelve grueling hours to tow his car back to New Jersey. Ben couldn't tow a car by chain on the Turnpike and had to pull it on heavily-congested Route 1, stopping at traffic lights every few miles.

Paris mediated on how much stronger and more self-reliant the stock which his father had come from was, compared to weaknesses he had witnessed in himself and his generation. How much more successful his dad would have been if he had received the same opportunities as his son.

The following week was bad. Tex Madison failed the written test, washing out of the Class "A" School. His break-up with Vera and excessive drinking took their toll. Before the week ended, he had orders transferring him to the Fleet.

"Shit, I don't have any regrets. Norfolk has played itself out. Time to move on. Like they say…see the world. Look me up if you get to Newport. I've been assigned to the *Stuart D.D. 714.*"

Paris failed his first performance test. He hadn't concentrated; too much was happening around him. He'd graduate near the top of the class, but not as the top student.

He made no attempt to contact Jennifer after the accident. Wednesday, he was called to the base commander's office for an urgent phone call. It was Jennifer; her voice sounded worried and her drawl was strained.

"Paris? Honey, are you all right? I haven't heard from you. I hate to call like this, but I got worried."

"I wrecked my car going home last weekend. Things went topsy-turvy," he explained, his voice flat.

"As long as you're okay and not hurt, that's all that matters."

"Without a car, I won't be able to see you."

"Honey, I can get a car. There's a small houseparty my girlfriend is giving this Thursday. I'll borrow a car and pick you up."

"No! I think it's better to leave it like this." He didn't know why he responded so sourly. Perhaps, it was what his dad had said, or down deep, he felt responsible for Tex's wash-out. It'd been Jennifer's girlfriend who caused Tex's downfall.

Jennifer was too well-versed in life not to pick up the finality in his voice. "You be careful," she said softly. "Don't let anything bad happen to you. I've got to go now."

Months later, after Paris was assigned to his ship, the radar crew flew to Dam Neck, Virginia for a refresher course. He attempted to reach Jennifer again. Thinking ahead, he took the number from a phone booth near the barracks that the team was assigned to during their two-day stay. Hitchhiking from Dam Neck to Portsmouth, he called from a drug store. A cold voice announced that Jennifer wasn't home and told him not to call again.

In a futile attempt to contact her, he violated her policy of never coming to the door. Walking a considerable distance to her home, he mounted the stairs to the porch and knocked on the door. A tall, thin man in his late fifties greeted him. Paris fabricated a story about having known a girlfriend of Jennifer Waters named Vera, whom he was trying to locate. He'd come to Miss Waters' home hoping she might help in his search. The tall graying gentleman placed a firm hand on Paris' shoulder and said slowly, "You mean Miss Thomas…Jennifer Thomas. I'm her father." His words had an icy tone.

Paris realized he had mistakenly called her by her married name, not her maiden name.

"She doesn't run with that crowd anymore. Now, if there's nothing else I can do for you, I'd rather have you leave now. It doesn't enhance our standing in the neighborhood to have a sailor calling at my front door."

Paris thanked him and descended the front steps. He walked toward the end of the block. A boy, not more than six, was playing near the corner. Paris had a gut feeling and approached the child.

"Is your name David? Is your mom's name Jennifer?"

"Yes, sir," the lad answered politely.

"I'll bet I could trust you to give a note to your mom. You mustn't let anyone see it. Give it only to your mom. Are you old enough to do that?"

"Yes, sir."

Paris scribbled down the number of the base phone booth and above it wrote, "Please call at 9:00 p.m. tonight." Purposely omitting any signature, he handed the boy the note, and the child continued playing.

That evening, Paris waited by the phone booth, constantly checking his watch. Precisely at 21:00, the phone rang. He picked it up. "Jennifer?"

"Yes! Who is this? I had a note to call."

"It's Paris, Paris Allison."

There was a long pause. Finally, she responded, "How are you doing, Paris? It's been a long time."

"They flew us down to Dam Neck for two days. I'd like to see you. Could you come to the base, even if just for a few minutes?"

"I couldn't. No, Paris. I can't."

They talked a few minutes before hanging up. Paris couldn't blame her. She had just reason not to come hurrying to him. He wondered if she was still "living it up" or had she settled down.

He'd never know. He never saw her again.

Radar school's June graduation came three weeks after the accident on Route 13. Because of his academic standing in class, Paris was second to choose his billet.

His fingers ran down the list of ships needing radar men. *D.D. 714 Stuart*, out of Newport, Rhode Island caught his eye. It had two openings. "That's the destroyer Tex Madison was assigned after washing out," he mumbled to himself. Hesitating, he almost decided choosing a ship out of Norfolk. Then, he thought, Tex was right. Norfolk had played itself out. He wrote his initials in one of the two circles next to D.D. 714. *Better to be on a ship where you know someone*, he thought.

Mickey Crowley ranked near the bottom of the class, but when his turn came, the second billet was still open, and he initialed the blank circle next to Paris.

"Damn! Why did you have to wreck your car? Now how are we going to get to Newport lugging our sea bags?"

"By bus, you idiot. How in hell do you think we got down here?"

CHAPTER 15

NORFOLK TRAILWAYS TERMINAL WAS CROWDED with vacationers arriving and departing. Vacation season had started and Virginia Beach, a few miles away, offered a temporary escape from the drudgery of monotonous jobs. Passenger lines formed before the doors of the big, sleek buses that would carry those leaving this resort area, and take them back to the northern cities. Final destinations in black lettering on vivid white backgrounds were identified on signs above the windshields of the vehicles, angle-parked along the curb outside the waiting room.

The hot July sun warmed the concrete parking area as passengers in line shifted uncomfortably, waiting for drivers to allow them to enter the cool green interior of the air-conditioned buses.

Paris and Mickey left their sea bags with the baggage attendant to load into the storage compartments. It was a relief not to have the heavy weights hanging from their tired shoulders.

"I miss Tex not being with us," Paris said to Mickey. "Doesn't seem right."

"Yeah! Too bad he flunked out. Should've stuck to his studies and left the boozing alone. You're right. It don't seem right, the three of us split up like this."

"Damn! This pavement's hot. It burns through the soles of my shoes," Paris said, moving to a shaded spot under the station's overhang.

"At least we're assigned to the same ship he's on, unless we heard him wrong," Mickey said. Good thing we're able to stick together. I'd hate reporting to my first ship by myself."

"Tex'll do all right." Paris shrugged. "He had a good head for mechanics. He can work his way out of the deck force and still strike for a rate. I hated to see him get fucked up. If Vera hadn't jilted him, he'd have graduated with us."

"That bitch didn't even look that good. Look! The doors are opening. New York, here we come."

I don't want to leave, Paris thought. *I should have picked a billet out of Norfolk. I could have chosen one of several destroyers home ported here. If I'd tried, I could've gotten back with Jennifer.* Hell, he contemplated, it wouldn't matter what home port he chose; all ships inevitably go to sea.

The passengers surged forward, eager to escape the blistering sun. One by one, they boarded the bus. Mickey was first to see the girls. He poked Paris as the brunette and light-haired blonde stepped up into the bus.

"Look at those cute pieces of ass. I'm going to have company in New York. You watch, Paris! I'll show you how it's done."

Paris caught a glimpse of both girls climbing the steps and proceeding to the mid-section of the bus. Mickey forced his way down the aisle, pushing and shoving the passengers trying to store luggage in the above-seat racks. Plopping into the seats across the aisle from the girls, Paris was forced to crawl over him.

"See! I saved the window seat for you."

"You've got a big heart," Paris answered sarcastically.

Hey, dolls...going to New York, too? That's where I'm going."

The blonde girl seemed lost in thought as she looked out the window.

Her dark-haired companion ignored Mickey's unsolicited chatter and busied herself arranging a small luggage case on the floor space by her legs.

"Girls, this ain't no way to treat the Navy," Mickey said with a grin.

The brunette sighed disgustedly. Suddenly she turned and looked Mickey in the face. "We didn't ask you to sit there, and you'd be doing us a big favor to leave us alone."

The venom in her tone hit Mickey as solid as a fist to his face, leaving him speechless. After a long pause, he uttered only one intelligible word: "*Jesus!*"

He sat back as the bus maneuvered from the curb and wheeled toward the bay. Finally, he mustered enough courage to look at Paris. A thin smile twitched at his lips. "They sure as hell aren't the friendly type," Mickey huffed.

During the ride to Chesapeake Bay from Norfolk, the bus kept continually stopping and starting until it cleared the city's congestion. The route ran parallel with the ocean to Little Creek, were ferries shuttled across the twenty-five-mile span between the resort beach area and the Eastern Shore.

The noise level in the bus diminished and the passengers settled in their seats to enjoy the air-conditioning and the view, read or snooze. Mickey napped, but Paris remained alert, his attention drawn to the pale blond tresses of the girl at the opposite window. The brunette, dozing in the aisle seat, blocked his view. Studying the reflection the blonde cast in the tinted window, he thought he saw sadness written on the portion of her face he was able to see.

Her profile indicated she was pretty, and her hair, in contrast with the tan of her skin, gave her a healthy look. Yet, Paris sensed, she was troubled. The hissing sound of air brakes interrupted his thoughts as the bus slowed to a halt.

Everyone napping snapped awake at this sudden intrusion and gaped out the windows to see what was happening. Lines of vehicles had formed, awaiting their turns for boarding the ferries.

The ferries' rigid time schedules required buses to drive on first. The driver butted the nose against the rear of the lead parked bus, secured his brakes, and allowed passengers to get off. The driver informed everyone there would be a three-hour crossing; time for them to go to the main deck and, if they chose, have supper in the ferry's dining room.

Mickey seized on this information in a desperate effort to create a rapport with the girls sitting across from him. "To show you we ain't bad guys, me and my buddy want to buy you girls supper."

Paris wanted to hit him for making this offer, knowing what little money they had to spread over the next 10 days. But, as the blonde turned in her seat, facing him, he was happy Mickey took such overt action. She was beautiful but appeared oblivious to what was happening around her.

"Carolyn! What do you think? If they want to buy us dinner.... It's their money, and I'm hungry."

"Beverly, we shouldn't...."

Before the blonde girl could attempt any further rebuttal, the brunette slid from her seat. "Let me warn you," she said, waggling a finger at Paris and Mickey, "you can buy us supper if you want to waste your money, but don't let that give you any ideas."

Paris formed his opinion of the girl called Beverly before they seated themselves in the dining room. He disliked her, sensing she was digging them for the cost of dinner and would laugh later to her girlfriend at how gullible they'd been to pay for it. When the menus were brought, Beverly scanned the entrees, ordering the most expensive meal. Paris watched Mickey's Adam's apple bobble when he looked at the prices.

No formal introductions had been made, but Paris had heard the brunette refer to her girlfriend as "Carolyn." He looked across the small table, expecting her order to be the same.

"I'm not really hungry. I'll just have a hamburger and a Coke, and I'll pay for mine," she said.

Carolyn wasn't interested in what was happening, Paris thought, and she's certainly not as mercenary as her friend.

"You're welcome to have anything you like." Paris spoke softly. "We asked both you girls to have dinner with us."

"No. A hamburger is fine. Thanks."

During their meal, the dominate conversation was between Mickey and the dark-haired girl, Beverly. Their verbal exchange was taking on an unfriendly tone. Paris concentrated on Carolyn, not realizing he'd been staring until she caught his gaze, and returned a nervous smile.

"Does anyone have a comb? I can't find mine." Beverly slammed her purse into the seat beside her.

Paris reached into his trousers' waistband and handed her his comb.

She reached across the table then, pulled back. "Ugh! It's filthy. The teeth are dirty!"

Paris' face reddened, but the fair-haired girl reached out and took the comb. "It's only cotton lint from his t-shirt. I know its bad manners to comb your hair at the table, but my hair feels like a mess. Let me use it," she said quietly. She stroked her thick, shoulder-length hair, while smoothing it with her hand.

"Thanks," he whispered gratefully as she returned his comb, aware of the light contact of her fingers as their hands touched.

She seemed to understand his dilemma. For a moment they looked at each other; then she dropped her head to look at the half-eaten hamburger, allowing her dark eyelashes to shield her eyes from his.

"Doll, you ain't putting on no airs with me," Mickey was saying. "I can tell just by looking, you've been around. So let's cut the shit."

"Excuse me, please," Carolyn said quietly, rising from the table. "I'm going out on deck for a while."

Paris glanced at the pair engaged in a verbal battle over Beverly's morality and Mickey's value of the meal. He followed Carolyn to the outer deck where she was seated on a bench toward the prow of the ferry. The sea breeze tossed her thick tresses about her face and shoulders. She was looking toward the horizon with her hand to her forehead, shielding her eyes from the brilliance of the sun. Clutched in her other hand was a furry toy he hadn't seen at the dining table.

He sat down beside her. "I apologize for my buddy's behavior. He's not always like this. He's relieved to graduate from radar school and he's showing it by coming on too strong. I want to thank you again for what you did in there."

"What did I do?"

"You used my comb."

"Oh…it was no big deal, and I could feel your embarrassment. Beverly can be rude at times. She doesn't usually behave this way either. The two of them rub each other the wrong way."

"You seem so distant…at times troubled." Paris spoke before realizing he was being intrusive.

"Now you're embarrassing me."

"I'm sorry…I wouldn't do that." He attempted to change the subject. "What's that in your hand?"

"That's my teddy bear. I won him on the boardwalk. It's silly to carry him around this way, but somehow I feel safer, like he's a security blanket, I suppose. Sometimes I feel so alone with no one to really talk to or share my feelings. It sounds crazy, but I find myself hanging on to it. Here! You take it, before I convince myself I'm completely insane." She thrust the stuffed animal into his hand.

"Suppose we share your security blanket," Paris said smiling. "I'll get laughed off the bus if I board it with a teddy bear in my hands, but I'll carry it for you if you'll let me sit and talk to you when we get back on the bus."

"I don't know. Bev and I are traveling together," she said hesitantly. "I don't even know your name. Anyway, it's senseless." Her eyes clouded. "There'd be no point, no reason in getting to know each other. It would only create more problems." She turned away and looked to the horizon, as if to cancel him out of her mind.

"My name is Paris…Paris Allison. I know yours. It's Carolyn. No one made any introductions when we all clashed together."

"Did you say, 'Parish'?" she asked.

"No, Paris. Like the capital of France."

"That's an unusual name."

"I'm not named for the city. It's from ancient Greek mythology. Paris was Helen of Troy's lover."

"It's beautiful…different." She fell silent for a few moments. "I like it."

"I think you're beautiful," he said quietly.

ADRIFT

"No, please don't." Fearful of what she felt was happening, she held up her hand to stop him from saying more.

"I'm sorry. I didn't mean to offend you."

"It's not you," she said quickly. "Perhaps…had we met another time, another place? It would've been nice knowing you, but not now. Please."

"I'm sorry" he repeated, hating the way she seemed to have closed a door and retreated within herself. "I'll go and leave you alone," he said getting to his feet.

"Wait," she said. "I've hurt you. I didn't want to do that. We can sit here and talk until the ferry docks on the other side. I don't want to go back inside anyway, not to listen to Beverly and your buddy bicker and fuss."

She motioned for him to sit down. Changing the subject, she said, "Look how beautiful the sky and water appear where they merge together!"

"Yes," he said, turning to admire the view. "The blues of the sky and water look like something an artist would paint. Where are you going when the bus gets to New York?"

"Oh, on to Connecticut. I live in a small section of North Hartford. Bev and I'll change buses at Port Authority and go from there. We came down to Virginia Beach for a week's vacation to get away from it all, or…," she hesitated, "to take it with us."

He frowned, not understanding. "I have leave before reporting to my ship. I've got a few days before I've got to report to Newport, Rhode Island. I'm assigned to a destroyer."

"It sounds exciting, traveling all over the world and leaving your troubles behind. I think I'd like that, if I were a man."

"You say that because you're a girl. With your looks, you'll marry some rich guy who'll whisk you all over the world, first class. You'll go on a luxury liner, not on a bouncing destroyer."

"I doubt that," she laughed.

As they talked, Paris sensed the earlier somber mood of the flaxen-haired girl had disappeared. She was now more at ease. There was no loss for conversation, and their subjects drifted from one topic to another.

Not since Jennifer had Paris experienced such camaraderie. As he watched the wind catch and toss her hair and listened to the soft sound of her voice, his eyes strayed to the fullness of her breasts and her long, shapely legs. *She's truly beautiful,* he thought, *not like a lot of pretty girls I've met, who became ugly after you got to know*

95

them. Carolyn, he decided, was as pretty inside, as out. The longer they talked, the more infatuated with her he became.

"Your eyes are blue, just like the water," she said suddenly. "So crystal blue. I'll always remember your eyes. They're kind eyes…mischievous, but kind."

"I'll always remember your face. I think you're the most beautiful girl I've ever seen. I mean that," he said, his voice breaking slightly.

The hours slipped by unnoticed, and the shore line appeared. The pier on Kiptopeak's eastern shore took shape, and countless sea gulls began flapping above the deck.

"Could I sit with you on the bus, Carolyn?"

"I don't think we should. I'd have to tell Bev, and that would go over like a lead brick. Then, there's your friend."

"Tell Beverly," he said.

They boarded the bus, *their hands clasped together*. The only rebuke encountered in the change of seating came from Mickey.

"Real smart…real smart. Just sit back and watch my mistakes, then move in. Real smart…."

Paris flashed him a look, stopping him mid-sentence. Mickey sat back in silence. Bev was happy to move toward the rear of the bus after giving Carolyn a knowing smile.

In the semi-darkness of the bus, Paris slipped his arm about Carolyn's shoulders and pulled her to him. She didn't resist. She sat with her head nestled against his shoulder, and she felt safe. They rode through the night, and only after the bus had become completely dark inside did Paris reach his hand under her chin and lift her face to his. He kissed her softly and felt moistness on her cheek. Looking into her face, he saw the tears clinging to her lashes. She was crying.

They rode cuddled together throughout the long ride through Virginia, Maryland and Delaware. In the early morning they were halfway up the New Jersey Turnpike. New York City was only a short distance away. Feeling the presence of the big city drawing near, Paris knew that, at this destination, their paths would separate forever.

Lack of time pressured Paris. He wanted more. Carolyn created a hunger he'd never experienced, not just a sexual response. He wanted her in *every* way. It could not…*would* not, end.

He listened to her soft feminine moans as they caressed, their mutual desires mounted. He cupped her breast in his hand gently, fearing he was moving too fast. She didn't resist.

Carolyn sensed a tenderness that made her not want to resist his touch. She felt no obligation or duty as she had in the past. Placing her hand on his, Carolyn then pressed his hand to her as they kissed. He was so unlike Tony, she thought. A sense of safety and security never known before stirred in her. It's so tragic to end now.

The bus pulled into New York Port Authority, and it took several minutes to unload it while Mickey retrieved their sea bags from the luggage carrier under the bus. "Come on, Paris...We've got to go."

"Wait for me by the main door. I'll be there in a minute."

Carolyn looked up into the sailor's youthful face saying, "I can't believe it's time to say good-bye. You're actually a stranger, yet I feel as if I've known you all my life."

Paris words almost echoed hers. "I feel we've always been together, too. Yet we know nothing of each other," he murmured against her cheek. "Please give me your phone number. Don't let it end like this."

"I can't...please...I can't....."

"I promise I'll call only once. If you don't want to see me, I'll never call again. I promise."

She pulled his face down so that his lips met hers. "Take care." She turned to walk away.

"No! I won't let you just go." The sharpness in his voice caused bystanders to look at him.

She saw the determination on his face. "All right, if you keep your promise to call only once." She hurriedly dug into her handbag, found a piece of paper, and scribbled down her name and phone number. She placed it into his hand. "Only call once, please. When I'm not looking at you...maybe over the phone, I can explain. Then you'll understand."

She again turned to go, but he reached to take her by the shoulders. He kissed her fully and felt her arms clutch his waist. "Take care of yourself...for me," she whispered softly. She turned quickly and walked away.

He watched Carolyn catch up with her girlfriend, who handed her a suitcase. They quickly disappeared into the crowded station.

CHAPTER 16

ANNA REACHED TO PICK UP the lacy panties hurriedly flung to the floor and, still in a supine position, raised her knees to fit them about her ankles. With a graceful motion and an arch of her back, she lifted her buttocks off the couch, allowing the panties to slip up and over her hips.

"You're getting pretty good at that," Paris said.

"You've given me lots of practice." Then, she added, "I only wish it were enough to satisfy you. You'll never be satisfied with just one girl. You'll always stray. That's the mistake I've made. If I hadn't let you make love to me, you'd still have that desire. That passionate desire we had is missing now."

Looking at Anna as he buckled his trousers, Paris knew she sensed something had been lost between them. Guilt felt for cheating was easier to cope with than the plaguing thoughts of the beautiful, troubled girl with pale golden hair he'd met on the Trailway's bus. Paris tried pushing her from his thoughts to enjoy this time with Anna while home on military leave. He attempted to cast off Carolyn as a melancholy soul who could only create problems in his life. Yet she haunted him like an invisible but always present specter.

"Don't talk crazy. I was afraid I couldn't pull out in time."

"There's something different between us. We lack the fire, that trembling excitement of our first time when it took our breaths away."

"Come on, honey. Drop it, please. If you don't hurry and get dressed, your folks *will come home and find you like this.*"

She laughed devilishly. "I'd tell them you forced me to submit, made me do wicked things, raped me."

"Fat chance you'd have explaining these hickies on my chest and neck," Paris said with a grin. "Come on now. Hurry up." He grabbed Anna's arms, pulling her to her feet, and playfully slapped her backside.

"I wanted to meet you at the station, but I knew your dad wanted to surprise you with the car," Anna said. "He spent hours getting it ready. An old Negro friend, who runs a body shop in Paterson, helped him and did the painting."

"My folks drove it to pick me up when Mickey Crowley and I got into Penn Station. After Mickey headed to Fort Lee, Dad grinned like a Cheshire cat showing it to me." Remembering the joyful event, mist formed in his eyes. "Well, I've got to go before your parents get home."

Anna's face dropped. "You have to leave now?"

"Yes, I've got a couple of things to do." Sensing he should give an explanation, he added, "I've got to call Mike. He wants us to get together since he and Lorraine are engaged now."

"You wrote me about their engagement," Anna replied. "You said you had a couple of things to do."

"I've got to write a letter to a buddy. He got fouled up with a girl and washed out of school. I want to let him know Crowley and I are assigned to his ship."

After Paris got home, undressing for bed, he searched his wallet for the phone number Carolyn reluctantly gave him. He studied the number; as if looking at it might uncover a clue about the girl who kissed him goodbye, whispering, "Take care of yourself for me."

He promised to make one call. *Maybe she's married*, he thought. *If that's true, she wouldn't have been foolish enough to give me her phone number.*

Wrestling with his thoughts, he finally fell asleep. Early the next morning he slipped downstairs, careful not to wake his family. It was too early to call, but he rationalized she'd be at home.

The long distance operator rang the Connecticut number and an elderly female voice answered, "Hello, hello."

"May I speak to Carolyn, please?"

"Just a moment. Carolyn…it's for you."

Moments seemed like hours to Paris, before he heard her voice.

"Yes, this is Carolyn."

"Carolyn. It's Paris."

There was a pause and he started to identify himself again. "Paris Allison. The Trailway's bus…."

"I hoped you wouldn't call," she said quietly. "I prayed you wouldn't. I shouldn't have given you my number. Oh, God. Please hang up. It was all a mistake."

He heard despair and helplessness in her voice. "If you're married and I've put you on the spot…."

"No, it's not that. I'm not married."

Paris sighed with relief. "I can't get you out of my mind. Since we met, since I saw you walk away, I've thought of you. I'll hang up and I'll keep my promise. But, before I do that, think, please think. If I've thought of you so strongly, what happened between us must have meant something to you. You wouldn't have allowed so much to pass between us and just walked away, only to forget completely about it."

"I didn't forget."

He heard the break in her voice, as if she were about to cry.

"What's wrong? What's so terribly wrong that you'd lock yourself up and throw away the key? Carolyn, I've got to see you. Give me your address. I've got several days left on my leave. I'll drive up."

"No. That's out of the question. Please don't ask."

"I promised to only call once and I'm running up my parents' phone bill. I've kept my promise. Just give me your full name and address, so at least I can write. I'll soon be aboard ship. It couldn't hurt to correspond with each other."

"There's something you must know about me," she began. Paris cut her off, fearful if whatever trouble or dark secret she might possess were known to him, it would destroy any hope of seeing her.

"Let me write to you. Just promise me you'll write back. I'll be satisfied with that."

"I'll write to you. I owe you that much."

Carolyn gave him her last name and mailing address in Hartford, Connecticut. "When I'm aboard ship, I'll write and send you my Fleet address. I've kept my promise, don't break yours. You said you'd write. You've made a promise."

"Yes, I've got to hang up now. Take care."

He heard the click as the phone was placed in the cradle. Still bewildered, he thought, *I know where she is. Now I can find her.*

The remainder of his time was divided between his family and Anna. Despite efforts to make his days enjoyable, the troubled face of that lovely blonde couldn't be erased. What started as a pleasant leave became a confinement.

Anna and his parents saw him to the train taking him from Newark's Penn Station to Providence, Rhode Island. Sea bag slung over his shoulder, he hugged his parents and then bent to kiss Anna's upturned face. The conductor called, "All aboard."

As the train began to move away, Anna started to cry sensing it was over. Looking back, Paris watched them wave goodbye as the train picked up momentum.

Paris met Mickey in Providence as he boarded the bus taking them to Newport.

"Goddamn! I'm glad we caught up with each other. I kept looking for you at the railroad station."

"How was your leave, Mickey?"

"Great! Just great! All the hometown girls wanted my pecker. The uniform turned them on."

Mickey hasn't changed since I last saw him, Paris thought, stifling a sigh.

"What'll we do when we get to Newport? How do we find our ship?" Mickey questioned.

"Orders are to report to the main naval base. They'll furnish transportation to the ship. I wrote Tex Madison we're coming. I hope he got the letter. I didn't know where he's assigned on the ship."

"Smart of you to think of writing. If I know Tex, he'll find us. He's probably waiting for us right now. How'd you make out with that blonde piece of ass? You were eating each other up on the bus ride from Virginia. Did you see her anymore?"

"I called. She promised to write when I send her my address. I want to see her again."

"Yeah! So you can wet your finger again," Mickey said.

"We might better get to the ship before I rip your damned tongue out," Paris warned.

Paris finished unpacking his sea bag and leaned against the chain-suspended cots opposite Mickey's berth. He ignored Mickey griping while stowing the contents of his sea bag into the foot locker beneath his bunk. Both had been assigned bottom racks in this small compartment that slept a compliment of nine radarmen and five radiomen.

"Shit! I'm not able to fit this stuff in my locker, and look at these metal hammocks. That's all they are: galvanized pipes around a wire grid. How the hell do you sleep on this? These dirty old mattresses ain't three inches thick."

101

"You'll do fine." Paris grimaced.

"I thought the double bunks in Basic were bad. Why'd we get stuck on the bottom, and why can't we use those upright lockers against that bulkhead?"

"Because you're not wearing a crow in your sleeve. You make Petty Officer, you move up toward the top rack. The higher the rate, better chance of an upright locker."

"I think we're getting screwed 'cause we don't know the ropes, yet."

"Mickey, you're full of...."

"Full of shit and hasn't changed since I last saw him," a familiar voice interrupted.

Neither heard him come down the ladder, but both recognized the deep voice.

"Tex Madison!" Paris grinned, shaking Tex's extended hand.

Mickey jumped from a squatting position, throwing his arm about their buddy's shoulders.

"As soon as we settled in, we were going to find you. I wrote we were coming, but I didn't know where you were assigned. Damn, it's good to see you. It's been over two months since you left school," Paris said.

"I got your letter. Shook me up you guys remembered the name of this ship and picked it as your billets. I'm up forward, up near the bow. I had everyone on the quarter-deck keeping an eye out for you."

"How do we get to the bow?" Mickey asked. "There's no hatches or passageways headed forward."

"The only way is the main deck or climbing up on the 01 level. This tin can was built at the beginning of World War II. It's a Fletcher Class destroyer with no through passageway. Old timers warned me in foul weather to stay off the main deck for fear of being washed overboard. Instead I should go hand over hand using life-lines on the 01 level. Several of these destroyers were lost during typhoons in the Pacific. They're top heavy."

"What you're telling us is we should have picked an aircraft carrier?" Paris kidded.

"Jesus Christ, Paris! It was your idea to pick this ship," Mickey moaned.

"Tex! Like you said, he hasn't changed."

"Mickey, I'm serious about this. You and Paris will be sleeping sandwiched between the magazines for the two five-inch gun turrets above us and the depth charges mounted on the fantail."

"Oh, shit!" Mickey groaned, rolling his eyes. "Paris...."

"What have they got you doing aboard ship?" Paris interrupted quickly.

"Right now, I'm in the deck force, but I've been playing poker with my First Class Division P.O. There's a chance he can get me trained as an engineer. I was always good with engines."

"I hope it works out for you, Tex."

"Check with your leading radarman about the duty list. If you guys don't have a watch at liberty call, we can go into Newport. There's a tavern — *The Blue Moon* — down by the waterfront on the lower end of town. Might be able to get us served and show you around. We head for Cuba in two days."

CHAPTER 17

OFF CAPE HATTERAS, THE STORM worsened. Torrential rains driven by gale force winds created huge swells, and the destroyer pitched and rolled violently. Massive waves smashed across the ship's mid-section. Its bow would rise suddenly, then dive into the churning Atlantic as the stern cleared the water, exposing the twin screws. Like the decrepit bones of an aging shrew, the keel creaked and moaned as tons of stress and vibration strained its rivets.

Making the dangerous route across the 01 level to reach the radar shack, Paris had left Mickey kneeling, heaving into the trough-like toilet in the rear head. Now, the un-relenting motion made Paris' gastric juices churn, bringing a foul taste of bile to his throat as he sat on a metal stool, staring at the rotating beam of light sweeping around the Surface Search Radar's scope. Heat generated from the electronic gear in the small confines added to his discomfort.

Should have brought a mop bucket to set alongside me, he brooded. *If I heave before I get to the main deck's rail, I'll have to clean it up. No one's going to do it for me.*

Remembering being sea-sick in his early teens when Mike's father had taken them deep sea fishing, he'd promised to never again get on a boat. "Shit!" he groaned. "Hope I can get through this watch and back to my rack."

"You look a little green, Allison." Lieutenant Walker spoke from the far side of the plotting table. "It's nothing to be ashamed of. When I assumed this watch, I saw the Skipper leaning over a rail, vomiting. Here's some saltines. Eat a few to settle your stomach."

"Thanks, Mr. Walker. I've had better days," Paris muttered weakly.

"Sometimes concentrating, putting your thoughts elsewhere, will get your mind off the motion. Nausea has something to do with the inner ear. Use mind over matter."

The Operations officer addressed all three radarmen standing watch. "We don't want to collide with anything that might be out there in this weather. There're three other destroyers in this squadron battling this storm, each less than a mile apart. To ease tension, I'd like to keep this watch informal. Talk freely, but keep a sharp eye when you're manning the radar scope. In this weather, that's our only eyes." Walker paused, looking at each man. "I don't think any of you have been to Cuba or on a shake-down cruise before. I'll brief you on both."

Paris looked up from the scope momentarily as the senior officer was speaking; the lieutenant looked and acted like a competent corporate executive, though he appeared to be no older than thirty. His self-confidence, matched with obvious ability and complete understanding of assigned duties, exceeded his actual years of service. The lieutenant had a reputation for fairness, and as a result was liked by his men.

Paris tried every remedy he could think of to alleviate the nausea. He attempted shifting his attention from the sickening motion, and he recalled the first day aboard when Tex Madison told Paris about the impending cruise. Tales from older crew members whetted his appetite for the excitement Cuba held for sailors on liberty. Still, the nausea persisted and the sea sickness failed to ebb. I'm glad I wrote Carolyn before we shipped out. Hope she writes back, he thought, remembering his reminder of her promise to answer. Knowing he'd be gone for weeks worried him. By that time, any relationship with her could be gone. *Damn! If we get through this storm and I ever set foot on dry land again....* His thoughts were abruptly interrupted.

Morrison, a dark-haired, ruddy-faced radarman, manning sound-powered phones, belched loudly. He clamped his hand tightly over his mouth as he frantically looked for a puke bucket. In desperation, he grabbed his white hat. Spittle clinging from his lips and dripping into his hat, he moaned, "I think I'm going to die." The stench permeated the area.

Without any inflection in his tone, Walker pointed toward the hatch. "Morrison, be careful as you throw your hat over the side. We don't want to lose you. There's a water cooler in the passage-way. After getting rid of your hat, splash cold water in your face and stand just inside the hatchway where the cold salt water spray will hit you. Breathe sea air and be back here to finish your watch in ten minutes."

Unruffled, Mr. Walker continued. "During a shake-down cruise, we'll spend time at sea in the Caribbean and north of the island in the Atlantic Ocean. Ships practice anti-submarine operations using evasive maneuvers. The gun crews practice anti-aircraft defense, firing at 'sleeves' trailing in the air connected to aircraft by cables. Call it war games, but each ship and the squadron are graded on their efficiency during these exercises. It's how combat readiness is verified." He looked at the abandoned sound-powered headset and motioned to Rogers, a radar seaman.

"Man those phones until Morrison gets back. We need to keep all communications open with the bridge."

"Sir," Rogers spoke hesitantly, his young oval face blushing with embarrassment and showing no signs of *mal de mer*, "Tell us about Cuba...er, the girls...you know? What's it like?"

"I can see your testosterone is rising. Yes! Cuba is a tropical paradise, and like any unstable country without many opportunities for work, young girls sell their bodies to survive. There's a great deal of political unrest under the present dictatorship of Fulgencio Batista. I fear Cuba teeters on the brink of civil war. Still, it's one of the most beautiful islands of the West Indies. It's called 'The Pearl of the Antilles.'"

"Sir, you going to get laid there?" Paris was stunned by Rogers' bluntness.

"No, Rogers," the lieutenant answered unemotionally. "I've made a firm commitment. I'm married. Just be careful. Don't bring anything back to the ship you can't wash off."

Arriving at the island of Cuba, the *D.D.714* moored to the main pier in the Bay of Guantanamo. Its three sister ships forming the squadron nestled alongside each other, their mid-ships abutting.

"Hard to believe we're only a hundred miles below the tip of Florida. Look at the peaceful green waters compared to that storm we hit off Hatteras," Tex observed.

"What's taking Paris so long, Tex? I left him in the shower 30 minutes ago. Liberty call's in five minutes and I don't want to waste time. I've got to get me some pussy."

"Crowley, you're sick. There's plenty of cat houses between here and Havana, and those 'ladies of the night' can look up a lot longer than you can look down."

"Who said anything about Havana? There's a local spot I've heard about, *The Red Barn*. I'm headed there."

"Here comes Paris," Tex said, disgust clouding his face over Mickey's narrow focus.

The influence of the United States Navy was evident. On the eastern end of the island, prostitution flourished, satisfying demands of hundreds of virile young military men from the Naval Base in Guantanamo and from warships tied to the piers. It didn't take long to find *The Red Barn*.

"Toulouse-Lautrec would flip over in his grave if he saw this dump," Paris joked as they entered the front door. "This is Cuba's answer to *Moulin Rouge.*"

Looking about the bar, young girls paraded about in panties and brassieres, most in their late teens and early twenties.

"I've found Heaven. In the States, to see a girl's leg above her bobby socks gave me a hard on."

"Mickey, you *are* a hard on!" Paris teased.

"First, let's get some beer from the bar. Beer must be made locally. Never seen beer called *Hatuey* with a label of a one-eyed Indian." Tex picked up an empty bottle from one of the tables to examine the label.

It didn't take long to realize there were no standards for beer making. Several beers could have no effect, yet another bottle might put the drinker into a stupor.

Paris received Carolyn's reply to his letter in mid-August.

Dear Paris,

I received your letter some time ago and it has taken me until now to get the courage to answer. But I did make you a promise that I'd write back. There's no way to explain this easily. When we met, I was pregnant. I didn't want to accept this fact and prayed somehow I was mistaken and things would change. There's no excuse of not knowing better or trying to pass the blame to someone I had known since high school. I felt I truly loved him and thought he loved me. By the time you and I met, I knew I'd been wrong about him, but I was too late in finding this out.

You called and I foolishly gave you my address. I was so afraid you would persist in trying to see me I tried on every dress in my closet trying to conceal my pregnancy.

My older brother is making arrangements to send me on a visit to "Grandma's." As young girls, we used to laugh at this cliché. Grandma's is a home for unwed mothers in Brighton, a small suburb of Boston. I'll leave for there next week before my friends and neighbors realize my condition.

I know as you read this, you'll hate me for deceiving you, but I honestly prayed my outcome would magically change. I never wanted to hurt you in any way. I know I'll never see you again, but if for any reason you want to ever speak to me again, I've written the number of The Home at the bottom of this page.

> *Take care,*
> *Carolyn*

After receiving her letter, Paris lost interest in Cuba. In early September, the squadron of four destroyers departed Guantanamo Bay and headed back to Newport. The crew looked forward to their return; however, at quarters each department was informed of the coming inspection.

The ship would be given a grueling Captain's Inspection the first Saturday after arriving in Newport. Leave and liberty were canceled until after the inspection.

After mooring the ship at Pier I along side the three sister ships of their squadron, the ship's crew turned to and for three days prepared the ship for the scheduled "White Glove" scrutiny.

Saturday morning the ship's complement stood at quarters on the main deck in their dress whites, spit-shined shoes, and regulation haircuts with spotless white hats tilted down on their foreheads.

Each division or department was headed by an officer or chief petty officer. The captain, flanked by his executive officer and first lieutenant, made his way slowly from bow to stern as a gentle morning breeze ruffled the ensign hanging at the fantail. The light wind flapped the pennants strung from the main mast supporting the radio and radar antennas, while small waves slapped lazily against the seaboard hull of the ship. The inspection encompassed the entire crew and ship from the main deck to the bilges.

Paris and Mickey stood at attention with the radar, radio, sonar, and electronics technicians who comprised Operations.

Grumblings among the younger sailors could be heard as the slow process continued and men tired from standing at attention. Whispered complaints of backs hurting, legs and feet falling asleep were made, accompanied with a command to "Tighten up, sailors," from the divisional officers.

Paris stood waiting for the review. To make time pass, he thought of traveling home, seeing his family, and returning with his car. He'd get to Boston, find this place called Brighton, and see Carolyn. He had the phone number she wrote in the letter and the address on the envelope she mailed.

Standing at quarters, no one knew what happened. Undetected at first, the deck began to list slightly to seaboard. The destroyer continued tilting as the inspection progressed; the captain's face looked puzzled. He turned to whisper to the executive officer as the ship failed to level. The executive officer leaned toward the first lieutenant, and the crew standing nearby saw the worried expression as his lips moved.

The first lieutenant broke ranks, motioning to the first division officer to accompany him. The two walked briskly to the main hatchway, quickly descending the ladder.

The vessel had now taken on a ten degree list. The vintage Fletcher Class destroyer was notorious for being top heavy with equipment, and the more experienced sailors and officers quietly began expressing their concerns.

Within several minutes, the two officers bounded through the main hatch to report back to the captain and executive officer. After a brief consultation, the CO headed for the quarter deck and immediately the public address system blared: "All first division damage control parties report to the quarter deck on the double. All other crew members secure from inspection and standby at your quarters to assist, if necessary."

The message was repeated; the urgency was clear to those assigned to the damage control parties. They scurried across the deck. Like the fine-honed edge of a razor, the repair parties "cut to the chase." Within minutes, the crew's countless drills and past training proved worthwhile.

Forgotten were the sparkling dress whites and spit-shined shoes as the men descended into the bowels of the ship in an effort to keep it from capsizing.

"Damn," Mickey swore to Paris. "We're gonna sink tied to the fucking pier. I don't believe it."

The repair crews worked below in the bilges, frantically closing off water-tight compartments and rigging emergency pumps to stem the sudden flooding. After several exhausting hours, the ship began to return to an even keel.

Later that day, Tex Madison explained to Paris that, in the midst of the inspection, an over-zealous junior grade officer, not realizing resulting consequences, demanded an inspection plate be removed and a sea cock valve, used for scuttling the ship in wartime to prevent its capture, be opened to test its working ability. Inadvertently, his actions almost scuttled the destroyer.

The *Stuart* was ordered to head north to Charlestown Navy Yard in Boston to determine damages. Overhaul of the ship's mess deck and galley, not scheduled for another year, would be moved up while it underwent repairs in dry dock. The crew would be fed in the chow halls at the Fraser Barracks located on the Naval Yard.

The incident was a career embarrassment for the captain, and the junior officer was quietly transferred to another duty station.

The situation couldn't have been more perfectly timed for Paris. He decided that, when he had weekend liberty, he'd phone Carolyn, go home and get his car, and head for Brighton.

Paris cursed as he downshifted while staying in the left lane of the one-way traffic on Boston's Washington Street. It was nearing five o'clock, and the sidewalks were congested with late afternoon crowds. Fighting bumper to bumper traffic and listening to honking horns from behind, he slowed to almost a stall, allowing time to scan passing faces on the sidewalk bordering the busy thoroughfare.

"She won't show up," he whispered. "She won't be there. This is stupid."

Her voice sounded uncertain when he telephoned. He hung onto her promise to meet him under the marquee of the RKO Theater located on the left side of the street. It was this trust that kept him from veering off in retreat down a side street.

Then he saw her. Carolyn was standing near the overhang, the mild September breeze teasing her blonde hair as she looked anxiously toward the oncoming traffic. A trembling sensation ran from his solar plexus to the tips of his fingers. *She's beautiful,* he thought. *I've never seen a girl as beautiful.* He blew the horn, waving out his window.

She waved back as her mouth widened into a pretty smile. Forced to double-park on the left side of the heavily trafficked one-way street, Paris ignored the curses and beeping horns as cars attempted to go around.

Carolyn worked her way through the pedestrians to the curb. Rather than risk her being struck by a passing car in the busy street, Paris opened his door and stepped out to allow her to slide in under the wheel. She looked at the narrow space between the steering wheel and seat and, with a worried smile, said softly, "I better go around to the other side. I'm afraid I can't slide past the steering wheel."

"I'm sorry, let me help you in on the other side, but be careful of the passing cars." He cautiously opened the passenger door to avoid being side-swiped. Carolyn slipped gracefully into the seat despite the additional girth she managed to conceal with her light tan, fall coat. Until seeing her swollen stomach, Paris had failed to register the reality of her pregnancy. Paris shut the door and hurried around the back of his Chevrolet to the driver's side.

"Gosh! The traffic is heavy," he said lightly. He glanced over his shoulder through the back windshield, waiting for a break in the traffic to let him pull out.

"I was afraid you wouldn't come. I kept telling myself how foolish it was to wait, that you would change your mind after you had given it more thought," she said, nervously twisting her handkerchief around her fingers.

Paris took his eyes from the wheel, glancing in her direction. "Carolyn, I had the same feeling all the way here. I kept telling myself you'd change your mind and not be waiting. I hung onto your promise you wouldn't stand me up. See, we're both bound by our promises." He smiled softly, shifting the lever on the steering column down to high gear. His right hand found its way into her lap, cupping her trembling hands.

"You'll ruin your handkerchief twisting it like that. Don't be nervous. The important thing is we're together. It's all that matters...all that will ever matter."

"Paris, I can only be trouble and embarrassment for you. Why do you bother?"

"Enough of that kind of talk," he interrupted. "I saw a quiet place where we can get a hamburger and maybe some hot chocolate. It's on the outskirts of town, but it's a nice drive. How does that sound? Are you hungry?"

"I'm famished. Maybe it's nerves. I'd love to take a drive, that is, if you really want to," she replied cautiously.

By the time they reached the diner, the initial nervousness had vanished and an unusual contentment engulfed them. They talked of their last encounter and of their fears of not seeing each other again.

Carolyn found it easier to talk of her pregnancy, and in Paris' presence, she no longer felt the shame that tormented her in the past months. She sensed no condemnation in his questions, only attempts to understand.

As they talked, he reached out to hold her hands protectively. Her face began to glow as he convinced her she was wanted as a person and not just for her body.

This troubled girl stilled his restlessness, never before quieted. He thought of what Anna had said: "You'll never be satisfied with just one girl...you'll always stray." How wrong she had been.

This flaxen-haired girl seated beside him was all he would ever want. Her pregnancy was consciously erased. When her time came, he'd think of a solution. Until then, he only wanted to be with her. On the way back to the city, he put his arm about her shoulder, gently pulling her to him. She rested her head against his shoulder as he drove.

"I feel all full inside," she said quietly.

"You're not sick?"

"No, not that kind of full…just complete. It's hard to explain. My mother said until you meet that special someone, you live only half a life; life isn't complete until then. I feel, even if we never see each other again, I've met that someone."

Paris pulled to the curb and gently embraced her. Their lips met lightly at first, and as they continued to kiss he could feel the moistness of the tears running down her cheeks. "Now that I've found you, I'll never let you go," he whispered.

"Let's be content with what we have today and not think of tomorrow. We'll think only of today," she answered softly.

The duty radioman piped a local Boston station into the radar shack. An instrumental arrangement of "Unchained Melody," the theme from the recent movie "*Unchained*," was playing. Its beautiful notes drifted out from the radar shack's speakers. Paris had seen the film with Carolyn. The first time hearing it, she loved the melody and called it their song.

Duty was lax in the radar shack, with no need to energize the electronic equipment while the ship was in dry dock; still, duty watches were scheduled. Paris took a chance shining his shoes near the end of the four-hour watch, pondering his future with Carolyn. *I've passed the Seaman exam and I'll be up soon for the third class petty officer. I could make chief in six years. It would be impossible to accomplish this in any rate but Electronics.*

He learned why the ship needed two radarmen, and he and Mickey were able to draw the same billet. The ship lost one radarman when his enlistment ended, and another went to officer candidate school. The latter re-enlisted for six years after being recommended for O.C.S. If he didn't wash out, he'd go on to flight school in Pensacola, Florida.

Four years of college and a lot of math are required unless I get recommended for O.C.S. and come up through the ranks, Paris thought. *I've always wanted to fly*. He imagined life with Carolyn as a Navy wife.

Paris didn't see Tex and Mickey step through the hatchway. Sounds of their voices startled him and, on the precariously tilted chair, he almost lost his balance.

"Hey! Let's hit the beach, Paris," Tex yelled enthusiastically.

"Hell! I almost fell and broke my neck! Let's put it off until tomorrow. I'm stuck with duty. That's why I'm holed up in here."

"Okay. We'll push it off 'til tomorrow. Then we're going to paint the town red. We'll celebrate being on the only destroyer in the Navy to try and sink itself at a friendly pier in peace time."

'Yeah, tomorrow you gotta go with us." Mickey grinned. "I've tried to get you on liberty with us for two weeks." To Tex he added, "I think he's got some piece of ass ashore and he's avoiding us. Now that we're together again, it'll be like old times."

CHAPTER 18

FALL BROUGHT WITH IT ICY, stiff breezes sweeping across the Charles River. As the leaves rapidly changed color, each passing day drew Carolyn closer to her anticipated delivery date; for Paris, each day brought him nearer the completion of the ship's repairs. Their precious time together was fleeting.

During the week, he'd hurry to her after the ship's workday was over. On weekends, if he had duty, he'd coerce buddies to trade watches, paying them to swap or taking their mid-watches in the early morning hours to be free with Carolyn in the afternoon. He was the first sailor to cross the gang plank at liberty call.

Carolyn gave him a telephone number for her room at the Brighton Home and he'd call just before he left the ship so she'd know he was on his way. She'd wait just inside the heavy door for his arrival. Occasionally, if she was late, he'd leave his engine running so the heater would keep the car warm for her. His heart always skipped a beat when she exited the huge oak door, her face beaming radiantly as she pulled her coat collar high to shield her from the chilly autumn wind gusting at her long blonde tresses.

On Navy pay, they were only able to take long drives and on rare occasions, see a movie. Being together was what mattered. They talked openly of the baby coming and how they'd cope with its arrival. Both were aware of the harsh criticism that keeping the child would bring.

At first, Paris pushed everything from his mind, but as time closed in, he cursed himself for not having the courage to marry Carolyn, regardless of her pregnancy, and toss aside any family and social stigmas. Now, the reality of her condition plagued him, yet he respected her reluctance to give the baby away for adoption. For Carolyn, any thoughts of casting her baby off like unwanted garbage to maintain social respectability were cruel and selfish. Yet keeping it would wreak havoc on those dear to her.

Sitting close to Carolyn in the movie theater, Paris studied her pretty face and the exquisite curve of her jaw line as she watched the poignant ending of *Love Is A Many Splendid Thing*. "It was beautiful...a beautiful story. I'm so glad you brought me to see it," she said quietly, her handkerchief discreetly patting away the moisture clinging to her long, dark eyelashes.

"You're just a romantic," he teased. "You're so sensitive. Moved by everything and everyone…so compassionate. Don't wear your heart on your sleeve. People will step on it and hurt you," he said affectionately.

"I have been hurt," she murmured almost inaudibly.

Paris failed to hear her words as he continued, "I don't care for movies with sad or tragic endings. I always feel they shouldn't end that way."

"Paris, life is full of tragedies. Things don't always work out the way we want them to."

"I don't know," he persisted. "I would have liked it better if it ended differently."

"But see, it was destiny…or call it fate. It couldn't be changed."

"I believe we make our own destiny," Paris rebutted. "I think we control our own outcome."

"Don't you believe in a Divine Plan?" Carolyn huddled close for warmth as they exited the theater into the cold night air. "A *raison d'etre?*"

"What does that mean?" Paris asked as they hurried toward the car.

"That there's a reason for being, for everything, regardless of whether we see or understand the reason. Everything we do, or not do, is part of a Universal Plan."

"I don't believe that." Paris put his arm about her waist, pulling her close to his side. "You're getting fat," he teased.

"Even my getting fat," Carolyn said seriously. "There has to be some reason to life and the mistakes we make. There has to be. Don't you believe in God?" She turned to look at his young handsome face.

"I think we're a mass of energy accidentally thrown together, plus electrical charges. Put them all together and under the right conditions, they spark and you have life."

"No, Paris. Even if what you are saying is correct, there must be a Supreme Being to make that initial spark to cause life, to create life."

Visibly shaking from the cold, Paris fumbled with the keys to open the door. Inside, he started the engine, and they huddled together as the heater warmed them.

"Anyway, I'm glad you enjoyed the movie. But more than that, I'm glad I met you." He tilted her face toward his and kissed her.

"You give meaning to my life, Paris. You gave me strength to go on when everything seemed so dark. I love you for that and for a thousand other reasons."

"So, is our being here now your Divine Destiny or my stubborn persistence?"

She took his face in both her hands, gazing into his eyes. "If nothing more ever becomes of us, our lives have touched, even if only momentarily, and its given my life meaning. The effect will always be there. Nothing can ever change that. There has to be a reason. It couldn't have been just by chance…for nothing." She kissed him softly, letting her lips linger against his. "For that, I'll love you. A part of me will love you always."

Back on ship, Tex and Mickey kidded Paris about his obsession to "*hit the beach.*" "Boy! That must be some pretty good stuff you're getting. Look at him, Tex, like a fly to honey. He can't get ashore fast enough."

"More like a moth to a flame," Tex said soberly. "Be careful, Paris, she don't burn your wings."

"Come on, guys. This is serious. Tex, let me borrow a razor blade. I'm fresh out."

"See? He just uses his friends. Use 'em and leave 'em. What's the matter, kid? Blow all your money on that piece of snatch? None left to buy razor blades?" Tex reached into his locker and pitched him a pack of Gillettes.

"He wants to be clean shaven. Don't want no stubble irritating her soft thighs," Mickey scoffed.

"A little hair pie never hurt anyone," Tex teased dryly. "When are your two best buddies going to meet this chick? You afraid of the competition?"

"Soon," Paris lied. "Now's not the right time."

"She's either a real beauty or you're fucking some old hag and don't want us to know it," Mickey joked, throwing his towel at Paris. "Go on. Take a shower and hurry off. Tex and I will go to that new Enlisted Men's Club and cry in our beer over losing our best buddy to some 'old piece'."

Seven fleeting weeks passed as the two young lovers continued their unique liaison. Finding a restaurant in the heart of downtown Boston, they were able to escape the bitter cold ushering in the start of winter. Sipping steaming cups of hot chocolate topped with marshmallows and secretly holding hands under the table, they whiled away hours, content just to be together, sharing their thoughts.

Carolyn tried desperately to control her emotions. Despite her condition and the events leading to their meeting, she found herself falling more and more in love with this young sailor whose eyes were the color of the bluest sea.

For Paris, Carolyn was all he ever wanted. The grass always seemed greener to him when dating in high school. No matter how nice or pretty the girl, he'd never been able to stop his wanderlust, never being content with what he had, until now. Watching this golden-haired girl with her soft smile and green eyes, Paris knew he was completely in love with her. "What's in the bag?" he said, motioning to a large, blue, canvas handbag beside Carolyn.

"Oh! That's a surprise. I wanted you to see what I'm doing when I'm not with you." She dug into the bag, proudly pulling out its contents. "I've been knitting. I've knitted a tiny pair of booties and I'm working on a small sweater, all in blue. I'm taking a chance on the color, but I feel sure it'll be a boy."

At this moment, seeing the tiny booties, the initial resentment of her pregnancy hit him. Up to now, Paris had successfully blocked it out. Her pregnancy was obvious, but other than her growing girth, he'd been able to push the inevitable from his mind. At night lying in his rack, he'd conjure up plans not including a baby. He'd thought of secretly marrying Carolyn and waiting until the baby was born, for her to give it to the Home for adoption. He'd announce to his family that he'd met a girl and got married out of state. There would be questions and criticisms about his sudden, unannounced marriage, but when they met Carolyn, she'd win them over.

He'd even considered waiting until she had the baby, then giving it up before bringing Carolyn home to meet his folks. They'd have a formal wedding. No one would suspect she'd given birth to someone else's child. It'd be their secret, joining them even more closely. His thinking was selfish, but his puritanical conditioning in choosing a virgin as a wife was deeply instilled in his upbringing. It was a classic situation. It was acceptable for a boy to sow his wild oats or even get a girl in trouble. However, if a girl made a mistake, she was branded a whore.

Until this moment, the baby had been something abstract, perhaps binding their union and making Carolyn more dependent on him. Now, witnessing her planning and preparing for the actuality of a boy baby, Paris felt his first twinge of resentment.

"What's wrong, Paris?" Carolyn asked, looking at the expression on his face. "I know," she teased, "you're jealous. I'll knit a sweater or maybe a pair of socks for you, too. I make a lot of mistakes, but it's the effort that counts."

"Yeah, I'd like that," Paris answered mechanically. "Have you finished your hot chocolate? We'd better go now."

In silence, Paris drove through the Blue Hill section of Boston as night closed about them. Finding a parking space on a residential street, he maneuvered the small Chevy sedan between two parked cars.

"Why are we stopping, Paris?"

"I want to sit and talk for a few minutes. It's hard to do while I'm driving."

"You seem so distant. Are you angry with me? Did I say anything to offend you?"

"No, honey. Show me your knitting again, please. Sometimes I don't know what comes over me." He forced a smile.

"I put the bag on the backseat." She turned toward Paris, twisting her body in an effort to grab the blue canvas bag.

"I'll get it." Paris reached back as Carolyn was attempting to retrieve the knitting. Her coat fell open, and with her arms stretched over the back of the seat, the maternity top raised high above the top of her skirt. It was the first time he'd seen a maternity skirt with a cut-out for a bulging abdomen. "What's that? It shows your tummy." He playfully rubbed the satiny fabric of the slip covering her stomach. It excited him to touch her there. Instinctively, he pulled Carolyn to him, kissing her lips roughly with a hungry mouth.

Her eyes widened, startled at the suddenness of his movements. She felt his hand cup her breast and her nipples hardened. A wave of warmth rushed through her as his hand reached under her skirt and her breath grew rapid. She tried pushing him away, but a flood of heat engulfed her. She suddenly felt lightheaded, unable to control the saliva trickling down the corners of her mouth as their tongues entwined. Her awkward shape was an encumbrance, and she squirmed in her seat, instinctively trying to mount his lap. She writhed and moaned, sounds of pleasure coming from deep inside her.

Paris tried to adjust his position, but her movements pinned him between the steering wheel and the door. With his hardness crushed beneath the thirteen buttoned frontal flap of his uniform, he made an involuntary cry of pain, "Ow!"

As if ice water had suddenly been cast on her, Carolyn broke free of his embrace.

"Oh, Paris. I feel so ashamed. After all the trouble that's been wrought by doing just what I was about to do...."

"Hey! Honey, hold on a minute. I started it and you responded. It's not your fault."

"Maybe that's what you really want of me. You wouldn't have to worry about getting a girl pregnant if she's already that way."

The words, so softly spoken, burned into his ears like a hot branding iron. He pushed her from him, "Yeah! All I ever wanted from you was just a quick piece of ass, with no worries."

"Oh, Paris. I'm so sorry. Please forgive me. Please." When he made no attempt to reply, she sensed the hostility she'd provoked. "Would you please take me back, now?" she quietly asked.

On the long drive back to the Home, neither spoke until he swung the car around the cul-de-sac at the top of the hill.

"Will you call me tomorrow...if you can?" she asked opening the car door.

"If I can," he answered tersely.

Leaning toward him, she kissed him softly on his cheek. "Take care." She closed the door and walked toward the big oak door entrance. Carolyn turned before entering, tears flooding her eyes, and watched him leave.

Without looking back, Paris put the car in gear and drove swiftly away. He nosed the car down the steep hill, thinking angrily that Carolyn believed sex was all he wanted from her. *It's early, too early to go back to the ship. Tex and Mickey talked of their good times at the new Enlisted Men's Club in downtown Boston. I'll go there and maybe run into the two of them. It'd take my mind off Carolyn and what she said. I need some real fun, some temporary escape from the pressing dilemma Carolyn and I face.*

After leaving Carolyn, Paris had no problem finding this new Mecca that drew young servicemen to its dance floors. The Enlisted Men's Club was built for that purpose. Uncle Sam put more than a million dollars into the building to keep its military off the streets, out of trouble, and away from Sculley Square's red light district. It offered live music, dancing, beer, and hard liquor. If a serviceman's identification failed to prove his drinking age, soft beverages were available to quench his thirst.

It was after nine o'clock when Paris found a parking space and walked to the front entrance of the Club. He was awed by the crowd of young girls standing at the door, waiting anxiously to go inside. As he approached, someone tugged at the flap of his open peacoat. He turned to face a pretty girl in her late teens. She smiled candidly.

"Hey, sailor. Would you sign us in?"

"Whose 'us'?"

"My girlfriend, Terry and myself. I'm Joyce Shaw."

"What do you mean, 'sign you in'? Can't you just go in?"

"You must be new here," she teased. "We can only go in as your guests. Two girls are allowed to each serviceman."

"Not bad odds," he joked. "But there's one condition. If I sign you in, you stay with me for the evening. I'm not going in there to become a wallflower. Okay?"

"Sure, as long as you can dance, I'll stay with you," Joyce said.

Inside, the noise was deafening compared to the quietness outside. Enlisted men of all ages and branches of service churned on the dance floor with local girls eager to enjoy the music and atmosphere they normally wouldn't have been able to afford.

"There's a bar. You two girls want a soda? I can't get beer. They're checking IDs."

"Soda's fine," Joyce answered.

"Nothing for me," Terry said, laughingly. "I see somebody I know. Joyce, see you later. Have fun." She waved to someone across the crowded dance floor and disappeared into the crowd.

Paris danced and joked with Joyce throughout the evening. When fast dances played, she sensuously wiggled her hips, smiling provocatively at him. During slow dances, her pelvic bone press against his groin and he pressed back. He noticed her small waist, the curve of her saucy hips, and flat stomach…a complete contrast to the past months with Carolyn. A pang of guilt swept over him.

Perceptively, she looked up to see a frown come to his forehead as he held her close while they danced to "Smoke Gets in Your Eyes."

"What's wrong…smoke get in your eyes?" She winked.

He shrugged off his feelings, smiling down at her. "I was just thinking how cute you are."

"You're cute yourself. You remind me of someone. That smile and the dimples, like some movie star. I know…Guy Madison. That's it. You look like Guy Madison, with a tinge of an accent I can't place. Not from New York and certainly not Boston. You're from the West, aren't you?"

"No. I'm from deep Dixie."

"Your accent doesn't sound like any southern sailor I've ever met. You're pulling my leg."

"Nope, I was born in the South, raised in the North. I'm not pulling your leg, but now that I think of it, I'd like to." His eyes held hers.

"Do you have a car? Did you drive here from your ship?"

"Yes, I've got a car."

"Good. When we leave, you can take me home."

He passed Logan Airport and found his way back through Sumner Tunnel, after dropping Joyce off. She lived in a poor, dilapidated section of East Boston.

Feeling guilty, he thought, *What a hell of a day*, as he nosed the small sedan toward Charlestown. *In just a few hours, I started an argument upsetting Carolyn and left her crying. Now, I've betrayed her. I didn't expect to pick up a strange girl and, as a grand finale, get laid in the back seat of my car.* It all happened fast, and he remembered it vividly. Joyce had asked him to pull down a dark street and park. He thought it was for some heavy necking, but she had more in mind. She pulled up her tight skirt, revealing the crotch of her panties, and crawled over the back of the front seat for more room on the rear cushions.

She had laughed when he fumbled putting on a prophylactic. "Hey, Guy. You don't need that. It's my safe time. There's nothing to worry about."

He couldn't deny enjoying her. She had a cute figure and knew how to handle herself. He hadn't been sexually intimate with a girl since Cuba, and his testosterone was at a boiling point. Now, guilt haunted him as he reached the overhead El taking him high above the city to Charlestown. That uneasiness persisted as he approached the Naval Yard exit.

Finding a place to park on a side street, under an El overpass within a short distance of where "Old Ironsides" was berthed, he walked to the main gate, still wrestling with his conscience. *Hell! We both knew what we were doing*, he reasoned.

121

We enjoyed it. A quick lay, couldn't hurt anybody. I used every precaution, and like she said, it was her safe time.

The Boatswain's Mate announced the end of ship's work and the commencement of Liberty Call. Paris showered, shaved, and donned his dress blues. Racing to the quarter-deck to get his liberty card, he saluted the officer of the deck and the ensign mounted on the ship's stern as he crossed the gangway.

He called Carolyn from a pay phone on the pier to let her know he was on his way. He found his car and drove toward Brighton, fighting the heavy Boston rush hour traffic. As he rounded the final turn before the hill leading to "The Home," Paris caught a glimpse of her waving nearly a block away. Even at this distance, Carolyn's long blonde hair, tossed by the chilly breeze, identified her. He pulled to the corner until she neared, then reached across the seat to open the door.

Her face glowed as she got in. The cold wind had reddened her cheeks and the abundance of estrogen flowing through her young, fruitful body made her radiantly beautiful.

"Gosh! What are you doing way down here?"

"When you called and said you were coming, I hurried down here. There's several little shops along the street and I wanted to pick up something. I was afraid I'd miss you and you wouldn't see me waving."

"What was so important to walk all the way down here for? I could have taken you."

"Something special, but I'll tell you, only if you take me for a bite to eat. I'm starving." She smiled at him, grasping his hand.

"Okay, but I don't usually pick up strange girls on the street and take them to eat," he teased.

He drove to a nearby diner they'd discovered, where prices were within his meager budget. Feasting on hamburgers and hot chocolate, they talked, holding hands across the table.

Carolyn wore a plain, soft tan-colored maternity top with a wide white collar curving at the base of her throat. She looked prettier than ever, Paris thought.

"I'm sorry we ended on a sour note last time we were together," Carolyn confessed. "I'm so glad you called me. I was worried you wouldn't."

"I was a little jealous when I saw the knitting. Guess I'm selfish enough to want all of your attention centered on me."

"Let's go back to the car. I want to show you what I've gotten, but please promise me…." She paused, as if uncertain of what she'd done. "Please don't be angry. If you don't like it, I can throw it away."

In the car, her slender fingers reached into a small brown shopping bag and pulled out a tiny blue velvet box. "I thought you seemed uncomfortable…in public…when we were together. I can understand the embarrassment you…you must feel when everyone looks at us," she stammered, handing the box to him. "It's only a pretense, not a commitment, and if you have any negative feelings about it, I'll understand. But, if you like it, you can put it on my finger."

"The thought of my being embarrassed with you, has never entered my mind," Paris whispered as he placed the ring on her finger. He tilted her chin as her eyes began to flood with tears, and he kissed her softly.

"I bought it at Woolworth's. It only cost a few dollars, but it looks like a real gold wedding band…."

Paris was sincere, speaking from his heart while still holding her hand. "Carolyn, I've worried about this since you first wrote of your pregnancy. I've tried to come up with a solution that won't hurt anyone. There isn't any. Now, I've made my decision about what to do. To hell with families and what people will say! I want to marry you. I'll take the baby as my own, if keeping it is what you want. *You and your happiness are all I want.*"

"Oh, Paris, I love you and want nothing more than to be your wife, but I think you're feeling pressured and being hasty. Please, give it some more thought, and if you still feel this way…regardless of what I decide about the baby…I'll marry you."

Two weeks later, the Stuart left the Naval Yard and headed into the Atlantic for sea trials. After 15 days, it returned to Newport, 70 miles from Boston.

The destroyer hadn't been moored long at Pier I when a sailor standing Quarter Deck watch, stepped into the radar shack. "Allison, there's a phone call for you. They say it's important."

Paris rushed to the phone temporarily mounted on the quarter deck for the crew's convenience. *It's Carolyn's time*, he thought. *It's too early…something must have happened.*

123

A cold sweat washed over him as he heard Joyce's voice on the other end. "Damn! How did you know how to find me? I never told you my ship's name."

"Never mind about that. I've got to see you. We've got a problem."

"What do you mean, we've got a problem?" Paris asked cautiously.

"I'm missing my friend."

"What the hell does that have to do with me? I don't know any of your friends."

"Dummy! I'm missing my period...I'm late. We need to get together to talk."

Paris was stunned. He felt he'd been hit with a sledge hammer. "I'll have to hitch-hike to Boston when I get a 48 hour pass. My car's still up there. Give me a phone number where I can reach you, and when I have week-end liberty, I'll get in touch. I'll come up, get my car and call. Then we can get together and discuss your situation."

"You mean *our* situation," she shot back at him.

CHAPTER 19

MIKE JOHNSON CAREFULLY PUT THE micrometer back into its soiled brown leather case, made a final adjustment to the turret lathe and was reaching up to pull the safety goggles over his eyes when he saw his supervisor framed in the shop office door. His boss' arm rose over his head in a beckoning motion.

He left his machine and crossed the noisy machine shop, carefully navigating between the powerful electric-driven lathes, drill presses, and milling machines. Squealing, discordant, nerve-shattering noises added to the mounting tension he was feeling. "What's up, Mr. Berman?"

"Personal telephone call for you. I don't usually accept calls on the job, but it's your mother…said it was important. Phone's on my desk. Make it quick. You're on company time."

Mike picked up the telephone as Sam Berman closed the door, muffling the disturbing outside noises. "Mom…everything all right?"

"I didn't want to call you at work, but the mail just came." She paused to catch her breath. "There's a letter for you from the Draft Board. I got nervous and opened it. You're to report for duty. Something about 'voluntary draft provisions'."

"Is there a date I have to report?"

"Yes, in two weeks. I'm sorry, but I got so worried. I shouldn't have opened it."

A wave of exhaustion swept over Mike. Lately, things were going badly in his relationship with Loretta. This draft problem would add coal to the fire. He wasn't sure how to tell her, and he didn't know what the effect it would have on their engagement. "You did right, Mom. Don't worry. Everything'll be okay. I'll see you this evening.

The past month, Loretta enrolled in a secretarial college in Paterson. Mike had no plans to pick her up after that evening's night classes, but decided it best not to delay telling her of his Draft notice, so after work he set off to get her. Traffic was heavy as he looked for a parking place near the school's entrance. Finding none, he circled the block.

It was seven o'clock and Loretta should have been coming out soon. Not wanting to take a chance on missing her, he put the yellow Ford convertible into second gear and crept slowly along Church Street. As he circled the block once again to approach the entrance, he saw Loretta. She didn't see him, and his hand moved to the horn to attract her attention. It froze in motion before making contact. The door of a car parked by the curb opened and Loretta walked up to it, a smile lighting her pretty face. She slid across the seat. Through the front windshield, Mike saw her arms wrap about the driver's neck as she gave him a long, passionate kiss.

Mike felt he'd been punched in the stomach. The car pulled from the curb, its occupants cuddled closely behind the wheel. Seeing this betrayal, he thought, *She's my girl. She took my ring and made me a promise.* Fighting his trembling knees and making no attempt to follow, he left the city heading north toward the Hamburg Turnpike. It took an hour to reach Greenwood Lake, and once there, he drove pass several popular dance clubs frequented by under-aged youths from New Jersey where the drinking age was 21, who came here knowing New York's drinking age was only 18. He pulled into Long Pond Night Club. It was crowded inside and the music deafening. Dense cigarette smoke irritated his eyes and they watered, hiding the tears already present.

Mike lost track of time at the bar. Things grew fuzzy as he tried to focus, and the loud music, no longer disturbed him. He knew he'd been drinking too much when he stumbled into a table as he made his way toward the men's room. Coming back, he knocked over his stool trying to mount it, and the bartender approached him. "Look, kid. You've had enough. No more…understand?"

"Yeah! Sure," Mike slurred. "I'm getting ready to go, anyway."

"Are you with anybody? Is anybody else driving?" the bartender asked.

"No. I'm by myself. I'm alone…all alone." Mike pushed his unfinished drink away and slid off the stool, almost falling. "I'm going."

"Go to your car and sleep it off. Don't try driving in the shape you're in," the bartender warned.

"Sure! I'll do just that," Mike yelled over his shoulder, elbowing through the crowd.

Like a sniff of ammonia, the cold night air momentarily cleared his head; he paused, leaning against the outer door. He spoke aloud to his girlfriend as if she were there beside him. "Loretta," he slurred, "you were wrong, but I forgive you. Just tell me you're sorry. Give in one time and everything will be okay." His tongue was thick as he concentrated on saying each word. "Say you're sorry and won't ever do it again."

He crawled behind the wheel, fumbling in his trouser pockets for the keys. The powerful engine whirled and caught immediately, a steady, even rumble resonating through the duel exhausts.

"I think we need some air, Loretta. I'll put the top down."

Mike unlatched the handle centered in the top windshield frame with his right hand, manipulating the lever below the dashboard with his left, as he torturously gunned the engine. The cloth top swung up and backward over his head.

"That's better...right?" he asked aloud.

The rear wheels spun, sending gravel flying across the parking lot as he engaged the clutch and sped away. He continued talking to the empty seat beside him. "Don't worry about your hair, Loretta. It's pretty with the wind blowing through it. Oh! I apologized to Paris and Anna about not going to Palisades Park when he was on leave...nothing to worry about. Just relax. Slide closer if you get cold. I'll see if this heap's as good as Paris said. You sit next to me, under my arm like you used to do."

The image of Loretta cuddled behind the wheel with someone else flashed before his eyes. Enraged, he pressed on the gas pedal. The convertible surged forward. Its heavy body swayed in the gradual turns descending the mountain side, the speedometer floating between 75 and 85. The car's power seemed magically transmitted to his own being.

He spun wide and side-slipped slightly in the next bend, accelerating quickly when reaching the crest of the curve. The car responded obediently. Approaching the straight-away into Ringwood Avenue, he saw ominous blinking red lights in the rear- view mirror. Far behind he heard the distant siren.

"Shit! Loretta...it's the cops. Don't worry. They won't catch us."

The speedometer needle was against the pin as Mike entered the next curve. Worn tires, hot from excessive stress, squealed against the centrifugal forces generated by the weight of the car.

"See, Loretta? Trust me...."

The steering wheel was suddenly wrenched from his hands as the right front tire exploded. The rag top flipped end over end, cartwheeling violently across the road as it disintegrated with sickening sounds of twisting metal and the smells of burning rubber, leaving parts of metal and human flesh strewn down the highway.

What was left of the chassis hurled from the road, wrapping its twisted frame around a large tree.

The patrol car screeched to a stop near the demolished convertible. "Did you see that?" the blue uniformed officer asked his partner, "That joker was clocking over a hundred when he flipped…must have blown a tire. He never had a chance."

"Don't get close, Jim. What's left might explode."

Stepping from the cruiser, the patrolmen walked cautiously toward the wreck. "Nobody could make it out of that."

One officer's foot kicked something in the road and he shined the flashlight near his feet. "My God! It's a head. His head's cut off." Aghast, the patrolman retched convulsively by the side of the road.

Paris Allison received word of his cousin's death by telegram from his mother, and with the aid of his operations officer, received emergency leave to attend the funeral. The shock of Mike's death devastated him. They had grown up together, sharing their most intimate thoughts, dreams, and hopes. Paris couldn't accept something as final and unforgiving as Mike's death.

Too many things yet to be discussed could now never be spoken of. Mike's death was senseless. "Why?" he repeated to himself.

Paris called Carolyn to tell her of Mike's death and to let her know he had 3 days emergency leave to attend the funeral. He'd drive to Boston to be with her, when he returned.

A light November snow had begun to fall when Paris returned to Newport from the funeral. He'd just come aboard when he received another phone call from Joyce. She was more insistent in her demands to see him, threatening to speak with his Captain and notify the Red Cross of her condition.

He made another trip to Boston to see her. It angered him to be so near Carolyn, yet she must never know of these clandestine trips.

As they ate at a local restaurant, Carolyn noticed long lapses of silence in her conversations with Paris, which she understandably attributed to the pain he felt after attending the closed coffin funeral. Paris confessed to her of his guilt in being instrumental in his cousin's death by selling him a car that ultimately brought about the tragedy.

A culmination of events triggered changes Carolyn sensed in Paris. Mike's sudden, untimely death and the guilt Paris felt all were possible causes for the uneasiness she perceived in her young sailor. But, down deep, she feared the tragic reunion with his family and friends had awakened a realization of another pending crisis: his serious consideration of marriage to an already pregnant girl. Pregnant by someone else.

Carolyn tried not to dwell on this thought. Her confusion and indecision about the baby she carried tore at her. Could she keep it and survive obvious criticisms, or when her time came, would she have courage to give up the baby? She suspected Paris' true feelings about keeping the child. *I'm sure the emotional stress of the funeral has caused him to re-evaluate his feelings for me*, she thought, attempting to discern his changes as something more than figments conjured up in her mind. She remembered Paris describing a lesson his father taught him as a young boy. *"The hunter hiding in ambush, who stares too long at his prey, will bring about his own detection."* To dwell on doubt very long, Carolyn prophesied, could cause it to manifest into reality.

"Paris, what are you thinking about? You seem so troubled. Is it something you'd like to discuss?" she asked.

"I'm sorry, Carolyn. I'm just a little tired." He ran a hand through his hair and sighed. *How can I tell her all that's happening?* He brooded. *My thinking's filled with so many confusing things that don't add up: Mike's death and Joyce's surprising revelation of having missed her period and more. After rolling it over and over in my mind, I believe there's no way I could have gotten a one-night stand in trouble.* He also knew something had gone wrong back home; he had felt it at the funeral. Mike never drank excessively. Everything he did centered around Loretta. It didn't make sense, taking off by himself, driving all the way to Greenwood Lake to get drunk, then attempting to outrun a trooper. Nothing made any sense.

Paris recalled that, when Loretta left the funeral site, she refused an invitation to ride with Mike's family, saying she needed to be by herself. But Paris had caught a glimpse of a dark-haired guy standing by a car parked off in the distance. Loretta walked to the car, got in, and slid over next to the driver. Then they drove off together. No one else had noticed. Suddenly, he realized someone was touching his hand.

"Paris…are you all right?"

He looked up at Carolyn seated across the restaurant's small table. "I was thinking of how much I wanted you to meet Mike. That can never happen now."

"I'm so sorry, Paris. I love you so. I wish I could take away the pain."

Paris looked away, his thoughts drifting again. *Michael seemed so dependent on me for support in any crisis. Now, with what's happened, I could really use his support. What a mess I'm in. I think it's called a paradox: All the time, it's the weak who supported the strong.*

CHAPTER 20

THE DESTROYER SQUADRON MANEUVERED A fortnight with the carrier *Leyte* in the wintry North Atlantic during naval exercises. At sea it was impossible to alter the eddy of events Paris was caught up in, and he hated this time.

Endless hours spent in a world of constant motion nauseated Paris, and he mentally fought to keep from retching. But so much cluttered his mind that he couldn't rely on willpower to combat the mal de mer. He stood watches at the radar scope with a bucket by his metal stool in case he had to regurgitate. Foul smells of diesel oil when refueling at sea added to his seasickness.

Other than two letters from Carolyn, in the mail flown in to the carrier and dropped by helicopter to the destroyer, he'd been out of contact with her. He wanted to see her and hold her. Midway through operations at sea, a personal telegram received in the ship's Radio Shack was brought to him. It read:

Marriage urgent - Stop -
Need Medical I.D. - Stop -
Contact me immediately - Stop -
Joyce

The lieutenant stepped through the hatch onto the pitching deck for a breath of air as the U.S.S. *Stuart* plowed its way through the rough North Atlantic.

Using handrails, Paris approached. "Mr. Walker, may I speak with you? It's something very personal."

"Sure, Allison. What's on your mind?"

"Sir, I'm in a jam and need advice. You're versed in most everything."

"Not everything." Walker grinned, balancing himself with the ship's movements.

Paris handed him the telegram, careful not to let the wind carry it away.

Reading it, a frown formed on the Lieutenant's brow. "You've gotten a girl in trouble," he stated flatly.

"Sir, she's pregnant…says it's mine. I had sex with her once and used a rubber. She said it was her safe time. She's threatening to notify the captain and call the Red Cross if I don't marry her. Sir, I don't love her."

The telegram was getting wet with ocean spray spattering their faces as the ship rolled from starboard to port. Both held the rail tightly to prevent slipping off the deck.

"We'd be safer in the passageway. Standing out here, we're asking for trouble," Mr. Walker said, motioning toward the hatch. Inside, he continued. "She's got you behind the eight ball, whether you caused her pregnancy or someone else. I can tell you what *can* happen militarily. For any other course of action, you'll need a lawyer. I can set you up to see a Naval chaplain. It might be a good idea."

Paris' mind raced as he listened to his officer.

"As a G.I. or Government Issue serviceman, you're not protected by the Constitution but are bound to adhere to the 'The Uniform Code of Military Justice.' That means the onus is on your shoulders. You had intimacy with this girl…she's pregnant. By notifying your superiors and the Red Cross…." He paused. "I might add, if she's a young girl about your age, someone's advising her on what action to take. She didn't come by this knowledge on her own. In any case, the Red Cross working in conjunction with Uncle Sam, can force you to marry her…."

"That's not fair," Paris interrupted.

"Fair or not, Uncle Sam matches half a monthly paycheck toward an allotment to be mandatorily sent to support a wife and family. The only way this match, along with half your month's pay, can be allocated is to a lawful wife. Here's 'catch twenty-two;' using a lawyer might help escape marriage, but without a legal wife, the government will not match one-half. A civil judge could garnish all but a pittance of your pay for what the court perceives as your responsibility."

"Mr. Walker, I've listened to older sailors talk about 'camp followers' willing to do anything to marry a serviceman just to receive an allotment check. Damn it! A shotgun's being pressed against by back."

"I can't sit in judgment against this girl. I don't know her," Mr. Walker replied. "This often happens, and many indigent women spread their legs for money, but no one forced you to have sex with her. You made that choice. I had an uncle stationed in France during the last World War, who was flown back to the states by the Red Cross and forced to marry a pregnant girl claiming he was the father of her

ADRIFT

child. Divorce is difficult. They remained married and until the day he died, he doubted the child was his."

"Sir, how can I prove it's not mine?"

"During the last World War, wounded servicemen were mysteriously dying after blood transfusions. This prompted more blood research. Discovered, along with the four major blood types, was another important factor. It's called the RH factor, after the Rhesus monkey used during the research. After a baby is born, blood samples can be taken to test for type and RH factor to try disproving paternity. But this isn't a legally recognized method. Someday, doctors will find an accurate test to determine paternity. But today, there's no absolute way."

"Sir, she wants to get married right away so a Naval hospital will cover the necessary expenses. I can't wait until the baby is born to get blood samples that might not work." Paris thoughts raced. "What if I married someone else? Then I couldn't be forced to wed her."

"Allison, your service records show you're single, but if you were to hurriedly wed someone else, the courts, with the Red Cross' encouragement, could still award the girl...." Lieutenant Walker checked the telegram to reaffirm the name. "Joyce, adequate child support. With what little Uncle Sam pays you now, you'd be in a financial mess. Did this girl, Joyce, have a rabbit's test?"

"Sir, what's that? I've never heard of a test called that."

"It's a medical test verifying pregnancy. I keep forgetting how young you are. What's your age? Eighteen, nineteen?"

"Eighteen, sir," Paris replied.

"The girl's claim of pregnancy may be a hoax. If not, she might have a miscarriage or decide to secretly abort. Then, your worries would be over. See a Naval chaplain and try to find a reasonably priced lawyer to help you. I'm sorry, Allison, for not knowing a solution to get you out of this fix, but in today's world, with you in the military, a pregnant woman has the upper hand. I hate to see you caught up in this predicament. You're a good radarman and highly thought of by those working with you. I've already spoken to the Skipper about you possibly entering Officer Candidate School and wanting to fly. I hope things work out and this mess clears up." Mr. Walker handed Paris the damp telegram. "Hang on to his. You might need it." Then, as an afterthought, he added, "If it's any consolation, you're lucky to be enlisted. If you were an 'officer and a gentleman,' by Congressional appointment, any character blemish on your record would force you to resign. On the other hand, as an enlisted man, having an affair with the wife of an officer could get you twenty years in the Federal Prison in Leavenworth."

"Thank you, sir, for listening and trying to help."

What do I do? Paris thought. Crumbling the message in his hand, he felt helpless at sea, as events closed in. He weighed the moral and financial decision the military and society obligated him to make. *Maybe it'd been a full moon. I've heard my dad tell of people going off the deep end when the moon was at its fullest.* His irrational jealousy caused this catastrophic event, which threatened the destruction of his cherished love for Carolyn. He could spend the remainder of his life regretting a few minutes of passion.

It was one of those crisp cold days in December, and the sun glistened on the newly fallen blanket of snow. Carolyn asked if they might stop for a moment when they first saw the small, seemingly forgotten park, nestled on the outskirts of the city. Strangely now, she seemed embarrassed to ask even the smallest request, as if her condition forbade her any liberties, no matter how slight.

Paris watched as she stepped from the car. Although her time was drawing near, she was able to maintain a natural gracefulness in her movements. Playfully, she hurried ahead and scooped up a handful of fresh snow, but undetected by Paris, brought it quickly to her cheeks to hide the tears beginning to form.

"Would you like to sit on the bench? The sun's dried it off," he called from the car.

"Oh! Do you really think there's time? They're so strict about being late. But if we could rest just for a few minutes...."

He walked up to her and they sat, unconsciously moving close to each other, as if together they might ward off the pressing time. He held her close and smelled the freshness of her hair as its pale golden strands brushed lightly across his nose. He reached to touch her left hand, and his fingers traced the small band of imitation gold she wore, recalling the day she purchased it, and how she had explained she'd wear it only when they were together. "Paris, this is 1955. People are eager to condemn an unmarried pregnant girl and cast stones at the male they assume is the cause."

"Let's get married right away, Carolyn, before the baby is born. Let's not wait for anything. There's going to be money problems, but I'll work those out," Paris added, thinking of his conversation with Lieutenant Walker. "We could get by. The important thing is, we'd be together. There's still time to have your delivery in a Naval hospital, if we hurry and do it."

Carolyn shook her head. "Paris, you're sweet, even when you're not sincere. My family brought me to Boston to save them any disgrace; now you'd ask me to saddle your family's only son with a wife carrying an illegitimate child. Tsk! Tsk!" Carolyn made a mocking sound, playfully chiding him for being foolish. "Isn't it obvious? I'm a sinful woman!" She ran her hand over her rounded stomach.

He couldn't help loving Carolyn. In her, he perceived no selfishness.

Carolyn's brow furrowed. "Paris, I've a decision to make. We've talked of this and still, it's something only I can do. The Home will make arrangements for putting my baby up for adoption, but once I've consented, my baby will be taken from me and I'll never know who has it. Never be able to see it...never be able to hold it or love it...." Her voice trailed off and she began crying softly. "Can't you see? The only way we could be together without bringing shame and disgrace to your family would be for me to give it up so no one would know I'd ever been pregnant. I don't think I can do it. I don't think I'm strong enough or cold enough to carry it inside me...feel it move...have it and just give it away. You're the exact opposite of the baby's father. He's Italian with dark curly hair. You're fair and blond. There's no way to make anyone believe the baby's yours. We couldn't live such a lie. It's a losing situation, either way." She tossed her head back proudly, her beautiful thick hair caught up in the stiff wintry air. She reached into her coat pocket for her handkerchief and hurriedly wiped her eyes. "Please take me back now," she asked softly.

On the drive back to Brighton, they hardly spoke, as both were absorbed in their own personal conflicts. His free hand grasping hers, he drove beside the intercity trolley tracks and entered the prim subdivision on the Northwestern edge of Boston.

Slowing for a right turn at the corner gas station, its surrounding sidewalks lined with freshly-cut pine trees, he saw a strand of red and green lights illuminating a crudely painted sign: "Xmas Trees For Sale." Releasing her hand to downshift, he frowned, unconsciously shaking his head, thinking: *I wonder what drastic changes will be made in our lives by Christmas?*

Carolyn misunderstood his movements and tears streamed down her face. "Paris, you've changed. You're so distant. If you've stopped caring, please don't think you're obligated to me. Because our lives have touched, we'll always be a part of each other. You once asked the meaning of raison de etra. There is a reason for all that's happened…there has to be. It's like making a ripple with your hand in a large pool. That ripple affects all the water in the pool, every molecule. It doesn't necessarily mean we, ourselves, will benefit by having met. But the effect created by our meeting will be felt in someway, somewhere, sometime by others in our lives, whom we come to know."

He cradled her head in the crook of his arm and gently pressed his fingertips to her lips to silence her. "Carolyn, I love you and I always will. Nothing about that has changed. Nothing concerning the baby and nothing about my loving you will ever change. Now, hush."

The engine labored on the steep ascent toward the Gothic structure looming at the top of the hill.

"You have my ship's phone number. Promise me you'll call if anything happens?"

"I promise. I'm not due for two more weeks. Please don't worry about me so," she said, drying her eyes with the back of her hand.

Paris made a wide circle in the cobblestone cul-de-sac bringing the car close to the main entrance. Then he started to get out and walk her to the door.

"It's better if I walk in alone. It's late." He drew her close, kissing her on the lips. "Take care," she whispered. As long as they had known each other, she never failed to leave without this tender adieu. She opened the car door and walked toward the large front door. About to enter, she turned, bringing her fingers to her lips, and blew him a kiss.

He engaged the clutch and began descending the hill.

Carolyn stepped inside and closed the heavy oak door. For a moment, her strength drained from her and she leaned back to rest against the door thinking that her life had become chaotic. Would she ever know an end to the shame and embarrassment she felt? The sharp pain hit her without warning, its intensity so severe she doubled over gasping and sank slowly to the floor.

Paris' thoughts were not on driving, and only after the car began to slide out of control on the icy hill did he snap back to reality. Quickly, he down-shifted to second gear and pumped the brakes several times. The small Chevrolet trembled as the wheels gripped the road; then it slowed.

Passing the corner gas station, Paris glanced again at the trees being sold for Christmas. The painful reality of what he must do was etched into his mind. When he last proposed marriage, he felt Carolyn detected insincerity in his voice. He loved her and would always love her, but now, locked in the inner recesses of his mind was an inescapable financial obligation. It meant nothing to him, only a physical release, a hurried toss in the car's back seat, and even during the passionate embraces, he had thought of Carolyn.

"God," he said aloud, "Joyce said it was her safe time. I couldn't believe it when she called to tell me she was 'missing her friend.' What a hell of a way to put it. Not, 'I'm in trouble, I'm pregnant,' or any logical explanation…just, '*I'm missing my friend*'."

At first, he assured himself her period was only a couple of days late, but as days dragged into weeks, the ominous threat of her pregnancy became a reality. After her disclosure, Paris avoided making contact with her. He'd been unfaithful to Carolyn and, in a strange, twisted kind of logic, hoped, by not calling or seeing Joyce again, the result of his lack of discretion would disappear.

Paris' thoughts retraced the last months and he spoke aloud. "What a Goddamn mess! I love a girl carrying someone else's child, and I'm accused of knocking up one I don't give a damn about." He cursed himself for feeling self-pity. "Damnit! I've only myself to blame. Nobody forced me into the backseat with her." Maybe seeing Carolyn pregnant, knowing the pleasures her beauty and body had given someone else, had driven him into this act with Joyce. He erased this from his mind. That would be blaming Carolyn for his own misconduct.

Joyce was in possession of a great deal of perseverance, as well as a growing embryo. After her first call through the phone on the quarter deck, Paris deduced Joyce got the ship's name from the sign-in list at the door of the Enlisted Men's Club.

Remembering how he hurried to the quarter deck, thinking it was Carolyn, he felt his face drain of color. Then came Joyce's additional calls and threats: "If you don't come to the phone when I call, I'll demand to speak to your captain. You had your fun, and now you're going to pay for it. I'll call the Red Cross. They'll see you marry me and give me my allotment. What do you mean, is it yours? You're damned right it's yours. You can't deny it. You've got to marry me, so I can have your child in the Naval hospital." Paris was convinced Lieutenant Walker was right. Joyce was being given advice by someone.

He didn't believe the precautions used had failed. In spite of her saying it was her "safe time," he had used a rubber. Paris saw no escape from this dilemma. He was being forced into an obligation to Joyce and the baby she was carrying. But he didn't love her, didn't want her.

Miserable about seeing Carolyn while trying to pretend everything was all right, he prayed a miscarriage would change the outcome of Joyce's pregnancy. *I don't have the guts to tell Carolyn*, he anguished, *regardless of my love for her. How could I admit what happened and that I'm being morally and financially forced to marry Joyce?*

It was late evening when he arrived at the Y.M.C.A. across the street from Newport's small park. He contrived a way to destroy any feelings Carolyn had for him. It would be cruel, but far better than devastating her with the truth.

Snow was piled along the curbs, so he parked a block away and walked to the building. Inside, he heard familiar sounds of games being played at the pool tables and the steady hum of the servicemen's voices in mundane conversations, as they attempted to conceal their loneliness. He'd find stationery to write a letter in the serviceman's home away from home.

He walked to the writing stands, finding the standard supplies of stationery and several fountain pens chained to the upright desks. Not hesitating, knowing if he faltered, he wouldn't have the courage to do it later, he began writing.

Dear Carolyn,

> *I know I could never forget the thought that you had been with another man and bore his child. I pretended to you and myself I could marry you and forget, but I know now it is impossible. Please forgive me for deceiving you.*
>
> > *Paris*

He addressed and sealed the envelope, purchasing a three-cent stamp from the stamp machine. He paused at the mailbox, envisioning Carolyn's lovely face, beautiful smile, her soft voice, reliving, as in a fast-forward movie, the countless events they had enjoyed and the wonderful times they'd spent together.

He shook his head, gritting his teeth; jaw tightened with determination, hand trembling, he dropped the letter through the slot.

CHAPTER 21

CAROLYN, HER HEAD PROPPED UP on pillows, looked down at the white sheets covering her flat stomach. She'd carried the awkward bulge so long, its disappearance astounded her. Running her hands over her abdomen, it was as if she'd lost a part of herself.

The baby's delivery was difficult and had drained her strength. Dark circles under her eyes and an unnatural whiteness to her skin evidenced the toll the seven pound, 12 ounce baby boy's birth played on her. Her deep green eyes scanned the bleak walls, noting the hour as she focused on the clock, anticipating the feeding time when the small wrinkled form with dark curly hair would be brought. She nursed the baby, despite rumored bad effects that breast feeding might harm her figure.

At seven a.m. the nurse entered the room carrying the hungry bundle. Its tiny cries reached Carolyn's ears as the door opened. As the baby was placed into her waiting arms, she noticed the cold expression on the nurse's face, thinking professional conditioning created a hard shell in her personality, preventing any personal involvements.

The soft cries ceased as the baby's mouth closed about her nipple, feeding hungrily. This attachment seemed identical to the nourishing lifeblood her body supplied through the umbilical cord while carrying him in her womb.

She held his small hand between her thumb and index finger, studying the tiny digits, whispering softly, "In all the world, I'm the only one who loves you…there's no one else. Your father proved his insincerity, fleeing responsibility and hiding in the wealth of his family. His plans didn't include being burdened by us, and in my family everyone wishes you didn't exist. Well, my beautiful little boy, you do exist. I love you with all my heart. I won't give you up…I can't."

Carolyn remembered her talk with Paris in the small park on Sunday; Carolyn had sensed insincerity in his voice. She wanted to believe it'd been her indecision about keeping the baby that brought the changes in Paris' personality. *How different our lives might've been*, she reflected, *if I'd known him before becoming involved with*

Tony. Yet we could have a marriage including my baby. Together we'd overcome the wrong I've done.

"I can't give you up…I can't," she whispered to her infant.

Carolyn had fallen deeply in love with Paris during the past months. Recalling the memories of her youthful years since her father died, she longed for someone strong to love and rely on. Fate brought Paris to her and, though her pregnancy was an obstacle, their love would surmount it.

She thought of Paris, wanting to call him and let him know of the baby's birth. But, with her child in her arms, she had an overwhelming compulsion to keep anyone who might influence her to give him up at a distance. Even Paris.

When she unscrambled her thoughts, she decided to write to Paris. In a letter, it'd be easier to explain her feelings for him and her baby than on a phone.

The temperature plummeted and heavy clouds hung low, sagging like bedding on the underside of worn upholstered furniture. Rain beginning to mix with snow splashed the window panes facing the cobblestone street.

Carolyn stood at her window, her concentration focused on the framed glass squares. A trickle of moisture clung to a pane and, as if by a prearranged plan, broke free to begin an irregular journey down the glass, finally destructing into a small puddle accumulating on the window sill. She watched the droplet, thinking of her life and how she'd allowed it to self-destruct. Like the raindrop spattering into a common puddle, she had permitted her troubles to mire down those she loved.

Having been informed of the birth of the baby, her brother Ralph would drive her mother from Hartford, arriving this afternoon. A full day had passed since Carolyn delivered, two weeks sooner than predicted. Ralph had to make hurried preparations at his job to get time off.

Carolyn showered and combed her hair, preparing for their arrival. Donning bathrobe and slippers, she applied make-up, realizing how drawn she looked. She decided against using rouge as it made her appear clownish because of her pallid complexion.

Startled at the sound of a door slamming shut, she looked from her window and saw her brother help their mother from the car. Ralph parked in the circular cobblestone drive in the same spot Paris had when she left him Sunday.

Her mother had aged since seeing her last. Ralph was able to drive up from Hartford only once a month and the physical changes in her mom since their last visit were noticeable in her stooped frame and slow movements. Carolyn blamed herself for having caused this.

She met them downstairs in the visitors' sitting room. Her arms encircled her mother. She couldn't restrain the sobs shaking her body. "Momma, I feel so ashamed, so confused."

"Everything will work out." Her mother's voice was weak, almost inaudible. "Can I see the child?"

Before she could answer, Ralph's voice grated her ears like a coarse file rubbing across jagged metal. "What have you decided regarding the baby?"

"I…I want to keep him…I can't let him go. I can't give him away."

Ralph, stood up. He was tall and painfully thin; his thinning, premature gray hair topped an intellectual face. Known for his sagacity and moral convictions, he spoke in the authoritative manner he had adopted since the passing of their father. Carolyn dreaded the resolve carried in his tone, though she knew he was thinking only in terms of the family and her best interests.

"Don't you know what the child will be called?" He thrust the words at her like a saber. "A bastard…and you a whore." Is this what you want? It's best to let this place take care of everything."

"No! Look at my little boy. Tell me that, if he were yours, you'd give him away." Carolyn spoke in a trembling voice.

"Please, I'd like to see him. He's my grandson and my daughter's child. She'll do what she feels she must." Her mother's soft voice took command.

The nurse brought the baby, wrapped in a blue blanket, into the room, and Carolyn's mother took him in her arms.

"He's beautiful!" She looked at her son while speaking to Carolyn. "Whatever you decide, we'll all stand behind it."

Ralph hesitated, started to speak and nodded. He couldn't argue with his mother.

"Momma, Paris says he loves me and wants to marry me. He'll take my baby as his. You'll see. If we pray, it'll work out…it has to." Carolyn's voice broke.

"What of Paris' family?" Ralph probed. "Do they know everything?"

"Not yet, but Paris is sure they'll understand…."

"You seem so sure of this Paris fellow. We've yet to meet him. Sis, don't put all your hopes in one basket. The bottom can fall out."

The weather worsened by the time visiting hours ended. Ralph used the telephone in the foyer to make reservations to stay overnight at a nearby motel. Then he and his mother left with plans to return the next day to verify Carolyn's decision about keeping the child.

Carolyn had supper in her room rather than join the other girls in the dining hall. She didn't feel physically or mentally strong enough to be subjected to prying questions regarding her baby boy and his immediate future.

When first arriving in Brighton, she considered herself an outsider, alone and apart from the others. Some unwed, prospective mothers took their situations lightly, as if invaded by a bothersome cold that would soon end, allowing them to resume their lives. A few talked of keeping their babies and concocted stories of husbands being killed in Korea, planning to return home to live out their fabrications. Others had been whisked away by parents, to "out of state colleges" or to "Grandma's" for extended stays, before signs of pregnancy were noticeable. Most would give their babies up for adoption. The Home in Brighton provided legal facilities for this. To Carolyn's disbelief, a few didn't know who the fathers were, openly discussing their pre-marital affairs. As an idealistic young girl, Carolyn grew up with a dream of romantic love. Sex was an expression of that love: monogamous, private, and held in the highest esteem. The deceptive sorcery of Tony's charisma and good looks had enchanted her. Young and trusting, she was impressed by his new convertible and endless supply of money. She was certain he intended to marry her. Tears came to her eyes, remembering her humiliation when she revealed her pregnancy to him and his denial of the child being his. This still burned her ears as she recalled him accusing her of "screwing around with other guys and getting herself in trouble and trying to nail him because of his family's wealth. His parents would produce several men to admit having sex with her if she pursued any steps toward marriage."

"They'll say they paid you to get laid," Tony had threatened her. "I'm not being pinned down. I've got plans, and my whole life is ahead of me. You're not tying me down."

He wanted her to see a doctor who'd perform an abortion. Carolyn couldn't believe this cruel, selfish man was the one she had loved. She never wanted to see him again. Then she had to reveal her pregnancy to her family. The hurt on her mother's face was etched in her memory; the agonizing disgrace would never be forgotten. Guilt and shame burned into her like a branding iron. She would never forgive herself for exposing her family to such scorn. Abandoning her upbringing had been a grievous error.

Upon being informed, her older brother, Ralph, was coldly understanding of his sister's dilemma and assumed the task of making necessary arrangements for Carolyn to come to Boston to bear her child. Carolyn felt The Almighty was punishing her for creating so much hurt for those she loved. Then, as though by "Divine Plan," Paris entered her life.

Carolyn sat on the side of her bed, struggling to write Paris and express her deep love for him, as well as for her child. Baring her pride in the contents of the letter, she opened her heart and wrote:

> *Dear Paris,*
> *I need your love now more than ever before.*
> *I've had a baby boy....*

When finished, she folded the letter, placed it into a stamped envelope, and wearing pink lipstick, kissed the sealed flap. She descended the stairs and dropped the letter into the foyer's mailbox.

That evening, as Carolyn lay in bed reading, the nurse came to remove the supper tray and brought her mail. "This came for you earlier. I thought it better to give it to you after your visitors left."

"Oh! Thank you." Carolyn placed her tattered book, A *Collection of Edna St. Vincent Millay's Poetry*, on the nightstand and took the envelope. Recognizing the handwriting, her heart beat rapidly. *Paris!* Waiting until the nurse gathered up the tray and left the room, she tore open his letter and read the short contents. Her heart fluttered, then, almost stopped. She gave an anguished cry. She'd been deceived into believing he loved her.

She now faced the naked truth: Everything was a lie. His expressions of love, feelings he said they shared, dreams of a future together, had all been false.

She fell against the pillow, crushing his letter in her hand. "It was all a pretense," she sobbed quietly, not wanting anyone to hear. *Everything he lead me to believe was a lie, just as it had been with Tony.* "Oh God, my baby...Momma and Ralph will be back tomorrow. I don't want to live without my baby...without Paris. It was all a lie. Paris, why?"

She burst into tears, sobbing openly, "I've been such a fool. There is no answer. I can't give up my baby and go on living."

The lines from Edna St Vincent Millay's poetry she had been reading flashed in her mind:

"You love me not at all, but let it go.
I loved you more than life, but let it be."

CHAPTER 22

IN THE DARKNESS, SILVERY-WHITE CAPPED waves slapped ominously against the seawall as a thick fog crept over Newport's lower waterfront, blanketing Thames Street. The heavy mist caused the lighted neon sign suspended above the entrance of the *Blue Moon Lounge* to cast an eerie glow.

Inside, secure from the cold dampness, the band played music that was almost deafening. Sitting near the dance floor, the trio watched couples move to the beat of "Night Train." One pair gyrated close together, their hips touching, while dancing the highly provocative "Dirty Boogie." Tex Madison and Mickey Crowley's eyes were riveted on the girl's pelvis while she performed slow bumps and grinds to the sensual rhythm.

The last few days were a blur and Paris had trouble recalling events placing him at the lounge. Too many beers and dense cigarette smoke blurred his vision. Squinting, he tried focusing on the dancers.

Though excessive drinking clouded his mind, the words written in the letter and mailed to Carolyn were still clear, eating at him like a cancer. He remembered returning to the ship and paying little attention to talk among the crew about a Mideast crisis. There was always scuttlebutt. He thought only of the pain he'd caused Carolyn and the dilemma with Joyce. Tex chastised him saying, "You've changed, Paris, since you got back from Boston. You're too damned quiet and irritable and you keep to yourself. I've got duty tomorrow and this'll be my last night to go ashore. I went to a lot of trouble getting false I.D. cards so we can get served locally, and you're letting me down. You two pussies stand your watches snug and warm in the radar shack, while I freeze my ass off in that motorized canoe. Don't screw this liberty up for me."

"You guys go. I don't feel like going ashore." He had sat on his tiered bunk, staring down at his bare feet.

"The three of us are going to hit the beach together, or none of us are going." Tex's face had reddened like a neon sign, flashing between concern for his buddy and frustration.

Mickey joined in. "What's wrong with you? You seem so fucking moody…not like yourself at all. You got clap or something?"

"Look! Get off my back. I'm tired of this bellyaching. Goddamn it! I'll go if that's how you both feel."

"We'll have a good time, Paris," Mickey had said amiably.

"Don't go crying in your beer if we don't," Paris had snapped.

Temples pounding, the smoke and noise grated his very nerves as anger swelled in his chest and his throat muscles tightened with an urge to strike out at the world that had taken Carolyn from him.

A blonde girl walked by the table. For an instant, he thought it was Carolyn. Realizing he was wrong, he reached for his beer.

"Be careful," Tex warned. "We're drinking on false I.D. cards. Don't overdo it, buddy. Make any trouble, and the Shore Patrol over by the door will hang our asses up to dry."

"Yeah! Ours and the yeoman who made the I.D.s for us," Mickey added nervously.

An unattractive brunette seated at the next table smiled when the band swung into a new tune. Grinning, Mickey squeezed from the table and sidled over to ask her to dance.

Tex slid his chair closer to the table and pushed his white hat to the back of his head; black strands of oily hair fell against his forehead. He formed his massive hands into a praying position on the table before him and breathed out heavily. "Paris, it's none of my business, but if you've got yourself in a jam, it's sometimes easier to share your problems. I've been down some rough roads myself."

Paris' thinking was saturated with alcohol, but he knew the raw deal his friend had gotten with the red-haired Vera. Tex never spoke of her but had never gotten over their breakup. Paris, staring down at the beer spills on the tabletop, finally looked up at his friend. Seeing the concern on Tex's face, he nodded.

"I've gotten myself in a mess with two girls, Tex."

"What kind of mess?"

"They're pregnant."

"Both?"

"Both."

"Goddamn, man. You been eating Spanish fly? You mean you've knocked two up at the same time?"

"No," Paris said, finding it hard forming the words. His tongue felt thick, like it was covered with cotton. "One's mine...I think. The other's not, that's for damn sure."

"So what's the problem?" Tex slapped his hand on the table. "You got feelings for the one carrying yours?"

"I said, I *think* it's mine. I got in her pants all right, but damn, I can't figure out how I knocked her up."

"Shit, man! You're old enough to know how to knock up a piece of ass. It's sure not with your tongue." He punched Paris on the shoulder.

"No, I mean it. I didn't take any chances. I was careful. I didn't slip up."

"Do you care for her?"

"You mean if I had a choice between the two?"

"What do you mean...if you had a choice? You said the other broad's pregnant, but it's not yours."

"You don't understand." Paris' words were slurring more noticeably. "That's what I've been trying to tell you. I love that one."

"Jesus! You're a glutton for punishment." Tex shook his head. "Sometimes advice is good and sometimes it ain't. I'm going to give the best advice I can offer and I mean it." He affectionately poked Paris in the chest with his forefinger. "You do what *you* feel...here, right here in your heart, nothing else. Don't give a damn about anything except that. Don't let anyone pressure you or put a shotgun in your back and march you to the altar."

The table rocked as Mickey stumbled against it. "She's an ugly little bitch, but when she pushes her snatch against my leg, she looks like Cleopatra." He threw himself into the chair, rocking back on its rear legs. "Ain't you guys going to dance, or you gonna sit and bullshit the night away?"

"We're talking about something pretty important," Tex scowled.

"Hey! I'm sorry I'm alive!" Mickey threw his arms up in disgust. This over-zealous gesture, with his chair tilted, sent him toppling back against the next table, knocking over several glasses and bottles of beer.

"You dumb son-of-a-bitch," yelled one of the sailors seated at the table. As Mickey fought to regain his balance, the irritated sailor pushed him, knocking him to the floor.

"Hey! What the hell did you do that for?" Tex jumped to his feet. "It was an accident. His chair slipped and he fell backward. You didn't have to push him."

The two Shore Patrol officers stationed by the door looked across the crowded floor toward the commotion.

Tex moved to help Mickey up.

"Maybe you'd like to do something about it?" The burly sailor rose from his chair, his square jaw jutting forward. He outweighed Tex by 30 pounds, and his confident expression announced he felt the odds were in his favor.

The loud, threatening hostility jolted Paris from his drunken stupor. "Hey!" Paris got to his feet. "It was an accident. Sit down and I'll buy a round to make up for the spilled beer."

"Look, fuck-face! Keep out of this or I'll have to stomp your ass too!"

Paris only saw a glimpse of the face: eyes small, dark, lacking intelligence; nose broad and flat, and jaw dark bristled with needing a shave. The pent up anger choking him for the past two days, exploded. Paris threw his entire weight behind his punch. All hell and bedlam erupted in the brawl that followed as the Shore Patrol moved in.

In the sudden fracas, amid the over-turned tables resulting from the melee, the Shore Patrol hadn't gotten to them. Tex had lifted Paris, pushing into the crowd, where they mingled in the confusion. Mickey made it out a side exit and Tex, supporting Paris under his arms, followed.

"Goddamn! We were lucky to get out of there."

Tex balanced Paris' dead weight across his shoulders, his head and arms hanging limply down his back. After hiding more than 20 minutes in an alley adjacent to the bar, he continued carrying him using a "fireman's hold" for several more blocks.

Paris remembered nothing of the aftermath.

"Damn, he's out cold! Never seen anything like that before. His reflexes are like a cat's. He broke that hard-on's nose with a round house and then passed out." Tex's back and legs were aching under the prolonged weight. "I think it's safe to put him down and rest."

"Are you sure?" Mickey moaned.

Paris woke sick to his stomach, his dress blues soaking and smelling of puke. He couldn't identify his whereabouts and felt his head would explode. He reached out to touch the wet walls seeming to be pressing in on him. Slowly looking up, he rec-ognized a nozzle. He was lying in a shower.

Groaning, he forced himself up, removing the foul-smelling uniform and his shoes. Naked, he stumbled from the shower and through the hatch leading to the compartments below. Finding his locker in the semi-darkness, he groped for a towel and a bar of soap, then made his way up the ladder to the showers. Allowing the cold water to pour into his open mouth to cleanse the foul taste, he showered and scrubbed his uniform with the soap, cursing as the exertion made his head throb.

Back in the compartment, using a fresh towel, he carefully rolled his uniform in it while trying to remove any excessive wrinkles. He'd try later to get the ship's laundry to steam press it. He scrambled into his rack and closed his eyes.

Paris opened his eyes at reveille. Because of the nausea caused by his heavy drinking, it took him considerable effort to get from his rack and join his mates preparing for muster. He found Tex and Mickey below on the mess deck. While lis-tening to their teasing, he tried downing a cup of black coffee.

"Boy! You tied one on last night. Remember hitting that bastard in the bar?" Mickey grinned.

A vague memory fuzzily came to Paris. "He must've hit me back one hell of a wallop. I'm still reeling."

"No," Tex smiled. "He didn't do any hitting back. You broke his nose and took two tables down with him. Damn lucky in the confusion we were able to get out of the place. Shore Patrol was right on our asses."

"I don't remember much at all. How'd I get to the ship, and who the hell threw me in the shower?"

"I did," Tex stated. "I carried your drunken ass all the way. When you began heaving, I dumped your butt in the showers and turned it on to kill the smell. Boy! You look like hell."

"Thanks. I owe you one."

"I hope I never have to collect."

They broke for muster at 0800. Tex fell in with the First Division; Mickey and Paris stood quarters with the men of the Operations department, outside the radar shack.

By mid-noon, the ship began bobbing at its mooring. The sky turned dark and the shoreline, only a mile away, grew hazy and hard to distinguish. The sea became choppy, and white caps slapped against the vessel's hull.

Mail call was at 1500 hours. Knowing the letter was from Carolyn when he saw the kiss on the envelope, Paris didn't need to look at the return address. He tore it open. The love and tenderness she expressed and the shock of the baby's coming so soon, caused his hands to tremble. He tried to push her from his thoughts but had failed miserably. He needed her as badly as she, in her confession in the letter, needed him.

Long months together as she carried the baby had made the child his. Despite his drunken stupor from the previous night, he remembered Tex's astute words. He must do what he had always felt in his heart, even if it meant a confession to the world. He'd see Carolyn and explain everything, just as she had to him. He'd do whatever was financially necessary to help Joyce support her baby. But now, he had to go to Carolyn.

Everything was suddenly crystal clear. A memory when he was a child, no more than seven, of a rare instance of open affection seldom witnessed, flashed across his mind. His father sat across the kitchen table from his mother with a cup of hot, sweetened coffee before him and reached out to touch her hand. "It seems like yesterday when I hoboed into Bainbridge on that Sunday morning. I jumped off the freight train and walked toward the sound of singing coming from a little white Baptist church. I peeped through the window and saw you. I said to myself, 'That's the girl I'm going to marry'." Just as his dad had done when he fell in love with Mom, no obstacle could have stood in his way. His father would've met any dilemma head on, telling the truth, not running from it. Had he leveled with Carolyn, she would've understood.

His thoughts froze. The letter mailed to Carolyn Sunday evening from the YMCA would've been received by now. He looked at the postmark on the envelope in his hand. It was dated Wednesday P.M.; Carolyn's correspondence had traveled through the Fleet Post Office to reach his ship in Newport. His letter reached her at least a day ago. *My God*, he thought, *my letter must have gotten to her. I mailed it Sunday night. I've got to get to her, to explain, to straighten everything out and tell her I never wanted to write it. I could never hurt her.*

He'd draw his liberty card and go to her. No, he'd call her first. He had to get himself ready. He thought of his uniform. It was a mess and still damp. He'd never get off the ship wearing it in that condition. He'd try to borrow Dress Blues. Mickey was close to his size. His uniform would fit, and they both wore the same rate. Paris raced to find his friend.

CHAPTER 23

LIBERTY CALL CAME AT 1600 hours, and Paris reached the quarter deck in borrowed blues, in time to see the first liberty boat pull away.

The sky blackened and a fine snow was falling. The sea turned rough and as the small boat rode the top of a wave, he spotted Tex at the engine controls. The coxswain hung diligently to the rudder bar while the bowman knelt near the prow.

Yells and frightened laughter crossed the water from the liberty party as the boat dipped its bow into a swell. Soon, it was impossible to see the craft when it disappeared, riding in the gullies of the mounting waves. Only an occasional *ding* could be heard in the darkening distance as the tiller rang his bell to order up engine speed.

It was after five o'clock when the rumble of the boat's engine could be heard returning. The storm was getting more severe and by now, snow fell heavily in large flakes from the blackness closing about them.

Because of the severe weather, the officer of the deck considered canceling liberty for those still aboard. Paris paced the deck, fearful this would happen. The crew lashed the boat and climbed the ladder to the quarter deck to warm up with hot coffee.

Paris moved quickly toward Tex. "Try hurrying them along, Tex. The O.D.'s going to cancel liberty any minute."

"When I tell him how ragged that's engine's running, he's gonna cancel it anyway. Hell, I didn't think we'd make it back this time."

"Tex, I've got to get ashore. I just received this letter and I've got to go to Carolyn."

He handed it to Tex, who held it up to a light suspended above their heads and scanned it quickly. "Shit, man...she'll keep. We'll be risking our necks to make another trip."

"I wrote her a nasty letter; she's got it by now. I've got to go to her. Remember what you said last night? I screwed up royally and I've got to see her, to explain."

"Snatch! They'll be the death of me yet. I wish somebody would figure out a way to dehydrate pussy. You could carry it around in a box and when you needed

some, you'd just add water. If that happens, I'll never look at another bitch again."
Tex sighed noisily. "Don't worry. I won't say anything about the engine. Get your
ass aboard and I'll get you ashore. Gimme a minute to hustle 'em up." Before there
was time for complaints, Tex hurried the two crew members into the liberty boat
and began revving the engine.

The O.D. leaned over the lifelines, yelling down to the crew, "We'd better call
it quits. It's getting too rough."

Tex responded quickly, "Sir, it seems worse than it is from up there. This liberty party's been waiting an hour to go ashore. It's good experience for us. It's a
piece of cake."

"I don't know," the young ensign hesitated, then relented. "Okay. I haven't
heard any cancellations on the ship to shore phone, but make this the last shuttle."

The engine ran rough and Tex fought the throttle adjustments to maintain
power as the small craft pitched and bounced. Someone yelled out light-heartedly,
"Piece of cake...my ass," and everyone aboard laughed nervously.

The motor whaleboat struggled, finally making it to shore. The liberty party
climbed the ladder one at a time, while the bowman held the boat against the pier
with the bow hook.

Paris, reaching the top of the ladder turned, cupped his hands around his
mouth, and yelled down to Tex, "Thanks! I owe you!"

"That's what buddies are for," Tex yelled back. "Hope she's worth it. The ones
I've known aren't."

The coxswain shoved off and in the howling wind, Paris heard the irregular
sound of the engine and ringing of the bell, long after the boat disappeared into the
snowy darkness. He trudged along with the liberty party in the deepening snow and
luckily caught a ride to the main gate with a sailor driving to Newport. The falling
snow blanketed the windshield. Seated in the front passenger seat, he only saw the
road when the wiper blade made its arcing sweep.

"Here's Two Mile Corner! This is as far as I can take you," the driver said. "I
pity you if you're heading to Melville Landing. Better change your mind and go
with me, into town. The Shore Patrol's canceling liberty and advising everyone
ashore to head to the YMCA."

"Thanks, but I've got to get my car. I'll get out here. Maybe I'll get lucky and
be able to thumb a ride to Melville."

Paris stood on the deserted road, unprotected from the blowing snow and frigid wind. Shaking from the cold, he pulled his white cap tightly over his head and partially buried his face in the up-turned collar of his peacoat. He grimaced, realizing he could freeze. It'd be ironic, he thought, his teeth chattering, if no one picked him up and he froze to death. Carolyn would never know of his efforts to see her.

A tractor-trailer slowed to make the turn and hissed to a stop. The driver honked his horn and Paris jogged awkwardly toward the rig, his shoes sinking deep in the snow. His feet burned from the wet cold.

The driver grinned. "I barely saw you on the corner with the snow coming down so hard. Where you headed?"

"To Melville. I left my car there."

"You picked a hell of a night to get it, but you're in luck. I'll let you off at the entrance to Melville gate. Damn good thing I picked you up. Way it's snowing, I don't think any car could make the trip." He laughed. "It's got to get deep before I bog down."

Smiling gratefully, Paris sat quietly, his feet warming against the heater.

When the driver dropped Paris off, he had a quarter mile walk to his car. He heaved a sigh of relief. Fortunately, he was able to move the vehicle without digging it out with the snowshovel stored in the trunk.

His gloved hands swept the windshield, then slid the key into the door lock. The thumb latch popped up. Luckily the lock hadn't frozen. Crawling into the front seat, he pumped the accelerator while pulling out the choke. Making a silent prayer, he turned the key to the start position, listening to the engine begin to crank. It turned slowly at first, as his stomach tied in knots. The battery was weak. It had sat here in the cold too long. Finally it began to spin more freely, sputtered several times and caught. He played with the accelerator and choke until the engine ran more smoothly. When he was sure it wouldn't stall, he put the car in gear and drove slowly through the deep snow. There was no moving traffic on the main road, but the sides were strewn with abandoned cars. He continually stopped to wipe the windshield and clear the snow that the vacuum driven wipers couldn't push aside.

Tension caused aches through his shoulders and neck, and his temples pounded with an intense headache from driving in these severe conditions. The snow was so deep, it was possible to move only in the ruts already formed. Miraculously, he fought his way to Boston.

Paris turned on the overhead light to look at this watch. It was past 8:00 p.m. Ahead, he saw a phone booth. Leaving his engine running, he waded through the snow to the booth. Dialing repeatedly, he gave up in disgust, hearing a continuous busy tone, then only silence. The phone had gone dead.

He continued driving, but snow piled high on the roof of the car and his headlights grew dim, starting to ice up. He got out several times to wipe them off for better visibility. The tracks used by electric trolleys divided the east and west bound lanes of the main street through Brighton. Paris recognized the surroundings, peering through fan-shaped openings made by the wipers. He strained to see ahead, afraid of missing the right-hand turn by the gas station.

So intently focused on not over-shooting the turn, he unknowingly began to drift to the left-hand side of the road. His front left tire hit the tracks diagonally before there was time to correct his direction. The tire slid over the rail, locking against the inside of the track. He turned the steering wheel to the right, but the front left tire just slid forward, guided by the tracks.

Frantically, he turned the steering wheel, trying to position the front left wheel at various angles to get the tire back over the rail. Ahead, through the driving snow, a single light was coming toward him. He panicked, seeing a flash of sparks above the light. *Oh my God*, he thought, *the trolley is still operating and I'm caught on the tracks.* On a collision course, the bright light bore down. Now, not more than two hundred feet away, the streetcar's high pitched horn continually sounded its warning. It was impossible for it to stop in time.

Paris reached for the door handle, about to jump, as the front tires hit a dry spot. The left tire rode over the rail and the car pitched to the right, veering from the path of the oncoming train.

His heart was still pounding when he reached the turn-off. Gradually accelerating, his rear tires began spinning as he attempted to gain uphill speed. He made it less than half way. Backing all the way down the steep slope, he took another running start. With tires whining, the car fish-tailed sideways and inched its way up the hill to little more than mid-point. He tried repeatedly, until the smell of burning rubber from the spinning wheels brought attention to the lighted instrument panel. The temperature gauge had climbed to the danger point. The Brighton Home lay at the summit, its lights like a distant beacon.

He abandoned the car against the curb and stepped into the deep snow. Paris glanced at his watch. Almost nine o'clock. It was late, much too late! He began running, the falling snow beating at his face. He fell repeatedly, causing snow to pack about his wrists and into his gloves. His hands and feet were freezing, and only determination to reach Carolyn kept him moving.

The summit seemed an eternity away. His feet and fingertips no longer had feeling. Both legs of his woolen bell bottoms were crusted to the knees with frozen snow. When he reached the front door, each breath burned with excruciating pain through his chest and throat.

Paris pressed the bell next to the door. It was too late for visitors to be received. Other than the night-light above the entrance, darkness had closed about him and snow was still falling. The accumulation now exceeded eight inches. The New England area was paralyzed with the storm that had blown in that morning and Boston, including all surrounding suburbs, had come to a standstill. Nothing was moving.

He pressed the bell again and, in desperation, pounded the heavy oak door with his fists, barely feeling pain to his hands. The door opened slightly and he saw only part of a female face peering out at him.

"What do you want? Visiting hours were over at eight."

Paris was so cold he couldn't stop shivering. His jaw chattered, making it impossible to speak.

"My God! You're freezing! What are you doing out so late in this weather? Did you get stranded? Come inside, before you freeze to death." She flung open the door, allowing him entrance into the large foyer. "You can use the phone on the table to call for assistance, but I don't think you'll get anyone until the storm lets up."

She was a small woman, in her mid-forties, dressed in a nurse's white uniform and wearing black horned-rimmed glasses. She moved quietly across the dark marble foyer, the heavy crepe soles of her white oxfords muffling her footsteps. "You can't stay here very long, but at least you can get warm before going back out. I'll get you something hot to drink."

Still gasping for breath, his chest and throat burned and he bent over, placing his hands on his knees to ease the racking pain.

"Wait!" he finally managed to say, holding up his right hand in a motion to stop her. "It's important! I've got to see Miss Stevens."

"Miss Stevens?" The nurse stopped abruptly, turning toward him. "Miss Carolyn Stevens?"

"Yes. It's urgent." Paris struggled with his speech, his chin still quivering. "I tried calling but couldn't get through. Phone lines are out...lines down all over." He straightened to a more erect position as breathing became less painful. A puddle was forming at his feet as the snow from his trouser legs and shoes started to melt.

"It's impossible to see her. Absolutely impossible," she snapped.

"She's still here, isn't she? She hasn't left yet?" Fear she'd already been discharged and allowed to leave before he saw her streaked through his mind.

"What relationship are you to Miss Stevens?" the nurse probed suspiciously.

Paris hesitated as his mind raced. *If I tell the truth, I'll be asked to leave.* The consummate lie spewed from his lips. "I'm the father. She's the mother of my son. I've just received her letter, telling me he was born."

"I see," she said studying his face. "Wait here." She disappeared, leaving him alone.

The large foyer was paneled in rich mahogany, its entranceway a dark brown stone. Above him hung a huge Gothic chandelier, and off in the distance was a large drawing room fitted with dark brown and green leather chairs with several long settees. Deep green velvet drapes covered the long windows in the drawing room, and the floor was tiled in large black and white squares. To the right was a wide, elaborate staircase that, he assumed, led to the girls' rooms upstairs.

He tried to imagine Carolyn in these surroundings. They appeared rich, yet coldly impersonal. A chill went through him as he thought, *It's an elaborate prison, where one does penance for affronting society with the sins of human weakness. What a price we pay, to keep our mistakes from being known.*

Hearing footsteps coming down the stairs, he looked up and saw a tall, lanky figure approaching. The gentleman appeared exhausted; thinning gray hair barely covered his scalp, and both shoulders sagged as his arms hung down limply. He was holding a crumpled piece of paper in one hand. As he neared, Paris could see the pronounced weariness in his eyes.

"Miss Roget informed me that Carolyn had a visitor." He offered no formal introduction and spoke so quietly that Paris strained to understand, reading his lips more than hearing the words. "Under the conditions, she's been generous enough to provide accommodations for Mother and myself. Mother is with Carolyn now." The man was in his late thirties, but exhaustion, made him appear much older.

"Did you write this?" There was no tone of anger in the voice. Paris studied his haggard countenance before looking at the wrinkled paper handed to him.

Something was wrong. It was the letter he had written to Carolyn. "How did you get this? Who are you?" he asked angrily.

"My name is Stevens, Ralph Stevens. I'm Carolyn's brother." His tone hadn't changed, but he seemed wearier, as though lacking strength to pursue the ordeal confronting him. "Your name is Paris Allison. I know of you, through Carolyn. She often spoke to Mother and me about you."

Paris remembered Carolyn referring to her brother, Ralph. *My God*, he thought, *he looks old enough to be her father, not her brother.*

Anger swelled in his throat. He didn't give a damn how the brother had gotten his letter. He owed his explanation only to Carolyn. "Where's Carolyn? I've got to talk to her," Paris demanded. He would have unleashed his full anger, but looking at Carolyn's brother, he saw the shiny mist of tears in his tired eyes.

Tormented words formed on lips that began to tremble. "Carolyn slashed her wrists…we almost lost her," Ralph said. "We're still not sure if she'll survive." Then, as if talking to himself, he continued. "The delivery weakened her and she's lost much blood." He regained control as awareness of the events presently taking place took priority. "My sister's attempt at suicide is a police matter, and for this reason I've met with you."

Paris was stunned. The words stabbed at his stomach, piercing him like a sharp dagger. He knew, holding his letter, it should never have been written. He'd come to explain his true feelings. He felt as if a tourniquet had been wound around his throat so tightly that he could not speak. A wave of weakness came over him, and he'd have collapsed but for the support of the paneled wall behind him.

When he could speak, the words were forced from his trachea. "The letter…I should never have written her. It's all my fault."

Ralph shook his head. "We're all to blame for what's happened, myself more than you. It was due to my pressure that Carolyn was shuttled here, away from her home. When she needed love and understanding, I exiled her from her family, and even though the baby was ill-begotten, it was hers, a part of her. But I kept insisting she give it up for fear of bringing shame to our family." In a shrug of disgust, he added, "I was so fearful of society's judgment, I may have destroyed her."

157

"No, Mr. Allison," he sighed deeply. "You're not entirely to blame, but the role you played in this tragic drama gave the *coup de grace*...the final blow, and for that you are accountable. You gave her hope, then at the last possible moment, you snatched that hope away. She relied on you. I tried to forewarn her, but your deceit was too convincing."

Paris listened to the words. All Ralph was saying was true, regardless of the reason for the letter. He'd fallen in love with her and, in spite of her resistance to him, had pressed her until she fell in love with him. He had no rebuttal. Having deceived her, he was accountable for the end results.

"Had the nurse not suspected something odd when she gave my sister your letter, it would all be over now. Thank Heaven, she returned to Carolyn's room to check on her. Now, all we can do is wait."

"She'll live. She has to," Paris cried out.

"As I stated before, it's now a police matter. They have in their possession a copy of this letter as evidence of your contribution to her attempted suicide. I go on record saying, as far as you are concerned, Carolyn is dead. Don't try to contact her in any way, for as long as I have breath in my body, I'll do everything in my power to place legal procedures against you. Don't ever attempt to see her again."

"I came to tell her how wrong I was to send this." Paris shook the paper in his hand. "To tell her how much I love her...need her."

"The damage you helped do is irreparable. For Carolyn's sake, I won't let her take another chance with you."

"But I need...." Paris was stopped before he could continue.

"Your needs are of no interest to me. The matter is closed," the brother said wearily. "Go now and get out of her life. If all goes well, we'll take her and the child back to Hartford and try to pick up the pieces. We'll share the baby with her. Her family truly loves her. We'll make her feel wanted again. If she dies, we'll take the baby as our own, to love it as she would have. Now, I want you to leave and never communicate in any way with her." He reached out and took the letter from Paris' hand. "As far as she's concerned, this ended it between you and her. She'll never know you came back. If you have any real feeling for her, you'll leave and give her up. Goddamn it! Can't you see? It's the best way." He turned and walked from the foyer.

Paris stood in silence, thinking. Carolyn's brother foresaw the hardships that lay ahead for his sister: criticisms from relatives, future accusations directed toward her and her illegitimate baby, society's condemnation, and her ultimate despair. If Paris failed her now, he'd fail her again in the future as a husband. Carolyn had already endured too much hurt.

Miss Roget returned quietly. "Mr. Stevens informed me you're to leave now." Her words rang with finality. She opened the door and Paris stepped out into the blowing snow. He was no longer aware of the bitter cold.

CHAPTER 24

IT WAS A BAD DREAM and he'd soon awaken to find everything normal. This subconscious defense protected him from mental collapse.

Paris had no recollection of reaching his car, nor could he remember details of the treacherous drive back. When he approached the freeway connecting Boston to Newport, the storm had begun to ebb. For miles, he followed a dump truck spreading sand on the road, its front plow pushing through the heavy snow.

Visions of Carolyn appeared in his mind. He'd see her face before him, then it would gradually fade. His hand unconsciously dropped to the seat to touch where she so often sat. He visualized her head resting on his shoulder as he drove.

He kept the car on the road and by some sixth sense, was able to maintain his direction toward Newport. Everything seemed surreal. He'd wake at any moment to find it had been a twisted nightmare, conjured up while he was in a deep sleep.

By early morning, the headlights picked up only swirling snow, caused by heavy gusts of wind occasionally rocking the small car. It was past three a.m. when Paris guided the car against the curb. Weak and nauseated from not eating for over a day, he left the car angle-parked in the deep snow in front of the only all-night diner in the small coastal town.

He'd get something into his stomach and wait for daybreak. He didn't want to start back to the ship in total darkness, remembering how rough the water was coming ashore the previous day. He consciously tried to collect his thoughts and analyze what had happened. Carolyn not surviving her attempted suicide was prevalent in his mind; he also recalled the beaten look on her brother's face and the doubt he had expressed.

His lack of experience with death made it easier to push the possibility of Carolyn dying aside, and he worriedly prayed she would be all right. *Nothing is going to happen to her, and I'll straighten everything out.*

"Time." He needed time. After the initial shock subsided, he'd talk to Ralph Stevens, her mother, and to Carolyn. He'd allow her time to gain back her strength, and he'd rectify everything. Mental and physical exhaustion crept over him, clouding his mind. Reality was no more than fuzzy thoughts, the sharp edge dulled by fatigue. "All I need is a little time and everything is going to be okay."

The diner was almost empty. A couple of drowsy-eyed sailors sat at the stools, facing the counter. Paris chose a booth where he could rest his feet on the opposite seat. When the waitress came from behind the counter to take his order, his chin was resting against his chest.

"This isn't the YMCA. You can eat here, honey, but you can't sleep."

"Give me a black coffee and a hamburger, please."

He fought to keep his head upright. She returned with his order, and he was jolted awake after searing his tongue with a swallow of scalding hot coffee. Glancing around the diner, he saw a clock. It was almost four a.m. If he headed back now, he'd be able to catch a little sleep before reveille. He hurriedly finished eating then, returned to his car.

Paris dimmed his headlights, squaring his hat as he approached the guardhouse at Midway entrance. He flashed his identification and liberty card for the Marine.

"What ship are you assigned to, Sailor?"

"The Stuart DD 714. She's anchored out at a mike."

"Not anymore. She lifted anchor to ride out the storm during the night. She pulled into Pier I an hour ago. She's berthed there. There's been some trouble. Drive on through, take a left on the main road and follow it around to Pier I. It's about two miles."

"What's the trouble?"

"Move it, sailor! This ain't a newsstand."

Paris swore under his breath. "Where the hell did they find these blockheads?" he muttered. "Give them a little authority and the pricks go wild."

He parked in the parking lot overlooking the long wooden pier. In the distance, Mt. Hope Bridge was a shadowy outline, hardly visible in the early morning overcast. Trudging through ankle-deep snow, he reached the gangway of the inside ship tied to the pier. He had to cross two quarter decks before reaching the *Stuart* tied up seaward in the berth. Saluting the Ensign and the Officer of the Deck, he knew something was wrong as he stepped aboard. *It isn't five and all hands are up*, he thought.

"Where've you been, sailor? Didn't you get word all liberty was canceled and to report to the nearest Naval station?" the officer reprimanded him.

"No, sir," Paris lied. "When I reached shore yesterday, I drove directly to Boston."

"It was announced every half hour on the radio. You couldn't have missed hearing it."

"Sir, my radio wasn't turned on. I didn't hear anything."

"You're damned lucky I don't write you up for missing ship's movement. Go below and get into the uniform of the day. There's already been enough trouble for one night."

"You mean the storm, sir?"

"I guess you *have* been out of contact. Our motor whaleboat's missing. It made the last liberty run yesterday and didn't return. When the storm heightened, we were forced to lift anchor and ride it out during the night. We hoped the boat would make it back to shore and wait out the night, but according to the Shore Patrol, it never came in. There's a search on for it now. Heaven help them!"

So much had already happened; Paris' knees almost buckled. In the CIC sleeping compartment, he quickly changed to his workclothes, carefully folded the Dress Blues he had borrowed, and placed them under the mattress of Mickey's bunk. Then, climbing the ladder, he made his way forward to the radar shack.

Mickey was sitting on the stool, studying the sweep of the Surface Search Radar. When he looked up, Paris saw he was crying.

"Tex is missing," Mickey said.

It was past ten in the morning, after the mist lifted and the sky cleared, when the patrols found the motor whaleboat. It had beached on the rocks off Martha's Vineyard, leading toward the open Atlantic. Apparently the engine faltered and stopped, and without power, the boat was swept out to sea.

Tex's hands were still gripping the controls. He'd tried to keep the engine running up to the last. The bowman and the coxswain were at their stations. All froze to death.

Paris closed his eyes, trying to shut out the horror of the report the captain was relaying to the crew over the ship's public address system. The sound of the tiller's bell rang in his ears as Tex headed back to his ship in the rough sea.

He shuddered, thinking, *My God, what have I done? I've destroyed the woman I love and I'm responsible for my best friend's death.*

Paris never attempted to analyze the reasons motivating his actions. It might have been guilt over Tex's death or a fatalistic determination that he couldn't stop what had been set in motion. In his heart, he knew his feelings for Carolyn were intense and maniacal, and had caused much pain and sadness; they could manifest nothing but unhappiness, eventually destroying the love they treasured. Conceivably, it was this fear of destroying their love that led him to his decision. *Carolyn's brother was right. If I love her, I'll let her go and never see her again. I can only cause her more grief.*

He called Joyce and arrangements were made the following week. When Paris asked him to stand up for him, Mickey's response was a puzzled one, "Are you sure you want to do this?"

Paris and Joyce were married in a private service performed by a local justice of the peace.

He stood at the hotel window looking out at the lights illuminating the busy highway. His thoughts were of Carolyn. He'd spend the remainder of his life filled with regret.

"Come to bed, honey."

He looked at his new bride lying in a provocative position on the white sheets of the dimly lit room. "In a minute," he said distantly.

"Look, let's make the best of it. I'll try to be a good wife," she said with a good deal of sincerity.

"Only for a short time. Remember, you're my wife only until the baby is born. I'll give the baby my name. Only my name."

"You bastard," she said, and rolled over on her side.

CHAPTER 25

A YEAR HAD PASSED SINCE the brutal snowstorm in December 1955, yet Carolyn's memory was always in his thoughts.

Guilt manifesting from the harrowing events leading to his hasty and unseemly marriage, wreaked havoc on Paris. The shocking death of his cousin Mike, the many complex conundrums associated with Carolyn's pregnancy, his foolish tryst with Joyce Shaw, his feelings of responsibility for Tex Madison's death, and finally, his undisputed culpability in Carolyn's attempted suicide, brought about the total destruction of their cherished love. These burdens weighed on his conscience and, like falling snow heavily accumulating in winter on a brittle branch, threatened a sudden snap. Those on ship in close contact saw the changes taking place. Paris too sensed he was nearing his breaking point when, a strange metamorphosis began happening. A hard outer shell started forming, which would eventually encapsulate and protect his inner emotions.

Contrary to the warning not to contact Carolyn, Paris had to know if she was alive. He had finally phoned her Hartford home. Reaching her mother and using a handkerchief over the mouthpiece, he identified himself as an insurance representative needing to speak with Miss Carolyn Stevens. Her soft voice answered and he hung up. She'd never know he'd called and he would never see her again.

Late June of 1956, in Gibraltar, he received a wire from Joyce informing him of the birth of a son. Paris never responded. He'd never forgiven her for trapping him in a loveless marriage. She'd get her monthly allotment check, nothing more. Joyce tried communicating by writing in a futile effort to make the best of their marriage, but he never answered. Divorce would be hard, but he'd find a lawyer to handle it. It was just a matter of time when his enlistment would be over, and the marriage would be ended.

Mickey Crowley remained his buddy, but after Tex's death, Paris' personality changed. The slow metamorphosis was complete. Inwardly, he was bitter and hostile, seldom showing emotion unless angered. If provoked, he'd fight savagely, using anything within reach as a weapon, possessing uncanny speed as his reflexes were spurred by a burst of adrenalin through his body. This inherit trait was passed to him from his dad. In a fight, it proved an asset, usually tipping the scales in his favor. The size of an opponent never entered his mind. By now, he didn't give a damn. Nothing mattered.

He sold the Chevrolet. A rod bearing was knocking, likely caused by the grueling abuse to the engine during that fateful snowstorm. He didn't want it anymore. It brought back too many memories, good and bad.

When stateside, he bought a used 1950 Oldsmobile with a V-8 engine. It had more power and speed than his smaller Chevy, and those daring enough to ride with him from New England to New York got there faster than with other drivers. Many riding with him for the first time reconsidered using slower and safer transportation to reach New York City on weekend liberties. One sailor confessed to Mickey, "He's a damn fool, that Allison. He'll stare ahead with those icy eyes and press the gas pedal through the floor. That man's asking to die, and I don't want to be holding his hand when he gets his wish."

Not yet 20, Paris had traveled throughout the Mediterranean, Caribbean and Europe. He attempted to burn himself out in brothels and hell ports, but no woman, regardless of how comely, could erase Carolyn from his mind.

In England he picked up a waitress working in a London pub near Piccadilly Circus. Seeing the barmaid's shoulder length blonde hair, he thought, *She walks proudly, like Carolyn.* She accepted his overtures. They soon left, heading to her girlfriend's flat in Portsmouth to escape the cold, damp wintry weather. Leaving Victoria Station, occupying a seating compartment unique to European passenger trains and certain they were alone, she disrobed. Passionately engaged, the compartment doors suddenly opened. The conductor, attempting to seat an elderly couple, caught them copulating.

The young girl screamed, frantically grabbing for her clothes, whispering to Paris that they'd be arrested and thrown from the train at the next station. Paris' cold, unwavering stare, caused the conductor to actually apologize. "Ex…excuse me," he stammered timidly. They were not disturbed again.

In a Portuguese brothel, Paris broke protocol, buying a dark-haired girl a drink after accepting her invitation for sex, then left her when he saw a blonde prostitute on the dance floor toss her hair about her shoulders, as Carolyn had always done.

Later, returning with the fair-haired girl, the abandoned brunette, armed with a razor, lunged at the blonde to slash her face for taking her business. Paris saw a blur of the coming attack from the corner of his eye as he heard screams and obscenities from the dark-haired girl as she leaped. His fist shot forward, hitting her squarely in her mouth; the razor flew from her hand. The two girls grappled on the floor bleeding, scratching and clawing as Paris found himself pinned against a wall by the proprietor's bouncers. The Shore Patrol escorted him back to his ship. Unknowingly, Paris shamed the prostitute by giving his business to another. He didn't care.

The incident put him on report and should have cost him his 3rd Class rate. "Something's eating at you," the executive officer observed. "You're good at your job. I've observed you under pressure. But you're ignorant of the customs in these foreign countries. You broke one of their taboos. I'm going to punish you by restriction to the ship during our stay here. Our job's to spread the goodwill of the United States, not make enemies. I won't blemish your record. You're up for 2nd Class Petty Officer and your operations officer speaks highly of you. He informed me of your interest in O.C.S. and wanting to fly. You're ordered to remain aboard ship until we leave Lisbon. I want you to find peace with yourself."

The Persian Gulf Crisis peaked in 1957. With slightly over a year left of Paris' enlistment, his squadron headed for Africa. In the Canary Islands, he'd find a scattering of blonde Spanish women, and in South Africa, light-haired English women and Boer -women, descendants of early Dutch settlers. Where the squadron was being ordered to patrol in the Red Sea, there would be nothing to remind him of Carolyn. Everyone there, to his knowledge, was black.

CHAPTER 26

LYING IN A FETAL POSITION, Francesca pretended to be asleep when Dominic awoke and got out of bed. Only when he completed dressing and after his footsteps could be heard descending the staircase did she venture to move.

Below, through the floorboards, the joking voices of Dominic and her father reached her ears. It was a daily ritual for her husband to stop for morning coffee and pastry before going to work. Still she waited, lying quietly until certain he had no reason for coming back. Then she threw back the thin sheet and swung her bare feet to the floor, her thick dark hair cascading loosely about her shoulders.

Dry flakes of once-green paint, bleached nearly white by the sun's torturous heat, loosened and spiraled downward as Francesca unlatched the ancient, louvered shutters covering the bedroom window. Clad only in a slip, which clung like a second skin to her young, voluptuous body, she propped her shapely hip on the sill and looked out across the flat roof-tops of the surrounding adobe structures, watching the village come to life. In the distance, sandy dust, caught up in the arid morning breeze, swirled in miniature tornados above the unpaved road leading to the marketplace. From there, she could hear voices coming from the many shops but couldn't comprehend the tongues or dialects above the hum of countless flies attracted to sweet fragrances drifting from her father's bakery below the small apartment she and her husband shared.

To the east, the sun reared its head like a blazing red fireball above the distant mountains. Soon, its stifling warmth would engulf the town. Scanning the far horizon, rising layers of heated air produced a wavy, mirage-like effect. She touched her throat; her fingertips felt damp. Perspiration was already forming on her olive-toned skin.

Francesca looked at the crumpled bed and her body involuntarily shook. Now 21 years old and having lived in this primitive area of Eritrea on the east coast of Africa for three years, she couldn't decide which she hated more, the country or her bestial husband.

God! I miss our home in Ravenna, and all my friends I knew there. Bitterly, she thought of her untroubled childhood in Italy; when she turned 18 and she had been sent for. She and her mother traveled by boat across the Mediterranean, through the Suez Canal to join her father here in Massawa. He and two brothers had ventured into several moderately successful businesses: shipping and trading in salt, a small restaurant, and an even smaller bakery. Her hand in marriage and a dowry totaling a small percentage of the enterprising businesses were given to her new groom. This was all because, in his youth, in Italy, her father made a promise to a close friend. She would never forgive her father for trading her off like some farm animal. Her prearranged marriage was made to Dominic Cabrelli, the son of a *campagno* from the *Old Country*. In disgust, she spat out the window. *No mention of love, no contesting my Father's wishes, and certainly, never a chance for me to think of divorce.*

Gazing out the window, she pondered her plight. It wasn't fair, she brooded. Neither knew the other. It was predetermined they wed and be contented with their parents' long, established plan. The High Nuptial Mass performed at St. Mary's Church in Asmara proved to be a farce in terms of joining them as man and wife. Dominic never thought of loving her. He possesses her, as he possessed his shares in her father's business.

Francesca had known no other man before her husband. Dominic proved savagely forceful. His new wife was his, to be used when his desires were aroused. Having no tenderness, and lacking understanding of a woman's emotional needs, he satisfied his lustful feelings in a selfish, brutal manner.

Francesca escaped mentally, reading love stories from books from her homeland, and when a romantic movie played in the marketplace's only theater, she'd sit in the darkness, eyes misty during the love scenes. As many of the movies were American made, she had difficulty reading subtitles written below the scenes in Italian, while following the poignant words spoken in alien English. She'd sit through a film several times, trying to match the words being spoken to the written words.

Her youth was being wasted in this primitive corner of the globe. She was condemned to an unhappy marriage that never satisfied her desires. There was no escape. She resigned herself to it.

In early March 1957, disturbances in the Middle East brought a crisis to the Suez Canal. At this time, Francesca's life took on a new meaning. She'd heard news of unrest to the North, but knew little of the strategic importance of the Red Sea, other than it channeled tankers and merchant ships north and south past Massawa, using the Suez Canal. A surge of excitement rushed through her as she observed the sleek American destroyer slide alongside the ancient pier. With girlish amazement, she watched American sailors move about the deck, mooring the ship to the rickety dock. Her intense concentration was abruptly shattered.

"What are you doing here by the docks…looking for trouble? Go home now!" Dominic commanded. His right arm shot out and he pointed toward the marketplace.

She hadn't seen his approach. "I wanted to see the warship from America. I've never seen one before."

"Go home, puttana. Now!"

She'd never seen him in such a rage. Fearful he'd strike her, she retreated quickly toward the marketplace. Trying to stem the flood of tears and the trembling throughout her body, she still heard the irate sting of his voice ringing in her ears. Approaching her father's bakery, she entered the stockade fenced courtyard through a private gate behind the small business and climbed the wooden staircase to the top landing to reach the apartment. Sweet smells of baked goods permeated the dark hallway.

As she entered the bedroom, a picture of Dominic on the corner of her dresser caught her attention; a small photograph of herself was tucked in the corner of the frame. "Even here, he dominates me!" she cried out, slamming the frame face downward against the dresser top, shattering the glass.

Francesca slipped out of her dress. In her brassiere and panties, in the safe darkness of the room, she lay across the bed, sobbing into her pillow.

After chasing Francesca from the pier, Dominic spent an hour drinking. From the day they were introduced by their families, he sensed she felt that he was beneath her standing. In three years of marriage, he was convinced that her long disappearances to the theater and the many hours she spent reading were an escape from him. In bed, he forced his desires on her in a brutal, psychological reaction to the lack of response from her.

Dominic derived sadistic pleasure from marital rape. In his mind, Francesca felt nothing for him, he compensated for this with a demented feeling of dominance during the sexual act. Seeing Francesca watch the young American seamen moor their ship to the pier triggered insane jealousy in him. Her fearful retreat from his verbal assault completed the sense of supremacy to his ego, which he fortified with a bottle of gin.

Entering the dim bedroom, he saw her stretched across the bed, her rounded buttocks in sheer panties and her back bare, except for the brassiere straps. Dominic leered down at her. Alcohol caused his head to ache and his temples pound, yet he grew hard looking at her semi-nude body. Unzipping his trousers, he bared his penis. She could try to escape from him in books and movies, but never from his bed.

CHAPTER 27

FOUR DESTROYERS LEFT NEWPORT, Rhode Island in early January 1957. Steaming south to Trinidad to refuel, they proceeded east 3500 miles to arrive at Freetown, Sierra Leone, West Africa, their fuel tanks nearly empty. Refueling, they headed south, crossing the equator, to Cape Town, South Africa. Rounding the Cape of Good Hope, they continued north into the Red Sea to Mombasa, Kenya, and then up to Massawa in Eritrea, Ethiopia on the east coast of Africa.

The Suez Canal closed in November 1956, and the squadron was to patrol the area and intercept all ships in the Red Sea coming from or going to the Port Said, verifying their nationality and type of cargo. This ensured no hostile traffic slipping through to aid the growing crisis. Massawa was to serve as the squadron's home base.

Two ships would patrol the Red Sea, one covering as far north as the Suez Canal, the other to the Gulf of Aden. This allowed the remaining two to refuel and replenish supplies before relieving their sister ships. Thus, the squadron maintained a constant vigilance.

After a month of patrolling, depression darkened Paris' mind. The illuminating light he knew as Carolyn was gone, and he was headed on a course of self destruction. At sea, he tired of cruising the aquamarine waters and seeing the distant sand dunes. The spectacle of flying fish soaring over and sometimes landing on the destroyer's deck had long ago lost its novelty.

Just once there was excitement. Manning the radar screen, he picked up two blips and reported sighting the contacts to the watch officer and to the bridge. General Quarters was sounded.

"General Quarters...General Quarters...all personnel man your battle stations. This is not, I repeat, this is not a drill."

The lethargic crew immediately responded to the call. In record time the Stuart was ready for battle. Several crew members dropped to their knees, praying.

Paris laughed at this irony. The rowdiest ones frequenting the black whorehouses of Massawa seemed the most devout when their asses were in danger.

Visual confirmation from the bridge identified the blips as two Egyptian torpedo boats. The gun crews locked the five-inch gun turrets in on the closing crafts. Seeing this, the torpedo boats turned and retreated, trailing white wakes behind.

In early May, Paris' ship returned to Massawa after being relieved. Massawa's blatant poverty and the wretched existence of the local populace added to his pessimistic attitude. Watching a native push a crudely fashioned wheelbarrow carrying his genitals, swollen to the size of small watermelons, through the unpaved streets, Paris shook his head, muttering, "Because of a simple hernia left untended, he'll soon die."

There was nothing for Paris to relate to in this dismal place. Alone, walking in the dusty, dirty streets, he'd whistle popular songs or music recalled from the States. Just humming or whistling a tune made him feel in touch with home and somehow closer to Carolyn. He made his own critique: If it couldn't be sung, whistled, or hummed, it wasn't music. He excluded jazz. To him, it sounded like instruments being tuned or warming up, each one hitting different notes and out of time with the other.

When he saw her, Paris' heart jumped and his stomach ached with a strange, hollow emptiness. Her dark hair hung loosely, midway down her back. His eyes traced her beautifully rounded buttocks. By the outline of her panties under the tropical skirt, he could tell that she wore no slip. "What a beautiful ass!" he whispered to himself.

Giving no hint of having noticed him, the woman crossed the main roadway of the marketplace.

In all Massawa, Paris had seen no one to compare with this Italian girl. He followed her, hoping to discover anything about this raven-haired girl, to insure seeing her again. *I'll content myself with the satisfaction of just looking at her*, he rationalized.

Paris crossed the street, keeping a distance behind her, thinking she'd turn and he'd get a glimpse of her face. If I get a close look, she'll be ugly, he told himself.

Without warning, she turned abruptly, reversing her direction. Seeing her face, an embarrassing weakness came over Paris. She was beautiful. A faint smile appeared on her lips, bringing a hint of intrigue to her face.

She passed within arm's reach, and Paris caught the pleasing scent of her perfume, which brought to mind some flower he couldn't identify. Her breasts and hips were full in contrast to her small waist, giving her a perfect hourglass figure. Then their eyes met. Each held the other's gaze for a moment, yet an unspoken understanding and desire surged through them like an electric current. She looked down, embarrassed that her feelings were so suddenly bared, and crossed the street.

Paris devoured her with his eyes, watching her until she rounded the corner at the end of the street and disappeared.

"Damn!" He cursed, reading the duty list. "I'm assigned to Shore Patrol." He wanted to go on liberty, hoping he'd catch another glimpse of the dark-haired girl he'd seen near the marketplace. "She's the only thing here resembling the Western World, and that I'd call feminine, since I arrived in this God-forsaken hole," he muttered, readying himself for Shore Patrol. He bent to lace the khaki spats over the lower legs of his white bell-bottomed trousers. Strapping the web belt about his waist, he attached the wooden nightstick and canvas-covered canteen. Slipping the S.P. armband over his right biceps, he mumbled, "This is going to be a hell of a long evening."

The S.P. party left the ship together and the duty officer paired up the men, explaining the areas of town they were to patrol. "It's going to be hot until the sun goes down." He pointed at their canteens. "I don't give a damn what you fill those with, but Heaven help anyone getting drunk on my watch."

Paris was paired with a shipmate from his radar gang, a fellow from the Midwest named Roberts. They had patrol in the section including the Cabaret, Alhambra, and Tracadero, the most notorious and rowdiest brothels in the village and frequented by all the sailors going into town. These were trouble spots where anyone on liberty could sip wine made from the vineyards in Ethiopia or drink Melotte Lager Beer, brewed in nearby Asmara. They also catered to sailors looking for sex with a black woman.

Paris winced. He had to keep order in the Alhambra Club, a dive he'd tried to destroy on his last drunk. He remembered the ribbing from his buddies for not wanting to "change his luck" by screwing a black woman. After drinking too much red wine, he was approached by a young black prostitute. He saw the whore as the antithesis of Carolyn, and in a drunken rage, wreaked havoc in the place, overturning tables and chairs, and heaving empty beer bottles at anyone trying to subdue him. After passing out, he was carried back to the ship by Mickey and another shipmate. It was a bad "drunk," and he had heaved until his stomach muscles were sore. He still cringed when he smelled wine.

"I hope none of these whores remember my face," he said grimacing. This futile thought was shattered as he and Roberts entered the Alhambra. The black females began laughing, while pointing in his direction.

The pair continued walking through the café. Above the noises from the patrons came scratching sounds from an old phonograph with a bad needle, which played "Davy Crockett, King of the Wild Frontier." Roberts jokingly questioned Paris. "Where in hell did they get that record and how'd it wind up in a whorehouse, thousands of miles from home?"

Paris shrugged his shoulders. "Probably given to the club by a swabby partying here from the ship relieving us."

As the darkness closed about them, dust from the dry, unpaved streets covered their shoes, and the white trousers above their spats took on a yellowish hue in the poor lighting from the oil lamps mounted in the store windows.

"We've been lucky," Roberts said as they headed toward the market area. "We've got about an hour left of our patrol, and so far it's been quiet."

Pleasant aromas of freshly baked goods from the small bakery at the street corner titillated their nostrils. As they neared the front door, sounds of a commotion inside reached their ears. The yelling was in Italian.

"Pazzo! Pazzo! Scioc 'chezza! Tagliare pene!! Tagliare genitali!"

As they stepped through the doorway, a sailor from their own ship rushed up to them. "You gotta help Wyatt! They're gonna cut him…gonna cut him bad!"

Paris scanned the bakery. By the far wall, two Italians held the arms of a crewman. A third man wearing an apron brandished a large knife in one hand, while his other pressed hard around the sailor's throat. The youth squirmed and struggled, his terrified face reddening from the choking.

Beside the display counter, the dark-haired girl Paris had seen in the marketplace cowered with her arms crossed over her breasts. Her flowered blouse was torn open to the waist, exposing her brassiere. Fear was etched on her pretty face.

"What the hell happened?" Roberts barked.

"Wyatt got a little drunk…too much to drink…saw those big knockers on that girl and couldn't resist trying to get a handful of her tits. Wyatt followed her in here and grabbed her. She screamed. I think all of these *Dagos* are related. They're gonna cut his balls off!" The sailor's voice rose to a screech.

"Get out of here and head back to the ship, now!" Paris commanded, seeing the large knife slicing toward the pinned sailor's groin. He lunged across the room, hitting the unsuspecting Italian across the wrist with a savage, hammer-like blow, sending the knife clanging to the floor.

The Italian swung to face the sudden onslaught, his eyes staring directly into Paris' icy gaze. For a second, neither flinched. Then, Paris uttered with cold authority, one word, "*Cessare!*" He knew no fluent Italian, just a few words remembered from his youth living in Paterson's "Little Italy." The irate baker turned and, with a puzzled expression, looked to his companions.

Pointing to his armband, Paris spoke slowly, accentuating each syllable, "*Ca po.*" He repeated the word again, "*Capo.*" Then, recalling two applicable words, he growled derisively, "*Mal Testa! Mal Testa!*" and slapped the sailor's red face so hard that a trickle of blood oozed from his mouth.

The aproned Italian nodded his approval, a small smile forming on his lips as he repeated the words, "*Mal Testa!*" and poked a finger at his own head. The two men released the youth's arms. Paris turned to Roberts. With a display of feigned authority, Paris ordered his partner to "Take him back to the ship." He pointed toward the door.

Roberts, understanding the necessary pretense, grabbed Wyatt's arm, placing it in a hammer-lock. "Don't say a word, you dumb ass. Just walk to the door. You'll be lucky if we get you out of here with your balls still attached! Brace yourself! I'm going to kick you in the ass to make it look like we mean business." He did so, with the side of his shoe hitting the sailor's buttocks hard enough to cause him to stumble.

When both sailors were out the door, Paris nodded to the three Italians, then looked at the dark-haired girl. For a brief moment, their eyes met again. She gave him a small, nervous smile. He knew that she remembered him from the marketplace.

"*Allacci 'are,*" one of the men commanded. Face flushing with embarrassment, she pulled her blouse together, trying to cover herself.

Roberts waited with the inebriated sailor down the road. "You were lucky as hell to pull that off. What did *Mal Testa* mean? I don't know Italian, but it saved this fuck-up's ass."

"I tried telling them he's nuts...crazy...sick in the head and didn't know what he was doing, but I don't know much Italian either. I think *Mal* means bad and *Testa*, head. Bad head or a headache. Seemed to strike them as funny and got us off the hook. That's what counts."

"Well, let's get our asses back to the ship before they change their minds," Roberts said.

"I think I'll stick around awhile, just to make sure," Paris responded.

"Hey, believe me, if they come for your ass, there won't be any cavalry coming to your rescue. Better for us to head back together. Lieutenant said stay in pairs. Remember?"

"Tell him I wanted to make sure there's no aftermath. It's my ass if he doesn't buy it."

"Like you said, it's your ass, not mine," Roberts said dryly. "I'll walk this pathetic shit-brain back to the ship to keep him out of trouble."

Unnoticed by Roberts, as they stood talking in the street, Paris saw the dark-haired girl leave the bakery and enter the stockade enclosure through a gate behind the establishment. *She must live above the store*, he thought.

Francesca trembled from the horrifying ordeal, yet none of what happened could erase the face of the handsome, young blond sailor with the unforgettable blue eyes that stopped her uncles from castrating the crazed, drunken sailor.

He's so unlike Dominic, she thought. *But his face seems sad and troubled. I looked at his eyes and saw no fear, only a deadly, commanding look. I've never seen my uncle falter, yet with just one look, he yielded. Perhaps he saw no fear of killing or dying, in the sailor's blue eyes. Never before have I associated fear with my uncle. Not until now.*

Proceeding through the gate leading to her apartment, she climbed the rickety wooden stairs to the bedroom. She crossed the room to pour cool water from a pitcher into a basin sitting on her dresser top. Removing her ripped blouse and placing it across the bed, she bent forward over the bowl and splashed water onto her face, dampening her throat and the tops of her breasts above her bra. *I'm thankful Dominic went to Asmara for two days*, she thought. *He'd blame me for what happened with the drunken American. He'd have found a way to twist everything and blame me.*

Loosening her skirt, she let it drop around her feet and stepped out of it. She walked barefoot across the room to retrieve a light cotton wrap hanging from a hook on her closet door. Passing the open window, she glanced down to the moon-lit street and saw him. He stood in the darkening street, looking up. The small white hat pushed to the back of his head exposed his blond locks. She knew it was him.

Francesca felt a hollowness in her stomach and a flush to her face. Her feel-ings were no longer rational. She was losing control of her emotions as she leaned from the window, her upper body clad in only a brassiere. She'd never done any-thing like this. Placing her left index finger to her lips as an indication for silence while motioning with her right hand toward the gate, she pointed in the direction of the stairs and then pointed to herself.

She saw Paris wait in the dim street for a moment to be sure he wasn't being watched, then he crossed to the gate, quietly opening it enough for his body to squeeze through.

Francesca eased the door open at the top of the landing when she heard a creak from the outside stairs. Paris reached the top step. Standing inside with the door slightly ajar, she beckoned for him to quickly enter, while holding a finger to her lips so he would know to be silent.

"*Fare silenzio...Bello uomo...Bello faccia,*" she whispered softly as she took his hand, gently pulling him into the room and, quietly closing the door.

Their passion flared with no premeditation, fueled by excitement and fear. Paris glanced at the open wrap, seeing she was wearing only her bra and panties. Without speaking, he put his arm about her waist and gently pulled her to him, first kissing her gently on the mouth, then her throat and the top of her breasts. His kisses were as soft as the silence in the room, and she quivered as he slid the straps from her shoulders and skillfully unhooked her bra. It fell to the floor as he maneu-vered her to the bed, his hand caressing her taut breasts and gently massaging the hardened nipples.

As he seated her on the bed, she felt lightheaded, as if she'd had too much wine. He eased the room's only chair against the door, its back tilted under the door knob to prevent intrusion. Returning, he unhooked the belt from his waist and hung his club and canteen over the foot post. He gently positioned her, as she sat on the edge of the bed, so that in a reclined position, his club would be in easy reach.

She laughed softly at the precautions and, putting her arms about his neck, pulled him to her, whispering, "*Fare l 'amore a al.* Make love to me."

She felt a hunger deep in her breast for this unknown sailor, an insatiable passion, she had never known or experienced before. Her blond, blue-eyed lover epitomized all the unrequited love that so many times in the past she'd felt watching the poignant moments in the cinema films. She felt herself grow wet, wetter than ever before, and her breasts seemed to swell. Her nipples stood erect as she felt her panties being eased down and gently removed.

She reached down to guide him, something in her marriage, *she had never done*. She arched her back and pushed her pelvis forward to meet his entry and had to suppress a scream of ecstasy. Biting the back of her hand to squelch her soft moans and cries as he moved rhythmically atop her, she felt a warm glow building inside herself, growing from her toes to the top of her head. This glow intensified, centering through her thighs and growing in magnitude until at last she climaxed, first in one burst, then in several smaller releases. Never before, even in her most erotic dreams, had she imagined such ecstasy, such complete satisfaction.

Her lover kissed the tips of her breasts and mouth before easing from between her legs. As he dressed, Francesca touched his face with her fingertips. Both knew, with hardly a word communicated, that each had given the other a warmth and tenderness that would be carried with them far from the darkened room.

She walked with him to the door and they cautiously checked the outside area. On an impulse, she turned and removed her picture stuck in the corner of the frame of her husband's photograph. Its glass was still shattered. She took it and, pointing to her name written below, pointed to her breast and said softly, "Francesca."

He took the picture from her and pointed to his chest. "Paris," he said, and kissed her lips a last time, then made his way quietly down the steps.

She saw the gate open and he disappeared. She spoke softly to herself. "I know now, that I can never remain here with Dominic. I've broken my marital vows. If I must steal from my husband and my family to leave, I'll do so. I must go seek and find the kind of happiness I have only just known."

CHAPTER 28

AFTER REACHING THE STREET, PARIS paused to place Francesca's small photograph in his wallet. Fearful of losing it, he repositioned his billfold by flapping it over his waistband, then pushed it over to his left hip so that his elbow felt its presence. "Why in heck did the Navy design a uniform without pockets?" he mumbled.

Less than an hour had passed since his romantic tryst with Francesca, yet it was a mile walk back to the pier where the *Stuart* was moored. Paris realized too much time had slipped away and everyone ashore had returned to the ship.

Darkness closed about him, and remembering the warnings given at liberty call, he knew he was violating strict safeguards walking alone. In this country, life had little value, and lone servicemen were found in areas like this with their throats cut and their pockets turned inside out.

He spoke aloud for assurance. "I'll be in a hell of a lot of trouble when I get back, but she was worth it. For a long time, I've felt I was losing my sanity. It wasn't just desire. We needed each other more than just physically." Making love to this Italian girl satisfied his greater hunger for beauty and warmth.

He thought of the many married sailors succumbing to African brothels for sexual release. No one would believe him if he were the type to brag of his conquest. He'd have settled for holding her hand and walking together. An image flashed before him of a small, snow-covered park and in it, Carolyn was holding his hand. He shook his head to erase this haunting memory. Besides her beauty and passion, Francesca possessed a tenderness he had needed for a long time.

The road became only a wide alley with decaying sandstone buildings casting dark shadows and blocking out the little light the moon gave. The alley snaked, curving ahead and disappearing into the darkness. Suddenly, Paris felt an intuitive awareness of impending danger. He heard an almost inaudible shuffle to his left about twenty yards ahead; he was not alone in the alley. Strangely, a dispassionate calm swept over him. He experienced alertness, not panic, calculating his distance from the noise and analyzing the sound. It wasn't heavy or hard, as a shoe would make, but more like a bare foot sliding across the ground.

With animal instinct, his senses sharpened. There could be no thought of running. That would be a mistake. To run in either direction meant turning his back on whatever lurked in the darkness. Retreat would be expected if the threat involved several people in an ambush.

There was no conscious deliberation or uncontrollable panic, only an innate defense process that couldn't be explained. His pulse slowed. He readied himself for whatever waited in the darkness before him. The Shore Patrol club hung at his side; his right hand closed about the handle, drawing it from his webbed belt. Now, he appreciated its value.

His teeth clamped together and his jaw muscles tightened under the pressure. He focused slightly to the right of the sound, a trick his father taught him when hunting at night. Doing this, his eyes better detected outlines in the blackness. His pace slowed as his steps carried him toward the sound. He had unconsciously become the hunter, not the prey.

A form lunged from the darkness. Paris caught a glimpse of something shiny thrust at his mid-section. Catlike, he pivoted to face the attack, feeling a burning pain in his left side as his arm arched upward and, with terrific force, brought the club down across the right shoulder and neck of the figure. The impact knocked his assailant to his knees and the knife fell to the ground, lost in the darkness. Now up close, Paris could distinguish his attacker. The native, stunned from the fierce blow, still remained on the ground.

With a split second to wonder about the pain in his side, he was sure the knife thrust had hit him. Abruptly, his attacker sprang to his feet, grasping Paris about his waist. The force of the lunge carried him backwards. He'd have lost his balance had a stucco building not been behind him. His club rattled to the hard ground, dislodged from his hand by the sudden impact.

Pinned against the building, he fought to keep from going down. The African's tall, lean body possessed overpowering strength, and Paris knew a fall to the ground could be fatal. His hands grabbed the assailant's shoulders to push him away, but the attacker's taller size and grip around Paris' waist gave him an offensive advantage. Paris' hands inched upward from the sweaty shoulders and closed in a vice-like lock around the native's neck. His fingers tightened and he dug his thumbs deeply into the black's throat. The Negro grabbed Paris' wrists to free the stranglehold.

The only sounds made were the grunting and shuffling of feet as their bodies raked the building. Now a gagging noise erupted as the native fought to breathe. He pulled violently at Paris' wrists, trying to break his hold. His attacker was drooling; Paris felt warm wetness on his forearms from a mingling of saliva and blood running from his own wrists as the native's nails clawed them to free the deathhold. A hard, bony knee shot upward into Paris' groin. At the sudden, excruciating pain, Paris released his hold; both men dropped to their knees.

Gasping for air, the black groped for the fallen knife. Paris' strength was drained by the sickening pain in his groin. He fought against unconsciousness. His right hand reached out and closed about a large stone lying in the dirt. With all the power he could muster from his position, Paris smashed the stone against his attacker's face. The stone crushed through nose and skull. A bewildered look widened the assailant's eyes, and for what seemed an eternity, the Negro stared blankly ahead. A dark red concave between his eyes replaced where his nose and forehead had been. Then, as limply as a rag doll, he collapsed into a lifeless heap.

Paris rose unsteadily to his feet. His left hand was pressed tightly to his groin and his right hand was still clenched around the bloody stone. If locals found he had killed someone, even in self-defense, his outcome would be uncertain in this foreign land. He'd heard that once someone was in jail, they threw away the key.

If the attack involved more than the one assailant, he would now be dead. Pain in his groin persisted, but he forced himself upright, taking several anxious moments to find his club in the dark. His white hat, knocked off his head during the initial attack, was easy to detect. The bloody stone was still gripped in his right hand; he had to get rid of it. Inspecting the darkened area to ensure nothing could be traced to him, he replaced the club in his webbed belt and made an inventory of his person. The Shore Patrol band was still about his arm, he had his canteen, and there were no tears to his uniform. Other than deep scratches on his wrists, he had no injuries that might be detected when he boarded the ship.

His left hand touched the wallet he kept in his waistband; there was a jagged tear across the leather. Pulling it out, he checked that none of its contents had fallen out. The wallet had caught the thrust of the knife and deflected it from his vital mid-section, leaving a long, angry scratch on his side.

He glanced at the lifeless form, then left, making his way to the ship as rapidly as the acute pain in his groin would permit. Pain had eased to a dull ache when he reached the pier. He drew back his right arm and hurled the stone far into the watery blackness.

Squaring his hat, he tidied his overall appearance, then crossed the gangway. He was thankful of the dark but apprehensive about asking permission to come aboard. In his present condition, questions would be asked.

Luckily, the quarter deck's lighting was dim, and he managed to board with only a disgruntled remark from the officer of the deck. "Sailor! A few minutes more and you'd be on report. S.P. duty was up an hour ago. Turn in your armband and club and go below. Get some rest; reveille's at 0500. We get underway at 0630."

Below decks in the darkened compartment, Paris undressed, putting his dirty uniform into the ditty bag strung from his bunk. Placing his lacerated wallet in his locker, he examined the contents again in the semi-light. Below the gash in the leather was the photograph Francesca had given him as he left her bedroom. Her picture wasn't damaged. *She gave me the love and warmth I needed to keep going*, he thought. *She'd never know that by putting her picture in my wallet and repositioning it at my side saved my life.*

Suddenly, he wretched and grabbed his white hat to keep from messing up the compartment deck. He sank to his knees, moaning. *I've brought heartache to everyone I've known. Now, I guess I've done the worst thing, something I can never speak of. I've killed someone. I'll live with this till I die.*

They came, and now were leaving. Their squadron was relieved; they could go home. They left Massawa and the Red Sea, proceeding to Aden, Arabia. After crossing the Arabian Sea to Karachi, Pakistan, the squadron headed south into the Indian Ocean, past Madagascar to Cape Town and up to Las Palmas in the Canary Islands. Their final leg would take them across the Atlantic, back to the States.

Having crossed the Equator, Paris was a seasoned "Shellback." He had crossed the Equator four times in less than six months. He advanced to the rate of Radarman 2nd Class Petty Officer. At 20, he felt old beyond his years.

Standing at the Dead Reckoning plotting table as they steamed from the Red Sea, Mickey joked. "Allison, you should've gotten some black pussy while you could. I hear the beauties in Arabia wash their hair in camel piss, and if they're wearing a veil, you'll get your balls hacked off if you look twice at one. Buddy, from now on, we're going to be beating our meat in dark passageways. Allison didn't get any black pussy back in Massawa, so he's used to beating his meat."

The radarmen on watch joined in. Even the Operations officer found amusement in the ribbing Paris was taking. He'd made himself a promise never to mention Francesca, but as the joking persisted, his tryst with her became his only defense. "Keep on laughing. While you fuck-ups were screwing that black stuff, I had the only beautiful white girl in Massawa."

"You mean that gorgeous, dark-haired Italian piece of ass wearing those tight white skirts? We all had her, in our dreams, our wet dreams," teased another radarman.

The Operations officer, trying to keep some dignity to the conversation, intervened. "Allison, if you said it was raining dollar bills, I'd feel I had to believe you, but that girl was untouchable. Some of the younger officers tried and couldn't get near her. I have to give you an 'A' for fabricating your defense, though. It was original."

Paris' Adam's apple tightened. He reached under his jumper and pulled the picture of the Italian girl from his damaged wallet. He threw it on the plotting board. Below her undeniably beautiful face was her signature: Francesca.

The operations officer dropped his protractor when he looked at the photograph. "Damn! I don't believe it."

CHAPTER 29

WINTRY GUSTS SWEPT ACROSS THE quarter deck as Paris waited for
Mickey Crowley. He leaned against the rail near the gangway, focusing down at the
dark foamy sea slapping against the ship. He didn't mind waiting; it gave him a
chance to think. The movement of the water acted like an opiate, clouding his
mind, making his thoughts drift into the past.

In a dream-like state, he reflected on the past years and the grief he had
brought to those his life had touched. He thought of Anna, his high school sweet-
heart; Jennifer, the first mature woman he'd known, Mike, his childhood companion, his close friend "Tex" Madison, who died helping him, and his beloved
Carolyn. "Yes," he whispered, "even Joyce. She pressured me into marriage, but
things hadn't worked out to her liking." All their lives were tragically altered
because of him. *I have a curse, a touch worse than King Midas. Everyone I touch is sad-
dened. I have a touch of sadness.* He deliberately shifted his concentration, thinking
now of Africa and the many hardships and the few good times on that cruise. *Funny
thing about feelings; you can't recall the actual sensation,* he mediated. *Good thing.... I
guess the virtual reliving of an emotion would drive you insane.* The images of a darkened alley and a slain native flashed through his mind. He involuntarily shuddered.

He thought of Francesca, the dark-haired beauty in Massawa, who in only a
few clandestine moments with her soft, warm, passionate embrace, had without a
doubt saved his sanity. What kind of sorrow would befall her for having known
him? His reflections returned to Carolyn. Deeply engrossed with these thoughts, he
failed to see Mickey Crowley approach.

Mickey picked up his sea bag by its long strap and hoisted the heavy load to
his shoulder. "Goddamn! You sure you didn't put the ship's anchor in here?"

"I'll take it across the gangway myself. You don't have to." Paris shrugged.

"Shit. It's Navy tradition. Your best buddy always carries your sea bag over for
the last time. If Tex was here, we'd be fighting over who's going to carry it."

"Yeah, if Tex were here." Paris took a deep breath. "It's about that time. I'm
ready."

"Goes without saying, I'm going to miss you, you ol' son of a bitch. You're going to write?"

"Sure thing. How could I forget the address?" They both laughed.

"Well, let's go before you rupture yourself."

Mickey carried Paris' sea bag across the gangplank and set it down on the pier. Paris followed, not looking back at the ship after he cleared the gangway. "Thanks, Mickey. You take care of yourself."

"Sure. Just don't forget to write. I'm stuck here for three more months before I get my discharge. Without you to bullshit with, I'll be clawing the bulkheads."

"You're a short-timer now. You're below a hundred days; the time'll pass by fast."

"You still write and let me know what civilian life is like."

"Sure thing." Both knew this was the last time they'd see each other. Their worlds were parting.

"Take care, Mickey," Paris said, squeezing Mickey's hand in a firm handshake. He reached for the strap, slinging the heavy bag over his shoulder.

Mickey shifted his feet, unsure how to act or what to say.

"You'd better get back aboard before you freeze your balls off. Come on now, this is a day we all look forward to."

"Okay. Good luck, Paris. I mean it…good luck."

Paris nodded back to his buddy. "Thanks. You too."

In more than three years, so much had happened. It seemed an eternity. Paris shifted the clumsy sea bag as the stiff ocean breeze sent a wintry chill through his pea jacket. It was a long walk to the dispersing center, and already the weight of the full bag was sending burning pains through his shoulders.

Strange, he thought, today should be welcomed. He'd watched shipmates depart on their last day aboard and listened to their boasts of the impending hell they intended to wreak on the unsuspecting civilian populace. That was before his mind became clouded and when his eyes had a clear, crystal blue color, instead of the deadness they now had. All Paris could remember was that much unhappiness had transpired in the past three years. He felt about as happy as a condemned man walking toward the guillotine.

PART III

CHAPTER 30

WITH A BACKGROUND IN ELECTRONICS, Paris found employment at a time when a recession enveloped the country.

Finding a job proved easier than getting a divorce. Joyce clung to the marriage, writing and calling, asking him to "give it a chance. It can work out." But Paris would never forgive her deception, nor could he erase his bitter memory of the loss of Carolyn.

Joyce refused to give in, pleading that their son needed a father. Reference to "their" son alienated Paris even more. "I've kept my word giving your baby my name. He won't be called a bastard; but as to his being my son, I've had good reasons for doubting he's mine. I won't subject the child to a blood test to verify if I am the father and shame you with the results. He's got my name and I'll support him as long as legally necessary, but I won't spend my life married to someone I don't want."

Her tenacity weakened over time. With its waning, she developed a wrath equal to Paris' feelings of losing Carolyn.

Divorce was a stigma in the fifties, carrying with it a sense of failure for both husband and wife. Couples breaking their oath to the Lord received society's condemnation and subtle ire; thus divorces were difficult to obtain. Reasons for the states granting them were limited to: proof of adultery, insanity, or severe conditions of cruelty. Once granted, a year or more wait was mandatory before the divorce became final. "Quickie" divorces in Reno, Nevada or Mexico were scorned and in many states not recognized as legal.

Paris was determined to be free of what he felt cost him his happiness; time and money were of no consequence. He didn't believe he'd ever find Carolyn again, knowing that moment in time when the sun shined brightest upon him was gone forever. He mistrusted the events that rose so quickly and irrevocably destroyed his life. Subconsciously, he constructed a protective barricade so thick it couldn't be penetrated by Joyce's pleas to make the marriage work. Allowing the walls to be breached, he'd have to admit it was not the events, but he himself who was responsible for destroying his happiness. With that hidden guilt and the reminder his marriage to Joyce held, divorce was the only solution. Without it, he'd never be free to seek his lost ecstasy.

It took two years to obtain an absolute divorce. The courts established monthly support for the baby, which Paris paid. He never made any attempt to see Joyce or the child. It was an episode in his life he wanted to forget, and willfully he turned his back on it. No one, outside of his immediate family, would know of his past or of a child he refused to accept as his own.

The steady hum of the ancient oscillating fan was lulling him to sleep as the old, gray-haired Italian barber snipped around his ears. No need to watch the skillful operation taking place; Pete had been cutting his hair since his first year in high school. He knew not to cut off too much. Paris wanted only a light trim to maintain a consistent look.

The old barber commented, "You can take it offa fast, but it takes longa time to grow back." Pete had resumed cutting Paris' hair after his discharge from the Navy, seven years ago.

The clanging noise of the door striking the bell suspended in its path startled Paris, but the sound was so familiar, he didn't bother looking into the mirror to see the customer enter. Pete finished shaving the back of his neck, removed the cutting apron and brushed Paris' clothing for any loose cuttings. As Paris got out of the chair, a sharp command struck his ears.

"Take some more off, sailor! Regulation's three inches, no longer."

The bark had a familiar ring. He turned toward the voice and looked into the grinning face of his old friend from boot camp. The years couldn't conceal his identity. "Steve…Steve Bakerman. What the hell are you doing here?"

"Paris Allison. You old son of a gun. Shit! I've been coming to this barber shop for years. Hell, I grew up on this edge of town. Damn, it's good seeing you. I thought it was you when I saw how particular Pete was cutting your hair."

"Yeah! He does a better job cutting hair than we got in Bainbridge."

"Yeah! Not nearly as short," Steve laughed, shaking his buddy's hand.

"Short! They almost shaved our heads!" Paris joked as they tugged each others' arms. "It's been over ten years since I last saw you," Paris recollected. "You went out west, to some Airedale School."

"Yeah, Norman, Oklahoma."

"How's civilian life treating you? You married yet?"

"Yeah! Hell! I bit the bullet after getting out of the Navy. Got two girls…four and five years old. What about you? You tie the knot, yet?"

"Yeah! I got out, settled in a job and met Deborah. We've got two boys. Deb wanted a girl, but no such luck, at least not yet."

"Damn, I've wondered whatever became of you. Funny how you make the closest buddies in the service, but once you're out, never see them again."

"Yeah. Like a book with a chapter of your life in it. Once read, it's never opened again. Maybe we can get together, give the wives a chance to meet. Deb would like that. I've often told her of you. What're you doing now for a living, Steve?"

"Things were slow when I got out. Recession in full swing. Fact is, I've often kicked myself in the ass for not staying in. I work at a small machine shop. Nothing great, but we're making ends meet. You've got to be doing okay, Paris. You always had a good head on your shoulders."

"I never had any brains. I lucked out in electronics, and it helped me to get started. Like you said, the recession knocked the hell out of finding jobs when we got out."

Sensing his friend's embarrassment concerning jobs, Paris veered the conversion to another topic. "I'd have figured you'd stay in the Navy…go for the full 20 years, Steve."

"I almost did, but I got screwed up out West. Met a girl…nice family. We talked of getting married. Trouble was the family was *too* nice…didn't want her to have anything to do with me. It blew my mind. I wanted out of the Navy afterwards, to try to find myself. Got out and got married before I realized it."

Now Paris flushed with embarrassment. "Shit, that's life. Real happiness is found only in fairy tales. Look! Deb's giving our younger boy a birthday party Saturday afternoon around two. Nothing special. Just small kids coming for ice cream and cake, with a round of drinks for the grownups. Bring your wife and kids. It'll be a great time for us to get together."

Paris pulled a pen and scrap of paper from his shirt pocket and scribbled down his address and phone number, handing it to his buddy. "I won't take no for an answer. Deb would break my legs if I told her we'd run into each other and she didn't have a chance to meet you."

"Well…sure…I guess. I'll check with the wife to make sure. Oh hell! You can count on me. I'll be there." Paris detected nervousness in Steve's voice.

Driving home, Paris reflected on the past. Seeing Steve brought back memories, many that he tried to forget, but some that had been pleasant. He thought of Deborah and how they met; a smile lifted the corners of his mouth.

His divorce wasn't finalized when they started seeing each other, yet she stood by him throughout the whole mess. She hung in like a trooper when he needed mental support. He was fortunate to have her. He loved her and the kids. Yet there was this restless urge, something he had to find, something lost, misplaced, that he kept searching for.

Steve Bakerman sat in the worn armchair, staring toward the bedroom where his wife, Margaret, was still dressing. It was getting late and he grew more fidgety the longer it took her to finish getting ready.

He felt sloppy. She'd neglected to press his pants, and the knees of his trousers bagged out like two puffed paper bags. A tie looked ludicrous with his wrinkled pants, so he discarded it, opening his collar to appear more casual. His two small girls scampered around the living room's dilapidated furniture. Even with the excitement of going to a birthday party, their small faces appeared pale, almost anemic in contrast with their dark eyes and hair. Their dresses looked as though they'd been washed and quickly ironed, without any semblance of starching, and their shoes were scuffed.

"Valerie," Steve called to the oldest. "Look in the hall closet and bring me the shoe-shine box. I want to shine your shoes and Terry's. You both look like you've been playing in the yard."

"My God! You'd think we're going to some command performance, the way you've been acting. Shit! It's just some old Navy pal you haven't seen in a decade. Why all the fuss?" his wife yelled from the bedroom.

"Hell, Margaret. I want my family to look respectable. Paris Allison comes from a good family; I don't want him to think poorly of us."

"Shit!" She answered. "He probably doesn't have a pot to piss in, either. You men! Always trying to appear to be something you're not. Wise up, Steve. The world's passed you by."

He didn't reply, just glanced through the open bedroom door as she stepped into her skirt. She had a cute figure, he observed, and a damn sharp tongue.

He looked about the room. *The house always looks untidy*, he noted, *like it needs a good scrubbing. The furniture needs cleaning and polishing and nothing is ever maintained.* Restless, he went to the kitchen to pour a cup of coffee and saw a large cockroach scurrying across the table.

"Damn it, Marge. I thought you were keeping up with the spraying. The roaches are taking over."

"They don't eat much," she shot back.

He poured himself coffee and whispered under his breath, "How in the hell did I get wrapped up in this mess?" It was obvious Margaret was no homemaker.

"Did you wrap the present? If not, I'd like to see what you got," he called to her.

"Hell! I forgot to get anything. It slipped my mind."

"Goddamn it!" Steve swore loudly, sloshing coffee onto the floor. "You said you'd pick something up. I'm not going there empty handed."

"Don't yell at me," she said as she stormed into the kitchen. "You've got as much time as I have. Why didn't you get it yourself?"

"I gave you money to pick something up. You said you would. Remember?"

"I needed it for something else, so I spent it," she flared back.

He attempted to soothe her sudden wrath. "I guess I can get a couple of cards at the drug store and put a few dollars in them for the girls to give," he said half-heartedly. "Are you ready to go now?"

"As ready as I'm going to be."

He looked at her standing in the doorway. She could've been attractive, but her dark eyes squinted, giving her a sinister expression. *She wears her clothes too tight,* he thought, rounding up the girls and starting to leave. Her dress was too revealing, and she appeared untidy, with her long dark hair always slightly disheveled.

In spite of his constant bickering, his daughters didn't have that sparkling fresh appearance other girls their ages seemed to have. He didn't outwardly criticize Margaret, but he did detect a difference in his family's appearance, and this gnawed at him. Hoping in the initial years of their marriage that his wife would cultivate interest in these things, he now was resigned to conditions remaining as they were.

While locking the front door, he remembered not shining their shoes. "Shit! The hell with it," he mumbled, slamming it shut.

The Bakermans arrived late. Seeing his buddy in the barbershop was one thing, but bringing his wife and family to the Allison home made Steve feel ill at ease. He thought of canceling, but he'd given his word. Steve pressed the doorbell. In a few seconds, the door opened wide and he was greeted by a beautiful, warm smile.

"You must be Steve...Steve Bakerman, and this is your wife and two girls. Gosh! They're little darlings. I'm Deborah." She extended her hand.

"This is my wife, Margaret, and this is Valerie and Terry."

"Paris has told me so much about you. He was so excited, seeing you again. Please come in and let me introduce you to everyone."

Deborah presented the Bakermans to three male guests seated in the living room. "Steve, Margaret, and their girls, Valerie and Terry. This is John Ferraro, Bill Appleby, and Tom Douglas."

The male guests stood up as introductions were made, and Steve felt a rush of embarrassment, observing that all the men wore suits, white shirts, and ties. Nervousness beaded his forehead as sweat ran down his back.

"Paris! Come see who's here," Deborah called out. "He's in the kitchen mixing drinks," she said to Steve. "Margaret, come and meet the girls. They've abandoned their husbands and are lending me a hand in the kitchen."

A pleasant aura about Deborah lessened Steve's initial discomfort. Warmth radiated from her, making him feel genuinely welcome. There was no pretense nor phony air. Not only was she pretty, there was honesty in her voice. He liked her immediately.

Paris emerged from the kitchen, carrying a tray of drinks. He quickly set the tray down to shake Steve's hand. "Steve, I'm glad you came. I was about to give up on you. I've been chewing Deborah's ear about you since seeing you at the barber shop. Did you meet everybody?"

"Yes, I think so," Steve said awkwardly.

"Good! Then you've got to bail me out. I've been helping in the kitchen; Deb's a slave driver."

"Help?" Deborah kidded. "He's ogling all the pretty wives while pretending to mix drinks. You men better keep him in here so the girls will be safe."

Steve's two young girls were still clutching the white envelopes in their small hands when Deborah reached out and put her arms around them. "I want to introduce your daughters to the other children. Margaret, let's leave the men to gossip. Come and meet everyone in the kitchen."

Steve sat down in a large armchair and glanced around the room. Everything was immaculate, the atmosphere bright and cheerful, and the fresh smell of furniture polish wafted through the air. Neatness abounded in the home.

Deborah ushered the wives and two well-dressed boys back from the kitchen and introduced them to Steve. "Betty, Joan, Dawn, this is an old Navy buddy of Paris'. Meet Steve…Steve Bakerman. And these are our two sons: Alan, the oldest, is almost five and here's our birthday boy, David. He's three years old, today," Deborah squeezed each of the boys. "Gosh! That makes me seem so old," she said, shaking her head.

Steve stood up to meet everyone, rubbing the good-looking boys' heads. The eldest had his mother's deep brown eyes; the smaller had a mass of golden tresses, like his father used to have.

He mentally appraised the women. Two were average looking; the girl named Dawn was strikingly pretty. *There are so many kinds of beauty,* he mused, *so many types of sexually attractive women.* His attention focused on the hostess. Of all the women there, Deborah appealed to him most. It was a combination of her smile, pretty face, dark hair and neatness. She was the epitome of his ideal woman. Looking about, he felt relaxed in the orderly surroundings.

"I don't know why we parents torture ourselves this way, but if we can stand the noise until the cake is cut, I have several games to keep the kids busy. Then we can all have a good drink. By that time, we'll need one," Deborah laughed lightly.

It took time to open the presents and cut the birthday cake. The grownups left the children with their games, and Deborah served the adults coffee in the living room. She continually checked the children, guiding them in their play. The wives soon migrated to the kitchen to be with Deborah. The husbands were left talking with one another, relaxing in their comfortable chairs.

Deborah peeked around the door. "Paris, don't just sit there talking. See if anyone cares for another drink," she scolded playfully. "I've got the liquor on the kitchen counter."

"You've got a fine-looking wife, Paris," the dark-haired man, that Steve remembered as John Ferraro, commented. "A real looker."

Steve nodded. "She's got a way of making you feel right at home. You've got some girl there, Paris. How'd an ugly son-of-a gun like you ever meet her?"

"I came to her rescue to save her from being an old maid," Paris said with a grin.

"She could never be an old maid," Steve answered seriously.

As Paris left to make more drinks, John Ferraro nudged Bill Appleby sitting next to him. It was obvious to Steve that they knew each other. *Maybe they work together*, he thought. Overhearing their whispered remarks, anger rose in his throat. "Bill, Deborah sure has a cute figure. Wouldn't mind having a little of that."

"With something like that to come home to, makes you wonder why Paris can't keep his pecker in his pants."

"It's hurt him professionally," John answered his balding friend. "They say he'd fuck a snake if he could get a grip on it."

"What he's getting doesn't look like a snake. That secretary he's been screwing is prime stuff. Every stud at work tried to get in her pants. I thought her pussy was sealed in a chastity belt. Allison spoke to her a couple of times and her panties fell to her ankles."

Steve's first impulse was to rap the darker one in the mouth for disrespecting Paris' wife. Strangely, he felt a compulsion to protect Deborah.

Paris' two "friends" accusations stunned him. The Allisons seemed perfect for each other. Looking at Deborah entering the room, he couldn't imagine being unfaithful to her. He saw Margaret standing in the kitchen and mentally compared the two.

If Paris is risking all this for a fast lay, his head needs examining, Steve thought. Pushing any hostile feelings from of his mind, Steve leaned back, sipping his drink as his throat muscles relaxed while reasoning that most men gossiped like old ladies; half of it was bullshit.

No one noticed and Steve would have missed it had he not shifted in his chair to reach into his pocket for his cigarettes. What Steve heard in the beginning of the evening had sharpened his senses or he would have let the incident pass, giving it no value. As he changed position, he glanced up, catching sight of the attractive wife named Dawn, standing by the kitchen doorway. Her lips puckered, forming a silent kiss. Discreetly, she blew the kiss across the room. Steve's eyes followed its course. Paris stood in its path, a smile warming his handsome face. His smile was directed toward Dawn.

During the evening, while conversing with the guests, Steve subtly watched Dawn's eyes embrace Paris. He continued to study Paris' wife. *The grass always seems greener in someone else's yard,* he thought. But his preference still rested with Deborah. His gaze took in the well-kept home and the neatness of their two sons. Paris had in his grasp everything Steve lacked in his marriage. He was certain by her actions that Deborah loved Paris intensely. He looked at Margaret, feeling ashamed. *I'd give my left ball to trade places. Paris has everything I could possibly ask for, yet he's not aware of it.*

By five o'clock, the party broke up. Everyone rounded up their children, said good-bye, and left. The Bakermans were the last to leave. Paris insisted they stay after the other guests left. He told Steve they needed undistracted time to rekindle their old friendship.

"Tell me, Steve, where'd you get that scar on your forehead? I don't remember you having that."

"Oh, this?" Steve's fingers touched the scar running above his left eye to his temple. "That's a little memento of my stay in Japan."

"I thought we stopped fighting the Japanese at the end of World War II," Paris said, laughing.

"It wasn't Japs. Two damned blacks tried to roll me as I was coming back to base. Bastards figured to cut my throat and take my wallet. I got one around the throat. Figured if I was going to die, I'd take him with me. His buddy picked up a damned two-by-four and broke it over my head."

"No shit!"

"Yeah! I don't remember much afterwards. I guess when he hit me and I still didn't let go of his pal, he ran. I came to in the hospital. The doctors said I almost choked the son-of-a-bitch to death. When the Shore Patrol found us, I still had him by the throat. Nothing ever came of it." Steve shrugged. "No military justice."

Paris looked for signs of exaggeration in what Steve related. There were none. In Basic Camp, he thought of him as his closest comrade. Now, he felt even greater respect for Steve for the courage he had shown.

"Paris! All bullshiting aside, the last girlfriend I recall you having was the Jewish girl that gave you a bad case of lover's nuts. How did you find a beauty like Deborah?"

"Lucky day for me, Steve. I'm proud of her. I met her at a roller skating rink. Couple of guys I knew back in school decided we'd pick up some girls by going there. I said I couldn't skate and had been riding waves while they were hitting the rinks. They promised not to put on skates. They lied. Soon as we got there, they rented skates and were on the floor, whizzing by with girls on their arms. I felt like a damned wallflower. I rented skates and practiced until I could keep my balance. Then, I looked for the prettiest girl I could find. Deborah was standing by the rail encircling the rink. I almost fell getting to her, but she thought I was horsing around. I asked her to skate around the rink. Half way around, she realized I couldn't skate, and she held me up until the music ended. I couldn't date her until I met her family. Steve, she's been holding me up ever since."

Deborah closed the front door softly after the Bakermans left and turned to Paris, who was picking up dirty drinking glasses strewn about the room. She sighed, weary from entertaining the grownups and watching over the children for hours. "I'm glad it's over. I'm worn out and still there's supper to make and a mess to clean up."

"Don't go to a lot of trouble. It's late. Let's have something light. Maybe soup and sandwiches? I'm not hungry, and the boys are filled up on ice cream and cake."

"I don't know. I'd feel like I was short-changing you," Deborah said guiltily.

"Nonsense. You need a break from the kitchen after handling that mob. What'd you think of Steve?"

"I liked him." Deborah walked over to her husband, putting her arms around his neck. "But I'm not sure about his wife."

"What do you mean?" Paris said, squeezing her tiny waist with his arms while still holding dirty glasses in his hands.

"Her eyes are peculiar looking, almost mean," Deborah reflected, "and she seemed to be giving the men the once-over. It's something I can't put my finger on and I shouldn't say, but they don't seem suited for each other."

"Hell! If he's happy, I'm happy," Paris said jokingly.

"Are you happy, Paris? I mean it, really happy?" she asked, her tone suddenly serious.

"Hey! What's this? You want assurance? Okay! Get the kids in bed early and I'll show you how to make the most of Saturday night."

"Promises! Promises!" Deborah whispered huskily into his ear. "Okay, Mr. Allison. I'll call your bluff, just to see if you're as good as you think you are."

"Oh! While I'm thinking of it, I asked Steve to get a babysitter for next Friday. Thought we'd enjoy going bowling together. You don't mind, do you? Think you can get to like his wife a little, even if she has strange eyes?"

"I don't dislike her," Deborah said, resting her head on his shoulder. She whispered softly, "I just wouldn't trust her. I feel a little sorry for Steve and the children. Call it a woman's intuition, but they just don't seem to belong together. Then, everyone might have been thinking that of us."

"Enough of that woman's intuition. Let's get supper over with and hustle the boys off to bed. I've got plans for you tonight, Mrs. Allison."

He held her in an awkward grasp for several more moments, the soiled glasses still in his hands, and, as if it were an afterthought, looked down at her pretty face. "Try to like her for my sake. I'd like to pick up the remnants of an old, almost forgotten friendship. Steve reminds me of my youth, when I was young and everything seemed black and white, with no gray matter in between. When I thought I had a purpose and knew what direction I was going."

She didn't answer. Mist formed in her dark eyes and they sparkled up at him for a moment before a tiny tear appeared in each corner. The tears belied her happy, outward persona she presented to everyone and attested to womanly intuition that had long sensed her husband's hidden restlessness.

"Hey! What're the tears all about?"

"I had hoped I'd make you happy…that you'd finally come to be content in the direction you are headed," she answered softly.

CHAPTER 31

CAROLYN GLANCED UP AT THE wall clock. It was past six, and she felt exhausted from lack of sleep and the long, busy day. Though her overall appearance displayed neatness and efficiency, dark circles under her eyes and an intense headache, evidenced the sleep deprivation of the past night.

"Tension and not enough rest," she mumbled to herself. "There's still a ton of filing and billings left and several blood work-ups to do." Today was hectic; only minutes earlier Dr. Graham had seen his last patient.

In the past year, Carolyn's mother developed trouble breathing, and lately her color had an ashy hue. Yesterday, her condition worsened, and Carolyn spent a sleepless night continually checking on her sick mother while mentally battling the guilt of knowing the tremendous burden that caring for Mark, her young grandson, over the past seven years had placed on the aging woman.

Without Mom's help and my brother Ralph's insistence that I obtain a useful career, I couldn't have made it alone, she thought. *Their help and love for my son have kept me going since returning from Brighton.* Carolyn stopped typing to massage her throbbing temples with her fingertips to help ease the pain of the severe headache. Despite her discomfort, she loved her job as Dr. Graham's medical assistant and receptionist. There was personal satisfaction being needed for her abilities.

At 26 Carolyn was an undeniably beautiful woman. Her blonde hair cut shoulder length, and the white uniform accentuated her well-shaped breasts, small waist, and rounded hips. Fatigue and an excruciating headache couldn't diminish her beauty, though worry of her mother's health sapped her stamina.

Over the past months she insisted her mom see a doctor, but she had obstinately refused. Carolyn and her brother observed no improvement. Last night it was apparent that this wasn't a minor sickness.

Dr. Graham entered from the examining room and, glancing through the office window, spoke in a pleasant voice. "It's begun to pour outside."

Carolyn looked toward the window. "Oh! I can't believe I left my umbrella at home. I'll get drenched waiting for the bus. But maybe the rain will wash away this terrible headache!"

"Nonsense! My car's parked outside. You're not getting soaked going home after the hard day's work you've done today. I'll take you home."

"Thanks, but it's better I take the bus. It'd be out of your way, and in this rain, the traffic will be heavy. The bus will be faster."

The doctor ignored her refusal. "You should've mentioned your headache earlier." He placed his hands on her shoulders and applied pressure up the back of her neck to the base of her skull. "Your muscles are as tight as a drum. Does the headache seem to register here at the temples?"

"Yes. I thought it'd ease by now," she said, feeling momentary relief from his fingers. "I've had a lot on my mind." She paused, fearful of annoying him with her problems. "And I didn't sleep well last night."

"I'll give you something to help you relax. It'll ease the tension in your shoulders and neck muscles, but whatever is on your mind, unless you speak out about it, I can't help you."

His voice showed concern. He was quiet a moment, then looked at her and asked, "Is it the job? Are you unhappy here, or is it your salary?"

"Oh, no, Dr. Graham! I love my job and the pay is certainly adequate. More than I've ever made before. I wouldn't want you to think I'm dissatisfied. My mother hasn't felt well lately," she explained. "She's having difficulty breathing. Her condition got worse last night. I've tried to get her to see a doctor, but she refuses. She makes sure everyone in the family sees one with the least problem, but she's the last ever to go. I love her, but she can be stubborn. I think at her age, I've given her too much to handle. I wish I'd been able to help her rather than be a burden."

Dr. Graham listened intently, then without answering entered his office. He returned carrying a paper cup of water and two white tablets. "Take these for the headache. I've got more for you in this bottle, for later on. Take two when you go to bed; it'll ease your headache by relieving the muscle tension. Now, put your work aside, young lady. I'm taking you home. I'll bring my black bag and we'll take a look at your mother."

"I couldn't let you do that. I really appreciate the thought, but…."

"I insist. Anyway, it's been a long time since I've made house calls. What's got to be done before we leave?"

"I've got to refrigerate these slides, but I can finish billing and filing tomorrow. I feel as if I'm imposing on you."

"Not another word about it. While you put the slides away, I'll get my bag."

They walked quickly in the rain to the car, Carolyn shielded by a large umbrella Dr. Graham held over them. His six-foot height made it necessary for him to stoop to protect her from the downpour. Worry overshadowed the embarrassment she felt because of her employer's unyielding willingness to assist her. She thought, *I'm too thin-skinned, but Mom would have to be on her death bed before she'd see a doctor.* She shuddered, fearing this thought might in some way endanger her mother.

"Are you cold? I felt you shiver." Dr. Graham put his free arm about her shoulders and hugged her close, clumsily balancing the large umbrella and the black bag in his other hand. Reaching the car, he released her shoulder and opened the door.

He drove slowly, switching the windshield wipers to high speed and still, at times, it was impossible to see more than a few feet beyond the hood of the car. He navigated through the busy town, following the tail lights of cars in the main stream of traffic. His car hit a puddle and water splashed across its hood, causing the engine to sputter as the wires got wet.

Carolyn apologized for the inconvenience as she gave directions. Dr. Graham shrugged off her apologies.

"Let me put it this way, Carolyn, he said. "If I was forced to wait for a bus in this downpour and you had a car, wouldn't you give me a ride?"

"That would be different." When she realized how illogical her answer was, they both laughed.

"Typical female logic," he joked.

Carolyn worked in his office a year and until now, had never given thought to how little she knew about her employer. The downpour had become a light drizzle when they pulled up to the small frame house in the suburbs of Hartford.

"I was worried we'd be walking when the engine started to stall."

"Please, let's go in. Mom's worried. I should have called and told her that I'd be late." Carolyn rang the doorbell and the door opened immediately.

"I was getting worried. It was raining so hard, and you'd left your umbrella at home," her mother said, her face flooded with relief.

"Mom, I'm sorry. I should've called to say that everything was okay. Dr. Graham was kind enough to give me a ride home. He truly saved me from getting soaked. This is my mom, Vivian Stevens. Mom, this is Dr. Graham." She hugged her mom and, seeing her young son, his arms outstretched toward her, knelt down, put her arms around him and kissed his cheek. "This is Mark, my son."

"Mrs. Stevens, I happened to grab my bag leaving the office. Carolyn mentioned you might be coming down with the flu or the beginning of a cold. While I'm here, I might as well take a look at you." He smiled reassuringly.

She started to protest, but Dr. Graham's gentle demeanor disarmed her resistance. "But your fee…," she began.

It's going to cost you a good, hot cup of black coffee."

"I'll make it right away. Won't you stay for supper? It's late and I know I've put you out." Carolyn spoke hesitantly, caught off guard by the warmth and friendliness of the man for whom she worked.

"No, this won't take long, just coffee will be fine. Now, Mrs. Stevens, let me take a look at you."

Shortly after he finished examining Mrs. Stevens, Carolyn saw Dr. Graham to the door. He stood on the lower steps to be level with her face and spoke quietly. "There are tests…more extensive tests I need to do, and there's a specialist I know. He's one of the best. I want you to bring your mom to the office tomorrow." He paused. "I could come by to get her."

"Oh, no. I'll call my brother, Ralph. You've done so much already, but I don't know if she'll go."

"I've told her it's a serious matter, and she promised not to make any trouble about coming."

Tears flooded Carolyn's eyes as she bit down on her lip trying to control her emotions.

"She's really a sweet person and understands her problem completely. You're lucky to have had her this long." He started to leave, then turned to face her, "I won't expect you before eleven. Oh! You have a handsome son. I never thought of you as married."

"I'm not married," Carolyn said, her words barely audible.

"I'm sorry. Divorce can leave bitter memories. I should've realized when you used your maiden name, Stevens, introducing me to your mother."

"I've never been married," she spoke more clearly.

Dr. Graham detected the tremor in her voice "You're very honest. These days, that can be a rarity. I didn't mean to pry."

"I've found honesty hurts less than living with a lie." She squared her shoulders, bracing for the answer to her question. "Do you want my resignation?"

Dr. Graham stepped up onto the concrete stoop and put down his black bag and umbrella. He placed his hands gently on her shoulders, looking into her troubled eyes. "Life can be cruel. Sometimes there's no sense or meaning in what happens, but life goes on. We have to pick up the pieces, glue them back together, and go on. Sometimes life shatters us, tears at our hearts, almost destroys us, but we must go on. Out of whatever happened in your life, you have a beautiful, healthy son. Two years ago, my wife was killed in a head-on collision with a drunk lunatic speeding on the parkway. It all seemed so senseless. I loved her very much. Life to me would've been meaningless but for our two daughters. Because of my two young girls, my life must go on. We both have to bury our hearts."

As if embarrassed by his vulnerability, he reached for his bag and umbrella. "Have your mom there by eleven or I'll bill you for a house call." He started to turn away, then hesitated and turned to face her. "There's a dinner this Saturday evening. I've been roped into going by some associates of mine. Seems everyone lately is beginning to form associations and they've asked me to join one. It's nothing formal, just friends, some doctors and their wives. I didn't want to go...not alone." He nervously cleared his throat. "Would you go with me?"

Carolyn looked up into the kind, soft brown eyes of this gentle being she had only begun to know that night. Tightness came to her throat, and she felt compassion for his tenderness. "I'd be honored to go with you."

In the early Spring of 1964, Vivian Stevens' death came quickly, though not quite unexpectedly. Sometime in the late morning hours, Carolyn's mother passed away. Her breathing had become increasingly difficult in the past months, yet she wished to remain at home, in spite of Dr. Graham's efforts to have her admitted to the hospital.

Carolyn, her two sisters, Ralph and Dr. Graham, hovered about her bedside. By late evening, Vivian Stevens seemed to rally, then her condition worsened. Dr. Graham called Carolyn and her brother together.

"It's very hard for me to say this, but I must be honest. Vivian is slipping away. She wishes to stay here with her family. To force her into a hospital now would be cruel and useless. I'm afraid she won't make it through the night, but that's in God's hands. She possesses a great deal of fortitude and could possibly hang on a little longer. I've got to leave now. There are pressing matters at the hospital I must attend to. Carolyn, if her condition changes, call the hospital and have me paged. I'll come immediately. Ralph, between you and Carolyn, explain to the rest of your family and ready them as best you can."

Carolyn continually checked on her mother throughout the night, praying for a miracle. *She's so tiny, resting there in bed* she thought, sitting on the side of the bed, *and seems so peaceful. She's not struggling for breath anymore.* Carolyn reached out to touch her mother's face, and realized that she was gone. She put her arms about the small, limp frame and pulled her mother to her breast, sobbing quietly. Shortly afterwards, she left her mother to inform the family.

Ralph, with Dr. Graham's help, made the necessary arrangements. The doctor helped Carolyn and her family in their sorrow throughout the wake. At the funeral, he waited until the services ended and everyone was leaving the grave site to approach Carolyn. "If there's anyway, I can help…please, just ask."

"Oh, Dr. Graham, you've done so much. You've been so kind. We can never repay you for your thoughtfulness." She fought back tears, biting her lower lip.

"Take some time off from the office. You'll need it to straighten things out, I know. Take as long as you need," he said compassionately.

"I'd appreciate that, thank you. I need just a couple of days to make arrangements with my sisters to see if they can take care of Mark for me and get him off to school."

"I want you to take two weeks off, with pay."

"I couldn't take advantage of you that way. You need someone at the office…."

Dr. Graham shook his head. "Carolyn, I'll get a temporary worker until you can come back. Now, go and be with your family. They need you near them. I'll call and check on you. Remember, take two weeks, and if you need more time, let me know. He stooped and kissed her tear-moistened cheek, then turned to leave.

Several months had passed since the death of Carolyn's mother and she was busy at her desk when Dr. Graham finished with his last patient for Friday evening. He approached her with a troubled look; his brows were wrinkled, and he appeared nervous, so unlike his normally calm composure.

"Is there anything wrong, Doctor?"

"No, nothing wrong, but I do have something to go over with you. Are you free to have dinner this evening? I know it's short notice," he added, "but it's important."

Carolyn's mind raced ahead. "I don't know. I'll have to find a babysitter. I could ask my sister. She watches Mark for me during the week, but I wouldn't want to ask her if she and her husband have plans."

"That won't be a problem…if you're free. I have a maid that helps at home and tends to the girls. I've already made arrangements for her to take care of your son for the evening. That is…if you have no other plans?"

"No, Doctor. I've planned nothing for the evening. Dinner will be fine."

"Fine! Then it's settled. I'll pick you up at six and we can bring Mark to my home. Don't worry about supper for him. He and the girls can eat together."

Dr. Graham picked Carolyn up that evening. As they drove to dinner, he still appeared nervous, as if he had a pressing problem.

"What's wrong, Dr. Graham?" Carolyn asked.

"Just something very important that's been on my mind. I think I'll feel better after we've eaten," he replied.

Seated at a grand piano, the pianist played Rachmaninoff's beautiful *Rhapsody On A Theme Of Paganini*. The music drifted across the richly carpeted dining room to their table beneath an elaborate glass chandelier.

Dr. Graham had chosen the finest restaurant and best table. The elegant décor created a perfect atmosphere. He'd regained his usual demeanor and they conversed through dinner. After eating, as they sipped their wine from long-stemmed glasses, he looked directly at her as he spoke. "I'm usually pretty good speaking at public lectures, but now I feel very awkward. I've given this a great deal of thought over the past few months…actually, since that rainy evening when I took you home and met your mom." He paused, as if not sure how to continue. "Would you consider becoming my wife?" Before she could answer, he added, "We both have reached a time in life when we need and appreciate each other."

Carolyn held her wine glass in her hand, about to bring it to her lips. Her eyes focused on her wrist and the long white scar. She put down the glass and didn't answer.

As if knowing her thoughts, he spoke softly. "We can never replace the losses known in the past, but we can fill the void left by those losses. Love has many faces. When we're young, it's that hot passion flooding our bodies that we call love. As we age and are mellowed by life's experiences, we come to appreciate another kind of love. Sometimes it takes the face of comfort, security, just being together and needing the other in companionship. In time, that face of love is more lasting and satisfying than the fleeting passion of our youth."

"What of Mark...my son?" she asked hesitantly.

"I'd adopt him as my own...give him a good education...help in setting a course in life in the right direction. I'd accept him as my son, as you would accept my daughters as yours. They need a mother and your son needs a father. I've grown to need you...to love you, Carolyn."

"I know," she answered simply.

He took her hand in his. "Carolyn, will you marry me?"

"Yes," she said thoughtfully. "Yes, Dr. Graham. I'll marry you."

His face lit up with relief. "You've got to stop calling me Dr. Graham. It's so formal. 'Tom' will do just fine," he said, smiling.

She looked into his kind eyes. "Yes, *Tom*, I'll marry you."

"Now that I've joined the Medical Association, I can more easily take some time off. Set a date for the wedding and choose where you'd like to go for our honeymoon. Florida...the Caribbean...Hawaii?"

She smiled at him, but her mind drifted for a moment and she spoke directly from her thoughts. "I'd like to go back to Virginia." At his surprised look, she added, "It's such a beautiful state, Tom. There's so much to see. It's so historical. There's Williamsburg, Yorktown, Jamestown, even Norfolk and Virginia Beach. I'd love to see the Chesapeake Bay and maybe cross it on the ferry once again."

"I think the ferries have been replaced by a monstrous engineering feat called a bridge-tunnel. I'd like to see that myself. It's settled. Virginia is where we'll honeymoon."

CHAPTER 32

DAWN SAT NAKED ON THE bed, watching as he stood before the mirror, knotting his tie. It wasn't until he was sure his appearance was presentable that he noticed she hadn't begun dressing.

"Honey, you'd better hurry, unless you plan going home to greet your husband in your birthday suit."

"You still turn me on after so many times together. For a man, you're even graceful putting on your trousers. It's not like being with Johnny. When I'm with him, I close my eyes and imagine it's you. I mean…in bed. I guess I shouldn't say it, but it's true."

"No, you shouldn't say it or even think it. It's bad enough what we're doing."

"Paris, I've done things in bed with you I can't do with Johnny. God! He and I've had bitter quarrels over that, and I've been married to him ten years."

"Dawn, we don't have time for confessions."

"Wait! Let me finish. What I said about closing my eyes, imagining it's you when I'm with my husband, it's true. I'm more honest about that than you are."

"What the hell brought this on?"

"I can't see you again," her voice trembled, worry twisting her pretty face. "I can't be used anymore, Paris. You don't realize it, but that's how I feel. I thought, in the beginning, we needed each other. God! I needed you and still do, but it's so one-sided. I've risked my marriage, children, self-respect…and I'd still gladly do it, if I knew I really had you. But you're doing to me what I do to Johnny."

He stood by the bed, looking down at her. He didn't interrupt.

"Heavens, I know I'm not your first affair; you were honest about that. But Paris, I see it in your eyes when we're making love. It's like you're looking for more, for something or someone else. I don't know what or who, but I can sense it. It's not my imagination. It's as if you've lost something and are trying to find it in sex. Maybe that's it. With all the affairs you've had, you look for a trait or similarity of some girl who hurt you in the past and you try to lose yourself, seeking this. There's no girl that can ever completely satisfy you. I know I can't. The risk outweighs the rewards. This is our last time." She paused then, added, "Oh, no one will ever know. We'll still be friends."

"I said in the beginning, no strings attached," Paris said flatly, displaying no outward sign of emotion.

When she stood and began dressing, Paris watched how provocatively she moved.

Despite the many times they had slept together, he still was aroused by her femininity.

He cracked the draw drapes covering the room's only window and, using the glow cast by the neon light above the motel, checked the parking area. He didn't want to run into any familiar faces. Dawn finished dressing, freshened her make-up and stood up, teasing her dark hair before the mirror.

He inspected the room to make sure they left nothing behind. As Paris unchained the latch on the door, Dawn glanced in the mirror for a final check, tossing her thick dark hair over her shoulders and patting it in place. Her movements stirred a distant memory. He quickly shrugged it off.

Safely away from the motel and back on the highway, Dawn slid close to Paris. "I care too much for you, Paris. Sooner or later someone would find out. We'll still be near each other and can keep the friendship we all had."

"There's an old saying, honey. 'Friends can be lovers, but lovers can never be friends.'" Paris took her hand. "Hell, remember the first time we held hands? You talk of risks. I think one of my greatest risks was the first time we met in your apartment and I had to step over Johnny's size twelve shoes at the top of the landing. With only one way in and one way out, *that's* a risk! But the reward outweighed the risk!" He grinned.

"What have you got planned for the holidays?" she asked quietly.

"I'm taking the family to the mountains to see their grandparents. Everyone's excited about going."

"I wish things could be different. We'll always be friends, won't we?"

"Sure. Like I said, no strings attached."

Arriving home, Paris unlocked the door and entered the living room. Deborah and the children would be asleep. He'd come home late before, using an excuse of having to finish some work at the office. Reaching the bottom of the stairs he saw that a light was shining in the upstairs bedroom. Ascending the steps, he pushed open the door. Deborah, her back to him, was sorting clothing laid out on the bed.

Funny, he thought, *to be doing this so late.* He scanned the room; the drawers of the dresser and vanity were open.

Deborah didn't turn, but he knew she'd heard him. Then he saw the brown leather suitcase. She spun to face him, vehemently spitting her words, "You bastard! I'm leaving. I'm not staying here another night."

Her words hit him like a blow.

"Working late again? Don't you think that excuse has gotten a little thin?"

"Wait just a minute…."

"I got a phone call…an anonymous friend." Tears streamed down her face. "Just wanted to let me know what kind of late work you were doing and with whom you were doing it."

"Some friend." Paris shrugged.

"I called your office. No answer. I kept calling…you bastard! Don't you think I knew all along you were cheating? I'm not stupid. I tried to pretend I was wrong, that you loved me. I tried kidding myself that no one else knew. Then, to have my face smeared in it like this…. I stood by you when you needed me. I thought that made us love each other more. Oh, I saw the flirtations, but I tried to pretend you were faithful. I don't deserve this."

"For what it's worth, it's all over…finished…done," Paris replied flatly. He'd made a rule never to intentionally hurt anyone, unless it became a question of survival. He'd hurt his wife, but it happened unintentionally. "Some do-gooder, this friend," he chided the informant.

"You're right. It's over…finished…done," she cried. "Look at you. I've watched you…felt for you. You're like some kind of Don Quixote, chasing windmills. You've chased a lost, impossible dream. I hoped you'd finally give it up and come back to me." She sobbed, "I never really had you in the first place. It's always been someone else. I can't take the hurt and the embarrassment any more. Keep chasing your windmills, but I'm not going to be here to come home to any more."

"Where will you go?" he asked sincerely. "What about the children?"

She looked dismayed, hopelessly lost. Deborah replied slowly, "I don't know. I have no place to run, no place to take the children." She slumped down on the bed, staring blankly at the floor, tears streaming down her face.

He sat beside her, and tried to put his arms around her.

"Don't touch me," she cried, pushing at his chest. "I don't want you to ever touch me again."

Despite her resistance, he pulled her to him.

"Why, Paris? Why?" she sobbed. "I gave you everything a wife could give. I do all I can for you. In bed, I thought I satisfied you. You said I did. I did…things I never dreamed of doing, because it was you and I thought we both loved each other. I enjoyed loving you. Was it all a lie? Were you making fun of me? Telling your girlfriends how pathetic I was at making love? Is that what you talked about when you were screwing them?"

He rocked her in his arms, trying to calm her. Better not to talk, he thought, better for her to get it all out. How could he convince her how much he needed her and loved her, yet could take another woman and love her also? Not in the same way, not equally, but nevertheless, for a short time, love her also? The affairs never lasted. There was nothing but sex to bind the relationships. It was the search, always the seeking that was important. The find was never fulfilling. His dad had said, "The hunt was better than the kill." It was true.

He kept looking, yet wasn't sure of his reason. He thought of all the girls he'd taken to bed. He barely remembered their faces. *Why do I keep looking? Why have I allowed myself to hurt the one dearest to me?*

"Stay with me, Deborah. Don't leave."

"I can't, Paris. I can't. I can't be hurt anymore."

"I won't hurt you again. I promise I'll never hurt you again."

"I want to believe you, but you can't…won't change, Paris. People don't change. You've said it before: People only pretend to be different. Your mold is set. I've got to go. I don't belong here anymore. I guess I never really belonged. I thought I did, but I was wrong."

"If not for me, for the kids. Stay through the holidays. At least let me try, until then." He kissed her wet cheek, afraid to take any further liberty. He felt a strange ache in his stomach. He had hurt her. Strangely, no affair held any importance to him. How could he explain to this trembling girl he loved her and yet could sleep with so many other women? "It's late. Stay at least for the night. I won't press you. If you want to leave in the morning, I won't stop you. Stay here. It's your home. If anyone leaves, I'll go. That's the least I can do for you and the boys. Stay tonight. I'll change, Deborah. I love you. I really love you." He pulled her closer. "I never intended to hurt you."

She rested her head against his chest, continuing to stare at the floor, her strength completely sapped. "Paris, I'm pregnant," Deborah said quietly.

For nearly an hour, the two stayed in this position. Finally, Deborah broke the silence. "I'll pretend, Paris. For the children's sake, I'll pretend for a while longer. No one will know. Your girlfriends...no one. I'll pretend to be the dutiful wife, but inside of me, something has changed. I love you...I always will, but you've taken something from me, something I valued, even if you didn't. I'll pretend for a little while longer, but Paris, one day I'll leave you. I won't stop loving you, but you'll force me to go."

She paused, then murmured quietly, "You're destroying what you've actually been looking for. What we had was special. It was never lost. It's better than anything you ever had or will ever find. What we have is special." She corrected herself: "What we had was special."

CHAPTER 33

PARIS GLOWERED AT THE BLISTERS on his sore hands. "Damnit, I should've put on working gloves. This raking is killing me," he called to Deborah. She was on her knees, planting flower bulbs along the edge of the porch.

She looked cute wearing tattered dungarees, her rump tilted up as she clawed in the dirt, unaware of her provocative position. "You're getting soft in your old age," she answered, not looking around.

Paris sneaked up behind her and rubbed the rake handle between her upturned buttocks. "Does that feel like I'm getting soft?" he laughed.

She shrieked and lost her balance, pitching forward on all fours. "Paris! Somebody might be watching. Stop that."

"You women," he laughed, "all ladylike in public, but wild as hell behind the bedroom door."

A tiny cry came from the front porch. "Now you woke the baby. I was hoping he'd sleep until I got the tulip bulbs planted. See what you've done, Paris?" Pouting, she rose to her feet. "Let's see if I can get him back to sleep."

He followed her to the porch where they'd placed the cradle, hoping the fresh air would keep their three-month-old baby asleep while they worked in the yard. "I give up with you," he said putting his arm around her waist as she quieted the child. "I give you everything I've got and you still can't make a little girl."

"Oh! I wouldn't trade him for all the little girls in the world," she said lovingly, placing the pacifier in the baby's small mouth. "There, there. Don't cry, Todd. Mommy's got you."

"Well, that's three boys. We'll have to stop trying before we have a full baseball team. Anyway, you've drained my youth. I feel like an empty shell, used and discarded."

"You're right," she whispered. "We have to quit trying. I'm too old to have any more babies. There's too great a danger of something going wrong after thirty."

"You're not old, certainly not too old to have more babies," Paris teased.

"No, Paris. This little fella has to be the last."

"See if you can get him back to sleep while I pick up that last pile of leaves," Paris said, turning to go down the steps, as a familiar car pulled up to their gate.

"It's Steve! Honey, would you put on the coffeepot?" Paris walked over to greet his friend. "This is a surprise. I didn't expect to see you until this weekend. Come to have me beat you playing chess?"

"Hi, Paris. No...I wanted to come. Just to talk."

Paris sensed something was wrong. Steve failed to call out a greeting to Deborah; he'd never deliberately ignore her. "What's troubling you, Steve? Need some money? I can let you have...."

"Margaret left," Steve interrupted. "Took the girls and left."

"Jesus!" Paris groped for words. "She'll be back when she cools down. You know how women flare up."

Steve shook his head, his face grim. She's been gone for two days. Anyway, I wouldn't take her back, not after all she's done."

"Come on in, Steve. I told Deb to put on some coffee."

"I don't want Deborah to see me like this. I haven't shaved or showered in two days. I had to tell you. I've thought of blowing my brains out...taking the deep six. She ran off with someone, Paris. She's been cheating on me."

It was more serious than Paris imagined. He called to his wife, standing on the porch with the baby in her arms. "Honey, forget the coffee. There's a bottle of whiskey in the cabinet over the refrigerator."

Deborah hurried inside. From the sound of Paris' voice and the expression on Steve's face, she knew there was trouble.

Steve Bakerman stretched, sinking into the softness of the big armchair. *My most cherished hours*, he thought, *are spent in the Allison home.* Following the break-up of his marriage, he found comfort being with Paris and Deborah. As years passed and the heartbreak eased, he'd plan these seemingly spontaneous visits, usually before Deborah made supper. It wasn't an intrusion; he was welcome, and Deborah always had an abundance of food prepared.

Steve would feign apologies for his timing, pretending he couldn't infringe on their hospitality, but Deborah's beautiful smile and insistent persuasion, always succeeded in "twisting his arm." After supper, he and Paris played chess while discussing world situations or their philosophies of life, while sipping wine, coffee or cold beer Deborah graciously brought them. During one visit, as they played, while engrossed in a contemporary conversation, Paris opened up to Steve of his first marriage and of the guilt felt in having caused Tex's death.

"Paris said, "When we were young, you had to promise to marry a girl to get laid. But, since the advent of the pill, 'nice' girls give themselves away on street corners. For a McDonald's hamburger and a milkshake, you get laid and blown on the first date. Nothing like in the 'fifties."

Steve nodded. "Back then, girls didn't have all these diseases they carry today. In the whorehouses overseas, we'd worry about a case of clap or syphilis. There are diseases today I never heard of: Herpes and Chlamydia. Hell, I read in some medical journal that there's a deadly, sexual disease originating in Africa that scientists have known of since 1959. It's called AIDS. If it reaches the United States, you might pick up a girl at a local bar, and she could give you something that'll kill you. Shit, since the girls started sowing their wild oats like the boys, things have gone to hell. They're giving pussy away, and now we're afraid to take it. It's safer to take a girl to a motel, and have her do a slow strip across the room while you masturbate on the other side."

"Yeah. Today, you can bring home something you can't wash off," Paris answered. "I remember if a girl got pregnant, you married her. That's the chance you took, getting laid. Now, they abort the baby and run off to screw again. There's no commitment for the guy that made her pregnant, either. In the military, if a girl got pregnant, she'd call the Red Cross and they stuck a shotgun in your back and march you to the altar. I never told you, but that happened to me."

Steve stared at the chessboard, studying his next move. He waited before speaking. "You're not talking of Deborah. I can't imagine her having to force anyone to marry her."

"Hell, no. Deb was a virgin the day I married her. I meant, before I got out of the Navy."

Paris told Steve of his meeting Carolyn and her unique dilemma. He told of his one-night stand with Joyce, followed by her unexpected declaration of pregnancy. He related the events leading to the tragedy of their buddy and his feelings of responsibility for causing Tex's death.

"Tex walked a thin razor's edge," Steve sighed. "If it's true that everyone is born with their days numbered, Tex didn't have many to start with. You can't hold yourself to blame, Paris. If the situations had been reversed, you'd have done the same for him. There are no guarantees in life…not even life itself."

"Right," Paris concurred. "Life offers no guarantees or real promises."

"Paris, being alone, without a wife and kids to speak of, gives me a lot of time on my hands. Time to think, read, and study. I've stumbled onto different aspects of theology, and I tend to believe more in Hinduism and Buddhism. Both answer a lot of questions for me about our debt in life. Every deed has an inevitable result. Perhaps this is the answer to all the turmoil, senseless tragedies, and internal sufferings we face. Maybe it's a past debt we owe and we pay for it in this life. We must take the responsibility for our past actions."

Paris took a sip of his drink. "What I'd like answered is what triggers our brains to bring on this insane, uncontrollable phenomenon called love. It can't be just lust. That would be over when we were physically satisfied. No, I keep looking for the answer to this self-destruction that shreds us up inside, rips out our hearts, and gnaws at our stomachs."

"I can't explain it. Men have been affected with it since the beginning of time," Steve answered, "Since Adam and Eve."

"What tears at me is that I never had a chance to explain to Carolyn. She'll never know. As for Joyce's baby, what if he's mine? I'd owe him a hell of a lot more than a monthly support check."

"Paris, if he is yours, you've given him the most valuable gift of all, life itself. Now it's up to the child to reach for that higher plain. Remember how you talked of your father and how little he had as a child? In spite of all that was against him, he raised himself to a higher plain. You shouldn't feel any guilt. It's entirely up to the individual. More and more, I'm inclined to follow the Hindu philosophy. It's how you live your life that counts."

"Well, anything I believe is better than what that Gypsy on lower Main Street told me years ago. Remember, the one doing the palm reading?"

"Yeah, I remember. That's back when we double-dated at Palisades Park. That was years ago. What *did* she see in your palm?"

"Nothing but bullshit for a dollar. She said I'd create my own short lifeline. I'm still here, so she was wrong."

CHAPTER 34

SOUNDS OF THE HEAVY CELL door sliding open penetrated his sleep. He tried focusing, wiping caked matter from his eyes as the stench of the urine-stained mattress beneath him and foul body odors inside the jail permeated his nostrils.

His mind registered distant, almost inaudible sounds. Something seized him and he felt his body jolt upward. A stab of excruciating pain across the bridge of his nose cleared his mind.

"Better not hit him anymore. You busted his nose with that last backhand."

"Who gives a shit?" the big, burly uniformed guard growled in a thick Irish brogue, holding the limp figure up by the front of his soiled shirt. "Look at this miserable bastard. He's just another fucking hophead who'd steal from the Holy Church to supply his habit. See those puncture marks on his arms?"

"Yeah, I see them, but the lieutenant said to turn him loose. He's banging this creep's old lady. Said for us to clean him up and release him. Maybe he's worked out something with the desk sergeant. Could be he's going to get some tail, too," joked the second guard.

"We'll hose the bastard down. By the time he dries out, his bitch mother can come for him."

"What about his nose? It looks broken."

"Gee, must've fallen flat on his face before we found him in the gutter. Tsk! Tsk! What a shame, and such a blessing for him we came along." The Irish brogue grew stronger, and as he spoke, his hairy fist tightened on the youth's shirt front. With a sudden upward movement, the guard rammed his knee into the man's groin.

An agonized cry exploded from the pathetic inmate's lips. He doubled over and collapsed onto the floor. Moaning, he rolled back and forth, both hands cupped between his legs, holding his groin.

"Hey! Lay off him, Clancy! You'll kill him!"

"I hate this scum. They'll do anything for a fix."

The hosing down with cold water helped ease the pain. But now, bitter despair crept over him. *Nobody gives a shit about me,* he brooded. *No, I'm wrong, my mother cares. She tried, but what chance did she have after my old man ran out on her?*

He heard salacious talk surrounding his mother all his life, remembering men visiting her in their cheap apartment on Boston's south side. His young life was filled with smutty jokes. Called a "bastard" and "the whore's son," he sympathized with his mother's plight and her hardships, working jobs in cheap bars and hustling for tips in restaurants. Many times there was no work or money for food. Oh, the support checks came every month, though never enough to cover their living expenses. The checks were a payoff erasing his father's responsibilities. All I've ever been to my old man, he thought, was a quick hump with my old lady and a god-damned cheap monthly payoff.

In his teens, James Allison found solace smoking pot. It freed him of emotional pain and made it easier to cope with his filthy environment and the constant teasing. He tried other chemical escapes: barbiturates, amphetamines, and cocaine, but they were expensive. Now, they were needed and he'd do anything to get them. The addiction sickened his mind, and he focused on the one he felt responsible for his miserable existence: his abandoning father. "The son-of-a-bitch made his monthly pay-offs until I reached 18; then that pittance ended," he muttered angrily. Stamped in his mind were the name and address found on the check. One day, he vowed, that bastard would pay for the shame and grief he'd caused.

It was some time before he was taken from his cell and led to the front of the precinct. Approaching the uniformed officer seated behind a desk, he saw his mother standing beside a tall, dark-complexioned man wearing a shabby-looking suit under a worn, dirty trenchcoat. A look of horror crossed her face. "My God! What happened to his nose? He's been beaten. You didn't let them beat him, did you? You didn't let them do *that* to him?" she cried out, hitting the plainclothes man on his shoulder.

"You can thank the lieutenant for his kind benevolence," the desk sergeant roared, "or your son would still be rotting in jail."

Overcome by helplessness, she felt her eyes fill with tears. She bowed her head, letting her shoulders droop, powerless to do anything.

"Here's your belongings." The sergeant emptied the contents of a manila envelope onto the desk. It contained a battered, empty billfold and a key ring.

"Mrs. Allison, sign this release, but let me warn you, anymore trouble and I'll throw the book at him."

As she leaned down to sign the release form, her son watched the plainclothes detective's hand rub across her rounded buttocks.

"I didn't hear you thank me and the sergeant."

Her voice quivered as she said, "Thank you, sergeant, thank you again, Detective Marino. I'll see he stays out of trouble. Come on, Jim. Let's go home."

"I'll be by this weekend," the plainclothes man said grinning, "to check on him and make sure you keep things straight."

As the impact of the lieutenant's last words struck the desk sergeant, he gave a yellow-toothed cackle.

Joyce and her son left the precinct, stepping out into the wintry air. It was two days before Christmas, despite the snow and the holiday decorations in the store fronts, neither had been aware of its coming. Neither cared.

James Patrick Allison lay listening to the sounds coming from behind the closed door of the next room, his dilated eyes staring up at the irregular cracks in the aging plaster ceiling. He'd been high on drugs, but they were wearing off. His broken nose and an uneven jaw line caused by missing teeth made him appear grotesque.

Around him, the room had whirled with vividly colored iridescent lights exploding as he experienced indescribable satisfaction and well being. But the illusion had passed, and lying there he felt the old despair, smelled the stench, and heard the disturbing, obtrusive noises associated with his life. He was back in a world of naked reality he feared and hated.

He rolled over, trying to shield his ears from the sounds in the next room, putting his sweat-soaked pillow over his head. At times, the voices became so loud they couldn't be muffled out.

"Roll your ass over. I want it the other way." He recognized the crude, gruff voice.

"Please, Frank. It hurts that way."

"Hey! Don't give me that shit. If I wanted straight sex, I can get it on any street corner without putting my job on the line. If that hophead son of yours needs a fix or gets arrested, who's the one you call? You call me…Frank Marino."

"But, Frank. He's sick. He can't help himself."

The guttural voice raised its pitch half an octave, mimicking his mother. "Frank, I'll do anything. Frank, please help him. Frank, don't let them lock him up again." The lieutenant's voice lowered. "Think what it costs and the chances I take keeping him in his habit. He's getting worse. I should drop your ass and get a steady hooker. It'd be a hell of a lot cheaper and a lot safer as far as my job goes. He's the true-to-life sequel of *The Man With the Golden Arm*."

"Please, Frank! Don't be angry," Joyce pleaded. "We need you. I need you…you know I'll do whatever you want."

"Okay! Just remember, I don't hold back on you and don't you hold back on me…ever! Understand? Now, roll over and let me feel some wiggle in that ass. Wiggle like you really like it."

James Allison lay listening to the grunts, moans, and occasional whimpers coinciding with the steady, dry squeaks of the ancient bedsprings in the adjacent room. "It's my fault," he moaned, "My mother's forced to submit to this humiliation. I'm 'dog shit.' She should've never had me."

He stared at the ceiling. Pressing the pillow against his ears as the noises gained in crescendo, he couldn't block the sounds.

He thought, no, it's *not* my fault. It's *his* fault! *He's* caused this. My old man dropped his load and ran off, leaving my mother and me. He never cared to look back at the misery he caused. That son-of-a-bitch is responsible for all this mess.

When he was too young for school, his mother worked evenings, leaving him unattended and stuck behind make-shift barriers in back kitchens to keep him from getting underfoot. There he remained until she had time to hurry and check on him. His childhood was spent in kitchens of dirty bars and cheap restaurants, awaiting his mother's return. He remembered the stench of his urine and feces while being confined. To cry out and ask for help was futile. No one cared to help him, except his mother.

Beatings were an accepted part of his life. In his school years, bullies worked him over and teased him, saying, "Go get your father." He was a punching bag to be beaten and laughed at. A broken nose, missing teeth, and a left ear puffed like a cauliflower evidenced his brutal beatings. Now at 18, James Allison's short, thin frame and drawn appearance belied his actual age.

When without work, his mother brought men home. If they stayed long, he would become an object for their hostility. Beatings would start, continuing until the visitor finally left. The cycle would begin when the next occupant moved in. There were years of pungent odors of stale cigars, spilled beer, and dirty laughter.

The next room grew quiet, but he lay motionless until he detected the steady snoring of his mother's companion. Slipping quietly off his bed, he crept barefooted to the door, cautiously easing it open. He stood several moments to be certain both were asleep. In the semi-darkened room, the only illumination filtered through the window from a street light. He studied the figures, partially covered with a wrinkled bed sheet. Marino's trousers were thrown over the back of a chair and the rest of his clothes lay on the floor.

He searched the trousers' hip pockets for the wallet, knowing he'd be beaten when money was found missing. That didn't matter. Carefully, he lifted the pants to prevent any loose change falling to the floor from the side pockets. The wallet was unusually thick because the detective's badge was pinned inside. Thumbing through the bills in the semi-darkness, it was impossible to count how much was there. James took half the contents, placing the wallet back into the trousers. Starting to drape the pants across the back of the chair, his hand brushed something hard and cold: a pistol. A strange power flooded through his veins as his fingers encircled the heavy grip. It was hard to suppress a hysterical impulse to laugh as he drew the six-inch barreled Colt from its holster.

Sensing a surge of unfamiliar strength while holding the heavy weapon, his purpose was suddenly very clear in his mind. He knew what he was going to do.

CHAPTER 35

STEVE BAKERMAN LEANED BACK IN the recliner, his senses savoring the warm, pleasant surroundings in the Allison living room. Strong scents of freshly cut pine wafted from the overly-decorated Christmas tree standing by the front window. Gnawing at his conscience were the sharp teeth of guilt as he thought of the years he'd harbored an unrequited love for Deborah. She'd never know, he resolved. To think of her in that way was to betray Paris.

"Now that your bellies are full and the boys are upstairs studying," Deborah said, entering the room, "you'll both want to nap while I struggle with the dishes." In mock disgust, she shook her head at the two men stretched out comfortably in the cushioned chairs.

"We're male chauvinists," Paris quipped.

"Do you want a drink or maybe a cold beer?" Deb asked, looking at Steve.

"Thanks, Deb. A stiff drink would be fine."

Deborah turned toward Paris. "Honey, can I get you anything?"

Steve sensed Deborah's love for Paris. How he envied his friend.

"Why don't you make yourself a drink and come in here and join us?" Paris asked.

"A little later. Let me get the dishes first."

"Hey, we'll help with the dishes." Steve made an effort to rise, but Deborah's small hand pushed against his shoulder.

"No. I want you to relax…enjoy being together. I'll go make the drinks."

Deborah soon came back with two iced-filed tumblers of rye and soda, then returned to the kitchen.

Steve raised his glass in a gallant salute, "To Deb," he said, taking a large gulp. "They don't make them like her anymore. Paris, you're lucky."

"You're right, Steve."

Steve took another sip of his drink, then placed it on the table near his arm. "It's been years, but remember when Margaret left? You and Deb were working in the yard when I drove up to tell you she'd run off. If it hadn't been for you two, I would've cracked up. I'll never forget the comfort you gave by being close friends and letting me cry on your shoulders."

Paris said quietly, "We cried on each other's shoulders after we killed that bottle of hundred proof whiskey."

"Looking back, I wonder what I saw in her. It was the biggest mistake I ever made...next to joining the Navy." Steve laughed loudly.

"Shit! We've all made big blunders in our lives. If we had an advance inkling as to the outcome, we'd have done lots of things differently," Paris said soberly.

"Yes, but the way she left with no warning...the total deceit...Hell, it started as a pretense of a part-time job to help save for a home. There was no job. It was an excuse to go out and whore with her boyfriend. She played me for a sucker for two weeks, telling me the first week's pay was always held back. She had no excuse for not having a check the second week. That's when she left.

The prick left her before the month ended. The son-of-a-bitch left town, leaving dirty pictures of her in my mailbox. Paris...at the time I would've killed them both, but I look back now and laugh. I miss my girls. I don't see them as often as I'd like, but they should be with Marge. Regardless of what happened, she's their mother. I've never tried to take them from her."

Steve reflected quietly. Then, picking up his drink, he took a long sip before setting it back on the table. "You're lucky to have Deb. Hey! Whatever happened to that Jewish girl you dated in High School? The one I met on Visitor's Day, when we were in Boot Camp? I think her name was Ann."

"Oh, you mean Anna," Paris answered. His thoughts drifted. "She married a rich kike and is living in upstate New York. I saw her five years ago at a class reunion. She came alone. One of her in-laws passed away and her husband couldn't come. It was funny she hadn't stayed with her husband for the funeral. Said she didn't want to miss seeing some of her old classmates. She hadn't changed, just put on a few pounds, but still pretty."

"Was she as pretty as you remembered her?" Steve asked sincerely.

"Oh! I don't know. Time plays hell with beauty; she hadn't changed in personality—that's what really counts. Steve, it's what's inside a woman that counts. Today's young women have no values. Everything's based on pot, cheap thrills, and fast lays. A lasting emotion is unknown to them. They'd screw Quasimodo to try something different. There was one that reminded me of someone else, and I thought I'd once again found the perfect girl." He stopped mid-sentence.

"What do you mean, 'once again found the perfect girl'?" Steve probed.

"Oh! Just a slip of the tongue."

"No! You meant it. You said, 'once again found the perfect girl'."

Paris parried Steve's inquiry. "The pretty bitch had me fooled, just as Marge tricked you. That's women for you," Paris shook his head disgustedly. "They're like decorated chocolate Easter eggs. Open them up and they're hollow inside."

"Not Deborah," Steve said defensively.

"No, not Deborah, she's special," Paris agreed. "No, there was one more special…," Paris added thoughtfully, and Steve knew once again his friend's thoughts had drifted into the past.

Steve interrupted the long silence. "Are you folks going to be home for Christmas?"

"We've made plans to head to the mountains to see my folks."

"Oh!" Steve's disappointment was obvious. "I was hoping we'd be together to exchange presents."

"Hell! You're coming with us. You didn't think we'd run off and leave you alone at Christmas."

"No. I can't go. I appreciate your asking, but I'd be imposing."

"It's all settled," Deborah reappeared in the doorway. "The arrangements are made. We'll put the presents in the trunk and ride up together."

"Gee! I don't know. I really like Paris' dad. I like talking to Ben; we seem to hit it off. I've often thought of the hard times he had during the Depression. Imagine not having money for a casket for their first child and making it himself. Each generation gets weaker. Nothing like the strong stock, in your dad's time. We're a generation of wimps. I'd like to see your folks, but…." Steve, feeling he'd be intruding, started to make an excuse not to go.

"No one would be happy if you didn't come with us. It's settled. Refusing to go is out of the question," Deborah said.

Steve searched her pretty face for an indication of pretentiousness; all he detected was sincerity. "Okay! You've twisted my arm. I'll go."

"Let's drink to it," Paris responded, emptying his glass.

"I'll freshen those drinks for you." Deborah picked up the tumblers and retraced her steps to the kitchen. The two leaned back in their chairs, savoring the moment and remembering old times.

"This is great." Steve smiled profusely. Thinking for a moment, he burst into laughter. "I remember. Anna gave you a bad case of lover's nuts, and I had to physically carry you to the base."

Both broke into laughter, tears coming to their eyes.

"She got me almost as horny as that cute ass working at the Navy Exchange got you," Paris said, still laughing.

"Damn! I close my eyes and still see her ass. I swear, Paris, each time she saw me, she'd find an excuse to turn around and bend over."

Their reminiscences were shattered by the sound of the kitchen phone ringing.

Deborah picked it up and called to Paris. "Honey, it's for you." She came to the arched doorway. "I asked who was calling, but he didn't answer. I'd be suspicious of you if it hadn't sounded like a young man. Unless you've had a sudden change in your tastes," Deb joked.

"Excuse me, Steve. I'll go answer it."

Paris rose, and passing Deborah, playfully slapped her backside with his open palm, leaving her rump stinging.

"Ow!" she screeched.

"Hello, this is Paris Allison.

The voice on the other end sounded tired and weak, straining to speak, the words slow and deliberate. "You'll pay for what you've done, you bastard. Your days on earth are over. Hell awaits you."

Before Paris could respond, the caller hung up.

"Who was it?" Deb asked, looking at the stunned expression on her husband's face.

"Oh, no one you'd know. Someone from the office wanting to wish us a Merry Christmas."

Steve knew the phone call had upset Paris. The call shattered the pleasant evening and it was best now for him to leave the two alone. Slapping both hands on his knees, he rose. "It's late. I'd better head back to the apartment. Deb, thanks for a great supper. It's been a beautiful evening. If you ever decide to leave that shithead, my door's always open." As an afterthought, looking at Paris, he added, "It goes without saying, if you need me for anything, just ask…for anything."

"It's early. There's time for a game of chess," Paris responded half-heartedly.

"I'll catch you next time." Steve went to the hall closet and retrieved his coat. He leaned down to kiss Deborah on her cheek. "Remember, if either of you need me, all you have to do is ask."

After the front door closed, Deborah put both arms about Paris' neck and laid her head on his shoulder. "What was the phone call really about? Is some irate husband making threats now?"

He tilted her chin upward to look at her face. He'd failed her for years, and a sickening guilt swept over him as he spoke. "I'm sorry for ever hurting you. Not one was worth it."

He saw tears forming in her dark eyes and watched her long lashes close in an attempt to halt the flow down her cheeks. "Just as long as you keep coming back, I know you haven't found what you've been seeking for so very long. What I'm afraid of is that one day, you'll find her again and not come back."

"Deb, I love you, and not until it hit me squarely in the face how I've been hurting you, did I realize how much you mean to me." He kissed her lightly on her tulip shaped lips, tasting the salt from the tears streaming down her face.

"The call…. What was it about?"

"I honestly don't know. I've gotten two calls in the past few days. Sounds more like a teenager than a man. Voice sounds sick, *really sick*."

"What does he say?"

Paris shrugged, looking away.

"Tell me, Paris. What does he keep calling about? Who is it?" Her voice was slightly raised in alarm.

He knew she wouldn't be satisfied with anything but the truth. "He says, my days are numbered. He threatens to kill me."

"Oh no!" Deb gasped, growing limp in his arms.

CHAPTER 36

THE BITTER COLD CHRISTMAS DAY couldn't dampen the festive spirit of those sitting around the table. Steve Bakerman, bathed in contentment, helped himself to a second portion of apple pie, wallowing in the warmth of the Allison family.

It'd been an enjoyable holiday weekend, and he was thankful for being coaxed to come. He relaxed on the drive to the Northwestern top of New Jersey, where Paris' parents made their home after Ben retired. High in the watershed mountains supplying reservoirs for metropolitan cities, he felt close to nature, more able to find himself. Here, the air was cold, clear and free of dusty impurities belched by smutty smokestacks necessary for the survival of the industrial cities below.

It was a beautiful, desolate location, bordered by tree-covered mountains, whose bases were lapped by the icy cold waters of several large lakes. The remoteness of the area drew everyone closer together.

Steve pushed his chair from the table and rubbed his stomach. "I'll explode if I have another bite, Mrs. Allison. I don't know what I enjoyed most, dinner or the dessert."

"Deborah baked the pies," Mrs. Allison said proudly, sharing the bouquet of compliments. "She's a much better cook than I am."

"Mom's trying to flatter me into doing the dishes. Actually, she taught me how to bake, but my pies can't hold a candle to her turkey and dumplings." Deborah said cheerfully, rising to clear the table.

"It's good her cooking's appreciated. That's the only reason I keep her around." Paris reached out playfully to pat his wife's well-shaped bottom.

Deborah maneuvered beyond his reach. "Mom, make your son behave!" She cried out, pretending complete exasperation.

Steve watched, smiling, trying to erase erotic thoughts racing through his mind as he focused on the feminine movements of Deborah's hips. He gave several dry coughs to regain his composure. "Anyone mind if I smoke?"

"Go ahead. Give yourself lung cancer," Deborah kidded.

Paris, occupied in the conversation about the table as they finished having coffee, failed to see Deborah shaking her head as she spoke to their 13 year old son, David. She left the dining room, carrying dirty dishes to the kitchen.

After his mother left the room, David sidled up to his dad's shoulder. Cupping his hand to Paris' ear, he whispered to him. "Okay," Paris responded. "Be back in an hour. It'll be dark soon, so stay on this side of the lake and keep the leash on Grandpa's dog."

Deborah returned from the kitchen and immediately realized her son was gone. The oldest and youngest sons were playing games by the Christmas tree. "Where's David?" she asked worriedly.

"Oh, he asked if he could walk his grandpa's dog down to the lake," Paris answered, interrupting the conversation with his Dad and Steve.

"He didn't! The little bugger just asked me if he could go out and I told him no. Paris, you shouldn't have let him go. It's cold outside and getting dark."

"Deb, he's dressed warmly, and I told him to be back in an hour. He'll be all right. He just wanted to walk Prince. Don't be so overly protective; he needs some growing room," Paris chided her, casting Deborah's worry aside and resuming his chat. Steve, seated across the table, observed the anxious frown on Deborah's pretty face.

The men moved from the dining table into the living room to sit before the roaring fireplace and sip their strong drinks. Their conversation ranged from politics to present economic situations, each giving his opinion for ways to solve the country's problems.

Deborah entered the room, her expression capturing Paris' attention. "What's wrong, honey?"

"David's not back and it's dark outside. Paris, please go get him. I'm worried."

"That's not like him. You're right. He's been gone over an hour. Get your coat, honey; we'll walk down to the lake together. I need to stretch my legs. Steve, you and Dad relax. We'll be back in a few minutes. Looks like David lost track of time. I'd hate to paddle his tail on Christmas Day, but I did tell him to come right back."

Deborah had gotten her coat and she handed Paris his. "Honey, please hurry."

Vaporized condensation came from their mouths when they spoke in the cold night air as they walked toward the large lake. Pacing the dark shoreline, they called to their son and Ben's dog, Prince.

The moon cast a faint glow across the water, but no sounds could be heard other than their own. Paris put his arm around his wife's shoulders, feeling her body beginning to shake.

"Don't worry, honey. David's just stopped at one of the neighboring homes. He's probably having hot chocolate and showing off Prince. He loves that dog. You're shivering, and I'm taking you back to the house. Stay inside and keep warm while I get the car and swing down by the lake so I can use my headlights to see better. Call all the nearby homes to make sure David hasn't just dropped in to say hello."

"Paris, something's wrong…I know it." Deborah began to sob. "You shouldn't have let him go out."

"Deb, stop. That's not going to help. You make the calls and I'll get the car started."

Initially, Paris had no real concern of their son's safety. Now the reality of the perils that might endanger their boy's safety raced through his mind. Back at the house, Paris studied the expression on his mother's face as she called the few neighboring homes to inquire if her grandson was there. He could tell by the growing worry in her voice as she completed each call that the possibility of his son being warm and safely inside a neighboring home was exhausting itself.

Steve and Ben Allison left the house and walked in separate directions along the lake's shoreline, calling out to David and the dog, while Paris swung the car around to allow its headlights to beam across the lake. Deborah refused to stay at the house and sat trembling beside Paris, her face pale with worry. Steve retraced his path to meet Ben at the mid-point of the lake's shoreline.

"If they're in hearing distance, Prince would've come to me when he heard me call. David must've gone around the lake over to the other side, or tried to cross the ice."

Steve looked at the lake, knowing the older man's thinking. "Ben, David's too smart to try walking on that ice. It's too thin in spots. The lake isn't completely iced over…wouldn't make sense to walk out on the ice if he couldn't get across."

Paris drove mercilessly over the rocks and rough terrain by the side of the lake, scanning down the twin beams of light in hopes of seeing some sign of his boy. Time was working against him, and David could be in serious trouble. It was too cold, high up here in the mountains, for anyone to be exposed for any length of time, and David was just a young boy. He thought of his son's tousled curls, small hands, and mischievous smile, then mentally shook himself. Emotions couldn't master his thoughts. He'd find his boy.

He bumped the car over the uneven ground, pulling alongside the two figures standing beside the lake. Paris left Deborah sitting inside and approached his father and Steve. "Dad, it doesn't look good. The wind's picking up, and it's been hours since the sun went down, so it's bitter cold. You and Steve take the car and drive Deborah back to the house. We can't wait any longer. Call the State Troopers and I'll keep looking until they get here. There's been some snow, but with all the hunters out this week, it'll be hard to track new footprints."

Paris searched the ground for fresh tracks of his boy and the dog. In less than an hour, he heard sirens and saw red flashing lights coming from where he'd begun his trek to the far side of the lake. He worked his way down the slope and through the underbrush surrounding the lake, hurrying to join up with the searchers. The State Troopers had already radioed for assistance from neighboring volunteer fire departments, and a band of civilians and uniformed men huddled together, receiving instructions from a State Police Captain.

Paris emerged from the woods, and nearing the clearing, heard his father's voice describing his grandson and his dog. "The boy's name is David Allison. He's a small boy, 13 years old with light brown, curly hair. He's wearing a heavy brown coat with a hood. And remember, my dog answers to the name 'Prince.' Don't be scared if you see him. He's big, close to ninety pounds…cross between a shepherd and collie, with long hair. If he hears you call, he'll come to you."

The tall, uniformed captain spoke out loudly to allow his voice to carry above the howling, icy wind. "We'll set up this site as the main base. From here we'll break up into individual search parties, groups of five to six men using lighted flares. With the wind picking up, I don't know what range we'll get with the walkie-talkies, especially once we're over the crest of the mountains. In any case, there's not enough radios to have one with each group, so we'll rely on using the bullhorns for close contact to call out to the boy and the dog. If a group locates them, signal the next nearest group by radio or bullhorn. Those carrying sidearms, fire two shots in the air. That way we set up a relay system. If…." The captain paused, realizing the elder Mr. Allison was listening, then continued. "When we find either the boy or dog or both, and word is relayed back, we'll sound two blasts on the siren from one of the fire trucks. That'll mean for all groups to come back to this base point. Remember, two blasts means they're found. We don't want any-one else lost tonight, so keep together in your group."

One volunteer asked loudly, "Shouldn't we set up some sort of signal if we find them alive?"

"No matter the outcome," the captain said, hesitating, "or the condition, two blasts or two shots. See if you can get some of the neighboring women to keep some hot coffee brewing. Maybe the fire station has a large pot."

One of the firemen stepped forward. "I'm Fire Chief Davis from Volunteer Station Number Five. Our truck has an AC/DC adapter, so we can plug in the large electric coffee pot we keep at the station. I'll send for it and some cups. We'll need something hot to keep our insides warm."

The captain added, "Oh, one more thing, Chief Davis. Could you have one of your men take a smaller truck and continuously circle the main road at the base of the mountain…maybe along Oak Trail? Have him keep his lights flashing. That'll give the men some sense of direction and keep anyone else from getting lost out here tonight."

"I'll see to it."

"All right, men! Move out and be careful." The captain added encouragement to the searchers and the family, saying, "We'll find the boy. Okay, that's it," he shouted over the blowing wind.

Paris saw Steve standing near his parked car and called to his dad to follow him. Deborah, refusing to remain at the house, sat inside the car. Her strained expression showed disbelief in what had happened so suddenly. She stared ahead in semi-shock.

"Honey, I promise he'll be all right," Paris said. "Don't worry, everything will be okay. Steve, you stay with Dad. He knows the woods. I'm going to start back to the other side and join up with one of the groups. Dad, be careful."

"I'll take Steve with one of the parties and start working my way around the right side of the lake," Ben said.

The mountainside appeared to be swarming with fireflies as search parties' flares and flashlights lit the area. Women from neighboring homes and some attending a Christmas party at a distant ski lodge had gotten word of a lost boy and came to help. Some were still clad in party dresses and gowns, covered up in expensive coats or furs. They crowded around the fire truck, serving coffee from the big urn and baked goods brought from their kitchen tables.

The women kept encouragement going to the search parties returning to briefly warm up and go out again. Some men made a huge fire with fallen timber and broken limbs collected in the immediate area, and shimmering sparks rose high into the black night as the fire crackled and snapped, giving welcomed warmth from the frigid wintry wind.

"It's too cold to survive out here," one searcher in Paris' party said to his companion, shouting above the howling wind. "The boy doesn't stand a chance. I've hunted these woods. We won't find him…not alive."

"Careful," the other cautioned. "That's the boy's father. Don't want him to hear us."

Too much time had passed. Paris refused to return when his search party headed back to warm up and continued looking. His voice was hoarse from yelling for David and Prince. He scanned any pile of leaves or mounded snow resembling a fallen human form, using his feet to scatter and break up the clumps to make certain nothing was buried in them. Paris thought of Deborah's torment, wishing he could comfort her now, but time was working against his son's survival. He had to find him.

It was near midnight, and still the searching continued. One party returned to warm up, exhaustion showing on their faces. "That old man Allison is wearing us out," one groaned. "Hate to say it, I thought I kept myself in pretty good shape but I can't keep up with him. He knows these woods and he's gotten some crazy notion the boy and his dog crossed over to the other mountain range. Said if the dog was in hearing distance, he'd have come to him. Myself, I think the dog and boy are beyond help. Couldn't say that to him, though. I left him with another group. He wants to take one of the four-wheel drives to the other mountain range to look. He's nuttier than a fruitcake if he thinks a small boy and a dog could get that far over this rough terrain. Everybody was against his idea, but he said he'd go without them if he had to."

Paris was several miles away, almost at the foot of the far range of mountains, when he heard two faint sounds of gunfire. The meaning was clear. His son—or Prince—had been found. As he hurried up the mountain side, he had no way of knowing if either was alive or dead. It was the longest journey of his life.

Almost 45 minutes passed as he made his way over the crest of the mountaintop to descend toward the flashing lights of the base camp. He heard two blasts from the siren on a fire truck. There was no doubting the meaning. He prayed his boy was alive.

As he broke through the brush and rounded the lake, a figure ran toward him. It was Steve, yelling and waving, completely out of breath. "He's alive! David's alive!" He ran to Paris, throwing his arms about him. "Paris, he's alive! Your dad found him…David and Prince. Both are fine! Nobody believed him when he wanted to go way over to the other range. Thought he was nuts, but that's where they were. Your dad called to Prince and heard him bark. The dog wouldn't leave David though…good dog. David slipped and was up to his waist in cold water just before your Dad got there. A few more minutes and he'd have frozen."

"Where is he? Where's Deb? Dad?"

"They took David by ambulance to the hospital. Just a little hypothermia, that's all. Boy, it's a lucky day."

"Let's get to the hospital." Paris suddenly felt the last ounce of his energy drain from him.

"Shit, man. Better get you there and have you checked out too."

"I need to see David…to see Deborah…and to thank my Dad."

CHAPTER 37

HE WAITED ACROSS THE STREET, hunkered behind a row of thick, snow-laden evergreen shrubs. His worn, wet shoes provided no protection in the ankle-deep snow. The agonizing, burning sensations he had felt earlier in his toes had dulled to numbness. The dark sky gradually lightened to charcoal, then slate gray. Small wrens nesting in the surrounding oak trees began chirping, heralding in the first signs of daybreak, but his presence and occasional movements cut short their ritual. The enfolding silence was leaden.

James Patrick Allison had exhausted the money stolen from his mother's boyfriend. Some went for the bus ticket from New England, most was spent on drugs. With cash, it'd been easy to make contacts in Boston. But here, he was a stranger; his cocaine supply was exhausted and his nerves were raw.

Finding the Allison house was easy. Still, he repeatedly checked the address taken from his mother's last support check. There could be no mistake.

Arriving the day before, he located the house before the wintry darkness mantled the area and approached a neighboring resident coming home from work, claiming, "I'm looking for Mr. Paris Allison. He has some work for me to do around his house. It's getting late and I don't want to bother him, but I'd like to see him before he leaves for work in the morning. Is that his house?" He pointed to the Allison home.

The neighbor scrutinized the boy, studying his broken face, torn clothing, and tattered shoes. He couldn't imagine Mr. Allison doing business with anyone looking so poor and needy as the youth standing before him. Perhaps a touch of a lingering Christmas spirit or the idea that the respected Mr. Allison might be trying to help someone truly in need prompted the neighbor to volunteer information.

"Yes, that's his house. Probably wants the walkways shoveled, though he always does his own work about the place," he answered, studying the pitiful creature before him.

"I just need to earn a little...a few bucks will help."

"Well, when Mr. Allison is finished with you," the neighbor smiled charitably, "come see me and I'll pay you to do a few small jobs, myself."

"I'd appreciate that. Could you describe him? I wouldn't want to approach the wrong person."

"Sure, son. You can't miss him. Parks his car right in the front of his house. You can set your clock by him; leaves just a little after eight every morning. Neat looking man with a full head of hair."

"Thanks. I'm sure I won't miss him."

"Don't forget to come by for those extra chores when Mr. Allison is done with you," the neighbor reminded. "I live two doors further down the street."

"Sure thing. As soon as I've finished with Mr. Allison."

Sleeping a few hours on a bench in the city bus station, James Allison returned in the early morning. Now, by the brightness of the sky, he knew it was almost time. Soon it would all be over; the debt owed his mother, finally settled.

He pulled the heavy pistol from beneath his worn coat, remembering Frank Marino saying, "I carry a long-barreled Colt. None of those snub nose guns for me. You can't hit shit with one if you're standing in it. The longer the barrel, the more accurate."

He didn't have to wait any longer. Across the street, the front door opened and someone stepped out onto the porch. The sun's glint reflecting from the glass storm door highlighted a full crown of hair. The figure paused, as if to take in a breath of morning air, then stared directly across at the bushes.

James Allison rested the barrel across a small branch, sighting down the six-inch barrel, both hands steadying the weapon. With his right thumb, he pulled back the hammer. In the morning stillness, the *click* sounded like an explosion to his ears.

He felt sudden panic as the figure reacted to the noise, and he saw the blur of an arm come up. He squeezed the trigger. He didn't bother to recock the hammer, but pulled back hard on the trigger and fired again. *It was so easy*, he thought relieved. *The score is settled. My troubles and my mother's have ended with just a pull of my finger. Our years of embarrassment and suffering are over.*

James Patrick Allison was laughing when he put the barrel into his mouth.

Paris did his most concentrated thinking while shaving. It was a time when all pressing matters were pushed aside and he could devote a few selfish minutes totally to himself.

He contemplated the recent terrifying events. During the hunt for his son, he'd done a great deal of soul searching. With so much at stake, realization of what he'd allowed himself to become hit him like a bolt of lightning. He'd looked so long for something not lost. Carolyn's words echoed in his mind: "We've given each other the ability to love and in doing this, a part of us will always be with the other, a part that can never be destroyed. In that way, we'll always have each other."

It was true. Their lives had been destined to meet, then part. In their brief encounter, each benefited and each had grown. Carolyn tried to teach him the importance and meaning of an unselfish love, only it had taken him almost a lifetime to understand. With each subsequent affair, he'd looked for another Carolyn. Even with his wonderful Deborah and their sons, he continued to look for the proverbial pot of gold at the end of a rainbow. It had taken this near tragic mishap of losing a son to bring sharply into focus the simple truth: His wife and sons were all the treasures he needed and wanted. He'd spend the rest of his life showing them how much they meant to him.

He finished shaving, frowning at his reflection in the bathroom mirror. The ordeal had taken its toll. What at one time had been a youthful countenance, now showed signs of aging and wear. His hair was graying at his temples and sideburns. Slight creases were beginning to show across his forehead, and his finely chiseled face had some sagging at the jaw line. "Goddamned character lines," he cursed softly. "I'm getting too much character!" He wiped away the excess lather and winced as he applied stinging after-shaving lotion to his face

"You're a lucky bastard," he said with a grin, speaking to his reflection. A fleeting image of Mike came to his mind. "Poor Mike, never had a chance at life or to make babies, but it was me who fouled things up."

Paris glanced out the bedroom window. It was a bright day and the sun's warmth was beginning to melt away the snow. *I'll have just a light breakfast before going to work*, he thought, descending the stairs.

His hugged Deborah, who was in her housecoat, preparing breakfast. She flipped eggs in the frying pan. "What's that for? It's too early for romance, and you can't take care of me and make it to work on time," she teased.

"I wanted to hold you for a minute," he murmured, inhaling the sweet scent of her skin and hair.

"There's plenty of time for that tonight," she purred, turning, her arms encircling his neck. The burning eggs disrupted their kiss.

"When I get home tonight, let's take the kids to a movie. It'd be good for us to go out."

"Only if you scrub this frying pan. I'll save it for you."

"You've got a deal, provided I get an incentive bonus." He playfully patted her rump.

Deborah fried fresh eggs for Paris and placed a plate of sausage and a cup of coffee in front of him.

"This is what I call service," he said smiling appreciatively. "Everything, even the newspaper. Anything interesting?"

"Same old stuff," she shrugged. "Crime and politics. Oh! There's a picture of a new Italian discovery about to marry a big movie producer. You'll like her. Her picture's on page three. Real cheesecake shot, but I think she's too mature to appeal to the younger studs."

Paris clumsily turned to the page and studied the picture. It was a distant shot, yet for a moment he thought he recognized the face. No. It's not possible, he thought, looking at the name "Francesca" in the print below the picture. It's purely coincidental.

Before leaving, Paris held Deborah for a long time, kissing her repeatedly.

"That's some goodbye and off to work kiss," she moaned softly.

"That'll hold you till I get home."

"I don't know. You've gotten me so excited, I'll probably attack the milkman."

Paris opened the door and stepped onto the porch. He took a deep breath, taking in the fresh, cold air. The sun's brilliance on the melting snow momentarily hurt his eyes and, as he squinted to focus, a shiny reflection in the bushes across the street caught his attention. Strangely, everything seemed so quiet. The birds nesting in the trees had stopped chirping.

Something was amiss. His senses sharpened for a split second. Time reversed itself and he was again in a darkened alley in far-off Africa. The hair on his neck tingled as his ears detected a sharp metallic click. Instinctively his cat-like reflexes brought his right arm up in a defensive position. The motion was wasted. The first impact caught him high in the chest, propelling him backward against the storm door. The next hit him squarely in the chest, sending him crashing through the glass.

He lay sprawled amidst the broken glass, knowing he was badly hurt as a wet, red stickiness bubbled from his chest. He heard what sounded like a sharp backfire and then screams coming from inside his home. Initially, there was a sudden shock, as if he were hit by a freight train, followed by excruciating pain. Then his body was enveloped in a peculiar dullness; a compelling tiredness engulfed his entire being.

He felt his head being lifted, and through rapidly blurring vision, detected Deborah's shadowy image. Tears running from her cheeks fell against his face. He tried to lift his hand to her face to comfort her, to tell her not to worry, that he loved her and everything would be all right, but his arms wouldn't respond. He felt the spasms of her body as she sobbed hysterically, rocking his head in her lap. For a fleeting moment, Carolyn's face appeared before him, only to quickly fade. Then, Mike's face emerged, but it faded.

An image was far off in the distance and, oddly, it was beckoning him. The form drew nearer, but the features were indistinguishable. It seemed to be coming nearer and nearer; still he couldn't discern any features, but the figure continued to beckon him to follow. The figure was close now, and Paris shuddered when he recognized the dark, bloody depression between the native's eyes.

The native beckoned once again. Paris' body shuddered, and darkness closed about him.

CHAPTER 38

STEVE BAKERMAN AWOKE TO THE bright sunlight shining through the yellowed, tattered window shade. It took several minutes to shake away the lingering sleepiness. *Funny,* he thought, *on the weekends I'm wide awake at five-thirty, but if it's a work day, I have trouble getting out of bed by seven.* He threw aside the old Navy blanket and swung his feet to the floor. Yawning, he scratched his hairy chest and reached for the pack of Camels on the rickety night table.

"Damn it!" he swore, as the "Little Ben" clock suddenly sounded its alarm from across the room. An unlit cigarette dangled from his lower lip as he scurried to the scarred dresser and fumbled for several seconds to find the shut-off lever on the back of the brass clock.

Since living alone, he always placed the clock on the dresser across the room. Too many times, he'd reached over to the nightstand next to his bed and shut it off, only to fall deeply back to sleep.

Standing in his shorts before the cloudy, badly streaked mirror, he ran his fingers through the few remaining strands of gray hair faithfully clinging to his shiny scalp.

"You look like shit," he said sourly to his reflection.

Despite his demeaning soliloquy, Steve was looking forward to a quiet evening after work with Paris. Pretending it was *only* the pleasure of Paris' companionship, he was able to consciously dismiss his guilt in wanting to be near Deborah.

He was content being near Deborah, and when the three were together, his life seemed complete. This way, he satisfied a need to love someone who wouldn't threaten his existence. Steve channeled his expressions of love to one focal point: Deborah. It was safe to love her from afar, without fear of the ramifications like those that shattered his ego in the downfall of his marriage. He accepted his life as it was, purposely renting this apartment a few blocks down their street to be near the two people he held dearest.

I'm lucky, he thought, *to have a friend like Paris, and for us both to love the same girl.* The work day at the machine shop would pass rapidly with pleasant anticipations of the coming evening. This would be their first get-together since the near tragedy involving Paris and Deb's son. *God* he thought, *I'm thankful Ben Allison found David in time.*

Steve shaved and showered, hurrying to have a donut and a cup of coffee at the local diner before going to work. Steve breathed in the stiff wintry air as he descended the steps from the apartment. He was fumbling with the car's door key when the first black-and-white raced by, its siren wailing. He opened the driver's door and was about to get in when a second black-and-white sped past. An ambulance, its red lights flashing, followed. He froze in his steps. They had come to a stop down the street.

"Hell! They're stopping in the same block Paris and Deb live," Steve muttered, his eyes straining in the morning sun. "The police cars and ambulance are too close to their home for me to ignore. I'll skip breakfast and drive past to make sure everything is okay."

His thoughts raced ahead of his movements, and he heard grinding, metallic sounds as he hurriedly shifted gears in his vintage automobile. He reached the block where Paris and Deborah lived, but traffic was being stopped by two uniformed policemen.

Steve recognized an elderly neighbor taking his morning stroll. He slowed the car, and rolled down his window. "What's happened?" he yelled.

The old man looked up, a perplexed expression on his face, but failed to answer Steve's question.

"Do you know what the hell's happened?" Steve hollered, angry at getting no response.

Disbelief showed on the gentleman's face. "Some hippy bastard shot Mr. Allison. What kind of sick nut would hurt such a nice man?"

The words exploded in Steve's mind. Shocked, he bounced the tires of the aging car against the curb as he frantically parked. The vehicle jolted as he lifted his foot from the clutch before the engine stopped. He ran, pushing his body through the growing crowd.

"Let me through. Goddamn it! I've got to get through."

He made it to the porch steps before being restrained. "Hey, Buddy! Where in the hell do you think you're going?" one officer snapped.

"My friend lives here. Someone said he was shot."

"Did you know Mr. Allison?" The question rang with such finality that Steve looked into the officer's inscrutable face.

"I'm Paris' friend. If he's hurt, he needs me. His wife, Deborah…. Where is she?"

His eyes scanned the shattered storm door, broken glass, and the body covered by a black rubber sheet. A dark puddle oozed from beneath the covering, staining the porch.

"Your friend's dead. His wife's in the ambulance; they're attempting to sedate her. She's hysterical," the office said quietly.

"Who would do this?" Steve cried out, tears streaming from his eyes.

"Across the street," the officer motioned with his head, his grip still firm on Steve's arm "Apparently, some drifter ambushed him, probably high on dope. Who knows? The bastard blew the top of his own head off after opening up on your buddy. No apparent motive, but we're running a check on him."

Steve looked across the street. Two plainclothes detectives and several uniformed policemen stood over another covered body, partially hidden behind some snow-covered bushes. Old, worn shoes protruded from the edge of the rubber sheet.

"Let me go to his wife. She needs someone with her."

The officer studied his face, then loosened his grip on Steve's arm. "Let him through. Let him go to the ambulance!" he called out.

Steve stepped up into the back of the long white vehicle. Two white-jacketed paramedics stood over Deborah who was lying on a cot, held down by restraints, "Who the hell strapped her down?" he demanded.

"We had to. She wouldn't leave the body. She's hysterical."

The sound of his familiar voice reached Deborah. She looked up at Steve "Why? Why?" she asked.

The black veil did little to conceal the dark circles under Deborah's grief-stricken eyes. Her world had suddenly been destroyed. Seated with her children and Paris' grieving parents during the grave-site service, she trembled convulsively.

Standing with the pall-bearers, Steve looked from the steel blue casket to Deborah. Still shocked by the cataclysmic tragedy, he felt the pain of the loss of his friend like particles of glass ground into his heart. Yet how much worse it was for Deborah, he thought. He and Paris had discussed their personal lives, and Deborah was aware her husband told him of his first marriage and of a son he never accepted as his own. This was a secret kept by Deb and Paris' parents, known to no one else and never alluded to. He hoped Deborah would forget all else and remember only what had been good in their lives. Steve knew the pathetic assassin carried no personal identification, and it was through tracing the serial number on the stolen police pistol to the registered owner, a detective friend of the mother, that a positive identification of the body was made.

Steve studied the casket. It was such a waste, he thought. Such a goddamned waste.

When the service ended, he made his way through the gathering. Putting his arm around her shoulder, he tried gently to move her away from the burial site.

"No...not yet," she said softly. "Not yet." Her hands reached to touch Paris' coffin, her slender fingers seeming to give a last caress to her husband. She kissed the fingertips of her left hand, then again touch the casket's surface.

"Deb, it's best we go now."

"Yes. Paris' mom is almost in total collapse. His dad is with her and the boys. He's so hurt, but doesn't say a word. He's always been strong...." She paused, raising her eyes to scan the site. "I picked this spot by the large oak. It seems so restful here. My place is alongside. Paris would've liked it here. I wanted him near Mike. They grew up together; just cousins, but more like brothers. Mike's buried over there." She pointed to a small headstone nearby. She began to sob, and Steve tightened his grip about her shoulders.

"I'm all right," she said, forcing a tremulous smile. "In spite of all that's happened, I can't help feeling sorry for the boy's mother. She flew down from Massachusetts, just herself and a detective friend, to claim her son's body. She seemed so alone. She must have been such a pretty girl when she was young...when Paris knew her. She's still attractive, but you can tell her life has been hard. I understand she made arrangements to have her son's body cremated locally. I don't think she had money or insurance to cover funeral expenses or have him flown back. Paris never acknowledged the boy to be his. He just paid the monthly support as long as necessary. He'd never discuss the matter, but I knew he felt bitter and guilty. To have it end like this...it seems so wrong."

She forced herself to think deliberately, to keep control. "I must go to my boys. They're confused and hurt."

"Deb, I'll always be near, if you need me," Steve said sincerely. "Paris is...was my best friend."

Steve watched as she walked off and embraced her sons. It wasn't wrong to love her. He never betrayed his friend, and he'd keep his promise. He'd always remain near, in case she ever needed him. Paris would've wanted it that way.

No one was there to see the taxi slowly enter the cemetery through the large wrought-iron gates. Everyone had gone and it was almost dark as the cab made its way along the narrow, twisting drive to the fresh mound of earth. The grave site stood out in contrast to the snow-covered ground. Already, strong wintry gusts blew snow onto the fresh earth; it appeared to have been lightly sprinkled with flakes of frozen ice. Several wreaths still encircled the mound, honoring the site.

The cab pulled parallel to the curb, less than 30 feet from the grave, and both rear doors opened. Two figures started to step out, but one was halted by a quiet command coming from the door nearest the curb.

"Please. I want to be alone. Wait here."

"Okay, but hurry it up. It's a long way to the airport."

She stepped out into the cold, dressed in a worn two-piece black suit. She had no winter coat to ward off the bitter chill. Seemingly oblivious to the weather, concentrating only on the object she held carefully in her hands, she walked to the foot of the grave and stood quietly for several moments. Then kneeling, ignoring the dirt and snow soiling her skirt, she removed the container's lid and gently emptied the urn atop the mound, shielding the ashes with one hand to thwart the wintry gusts.

The urn emptied, she set it aside and with her hands intermingled the ashes with the earth. This done, she rose slowly, making a sign of the Cross on her breast, and gazed down at the fresh mound of dirt. Then she walked to the head of the grave and pulled one white carnation from a wreath. Holding it in her soiled, clenched fist, she turned to leave, but stopped and once again looked back.

"Come on, Joyce! It's late and it's a long way back to Boston. I'm already in hot water about not reporting my gun stolen."

"I'm coming, Marino. Keep your damn shirt on."

CHAPTER 39

SHE STOOD ON THE BALCONY looking out over the bay. The gentle breeze caught her hair and tossed it lightly about her face. Strands of hair that once seemed to hold the glimmer of the sun now teased her face like wisps of silvery moonlight. She seemed to be searching the horizon where the sky joined the sea and, engrossed in her visual quest, she failed to hear the footsteps behind her.

"There you are. What on earth is out there? You seem to have drifted off to another world."

"Oh! I'm sorry. Please forgive me. I was just watching the horizon...the point where the sky meets the sea. The colors are so beautiful, the blues so gentle. I guess it sounds mad, but I've always loved this bay."

"Not mad; melancholy maybe, but not mad. You've always had a love for this spot. I'm the one who's mad letting you convince me this was the shortest route to Maryland," he teased her as his arm encircled her waist. "One consolation, though. It gave me a chance to attend the Medical Convention at Eastern Virginia Medical School; otherwise, I'd have never found the time."

"We'll have to leave soon," she spoke softly. "I wouldn't want to be late for my son's graduation from Annapolis."

"Not *your* son's; it's *our* son's graduation!"

"You've never shown any partiality. I've been very fortunate," she said gratefully.

"You've always accepted the girls as your own, even after they married. Why should I be any different? We both love them all."

She studied his distinguished, kind face. "I'm very fortunate," she repeated. She put her arms around his neck and kissed him lightly. Her eyes glanced at the two white lines, one on each wrist. They had faded over the years, but would never completely disappear. The scars had been too deep, like her memories.

Holding him, her eyes looked back to the horizon. They held each other for several minutes, then he gently said, "I think we'd better get started now or we'll never get there on time, Carolyn."